WORST HOLIDAY EVER

A Family Drama Romance Anthology

KILBY BLADES   R.L. MERRILL   MARIE BOOTH

ADRIENNE BELL   EVA MOORE   KARI LEMOR

MEG BELLAMY   PRESLAYSA WILLIAMS

ERIN ST. CHARLES

ISBN-10: 0-9991532-3-4

ISBN-13: 978-0-9991532-3-9

CONTENTS

PART I
THE STORIES

Decked Out by Eva Moore

AN EXPOSED DREAMS SERIES SHORT STORY

"ARE YOU EXCITED FOR CHRISTMAS THIS YEAR?"

Natalie heard and felt Enzo's words rumble in her ear pressed against his chest. The lounge chair on his parents' deck was not meant for two. Nor was it generally called into service on December twenty-first, but they were making it work. Natalie snuggled into the warm V of his legs, draping her thighs over the side of his lap and tucking herself more firmly into his embrace. His hands stroked down her arm gently as if she were fragile and precious, even as his work-roughened skin caught at the wool of her poncho.

She knew that she was tougher than he believed, but she appreciated his tendency to pamper her, like when he pressed kisses into her hair and held her close. It was still such a novel experience. Carrying his twins was exhausting, and they were only just out of the first trimester. She toyed with the button on his flannel shirt while his heart continued to beat steadily beneath her ear, trying to find an answer she could say in the near presence of her six-year-old, Daisy, up in the tree house.

"Excited is one word for it."

"What's another?" He pressed, not letting her evade.

"Nervous. Terrified. Exhausted. Oh God." Natalie pressed her palms to her eyes as if she could block out the swirling images of her own personal Nightmare Before Christmas.

"Babe, what's got you worried?"

"I don't know. Meeting your entire extended family around a holiday packed with sensitive traditions and managing the expectations and sugar intake of an over-stimulated six-year-old while pregnant with twins? You're right. What could I possibly be worried about?"

Enzo's hand slid from her arm to underneath her poncho, coming to rest on her barely bulging belly at the mention of the babies. The warm weight of his fingers cherishing the lives they'd created eased a bit of her nerves. She was still new to this whole trusting-a-man thing, but this was Enzo. The man she'd fallen in love with, the man who had proven himself trustworthy, the man who was still by her side.

"You don't have anything to worry about. I'll be right here to help with Daisy and to keep my rowdy family in line." His hand shifted from her belly higher, cupping her sensitive and swollen breast beneath the cover of her wrap. "I've got a few plans to help you relax, too."

As much as she had longed for his touch throughout the day, she tugged his arm away.

"Stop it. Daisy is right there."

Enzo bent his head and pressed a kiss to the shell of her ear that made her shiver just as much as his words.

"So? She'll see that I really love her mama."

"I'm sure she already knows that, but we have to leave for the winter recital soon." She wiggled her hip against his already stiffening cock. "How do you plan to hide that?"

"Worried the other moms will be jealous?" He chuckled.

She turned and pressed a kiss to his lips before levering herself out of the chair.

"They already are, babe, but gloating isn't attractive."

As she turned to rise and get Daisy ready for her big night,

Enzo grabbed her hand and pulled her back in for another searing kiss. When she raised her head faster than her eyelids, he grinned.

"You are always attractive to me. Don't worry about Christmas. I have a few surprises lined up. It's going to be a big family holiday to welcome you and Adrian. All you have to do is sit back and enjoy."

"Surprises? Enzo, what surprises?" In her life, they had never been good. Enzo booped her on the nose as he rose to stand beside her.

"It wouldn't be a surprise if I told you, now would it? 'Tis the season for giving, Natalie. Let me give you this." He turned toward the tree house that still stood, sturdy and weathered, in his parents' backyard. "Come on, Daisy. Time to go."

ENZO SURVEYED THE SEA OF CARS IN FRONT OF HIS OLD elementary school. "Why don't you ladies hop out here, and I'll go park the car."

"Sounds good." Natalie hustled Daisy out of the car.

Enzo rolled down the window and called out, "Break a leg, *bellissima*," before slowly pulling away from the curb.

The neighborhood was packed for the winter recital, and he ended up parking four blocks away. The principal was up on stage making announcements by the time he finally squeezed into the packed auditorium. Enzo scanned the assembled parents looking for Natalie. He crept up the aisle, finally spotting her near the middle of a row. Flanked on either side by more parents.

She hadn't saved him a seat. He rubbed away the pinching in his chest. She needed time to adjust, he reasoned. Old habits died hard. He was trying to be patient, but every time she forgot to include him felt like a paper cut. Annoying, impossible to ignore, and painful when things got salty. He had a lot of lingering paper cuts. He'd almost prefer one big slice that he could heal all at once.

He waved to get her attention and gestured to the back. The

apologetic shrug she gave him didn't make the ache feel any better. He pushed it aside. They'd get there, once he became a permanent part of their lives...

As the first graders began to sing "Deck The Halls," he took a space standing behind the back row of seats. Daisy sang two more songs, one about eight kandelikas and another about dancing snowflakes. Had Daisy ever even seen snow? Maybe he could take them to Tahoe next year. Look at him, dreaming up family vacations for *his* family. It was all so new, but he couldn't wait to get started. Christmas Eve. He could be patient a few more days to set his plan into motion.

Daisy followed her classmates off stage and when she waved at her mom her little face fell. Nope. Not happening. Not caring if it was embarrassing, he cupped his hands and yelled, "Didi!" while waving madly. The grin on her face and her little wave made the rest of the stares worthwhile. He would yell across any gym so that little girl would know he was there for her, even if her mother had forgotten.

By Christmas Eve, Natalie was a nervous wreck over those stupid surprises. She'd been so distracted at the recital that she hadn't noticed when someone took the seat she'd been saving for Enzo until it was too late.

He hadn't said anything, but she could tell he'd been upset. She was still trying to figure out how to fix that. But tonight, she was simply too overwhelmed to think, let alone tackle heavy emotional conversations. She had to get presents to Jo's house for tomorrow morning, and get everyone dressed and out the door for a late Christmas Eve dinner and Midnight Mass. This Feast of the Seven Fishes was a cherished tradition, as was the late mass. She wasn't completely happy about keeping Daisy up into the early hours of the morning. Hell, she wasn't sure she was going to make it that long either, but it was an important tradition in Enzo's family, so she was going to try.

Enzo's entire family. She was going to meet even more of them. Plus surprises. Was it any wonder she was a nervous wreck?

A lifetime of insecurities threatened to rise up and drown her, but she clung to Enzo's love like a buoy. He'd found plenty inside her to love, and she would just borrow his confidence until hers showed the hell up.

They walked up to Jo and Dom's house, arms laden with bags of presents, bottles of wine, and the platter of fish sticks Daisy had baked all by herself. Daisy was so excited for her first real family Christmas, and Natalie wanted it to be perfect.

Thank goodness the reality show that had brought them together, Million-Dollar Starter Home, was on break for the holidays. She'd had time to indulge Daisy's enthusiasm.

The door opened, and they were immediately enveloped in hugs and noise, warmth and love. Natalie's nerves eased up a little. This family was amazing.

"Look, JoNana. I made the sticks for the fishy dinner all by myself! Well, Mommy took them out of the oven, but..." Daisy clearly shared none of her mother's nerves, chattering away as she disappeared into the kitchen with Jo and her casserole dish.

Enzo took the presents to put under the tree, before following Daisy back into the kitchen, leaving Natalie alone with her bottles of wine. Stopping for hugs with Zia Elena, Zio Tony, Seth, and Frankie, she made her way over to Brandy who seemed to be managing the makeshift bar next to the fireplace. Brandy's corkscrew curls glistened in the dancing light from the fire, and Natalie admired the young woman's style. The bright red sweater dress suited her to a T. She fit here in Jo's living room, all decked out with draping holly and ivy and gold accents. Brandy was an outside addition to the family, and if she could feel at home here, so could Natalie. Eventually. She was already holding out a wine glass of sparkling water by the time Natalie made it to her.

"I don't know how you're doing this without wine," Brandy

teased, taking the bottles of wine and adding them to the stash, before turning back to the cocktail she was mixing. Natalie nodded dramatically and took a long sip of her club soda, earning a laugh as an older lady toddled up beside them.

"Do you have my Manhattan done yet, girl?"

Brandy's back tensed, but she dropped in the cherry and presented the drink with a smile.

"Here you go, Prozia Dulce. Have you met Natalie yet?"

Dulce turned her attention to Natalie as Brandy had intended, looking her up and down. "You're Enzo's girl."

Natalie nodded.

"Hmm. Got yourself knocked up with twins, I hear."

Natalie's mouth dropped open, words deserting her. How did one respond to that? Apparently, Great-aunt Dulce did not require a response. She patted Natalie on the cheek and sipped her cocktail.

"Good girl. Now get a ring on that finger." Dulce turned her attention to Brandy. "You've been with Seth long enough. Why haven't you made any babies yet? You got something wrong down there?" The woman who had to be pushing ninety circled a finger meaningfully at Brandy's belly. Much to Natalie's surprise, Brandy gave the old biddy a civil answer. Her talent must have come from years of tending bar. Natalie didn't have that level of calm in the face of rudeness anywhere in her arsenal.

"We are waiting until I am out of my nursing program and my career is a bit more stable."

"Bah! Careers. A career is what you do until you catch a man. You two have already done that. Now get on with it. I want babies to cuddle before I die."

With another deep swig of her Manhattan, she toddled off to harass someone else.

"Rude old bat."

Natalie grinned. "How old is she exactly?"

"Don't attempt the math. It doesn't matter. She's so well pickled she'll never die. That's her second drink in under an hour.

I'm mixing a pitcher if she asks for another one." Brandy muttered and picked up her own red wine. "Come on. Let's step away, or I'll never be off the clock."

Natalie knew that Brandy had worked as a bartender during her off hours, but had thankfully been able to cut back significantly now that her nursing program had begun. Nat certainly didn't want the poor woman working through her holiday. They didn't make it far before Jo's voice rang out from the kitchen.

"Domenico Valenti, I swear if you do not get out of my kitchen this second, I will never make your pepperoncini ever again!"

There was no teasing lilt in Jo's voice to soften the threat. Dom must've caught that too, because he hustled out of the kitchen with a frown on his face, just in time to answer the next doorbell. Jake Ryland, show runner for the Valenti family's reality show, walked in, his arms weighed down with gift bags.

"Hi, Dom! Merry Christmas!" He accepted a clap on the back from the family patriarch as he moved further into the room to set down his gifts.

"What's all this? What are you doing here?" Frankie asked from her perch by the fireplace, her confusion clear.

"Frankie!" Dom chided.

"No, it's okay, Dom. Your father found out I was going to work through the holiday, and he invited me to join you all. *These*," he arranged the bags at the foot of the tree, "are presents to thank your family for having me."

"All work and no play." Frankie found her trademark sass quickly, pushing past her shock.

"I don't think anyone has ever called me a dull boy." Jake returned without missing a beat.

"There's a first time for everything."

Natalie practically heard the sparks flying as they clashed wits. *How long has that been going on?*

Their banter was interrupted by another peal from the doorbell.

The front door opened and the number of people in the room

doubled. The noise level tripled. Adrian and Sofia's arms were full of wrapped boxes, and Adrian's younger sister, Luciana, carried in several aluminum trays.

"Welcome! Welcome!" Dom relieved her of her burden, placing the food on the sideboard. "This smells amazing."

Adrian's mother, Graciela, followed behind Luciana, gripping her older daughter Mahalia's arm tightly. Her husband Rey was right behind them with little Jeremiah tucked in his arms. Adrian's middle sister, Aracely, shut the door behind them with her foot, her hand full of a large stockpot.

"Homemade horchata," she explained as she shimmied past hugs on her way to the kitchen.

"I made shrimp tamales. I hope they turned out. There are chicken ones for your freezer, too." Graciela looked a little spacey as she explained, and Natalie wondered what kind of medication she'd taken to overcome her fear of leaving her house tonight.

"I'm sure they'll be delicious," Dom said, offering his arm. "Come on back and say hi to Jo."

Luciana joined Brandy and Nat near the de facto bar.

"Wine. Any color. Any kind. My God, dealing with my family at Christmas should not be attempted sober." Brandy handed her a glass of red wine and grinned. Luciana drank deep and sighed before holding out her other hand to Natalie. "Hi, I'm Luciana, but everyone calls me Lucy. You must be Natalie."

Natalie nodded, and raised her glass of water in cheers. "Welcome to the mad house."

"At least we're all here now. We can just relax, eat some good food, and drink some good wine. Well, except for you, Preggo." Brandy teased.

"Don't remind me." Natalie sighed. The doorbell rang again, its peal sending a wave of confused silence through the room. Natalie was profoundly grateful that she stood near two strong young women, because when the door opened, she leaned on them, hard. A woman with heavy makeup and a face permanently set into a scowl stepped inside, followed by a tall lanky man with long black hair and a slimy smile.

What the hell?

Enzo came from the kitchen into the nearly silent living room. Seeing the two newcomers hovering near the door, he went to greet them, arms wide open. "Welcome!"

He pulled her mother into a hug. "You must be Portia. I'm so glad you could make it."

Natalie gasped. He knew who she was. He'd been expecting her. Had he invited her? No. No, he wouldn't have done something like that without talking to her first. Would he?

"And you are?" he asked, turning to the man standing next to her mother, the man she never thought she'd see again.

"Kyle, Daisy's dad, and I'm here to get my family back."

With a strangled cry, Natalie dropped her glass and dashed into the kitchen.

MAYBE NATALIE HAD A POINT ABOUT SURPRISES. ENZO certainly hadn't expected this when he'd invited Portia Carras to Christmas. He had wanted to meet her and get her blessing before he took the next step with Natalie. He'd hoped that news of the twins might help Natalie build a bridge with her mother. In his world, babies and growing families were events to celebrate. He certainly hadn't anticipated her bringing Natalie's ex-boyfriend along.

"Well, that's something we should talk about."

"I've got nothing to say to you." Kyle pushed past Enzo, and planted himself on the wall nearest the kitchen door, settling in to wait for Natalie.

Shit. When Enzo and his mom had brainstormed how to make this Christmas special for Daisy, they had both thought that having both sets of grandparents would be a nice surprise. God, how was he going to salvage this?

"Can I get you something to drink, Mrs. Carras?" he asked as he led Portia across the room to the spot her daughter had left vacant, all the while keeping one eye on the brooding tag-along.

"It's *Ms.* Carras," she winked at him before turning to Brandy, who had stepped back towards the bar. "And I'll take a vodka martini. Don't even look at the vermouth." Brandy shook, strained, and poured the requested drink, intently focused on the conversation in front of her.

"So how was the drive down from Lincoln?" Enzo asked, determined to be hospitable. Portia took a deep drink with her eyes closed before replying.

"Awful. When I offered a ride to Kyle, I expected him to be grateful. He's been asking questions about Natalie lately, so I thought he'd be excited. But all he did was bitch and moan the whole way." She knocked back the rest of her drink in one swallow. "After all that, he didn't even offer to take a turn driving. Can you imagine? Another." She set her glass back down in front of Brandy and snapped her fingers. Brandy sucked in a breath as her eyebrows drew together. Enzo hadn't seen her angry before, but he had no doubt that when that cool composure blew it would be impressive.

"Why don't you let me make that for you?" Seth stepped in front of Brandy, picking up the glass while simultaneously spinning his fiancé out of range. "Brandy needs to go help Tia Jo with the cioppino."

"Is that that fishy soup? Ugh. I hate fish." Portia wrinkled her nose in disgust.

Enzo's brain stuttered. She'd come to the Feast of the Seven Fishes and didn't like fish? Fucking perfect.

"The only seafood I like is shrimp. Not that there's anything shrimpy here." Portia eyed Seth and Enzo speculatively as she took her glass back, with a sauced wink. Enzo was sure she'd meant it to be saucy, but she'd already crossed into less than sober territory. He had to wonder when she'd started drinking.

"Oh, that's good then," Lucy chimed in, trying to ease the tension. "My mom made shrimp tamales."

"I don't eat Mexican food." Portia sneered, smoothing a hand over her waist to her hip. "So fattening," she added with a significant glance at Lucy's belly. "When are you due?"

Lucy's angry growl faded as Adrian wrapped an arm around her shoulder and pulled her away from the toxic woman. Enzo tried to salvage the situation. God, he hated conflict, and here he'd invited it in on Christmas Eve. He had to get her out of the house, even if it was just for a few minutes.

"I'm sure we'll figure something out. Let's get the rest of your things from the car. We're putting the presents under the tree." He heard Lucy muttering, "That bitch," to her brother as they walked past, and he couldn't help but agree. Natalie came back in from the kitchen then, and Enzo realized the full extent of his fuck-up.

Her face was blank and pale, eyes wide and glassy, as she crossed the room.

"Hello, Mom."

"Hello, Natalie." Portia looped her arm through his, and squeezed his bicep. His stomach churned with disgust. "This is quite the fellow you've caught. So nice of him to invite me for Christmas when my own child couldn't be bothered."

"And Kyle? Was he invited too, Mom?" Natalie asked, still not looking at Enzo. Yep, he'd definitely stepped in it this time.

"He's been asking about you and his kid."

Kyle stepped from the wall, but Natalie held up her hand to stop him.

"You mean, Daisy? Your granddaughter?"

"Really, do you have to rub it in my face that I'm a grandmother? I don't look like I should be a grandma yet, do I?" Good Christ, had she just batted her eyelashes and rubbed her breasts against his arm? Enzo disentangled himself with a shudder and didn't answer.

"So you just decided to invite my ex-boyfriend along for the ride?"

"You know I hate to drive long distances. If you'd sent me a plane ticket, I wouldn't have needed a car buddy." She turned her attention back to Enzo. "I've always relied on the kindness of the men in my life. My daughter has always been so ungrateful."

Natalie flinched at that jab. Enzo reached for her hand, and it lay limp and clammy in his grip. She still wouldn't look him in the eye. How on earth could he apologize for this?

"I'm sorry that raising me was such a burden." Natalie replied with a cold, flat voice. "While we're on the subject of the ways I've ruined your life, congratulations. I'm making you a grandma again. We're having twins." And on that verbal hand grenade, Natalie pulled her hand from his and walked away.

Kyle stepped into her path, putting a hand on her shoulder. Enzo stiffened, but when Natalie nodded, his heart fell to his feet. All he could do was watch her walk away with her ex trailing behind her. She'd given Kyle a nod, but she wouldn't even look at Enzo. He was so screwed.

The rest of the room was unnaturally silent. Even Buster, Frankie's black and white mutt currently curled up around her feet, seemed to be judging him with soulful eyes before looking away from the mangled train wreck he'd caused.

"Let's go get your stuff from the car."

"Oh, all I have is my overnight bag. Which room is going to be mine?"

"She can have mine," Frankie said. "You couldn't pay me to stay here tonight," she added under her breath, but loud enough that they all heard her anyway, to Jake who'd taken the seat next to her on the couch. "Where are you staying tonight?"

"I had planned on crashing here, maybe on the couch, but it seems like the house might be a little more crowded than expected," Jake said.

An awful thought flashed through Enzo's mind. Did Kyle think he was staying here tonight? *Over my dead body.* It may not be a very Christian sentiment, but surely there was room at an inn, somewhere far, far away.

"You can sleep at The Block. I'll give you a ride later." Frankie added. "It'll give me a chance to harass you about the new contracts while you're tipsy."

"That would be a solid plan, but I don't drink."

"Well, damn it. Then you can drive me home later. I have a feeling tonight is going to call for more wine than usual."

"Deal." Jake grinned at Frankie before shaking his head at Enzo.

Yeah, I know, damn it.

He didn't need the know-it-all show runner to point out that he'd messed up royally.

"The antipasti are ready." Jo announced as she and Aracely came into the dining room, bearing heavy platters of delicious snacks. "Who's hungry?"

No one had stopped her or questioned who she was with when she'd walked straight through the kitchen and out onto the back deck followed by Kyle. She hoped that meant she was trusted and not that they didn't care at all that she'd just left with someone other than their son. In her mind's eye, she flashed back to the last time she'd been on this porch and wished she'd pressed Enzo harder about his freaking surprises.

She owed them all a huge apology. She didn't doubt that her mother had been horrible to everyone in that room, well, everyone she didn't have a vested interest in charming. Natalie had spent her childhood apologizing for her mom and isolating so that no one else had to deal with it. All of the old guilt and anxiety came flooding back. She hadn't wanted to bring toxic drama into this house, but it had followed her anyhow.

At least she'd managed to keep Daisy clear of it for now. She hadn't wanted to go upstairs, but Natalie had insisted and Jo had backed her up with promises of extra presents if Daisy would hide out up in Enzo's room until Nat came to get her. If at all possible she was going to protect her baby from the jerk who'd abandoned them both. Arms crossed, she turned to face Kyle, praying for the strength to get through this.

"Well? What do you want?"

"Come on, Nattie. Don't be like that." He tried to brush the hair back from her face, but she jerked her head back out of his reach. He'd lost the privilege of touching her a long time ago. Seven years ago, to be exact.

"Cut the crap, Kyle. Did you forget that I'm well versed in all of your bullshit? Suddenly you want to see me, after walking away from us without a backward glance?"

"How would you know if I looked back? You disappeared."

"Correction: I built a life for myself and my daughter." Had he been looking for her all this time? No. The Kyle she'd known wouldn't have bothered. If he had cared, he'd have found them long before now. No, she wouldn't slip up and fall into giving him the benefit of the doubt.

"Listen, I know I was an ass back then, but I've changed. Don't you think you've kept her from me long enough?"

Natalie's jaw dropped. The nerve of this guy! Her stomach was churning over the fact that she'd ever let him touch her. That she'd ever fallen for his false charm. She had to get to the bottom of this before he undid all of the hard work she'd done to put herself back together.

"What's this really about?"

"I've been thinking..."

"A dangerous pastime." Natalie chuckled at the quote that flew unbidden from her mouth, but Kyle didn't get the joke. Of course he didn't. He hadn't spent the last six years immersed in Disney movies with Daisy.

"...And I want to give us another shot." Kyle finished his thought with what Natalie was sure he thought was a sexy smolder. All it made her want to do was smack him upside the head with a cast iron skillet. Definitely too much Disney in her life.

"Do you need money? Is that what this is about?"

"No! I miss you. I've seen your makeup videos on YouTube. You look good, baby, and I keep thinking that we should be doing that together. I'm way better looking than that dude in there."

Ah, money AND fame. Well, she had her answer. Her videos had crossed his screen, likely through a mutual friend on social media, and he was here for his cut. Now that she was getting some attention, he was ready to step back in front of her spotlight. He'd always hated being second best. Hell, he had never been any best, not for her.

Kyle stepped closer and put a hand on her shoulder while she was lost in thought. Did he actually think she was wavering?

"I want us to be a family," he murmured.

"What's her name?" Natalie asked.

"Whose name?"

"Our daughter."

He hesitated a moment too long, and Natalie knocked his hand away. He raised it again, catching himself mid-swing, his face crumpled with anger.

"Go ahead. Hit me, you stupid fucker, and see how fast your ass lands in jail."

"Mommy?" Natalie's gaze swung across the yard, searching for the source of her daughter's voice. Her little legs swung down from the tree house. Apparently, Daisy hadn't stayed upstairs. "Are you okay? Who is this? Where's Enzo?" she asked as she clambered down the rope ladder. She sprinted across the yard into Natalie's arms. The shaky panic in her baby's voice shot steel down Natalie's spine. This farce ended now.

"I'm fine, baby." When Daisy reached the top step, Natalie pulled her back against her midsection and wrapped her arms around Daisy's shoulders, as if she could protect all of her babies at once. "This is Kyle."

He got down on one knee, and reached a hand toward Daisy. She kept hers tucked behind her back.

Good girl. Natalie was damn proud that Daisy's bullshit meter was strong and accurate.

"Hi, Dana. I'm your dad." Kyle said, his eyes never leaving Natalie's.

"You might have donated the sperm that made her, but you will never be her dad."

"Think about it, Natalie. We were good once."

"You had it good. *We* were never good. And her name is Daisy. Go away, Kyle. We're done here."

Daisy turned to bury her head in Natalie's torso as Kyle stalked back into the house. She'd never stood up to him like that while they were dating. If she'd known how easily he'd back down, she might have found the strength to leave him sooner. But then she wouldn't have this little angel in her arms. So, no, no second-guessing. And definitely no looking back.

Natalie did just that though, in the next second, peeking over her shoulder towards the kitchen window and saw their future. Enzo stood in the glowing light, his expression unreadable. He'd clearly watched the whole thing and had turned to talk to Kyle. That would be an interesting conversation.

"Was that man telling the truth? Is he my dad? Why did he call me Dana?"

Finding out what was going on in the kitchen would have to wait until she'd navigated the minefield of these revelations with Daisy. Just how she'd imagined spending Christmas Eve.

"He is my ex-boyfriend. You know how we talked about how a boy part and a girl part have to come together to make a baby? He gave me the boy part that made you."

"And Enzo gave you the boy part for the twins."

They'd had several conversations down this path already since they'd told Daisy about the babies. Natalie watched her bright child piece together the data in front of her.

"That's right, but that doesn't make him your dad. That man will never be the father you might want him to be. That's why he can't remember your name."

"Do you think Enzo will be my daddy, like he will be for the twins? Or will he have to go away, too?"

Her precious child had already lost so much. Natalie hoped she wasn't lying when she answered.

"I hope Enzo will be your dad, and I'm sure he'll be around for a long, long time. Enzo is a good man who loves us very much. Kyle only loved that I loved him, so good riddance."

Daisy squeezed tighter around Natalie's waist.

"I love you, Mommy."

"I love you, too, Daisy. Forever and ever."

BACK INSIDE, ENZO HAD SEETHED AND PACED AS HE WATCHED Natalie handle the conversation with Kyle through the kitchen window. He was trying to calm down enough to ask Kyle a question without punching him in the face and wasn't succeeding. His mother had bustled around behind him, finishing dinner, but he'd barely noticed.

All of his focus was on Kyle. He'd dared to put his hands on Natalie. True, she'd shut him down, but when he'd raised his hand in anger, Enzo had almost charged out the door like a mad bull. When he'd dropped to his knee, Enzo had nearly gone through the window. He'd be damned if that asshole swooped in and beat him to the punch.

Only the rage on Kyle's face when he burst in the door and stalked through the kitchen made Enzo feel any better. This was his chance to corner the bastard. *Carpe diem, and all that.* Somehow Daisy had gotten involved and likely had questions, so Natalie was occupied. Enzo followed Kyle into the living room, where he'd just poured a stiff glass of tequila. The jerk knocked it back and poured another before deigning to turn his attention to Enzo, who held his temper in check by a thread.

"Worried?" Kyle asked. Enzo was dying to wipe that smirk off his face, but he refrained. His mission was too important.

"Not in the least. I'm going to marry her."

"Oh yeah? Funny, she didn't say anything about that to me."

Enzo refused to be baited or pulled away from his goal.

"I want you to sign over your rights to Daisy. I'm going to adopt her."

Kyle's eyes burned with hatred and Enzo grinned, aware that he was baiting the beast.

"Fuck you."

"No, thanks. You will never be that little girl's father."

"Oh yeah? Watch me. I'll fight for custody, and then Natalie will come back to me. She'll be so scared of losing her brat that she'll do whatever I say. And you'll be shit out of luck. No more YouTube videos. No more money. No more Natalie." Kyle got right up in Enzo's face, and it took all of his restraint not to head-butt the asshole. How had Natalie ever fallen for this guy? "I can't wait to fuck her again. She always was a hot piece of ass."

"I thought you didn't like fucking her pregnant."

The words left a bad taste in his mouth. Enzo hated talking about Natalie as if she was an object, but it was the only way Kyle would understand he couldn't have her. The simultaneous anger and disappointment on Kyle's face as he shook his head was priceless.

"No. No, she would have said."

"You can congratulate me. We're having twins."

Kyle looked around the room for confirmation, which Frankie gleefully supplied by nodding and asking, "So are you ready to be a daddy times three?"

"You son of a bitch! You ruined everything." Kyle growled and threw his tequila in Enzo's face. Undeterred, Enzo stepped right up to the challenge, and stated his bottom line.

"You are never going to get anywhere near either of them again. They're mine."

Kyle roared and lunged, and Enzo sidestepped so that Kyle glanced off his shoulder. Before Kyle could regain his balance, Enzo decked him with a right cross that sent him crashing into the Christmas tree.

Enzo leaned over the man and tried not to appear as pleased as he felt about the split lip.

"Now, are you going to sign the papers? Or are we going to do this the hard way?"

From his spot amidst the presents, Kyle spat blood at him and replied. "Fuck no, and I'll press charges for assault."

"You might want to rethink that." Lucy pointed to her cell-phone that she held up in her hand. "I got your punk ass on camera. I think a judge would say this was self-defense."

Enzo stepped between Kyle and Luciana just in case, and crossed his arms. "See you in court. Now get the hell out of my house."

Kyle crawled out of the presents and marched out the door, slamming it behind him.

Enzo was not one to go searching out violence, but he had to admit punching that asshole had felt good. A primitive power flowed through his system, setting his blood aflame. He flexed his fingers, absorbing the pain as his penance. Maybe with that jerk gone for good, he could get his plans back on track.

"Well done, big brother." Frankie clapped him on the back, before pulling him into a fierce hug. "What a jerk! What did Natalie ever see in that guy?"

"I have no idea." Enzo said, sarcasm thick on his tongue, emboldened by the adrenaline pumping through his veins. "He's a real winner."

"Once upon a time, he was a way out." Natalie said softly from the doorway, before she dropped her eyes to the ground and backed into the kitchen she'd just left. A tense silence filled the room. *Damn it, when was he going to catch a break?*

"So are you interested in filmmaking or the law?" Jake asked Lucy, breaking the stillness.

"Both," she replied with a grin.

"Well, I just hope no one got me anything fragile." Great-aunt Dulce sipped from a full Manhattan. "I'm not doing returns the day after Christmas because of that asshole."

"Dinner's ready," Jo called from the doorway to the kitchen before she saw the scene in the living room. "What the hell happened to my tree?"

Natalie wanted to crawl under the table as she helped cover it with platter after platter of food.

Fried salt cod in pasta, calamari, insalata di mare, poached lobster tails, cioppino, Daisy's fish sticks, and Graciela's tamales joined spaghetti, kale cakes, polenta, and a huge green salad on the groaning table. Her mouth should be watering now that she was past the hell that was her first trimester, but instead it was her eyes threatening to spill over.

Thank goodness Kyle had left, but Daisy was shaken by the destruction in the living room, and Natalie still had her mother to contend with. Somehow she would get through the rest of this meal and Midnight Mass. Maybe if she just kept her head down and her mouth shut. It had worked for large portions of her childhood.

"Would you please pass the baccalá pasta?"

"Sure. Does anyone need more wine?"

The conversation stuttered around the table as the Valentis tried to get their holiday back on track. People were trying to ignore what had happened, but their brains were so full of it, no one could manage more than basic requests and pleasantries.

No one except Prozia Dulce.

"Enzo, did I ever tell you that your Prozio Emilio was a boxer? I think you inherited his right hook. He was so sexy when he knocked the shit out of someone. It was usually some upstart who had the nerve to flirt with me, of course."

Prozia Dulce reminisced and didn't touch the food on her plate, but sipped from her full cocktail. How was it full again? What number was she on? Natalie had no clue how the woman was still awake, let alone remembering her husband from seventy years ago.

"Zia, please," hushed Dom. "There is a child at the table."

"Never too young to learn that a man who will defend you is one worth keeping." Natalie caught the meaningful look Dulce shot her but didn't rise to the bait. Portia did though, because of course she did.

"So you want my granddaughter to learn that violence is an acceptable response?" Portia turned so Natalie could see the disapproval on her face. "Natalie, I don't know what you see in these people."

Well, then it's a good thing I stopped caring about your opinion a long time ago. Natalie bit back her retort, and tried to change the subject.

"How's your dinner, Mom? Did you find enough to eat?"

Portia toyed with the lovely salad on her plate with a moue of distaste, before pushing her plate away and picking up her wine glass. *Great. More alcohol is just what this situation needs.*

"I'm sure it's fine for you, but I've lost my appetite. The smell of all this fish is turning my stomach. And really, who serves frozen fish sticks at a fancy meal? They look disgusting." She poked at one on her plate with her fork as if she was afraid it would wiggle off.

Natalie took an extra serving of the fish sticks, and looked at Daisy as she bit into one.

"These are delicious, baby."

"I agree," Jo chimed in crunching into her own fish sticks with enthusiasm. "I'd forgotten how tasty these are. Thank you for bringing them, Daisy. I think we should make them a permanent addition to the menu."

Daisy just stared at her plate, silent and still.

That did it.

Every nasty comment, every unfounded accusation, every pain-filled holiday memory of her childhood flooded into Natalie's mind. She'd spent large portions of her childhood staring down and wishing she were anywhere else. That desire to leave had driven her to overlook Kyle's behavior because he'd promised to take her away. It had taken her eighteen years to find the strength to cut her mother out of her life.

She would do better than that for her daughter. From the day Daisy had been born, she'd vowed to be a better mother than her own had been. Her bright and bubbly baby shouldn't have to put up with the same bullshit. Natalie had to confront her mother about her behavior. As soon as dinner was done, she'd kick her right back where she belonged. Out.

"Everything was delicious, Jo. Thank you again for having us."

"You are always welcome in my home and at my table, Natalie. You know that."

We'll see how you feel about that tomorrow morning.

Daisy came around the table and leaned into Natalie's side. She didn't have to say a word. Natalie could practically see her mind whirling with all of the questions tonight had churned up. Daisy had barely touched the fish sticks she'd been so proud of. Natalie rubbed her hand up and down her daughter's strong little spine, hoping she'd raised her with enough backbone to bear the coming turmoil. Inside, Natalie was seething. How dare her mother come in here and spread her crap all over this family?

"Why don't you let me take her up and put her to bed?" Enzo murmured, placing a hand on Nat's shoulder, jolting her from her thoughts. She hadn't noticed that almost everyone was done eating. She glanced at her watch. It was nearly ten! No wonder Daisy was fading. Better that she not witness the coming ugliness.

Natalie pressed a good night kiss to Daisy's forehead and let the man she loved lead her baby up to bed. If anyone had told her a year ago that she'd find a man like Enzo who she would trust with her whole heart, she'd have called them a liar. But here she was, even now, even after this horrible evening, confident that this man had her and her child's best interests at heart. They were going to have words about his idea of a surprise, but she still felt this welling up of love in her chest when she watched him walk away, hand in hand with Daisy. It was a miracle.

Natalie stood and began clearing the table, needing to order her thoughts before she approached Portia. She would never win if she went into the argument emotional. She had two hours before they had to leave for Midnight Mass. Half an hour washing dishes probably wasn't a bad idea.

"You don't have to do that, Natalie. I've got it." Jo protested.

"You've spent all day in the kitchen. You go sit and relax with your family for a bit. Besides, I think I've caused all the damage I can for tonight. Let me at your china."

The joke fell flat, and she backed into the kitchen with her arms full just praying for this night to end.

On the way upstairs, Enzo stopped Daisy in front of his family's nativity scene. At this point, it had its own table. Each year, new pieces were added, and everyone had their favorites. He pointed to the empty manger.

"Do you know this story?"

"I know baby Jesus was born on Christmas."

"Yes, and after Midnight Mass we'll put him in his cradle, but that's not the important part. God gave Jesus to Mary in a miracle, but he couldn't stay and help raise him on Earth. That's where all of these people come in, to welcome him. But Joseph, he was special." Enzo held out the carved figure of a man for Daisy to take. "Joseph loved Mary, and when Jesus was born, he loved him too. He adopted Jesus and raised him as his own."

"He wasn't mad that he had to raise someone else's kid?"

"No, he wasn't, and neither am I. I'd be so proud... This isn't how I imagined tonight going, but I have something important to ask you before you go to bed."

Daisy looked at him with world-weary eyes, too old for her little face. His mistake had put that doubt there. He hoped his apology could take it away again.

"Daisy, I want to be your dad. I want to marry your mom, and for us all to be a family. I love you both so much. But you should get to have a say in this too. What do you think?" He watched the words filter through her agile mind, and prayed she'd come to the same conclusion he had.

"Would we all live together?"

"Yes. You, me, your mom, and the babies."

"And that scary man will go away?"

"I promise I'll never let him near you again."

She dropped her eyes and her voice, suddenly shy. "And you'd be my dad for real?"

"With all my heart."

She hugged him fiercely then, tears streaming down her cheeks.

"Is that a yes?" Enzo had to be clear before he could set his next plans into motion.

"Do I get to keep JoNana instead of Portia?"

Though he wished he could agree wholeheartedly, he had to be honest.

"Well, Portia will still be your grandma, but yes, so will my mom. She will be so excited to be your nana for real."

Daisy's tiny face scrunched up with the intensity of her thoughts. Enzo thought that witch might be a deal breaker. His heart leapt in his chest when she stuck her little hand out solemnly.

"It's a deal," she said as she took his hand. He shook it seriously, before picking her up in a bear hug.

"Deal. Can you keep it a secret until tomorrow? I want to surprise your mom."

"Sure...Daddy."

His heart grew three sizes, filling his chest to the point of bursting. He carried her upstairs and got her settled on an air mattress before searching out Natalie.

His mother found him first in the hallway.

"Oh, Enzo, what have we done?" Jo moaned.

Enzo just shook his head and chuckled. They'd screwed up Christmas good and proper. Jo continued.

"I feel like I pushed for this big family Christmas. I had this picture in my head of how things would be. Poor Graciela has barely said two words all evening because she had to be sedated to come here. Midnight Mass might push her over the edge. And that woman, Portia, she's a piece of work! Who brings her daughter's ex along for Christmas and then proceeds to hit on every man in the room under forty?"

"I missed that last bit."

"I may have promised Seth extra tiramisu for tolerating her. Enzo, did I ruin Christmas?" Jo covered her face with her hands.

"No, Ma. You can't ruin Christmas. It's still the day God sent his love to the world. All we can do is try our best to do the same."

Jo pulled Enzo in for the best gift of all, a mom hug. "Those Sunday School lessons really sunk in, huh?"

"All this has made me really grateful for you guys. When Gabe died, our family could have fallen apart, but it didn't. Yeah, it's been hard figuring this all out, but we are doing that hard work together. I guess I didn't really appreciate how special that is until I saw what Natalie's had to overcome all alone. Which makes me feel even worse for dropping this nightmare in her lap at Christmas."

"You're a good man, Enzo. Intent matters, but now we have to fix this. I'm going to thank Graciela for coming and ask if she wants to go home. I think Rey can probably drive her. As for Portia—"

"Leave Portia to me and Nat. I'm learning that when we don't plan together, shit hits the fan."

"An important lesson to learn. Do you know what I've learned tonight? I am pretty damn grateful for our family, too."

"Can I ask two favors, Ma?"

"Anything."

He leaned in and whispered in her ear, earning a smile.

"Of course. They'll be ready and waiting first thing. And the second?"

"Will you kill me if I miss mass?"

"Go fix things with Natalie. I'll consider that penance."

"I love you, Ma."

"Love you too, baby. Merry Christmas."

ENZO FOUND NATALIE UP TO HER ELBOWS IN SOAPY WATER, scrubbing plates and glasses.

"Did she go down okay?"

"Out like a light. How are you holding up?" He rubbed a hand up and down her tense back.

"Honestly? Awful. I hate her. I hate my mom and the way she makes me feel. And I hate that it makes me feel like a terrible daughter."

Tears mixed with the sudsy water as she wrung out her sponge. His chest tightened at the sight. He had to fix this.

"I'm so sorry. I didn't know."

"You could have asked me, Enzo." Her voice broke. "You should have asked."

"You're right. I should have planned with you. I'm still learning to take more than one person into account."

"It's a shift, isn't it?" Natalie turned from the sink, wiping her cheeks with wet hands. "I forgot too. The night of the recital, I should have saved you a seat. It's been eating me all week. I had planned on it, but I got so distracted by your 'surprises' that I didn't notice when that lady sat down. I had picked up my purse to look for my phone—"

He cut her off with a kiss. "I still got to see the performance, and Daisy knew I was there for her. It's okay. Can you forgive me? Can you still trust that I will be there for you?"

"Is it just that easy for you?"

"I've had longer to get over it, and it was minor compared to this fiasco. But the way I see it, we are going to make mistakes over the next fifty years. If we can't talk about them and forgive each other, it's going to be a long haul. I am so sorry, Natalie. I promise I won't make this mistake again."

Natalie smirked and dried her hands on a snowman towel.

"Only fifty years?"

"Well, by the time we're as old as Prozia Dulce we'll have it all figured out, right?"

She smiled her real smile then and Enzo felt a flicker of hope ignite in his chest. She tucked her head under his chin and let out a sigh as she leaned into his strength. Maybe he could still salvage his plans for tomorrow morning.

"I really am sorry. It wasn't fair for Ma and I to spring Portia on you." Enzo smoothed his hand over her hair.

"Jo was involved?"

"She got it in her head that we should have a big family Christmas, and I got caught up. You know and love my mom. I wanted a chance to know yours, to know Portia approves of the man who loves her daughter. I thought the babies might bring her back into our lives. I never thought that we might not want her there."

"She never wanted to be a mother. Becoming a grandmother again only makes her feel old. It wasn't ever going to go over well." Natalie shook her head under his hand and pulled back. She began stacking wet dishes on the counter. Enzo snatched up a towel instead of the woman he loved, and began drying to keep his hands occupied.

"What was she like growing up?"

"Pretty much the same. When she's around, I go right back to being that quiet insecure kid who has to apologize for existing." Natalie's voice went higher and softened, as if she were that young girl again.

"I still can't believe she brought Kyle, although after tonight I have a better appreciation for just how desperate you must've been to leave."

"Apparently he got wind of the makeup videos blowing up and

he thought he could get his slice of fame by playing nice with me and Daisy."

"I'll admit it took all of my self-control to stay in the kitchen when he raised his hand to you." Enzo stacked the last dry plate in the cabinet and turned to face her.

"What stopped you?"

"You were handling it." He shrugged and added. "I'm kind of glad he came though."

"What? Why?" Natalie asked, incredulously.

"I asked him about renouncing his custody rights."

"Custody? That's a big step. Enzo, don't you think this is something we should have talked about first?" Natalie grabbed the large stock pot from the stove and shoved it into the sink, before snatching up the steel wool pad.

"It is. We are right now. Do you trust me to help parent Daisy?" Enzo stilled her frenzied scrubbing with a hand on her wrist, begging her to look up.

Natalie shook her head. "You know I do. That's not the point."

"The point is the opportunity presented itself, and I seized it."

"Is that what happened to the Christmas tree? You seized Kyle and took out Christmas?" Natalie finally looked at him, and there was a hint of hope and humor in her eyes.

"No, other way around, and that happened when I told him we were pregnant. Lucy got it on camera if you want the slow motion replay. But between that and the fact that he didn't pay support or ask for visits for six years, proving his abandonment should be easy in court.

Enzo skimmed the hair back from her cheek, and she leaned into his hand. He pulled her back into his arms for a hug, wet hands be damned.

"You've done your homework," Nat murmured against his chest.

"I'm serious about making a family with you. I want Daisy to be mine as much as those babies in your belly are."

"I want that too."

Enzo pulled back and then held out his hand. When she took it, his heart felt whole again. "Then we can figure out the rest as it comes. It's time for dessert."

SOME MUCH-NEEDED COFFEE WAS BEING PASSED AROUND THE table laden with desserts when Natalie and Enzo came back into the dining room. Natalie felt stronger now, having worked through things with Enzo. All she had to do was make it through this last course.

Mahalia and Rey had taken baby Jeremiah and Graciela back home, and Daisy was still resting, but everyone else was crowded around the amazing spread of sugar and chocolate. Portia sat like a duchess at a peasant table, her trademark sneer on her face.

"Jo, really it's okay." Adrian reassured Jo. "My mom was excited to try and come. We've been working on expanding her boundaries with the help of her doctor. Tonight was a good step forward."

"I just feel bad that I pushed so hard. I hope she wasn't scared." Natalie would add guilt to her list of things to worry about if Adrian's mother's recovery from agoraphobia was set back by the drama she'd tracked in with her.

"Nonsense. Graciela Villanueva knows her mind. If she'd wanted to say no, she would have." Adrian patted Jo's hand before Portia cut in.

"Really? I didn't think your mother knew that word. Is it the same in Spanish? After all, you have how many sisters and no father?" Portia delivered the barb with the tone of a joke, but everyone saw the ugly for what it was.

Dom half-rose from his chair to defend the now-absent Graciela, and Adrian looked ready to explode, but Natalie stayed them with a raised hand before facing down her mother.

"Is that what pisses you off, Mom? That you didn't say no my father and you got pregnant? That you didn't say it to any of the parade of men you traipsed through my childhood?"

The way her mother's face went pale made Natalie wonder if she'd struck the truth. A truth she'd never considered before. It would explain a lot if her mother hadn't consented to the life she'd been thrust into carrying.

"I'm not going to air our dirty laundry here in front of strangers."

"They aren't strangers. They are family. And don't pretend we've ever talked about my conception, alone, either."

"It's nobody's business."

"I'd say it's my business why my mother has barely tolerated me since birth."

"I did my best."

"Your best was borderline neglect. But you know what?" Natalie moved closer to the table so she could look her mother dead in the eye. "I forgive you. I forgive you for every nasty comment and every forgotten birthday. It's clear you gave all you had to give."

"I don't need your forgiveness." For the first time, the anger on her mother's face didn't hurt.

"No, but I need to give it and move on. I deserve to be loved and happy, no matter what you think. I have found that and more from the people around this table. I don't need it from you anymore. You're free."

"What do you mean I'm free?"

"I won't saddle Daisy with an awful father just because he happened to donate the sperm. I've chosen a better man for that, one who loves her, heart and soul. Why should I settle for anything less? Just because you gave me life doesn't mean you get to make it a living hell anymore. We're done."

"You think you can just toss away all those years, all the sacrifices I made for you?"

"No. I thank you for keeping me alive, but I no longer need your toxic mothering in my life. You can go now."

The shock on Portia's face was oddly satisfying, as if she'd never considered this possibility.

"Are you kicking me out? On Christmas Eve?"

"No, I'm telling you you don't have to stay."

"Daisy will be disappointed if I'm not here in the morning." She was clearly casting around for excuses, but Natalie wasn't having any of it.

"Why? Did you bring her a gift?"

"I didn't know I needed to buy her love."

"That's not what I meant. It's the only reason I could think of that you'd want to say for morning. But the fact that you didn't bring her a present on Christmas is typical. It's just more evidence of your narcissism. She'll see the grandma who loves her in the morning, whether you stay or you go." Natalie looked across the table at Jo, who nodded her support.

Portia took in the stone faces of everyone seated around her, before focusing her rage back on its usual target. Natalie's shield was strong and holding, though.

"You're going to regret this."

"No, I really don't think I am." Natalie turned her attention to Jo, emotionally and physically drained. "The panettone and those honey struffoli look amazing, but I'm exhausted. I think I'll go lay down for a bit."

Jo ran a hand down her back. "Go get some rest, baby. There will be more treats in the morning."

Enzo followed her into the hallway, his warm hand heavy on the base of her spine. As they reached the stairs, Natalie heard the front door slam and Prozia Dulce burst out laughing.

"This is the most entertaining Christmas you've had in years, Jo. Who's ready for mass?"

Natalie just caught Brandy's muttered, "How the hell is she still awake?" and grinned. She'd found quite the family for herself.

These people had welcomed her and her child in with open arms, and when her crazy past showed up for dinner, they'd simply hugged her in tighter and supported her while she figured out how to handle it. Warmth flooded her chest as the gratitude she felt reached out to touch each member of her new family. She wondered if they realized how special that kind of support and understanding was. Leaning into Enzo's shoulder as they climbed the stairs, she vowed to make sure they knew how amazing they all were. Starting with the man next to her.

"You are incredible." Enzo whispered against her neck as he shut and locked the door of his old bedroom.

"I'm just done. None of us deserve that kind of hate."

"The way you handled her was amazing." He smoothed his hands over her shoulders. "You are so strong." He kissed the top of her spine and felt the shiver beneath his lips. "So smart." He licked a path up to her ear and her head dropped heavily. "So loved." He turned her to face him and kissed her with all of his pent-up admiration and relief. "You know that my family is your family now, right?"

She nodded, her eyes glassy with tears.

"Natalie." He kissed her again, needing to chase away her hurts, but when he tasted her salty sadness on his lips, he pulled back. "What's wrong?"

"Nothing."

"Talk to me about this."

"Really, for the first time in my life, there's nothing wrong. The relief is overwhelming." She leaned back into his kiss, eager and sweet. "I think I've been a pretty good girl tonight. What do you say you give me my Christmas present early?"

Enzo grinned. "When we were kids, we always got to open a present early as a reward for making it through mass. You definitely earned a reward tonight."

"Your flexibility is noted." She kissed the hollow below his Adam's apple, and he groaned.

"Care to start unwrapping?" He held out his arms and she giggled, happy in his arms. Her fingers slowly worked at the long line of buttons down his flannel shirt. The anticipation was going to kill him before she even made it to his belt. Gripping either side, he tore his shirt open, Hulk-style.

"Oh. You're that kind of gift-opener? I don't think this is going to work." He raised an eyebrow as she slid her hands up his torso and over his shoulders, pushing the torn flannel to the floor. "You see, I like to take my time, let the anticipation grow, before I finally open the package."

"If you let this package grow any bigger before you open it, I might not be able to walk tomorrow."

She cupped him through his jeans and his hips thrust against her, instinctively reaching for more of her love. In the end, he gave her just what she wanted, a long torturous build up, tasting and savoring every new gift of pleasure, until they were both beyond frantic. When he finally gave her the gift that keeps on giving, she was out of her mind with pleasure. He kissed her hard to muffle her cries, but he was humbled by the joy she took from every stroke. She cupped his cheek as they came back down, and he knew everything was going to be okay. Exhausted and sated, she curled up in his old twin bed, tucking the cover under her chin and nudging his bare ass out onto the floor.

When soft snores emanated from the bed, he quietly dressed in his clothes for morning and headed downstairs. He had a few Christmas miracles left to pull together for the woman and children who deserved all of the love and magic he could muster.

AROUND THREE, NAT HAD WOKEN ALONE IN BED. SHE HAD tiptoed down the stairs and found Enzo passed out on the couch, fast asleep. After loading the stockings and leaving her own special gifts from Santa, she had pulled a crocheted afghan over him and went back upstairs to steal a few more hours of sleep. This time, she awoke to Daisy's giddy face two inches from her own.

"Wake up, Mommy! It's time!"

Her daughter bolted from the room, job done, leaving Natalie to tug on clothing and follow. She stumbled downstairs and into the softly filtered early morning light that edged the scene in the living room with a golden glow. The tree had been righted and presents had multiplied overnight. The mantel was nearly covered by all of the stockings.

Frankie and Jake came in the front door with fresh coffee from Starbucks. Sofia and Adrian were snuggled up on the couch. Brandy and Seth were discussing the nativity scene with Daisy, and Enzo was nowhere to be seen.

"Where's Buster?" Nat asked.

Frankie grinned. "For the safety of the presents, I left him home. He really likes shredded paper."

"Look, Mommy! I got to put baby Jesus in his crib. Now they are a real family." Seeing her daughter grin over the idea of family made Natalie's heart jolt. She was so close to being able to give this family to her baby.

Dom came in from the den with his hands cupped in front of him.

"Here, Daisy-girl. Add these to the scene."

He handed her a delicately carved little girl holding a flower and a figure of a mother cradling her pregnant belly.

"Did you carve these, Dom?" Natalie asked, watching the older man's eyes go shiny as he watched her daughter carefully admiring his work.

"It's just a hobby. Everyone has a special piece in the nativity."

"So these are for me and Mommy?" Daisy asked quietly.

"They sure are. You're part of the family now." Daisy hugged Dom around the waist and his tears ran over. He reached for Natalie, pulling them both into a bone-crushing hug. Swiping his eyes, he released them and coughed.

"Will you make ones for the twins next year?"

"You bet. Now, let's get this show on the road. Jo!" he bellowed towards the kitchen. "Are you ready?"

"Almost!" Came her hollered reply.

Moments later, Enzo appeared bearing a tray of cookies that

looked like they'd been cooked in a waffle iron and then coated with powdered sugar.

"What are those?" Natalie asked, her mouth watering at the smell of almonds and caramel.

"The first pizelles of Christmas." He shot a look at his sisters that Nat couldn't begin to fathom. "Don't even think about it, you two." He turned back to Natalie. "Someone once told me that I looked at you like the first pizelle of Christmas, hot off the griddle. That's when I knew this was serious. So it seems only fitting that you get the first this year."

Natalie grinned and took exaggerated care in picking one and biting in. "Mmm. That's delicious." She licked the powdered sugar off her lips slowly, teasing him deliberately, enjoying this relaxed and playful Christmas morning after the evening's turmoil.

"Come here and give me a taste." He leaned in to kiss her in front of God and family, and she happily let him.

Dom took the tray from the distracted Enzo and set it down on the coffee table, laughing as the hordes descended. Jo came in with a tray of sliced panettone and coffee cakes, and set it down on a side table, before sitting down next to her husband on the couch, to the shock and wonder of all. This was quite a reversal after the six months of near silence from the matriarch of the family. It was no secret that Jo and Dom weren't seeing eye-to-eye after the death of their eldest son, Gabriel, and Jo's subsequent retirement. No one was more surprised than Dom, judging by his dropped jaw and bulging eyes.

But when Jo dropped a hand on his knee, he unfroze and wrapped his arm around her shoulder. The tender kiss pressed to her temple drew them even closer together before he sat back, wiping his eyes again.

Christmas miracles were in the air. Daisy was tasked with delivering gifts to everyone. Dom's gift of a starter nativity set for each of his children was topped only by the framed set of three sonograms from Natalie and Sofia.

Jake's gift of a muzzle harness to Frankie prompted much

teasing and laughter.

"It's for Buster, so you can bring him on set again."

Natalie never thought she'd see the day her always-in-control boss man, Jake Ryland, turned beet red with embarrassment, but it was clearly a day for firsts.

Daisy was on cloud nine. She'd never seen a pile of presents so high and all of them bore her name. Natalie smiled indulgently as Daisy tore through the paper, uncovering a big sister t-shirt, a pair of binoculars, and a Fairyopolis book.

Natalie handed Enzo a big shipping box with a grin. "Here. This one's from me."

She grinned at the way he tore through the paper, remembering their time alone last night. He opened the huge box to find two smaller boxes wrapped inside.

"Well played, stinker."

He opened the first box inside and stilled.

"What is it?" Frankie asked.

"It's business cards for my new company. These are gorgeous, Nat. Where did you get them?"

"Sofia helped me design them. Open the other one."

He opened up the other small box and laughed.

"Sunscreen."

"Gotta keep my man safe from those UV rays. Airbrushing is so much safer than a real tan." He leaned in for a kiss that did nothing to quiet the butterflies in her belly.

"Keep going," Natalie said.

Enzo looked into the big shipping box again, eyebrows furrowed.

"It's empty."

"Yeah. So are half of the drawers and closets at my place. Maybe you could fill it with some stuff and move in?"

She'd done it. She'd reached for what she wanted, putting her desires out into the world. When he kissed her deeply again and Daisy began making gagging noises, she knew she'd won. Her smile broke their kiss and Enzo leaned away from her.

"Okay, your turn, you two."

He pulled a stack of gifts from beneath a table and Daisy reached for them eagerly.

"Wait! There's an order. Here, open this one first or it'll spoil the surprise."

"More surprises, Enzo?" Natalie teased.

"I've got a good feeling about these. Trust me."

Miracle of miracles, she did.

He handed Daisy a small shoebox wrapped with a candy cane bow.

"It's more fairy furniture!" Daisy crowed. "Two cribs, two stump chairs, and two little mushrooms."

"I made them so we can welcome the twins into our fairy family too."

"I love them. Thank you, Enzo."

"You're welcome. Now this one." He handed Daisy a flat box that looked like it would hold clothes. She opened it and paused, her eyes full of confusion. Natalie leaned over and in the box was a stack of papers and a charm bracelet. Enzo hastened to explain.

"Daisy, that's the paperwork to apply for adoption. I want to be your dad, but I'm giving you that to hold onto until you're sure." He lifted the bracelet out and fastened it around her little wrist. "See here? There's a charm for each of us. A daisy for you, a shovel for me, a lipstick for your mom, and two bottles for the twins. We can keep adding memories to it in the future. It's my promise to you that I'll always love you and take care of our family."

Daisy threw herself into his lap and cuddled hard. Enzo laughed, and Natalie had never seen anything more precious.

"Which leaves this for you." Enzo held a small flat circular present out to Natalie. It looked like a powder compact...and it was. She tossed the wrapping paper onto the pile on the floor and murmured, "Thank you," hoping she'd kept the disappointment out of her voice. She'd given him half of her apartment, and he'd given her makeup?

"Open it."

She looked into Enzo's eyes and saw the laughter and love dancing there. She opened the compact and inside was a sparkling little diamond ring. She was speechless, so Enzo filled the silence.

"It's not a big stone, but it carries a big promise. I will love you, Natalie Carras, for the rest of our lives. I might still make mistakes, but I promise to learn from them. Good times, bad times, I want to have them with you by my side. I want to make plans for our future. I want to parent these beautiful children with you. I want to sit in this living room surrounded by *our* family every Christmas morning. Marry me, Natalie."

Still struck mute by the best surprise, she nodded and threw herself into his lap too, pulling the two most important people in her life close to her heart. The rest of the room erupted into cheers and applause, and Natalie knew she was finally home.

THIS WOULD GO DOWN AS THE WORST AND HER FAVORITE Christmas ever. She grinned as she turned her hand back and forth, letting her diamond twinkle in the lights from the tree. Everyone had scattered while Jo made brunch. She and Enzo alone remained curled up on the couch. *A Christmas Story* played muted on repeat on the TV in front of them.

"You know, I always hated the holidays. They never lived up to the ones in the movies."

"I'd say this year was right up there with the Griswolds." Enzo ran a hand down her hair.

"Closer to *A Miracle on 34ᵗʰ Street*." Natalie grinned and snuggled closer into the security of his arms.

"Our love is a true Christmas miracle." Enzo kissed her forehead. "*Natalia*. In Italian, your name means born on Christmas," he mused.

"It certainly feels like I'm starting a new life today. I can't wait to get started."

A Perfect Fit by Adrienne Bell

✦

THIS IS THE SECOND CALL FOR FLIGHT 322 FROM SAN JOSE TO Chicago.

Cynthia rolled her eyes toward the textured beige ceiling as the announcement crackled over the gate's public address speakers. Deep down she wanted to sigh, but she didn't dare. Not while she was still on the phone with her mother. Not when she was only four hours away from having to spend her entire Thanksgiving weekend in the woman's house. That was exactly the kind of trouble Cynthia didn't need. So, she swallowed down her frustration and kept her sighs to herself.

"Mom, I have to go," she said, doing her best to keep her voice even. "They're calling for us to get on the plane."

"*Us?* Who is us?" her mother asked. "I thought you were coming alone."

"I am, Mom." Cynthia tightened her grip on the leather handle of her carry on. Her fingers trembled under the strain. "I just meant all us passengers. They need us to get off our phones and on the plane now."

Cynthia didn't know why she bothered. She'd talked to her

mother enough times to know that the woman wasn't actually listening to a word she said.

"Of course, your father and I would be over the moon if you ever did bring someone home," she said.

Uh, no. Even if she was in a serious relationship—which she wasn't—there was no way Cynthia would ever drag someone she loved into her parents' house during the holidays. Hell, she wouldn't even do it to someone she hated. Surely, torture like that went against the Geneva Conventions.

Okay, maybe that was a *little* dramatic. Normally, Cynthia did okay when dealing with the members of her family one-on-one. Sure, her mom was a little pushy, and her dad was closed off and silent, but nobody was perfect. It was only when the whole Ruisch family—her sister, her nephew, her aunts and uncle—got together under one roof that the situation became truly unbearable. Fortunately, that only happened once a year.

"Maybe if you finally lost some weight you'd be able to catch a man's eye," her mom kept going. "You really need to work on that next year. We'll talk all about it when you get here. I've been doing some research into different diet programs for you, and—"

This is the third and final call for flight 322 from San Jose to Chicago.

That was it. Even if it wasn't the last call, Cynthia had already had more than enough.

"Gotta go, Mom." She jabbed her finger down on the End Call button and marched toward the line.

She didn't even make it halfway to the woman scanning the boarding passes before a wave of guilt and regret washed over her. Damn. She was going to pay for that. Even if she had been able to blunt some of the annoyance in her sharp tone, Cynthia knew she would still find her mother nursing hurt feelings the moment she stepped through the door.

It was always going to be something. Every year, some little melodrama was destined to play out in the house. Last year, it had been the Disaster of the Ungrateful Overweight Daughter. The year before it was the Trial of the Unappreciated Parents. It looked like this Thanksgiving it would be the Tragedy of the Rushed Goodbye.

Cynthia's mood continued to sour with every step down the crowded gangway toward the plane. Every year she went through the same crap when she went home for Thanksgiving. There would be the snide comments about her career, her love life, her finances. And somehow her family would always find a way to bring the root cause back to her weight.

To hear her mother say it, you would think that thin people lived magical, problem-free existences. Except Cynthia knew that was bull. The only difference Cynthia could see between her life and the lives of her skinny friends were that they faced their troubles in a size 6 instead of a 22.

Of course, there were *some* things that were easier for those friends. They could buy the cheap seats on a plane, knowing that while they might be a little cramped and uncomfortable, they'd be able to fit inside the smaller space. Cynthia wasn't so lucky. Flying home on the busiest travel day of the year didn't just mean springing for an overpriced coach ticket. It meant she needed to upgrade to the section that came with a full—*eyeroll*—decadent inch of space and an extra hundred dollars on the price tag.

It didn't help her mood that everyone around her seemed to be just as miserable as she was. Cynthia looked around but didn't spot a single smiling face in the crush of people. The energy surrounding her in the cramped hallway was every bit as heavy and stale as the recirculated air. Nobody seemed to care that today was the official start of the holiday season. Then again, how could anyone in their right mind find the will to be jolly in a cheerless airport?

This wasn't some winter wonderland. This was hell, plain and simple.

Cynthia shuffled forward a step at the same time as the woman next to her, and their arms brushed against each other. Reflexively, Cynthia pulled her bag in closer to her side.

"Sorry," she muttered.

Apparently, the other woman wasn't feeling half as conciliatory. She shot Cynthia *the look*. The one she knew all too well. The look that took her in from top to bottom, and made it clear that she was taking up too much space. Space that could be better used by someone smaller. Someone thinner. Someone far more worthy.

Cynthia did her best to shoot the woman an apologetic smile. The same one she always gave when she received *the look*. She'd given it so many times, it was automatic, like saying bless you when someone sneezed. She wasn't exactly sure why she did it. She just knew it was expected.

Of course, there was a huge difference between expected and *accepted*. The woman made that abundantly clear. She muttered something under her breath about lazy, rude people before slipping to the front of the line.

Cynthia tried to shake off the twinge of pain that shot through her at the stranger's comment. She might as well get used to the jabs about laziness. By the time the holiday weekend was over, she'd be on the receiving end of too many *looks* and muttered comments to count. That bitch might think she gave good glare, but she had nothing on Cynthia's family.

Cynthia pulled herself in as small as possible as she entered the plane. She nodded a greeting at the flight attendant and did her best not to wobble as she trailed her carry-on bag behind her down the narrow aisle. Fortunately, business class was near the front of the plane, but the people that had boarded before her were already spilling their arms and feet into the aisle, making a challenging course for Cynthia to maneuver through.

She just needed to get to her seat. After that, she could get through the rest of her regular flying routine—sit down, press herself against the window so she didn't make contact with the person next to her, and stay that way for the next four hours until the plane landed. Sure, it wasn't her favorite form of travel, but at least she had a system that worked.

The only thing she really hated was when the aisle passenger got there before her. When that happened she had to go through the agony of making eye contact and asking them to get up so she could get to her seat. She hated that more than anything else, actually having to ask someone else to make way for her. But there was no way around it. Given how cramped the rows were there was no way that she could shimmy past anyone.

And because it looked like the devil was working overtime, that's exactly what happened this time. Cynthia's chest tightened as she spotted a man sitting in the seat next to hers. It didn't help that he looked to be a big guy too. In her experience, big guys didn't get the same treatment as plus-size women. They were usually cut a lot more slack. Especially the cute ones.

And the guy sitting in her row was definitely one of the cute ones. And the closer she got the clearer that became—short-cropped hair, gorgeous bronze complexion, and big brown eyes.

He sure was easy to look at.

Which was why Cynthia was quick to look away. She could already feel the heat creeping into her cheeks from just a brief glance. The last thing she wanted was to have to explain why she was blushing and stuttering as she asked him to let her slip past.

She did her best to keep her eyes focused on anything *other* than her seatmate as she moved the last few feet down the aisle. She looked at the other passengers, she looked for the emergency exits, she looked for an open compartment to stow her carry on.

Except she couldn't find one. Thanks to her mother's reluctance to say goodbye, all the ones on the way to her seat were already full. There was a little empty spot in the bin above her seat, so she lifted her bag up and gave it a try.

No luck. The bag was too big for the small space...and now that it was above her head, too heavy for her to balance with any kind of grace. Cynthia quickly scooted over to the next compartment to try her luck next, but today just wasn't her lucky day. She craned her head around trying to check the space behind her, but she couldn't see that far.

"There's some room over here," a voice said from over her shoulder. A deep, friendly voice. "Here, let me help you."

Suddenly, the weight was lifted from her hands. Cynthia turned around to see the cute guy easily carrying it down the aisle a few rows. He reached inside the bin, turning and pushing the other bags this way and that, until, just like magic, Cynthia's bag slid inside.

"There you go." The man turned toward her with a smile. "A perfect fit."

She was wrong. This guy wasn't just cute. He was downright hot. The smile he gave her lifted his cheeks and lit up his warm eyes...and threatened to bring the blaze right back to Cynthia's cheeks.

"Thanks," she muttered. Then she quickly seized the opportunity to slide past his empty seat and into hers. Cynthia kept her head down as she buckled up. Once that was done, she dug into her purse for the in-flight essentials—a magazine, her phone, and her earbuds.

Her earbuds.

Oh, shit.

Cynthia patted her pockets, all the while knowing that what she was looking for wasn't on her. They couldn't be because they were still in her carry on. She closed her eyes and let her head fall back against the seat. She could see them, clear as day, tucked into the outside pocket of her bag. She'd meant to get them out before getting on board, but she'd been so preoccupied with her mother's yearly pre-Thanksgiving call that she'd forgotten to take them out.

Well, it was too late now.

"Are you okay?" The hot guy with the friendly voice asked beside her.

"Yeah." Cynthia nodded but didn't dare look his way. The way her horrible day was going, she was bound to have half a salad stuck between her teeth. "I just forgot something."

"Something important?"

Only the one thing that made four hours in this flying tin can bearable.

Cynthia shook her head. "No. I'll be fine."

No matter how chivalrous Mr. Charming Smile had been helping her out with her bags, she wasn't about to ask him to get up just so she could fumble around with a carry on stowed a few rows back. She'd already had one person call her rude today. She didn't want to risk him thinking the same thing.

No, she was just going to have to wait until Chicago to listen to music.

She tucked the phone back into her purse and slid the magazine next to her leg. She'd wait until the silence became unbearable before she'd crack that bit of entertainment open. Now all that was left was to get into position. She turned toward the window, shifting her weight to her right hip, She draped her left arm across her lap far enough that her hand rested on the opposite leg. It wasn't the most comfortable position, but it wasn't the worst either. More importantly, it worked. As long as she kept her knees pressed together, there wasn't a single part of her that crossed over the dividing line of the center armrest. Now all she had to do was keep her eyes outside.

It was easy to do as the plane took off. That was her favorite part after all. There was something magical about those first few moments of flight, of pretend weightlessness, of watching the world slip away below you. Even though Cynthia understood the physics, there was still something unbelievable about it.

She watched the ground below as they rose and rose. The individual waves on the bay disappeared. The details of the cityscapes and hillsides faded into broad strokes. She stayed still the whole time, just watching. Maybe it wasn't flying she disliked, it was everything associated with it—the dread of visiting her family, the nasty looks from strangers, the cramped conditions.

Most times, she was able to grin and bear it, but this time something felt different. Maybe it was her mother's complaints. Maybe it was the nasty woman that had grumbled at her when she'd come on the plane. Maybe it was just the plain old holiday blues, but this time Cynthia felt more cramped and uncomfortable than ever before.

By the time the seatbelt light when off and the flight attendant made the announcement that they could move around, Cynthia realized that she'd been sitting stock still for over forty-five minutes.

For half a second, she started to move. Her arms relaxed and her knees fell apart just an inch. Her body ached, and she was dying to stretch out some of the tension in her muscles. But the second she caught sight of Mr. Hottie in her peripheral vision, she caught herself and draped her arm over her lap.

"Afraid of flying?" he asked.

Cynthia glanced his way. His eyes were just as warm and friendly as before—milk chocolate brown, and every bit as tempting.

"Excuse me?"

"I was just wondering if you were afraid of flying," he repeated.

Cynthia shook her head.

"Really?" There wasn't any cruelty in his voice. No disbelief either. Just curiosity.

"Do I seem afraid?"

"You seem...tense."

"Well, going home for the holidays will do that to a person."

"You must have one hell of a family then because you haven't moved an inch in an hour." He laughed a little and the light-hearted sound snuck beneath her defenses. Cynthia found herself opening up a little.

"You have no idea how right you are," she admitted. "Though the keeping still part is for your benefit."

His brows pulsed up just a bit in surprise. "Mine?"

"These seats are so small, and I'm...not," she said. "I've found over the years that people appreciate it if I keep myself—"

"Balled up tight?"

"Something like that."

His smile was back. And oh, she liked that smile. After the hell of waiting through seemingly endless airport lines, and absorbing all the tension hanging in the air above the fed up crowds, that smile was like a cool ocean breeze.

"Don't feel like you have to fold yourself into a pretzel for me," he said.

Cynthia found herself smiling back. "Really, it's no problem. I'm used to it."

"That's a shame," he said. "But stop. It's uncomfortable just looking at you."

Cynthia opened her mouth to say she was sorry, but stopped herself. Apologizing hadn't done any good before. Besides, he was right. She was uncomfortable. She inched her arm over toward the armrest. She even pulled her shoulder off the wall.

"Better?" she asked.

He shot her a funny look. One that actually made her want to laugh. The kind of look that said *you can't be serious*.

"We have another three hours," he said. "If you don't relax for yourself, do it for me. I'm getting a crick in my neck just looking at you."

"You don't really want me to spread out." It was a thought that had flown through her head a thousand times when people told her not to worry so much, but she'd never actually said it out loud before. There was just something about this guy—this stranger—that put her at ease. She couldn't explain it.

"Why? Are you afraid I'll get upset if we touch? Here." He leaned over in his seat until the top of his arm pressed against hers. "There. It's already happened. We've touched, and I'm not angry. Are you?"

"No." And she really wasn't. It was a strange realization. If anything she was amused. She couldn't remember the last time anyone had gone to such extremes to make her feel comfortable.

"Good," he said and leaned back fully into his seat. "Then take a real breath and relax for a minute."

And she did. It must have been something in his voice because it wasn't even a conscious decision. One second her chest felt tight and tense, and the next she was taking a real breath. One that filled her lungs completely.

"Better?" he asked.

She nodded.

He twisted in his seat just far enough to extend his hand. "I'm Javier."

"Cynthia."

"You live in the Bay Area?" he asked.

"Fremont."

The smile lines around his eyes intensified. "San Jose."

Something lit up inside her knowing that they lived so close, not that she was about to show it. "I figured you were local." She gestured to his orange and black jacket. "No one else would willingly admit to being a Giant's fan."

Dear God, what was she doing? Teasing him? This felt dangerously like flirting. Of course, it had been a *really* long time since she'd tried to flirt with anyone. The terrible thought that she was doing it all wrong rushed through her head.

Then again, maybe not. Javier's smile turned from friendly to downright playful. "You don't like baseball?"

"No, I love it," she said, her grin growing wider. "That's why I watch the A's."

He laughed loud enough for a few heads around them to turn their way. Reflexively, Cynthia retreated a little from the attention. Javier, on the other hand, didn't seem to notice. And if he did, he certainly didn't care.

"Well, no one's perfect," he said. "I bet you look beautiful in green."

Was he...was he flirting back?

He couldn't be. Her luck wouldn't allow it. She was having the kind of day where everyone scowled and grimaced at her. Not the kind where she was seated next to a hot, friendly big guy. He was probably just being nice. There was no way that he could actually be into her.

But whatever his motives, Javier certainly didn't mind talking to her. Or facing her. Or letting her take up the space next to him. And he was right. They were stuck together for the four hours. She'd be doing herself a favor if she gagged the nasty voices in her head, stopped overthinking everything, and just enjoyed the moment.

So, that's what she did.

"Are you off to visit family too?" she asked.

He nodded. "My *mami's* side. You?"

"My parents in Naperville."

"Ah." His eyes widened in understanding. "The 'burbs."

With anybody else, Cynthia felt the words would have come out judgmental and toxic, but Javier wasn't like anybody she'd ever met before. He sounded like he'd finally figured out the answer to a problem that had been puzzling him.

"That must have been where you grew up," he said.

"Oh God," Cynthia blanched. "Don't tell me it shows."

He cocked his chin to the side, just a little. He looked at her for a long moment, like he was really taking her in. Really seeing her. Usually, when people eyed Cynthia it made her horribly uncomfortable, but this wasn't *the look*. It wasn't even a stare. This was about as far away from those things as a person could get. The look in his eyes was warm, and comfortable, and kind.

"You didn't fit in there did you?" he asked.

She shook her head. "Not even a little."

"That's what shows." The smile still shone in his eyes and lifted his cheeks, but his voice took on a sympathetic note. "So why do you want to go back?"

"I don't want to. I *have* to." Javier arched his brows. His expression made it clear he wasn't buying it. Cynthia doubled down. "It's Thanksgiving. I always go and see my family for Thanksgiving. It's not like I have much of a choice."

"There's always a choice."

Cynthia chuckled. "Not with my family there's not. Trust me, if I don't show up tonight, chances are I'll wake up to the sound of my mother banging down my door tomorrow morning."

"Because she misses you that much?" he tried.

Cynthia shook her head. "Because without me there to pick on, the rest of the family would have to interact with each other, and that would be a bloodbath."

He smiled. "You're telling me you come from a family of violent badasses?"

Ha. Hardly. "I come from a long line of passive-aggressive jerks. It's much worse."

He laughed again. This one louder than before. More people turned around to look their way, but this time Cynthia didn't mind as much. There was something soothing about that rich laugh of his that took the sting out of the judgments of strangers.

A mischievous sparkle lit up his eyes. Maybe it was the effect of being so close or the sustained contact of their gazes, but Cynthia felt a tingle rush through her body at the sight.

"Well, then, I bet you could use a drink," he said.

"I'd love one," she said. "Too bad I don't know any good bars at thirty-five thousand feet."

"That's okay. I know a place." He gave her leg a single pat as he rose from his seat. Another thrill ran over her skin leaving goosebumps in its wake. "The selection might be a little limited, but that just means I'll have to take you to a nicer place the next time."

His words hung in the air as he moved up the aisle, and Cynthia was suddenly grateful he was walking away. Her cheeks were burning. Absolutely on fire.

Next time?

There was no doubt he was flirting now. Javier, with his adorable smile, warm demeanor, and downright gorgeous brown eyes, was *absolutely* flirting with her. Hell, he was off to get her a drink.

Cynthia fought the urge to watch him go. It was a losing battle. She didn't make it five seconds before she craned her head up just far enough to peer over the seat back in front of her. For a moment, she feared that Javier might turn back around and catch her sneaking a peek at him, but she soon realized that wasn't going to happen. Even walking down the narrow airplane aisle, his stride was confident. This was a man who didn't check around to see if he had someone's attention.

But on the other hand, he didn't seem cocky, or arrogant. Just self-assured. The man was obviously comfortable in his skin. And why wouldn't he be? It was dead sexy skin, after all. He was everything Cynthia was attracted to—soft and strong, plush and humming with vitality.

Cynthia dropped her head back down as he turned the corner into the flight attendant's alcove in the center of the plane. She took the moment to fluff her blonde curls and straighten her clothes. She even reached into her purse and pulled out her lipstick. She did her best to touch it up in the faint reflection that showed in the small oval window at her side. It looked like she could probably do with a little extra mascara and a touch up of foundation, but all that was stowed away in her carry-on bag.

But she couldn't help but feel that even this little bit of primping was ridiculous. A couple of cute quips and a sexy smile didn't mean much...but it didn't mean nothing either.

Besides, she found she liked this nervous flutter in her tummy. It felt good. Good enough to want to put a little performance into her flirting. There was nothing wrong with that. Was there?

Of course, there wasn't. After all, she wasn't some dour, humorless person. Not usually, anyway. Only this time of year. Only the third Wednesday in November when she had to fly halfway across the country to spend the weekend with people who were far more comfortable picking apart her problems than facing their own.

Even if nothing came out of this flirtation—and she was pretty sure that nothing would—at least she'd still have the memory of his kind eyes and deep laugh to keep her company as she endured her family's drama. The thought of his smile alone would be enough to get her through at least a few diet lectures and countless *looks*.

Cynthia had just finished flicking the last of the fresh lipstick off the corners of her mouth when Javier returned. In each hand he held a short, squat plastic cup. He handed her one before settling back in his seat. Cynthia looked down in mock horror at the aggressively bright red drink.

She couldn't hold back her chuckle. "Okay, I give. What in the world is this supposed to be?"

"The label on the can said strawberry margarita," Javier said.

"The *can*?" Cynthia gave it a sniff. It didn't smell like any strawberry she'd ever come across.

"The selection turned out to be a little more limited than I thought. It was either this or the 'traditional' lime version." The way he shuddered when he said *traditional* made Cynthia laugh.

"You're telling me it was worse than this?" she teased.

"You didn't see it," he said. "That green was...unnatural. Like the color of anti-freeze. Trust me, this was the better choice."

Cynthia glanced down at the fuchsia liquid sloshing in her cup. "That remains to be seen."

"But wait, there's more," he said, digging into his pockets. He fished out some packets—nuts, pretzels, and crackers. "Not exactly a Thanksgiving feast, but it should hold us over."

"It's great," Cynthia said. "Thank you for going to the trouble."

"Walking fifteen feet is no trouble." Javier raised his plastic glass. "To new friends."

"To new friends," she agreed and touched her glass to his. They both took a sip...and winced at the same time. The can might have said strawberry margarita, but all Cynthia tasted was sickly sweet corn syrup and the harsh burn of alcohol.

Javier gave her an apologetic glance. "Then again, maybe the anti-freeze wouldn't have been so bad."

She laughed. "I have a feeling there were no good choices."

He nodded. "Do you want me to toss it for you?"

Cynthia pulled her glass away, holding it protectively against her chest. He wouldn't grab for it there, would he? And would she even mind if he did?

What? Where had that thought come from? It wasn't as

though she could blame the drink. She'd barely choked down one sip.

"Don't even think about it, buddy," she teased him. "I was promised a drink, and by God, I'm going to have mine."

"Fair enough," he said, dropping his voice down low. "But I should warn you, the drink comes with a price."

Cynthia's arched a brow. "And you didn't tell me this before because..."

That mischievous twinkle was back in his eyes. Dang, she had a feeling that he'd broken a lot of hearts with that look.

"Because I didn't want to risk you saying no," he said.

Cynthia couldn't help but laugh at his boldness. "That's cheating, Javier."

"Javi," he corrected her. "All my friends call me Javi."

"Are we friends?" Funny. She'd meant the question as a joke, but she couldn't manage to keep the note of hopefulness out of her voice.

"We must be," he said. "Because I only drink with friends."

Cynthia pressed her lips together in mock consternation. "Friends don't lie to each other, Javi."

"I didn't lie," he said. "I just didn't reveal my true intentions."

"And what are those?" *Damn.* There was even more hopefulness this time. Hopefulness, and just a hint of longing. She *really* needed to work on her poker face.

"To know more about you," he said.

"*Really?*" Cynthia winced. Maybe it would have been better to keep that last word in her head. Especially since he seemed so sincere. He shifted in his seat and leaned in a little closer.

"Of course," he said. "It's a long flight, and you seem very interesting, Cynthia."

A quick rush of heat ran over her skin when he said her name.

"Well, I'm afraid you're in for a terrible disappointment," she said, "because there's not that much to know."

"Oh, no," Javi said. He shook his head. "I don't believe that for a second."

"No, really, it's true," she tried. "I live in Fremont. I work as a market analyst in Campbell. I like Chinese takeout, and I spend most of my time off watching movies and going for walks in the hills around my house. There, that took twenty seconds, and you know practically everything about me."

"Not everything. You forgot about baseball," he prompted.

"True," she conceded before taking another sip of her *margarita*. "I like baseball."

"How about football?"

Cynthia frowned as she shook her head. "Nope. It's also a no to basketball and soccer. I do like hockey, though."

"Interesting." Humor lit up Javi's eyes. "You like it rough. I wouldn't have guessed."

If it was anyone else, Cynthia probably would have found his words and tone inappropriate. But not Javi. She wasn't sure why, but he didn't seem like he was trying to diminish or embarrass her. Even more importantly, she had this feeling deep down that if she told him he'd crossed a line he would stop and not be upset about it. There was an instant comfort there. A sense of safety that she intuitively felt.

"Not rough," she countered. "Just intensely physical."

Dear God, what was she doing? A little flirting was one thing, but this was veering dangerously close to full come on territory.

"We should watch a game together sometime," he said.

"At a sports bar?" she asked, knowing she was toying with him. "Because I'm not really into sports bars."

Javi's smile grew. "Alone then. We should watch one together...alone."

Cynthia glanced down at her lap. Heat burned her cheeks. She couldn't pretend ignorance. She knew exactly what he was saying. And even though she knew he was probably just joking around with her, it was fun to imagine that he wasn't. Besides, she'd never played with anyone like this before.

And *playing* was the perfect word for it. Cynthia didn't feel a sense of expectation or pressure from Javi. When she looked in his eyes she didn't see any expectation that she needed to say a certain thing or act a certain way. They were just having fun.

Cynthia looked up, suddenly not caring if he saw the blush lighting up her cheeks.

"Maybe..." She let the word dangle in the air between them for a long moment. "But only if you promise not to bring any of this canned margarita crap."

"Well, that's a shame," he said, giving her an exaggerated frown. "And here I was just getting used to the stuff."

Cynthia quirked a brow. "Really."

Javi took another sip...at least he tried to. The moment the *"margarita"* touched his tongue his brow pulled together and his lips tightened.

"No," he admitted, letting what was in his mouth fall back into the cup. "This stuff is awful."

"Well, at least I know you have good taste." But that was about all she knew. Well, that and he had the power to make her blush just by smiling at her. "Now it's your turn to tell me about yourself."

"What would you like to know?"

Cynthia shrugged. "The basics, I guess."

"Javier Garcia. Six foot one. Two hundred and sixty-five pounds. Software developer. My favorite color is green, and if I was going to be any animal, I'd be an eagle."

She scrunched her brows together above her nose. "That might be a little *too* basic."

He leaned in across the armrest, pushing just a few inches into her space. "Then ask me a question. Tell me what you really want to know."

Cynthia thought about it for a second. She wanted something meaty. Something deeper than the usual superficial niceties. It wasn't a hard choice. She went for the one question she dreaded being asked year after year.

"Are you looking forward to spending the holidays with your family?"

Javi's eyes narrowed just a touch, almost as if he could sense that this wasn't some random question to her. He took a second to think before answering.

"I'm looking forward to some parts," he said. "There are some people I can't wait to see. Other parts, other people... not so much."

Cynthia understood that all too well. She shifted her body, so she could face him more fully, and then rested the side of her head against the seat. "Do you have a big family?"

He shrugged. "I guess so."

"How many will be there for dinner?"

He glanced up at the ceiling, rocking his head back and forth. "Twenty. Maybe twenty-five."

Cynthia's eyes widened. "Wow. That's a lot of turkey."

"How many will be at your parents'."

"Eight," she said without hesitation. She didn't need to shuffle through them in her mind. There were the same people there every year. "Me. My parents. My sister and her family. My aunt and uncle."

"That's it?" he asked with another big laugh that carried through the plane. This time though, Cynthia didn't feel any embarrassment. "The way you were talking I thought you had to face at least a dozen nasty relatives."

"Seven is enough, trust me," she said. "If you had to spend even a couple hours in my parents' house, you'd understand that."

"If you say so." He didn't look convinced.

She didn't understand why. If anyone had a right to be skeptical, it was her. "You're telling me that you get along with everyone in your family over Thanksgiving?" she asked. "All twenty to twenty-five of them."

"Well, not *everyone*," Javi admitted. "My cousin Bernardo, and I don't get along."

That sounded interesting. "Why's that?"

"Well, I think he's a drunk machismo pain in the ass. He thinks I'm a stuck-up, fat pig."

Cynthia unconsciously flinched at the nasty epithet. It didn't matter how many times she heard them. They still stung.

"How awful," she said. "I'm so sorry."

Javi shook his head. He didn't look hurt. Not even a flicker of shame showed in his eyes.

"Don't be. At least, not for me," he said. " If you feel bad for anyone, let it be Bernardo. He's the one who has to live his life as an asshole."

The funny thing was Javi looked like he really meant the words. He looked fine. Actually fine. Suddenly, Cynthia felt envious of his attitude.

"How do you deal with him?" she asked.

Javi shrugged. "I do my best not to. With a family as big as mine it's easy to avoid one jerk."

Cynthia smiled. She wished it were that easy with her own family. "Things get a little more complicated when there's only eight of you. There's no one to hide behind."

Javi leaned in even closer, resting his hand on the divider between them. Apparently, her answer piqued his attention.

"Is *everyone* in your family really that bad?"

"Oh, sweetie, you have no idea." Without thinking, Cynthia reached out and draped her hand over his. It was only after she felt the warmth of his hand under hers, the smooth texture of his skin, that she realized how intimate the gesture really was. They were sitting close together now. Practically in each other's space.

Javi must have felt the change of atmosphere too. He turned over his hand so that his palm cupped hers. Long, strong fingers wrapped over hers. "Tell me about them. What is Thanksgiving like for you?"

This was usually the point where Cynthia lied. It was easier that way. People thought they wanted to know, but they didn't. Not really. What they wanted were easy to digest sentiments. Brief details and not much more. So, that's what Cynthia gave them.

Oh, you know how moms are...

Well, family can be rough...

There's a reason they call it the most stressful time of the year...

Statements like that didn't just keep people comfortable, they also protected Cynthia from having to relive the painful truth.

But this time something was different. When Javi asked her the question, she *wanted* to tell the truth. That had never happened before. Just with Javi.

"Imagine a whole family of Bernardos," she said.

He winced. "Really?"

"Pretty much." Cynthia let out a long breath. She knew she could stop right there, and he would understand everything. Hell, she probably *should*. But now that she was finally speaking the truth, she didn't want to stop. "From the moment I walk through the door to the moment I leave, everyone will give me the *look*."

Javi raised his brows in question. "The *look*?"

"Oh, come on. You have to know the one." She was certain that he did. "The look that says if you even go near a tray of snacks, or a plate of food, you are committing the horrible sin of being hungry while fat."

The corners of Javi's eyes fell as the humor left his smile. "That's a real thing in your family?"

"Of course," she said. For the first time, Cynthia stopped to think that maybe the shame her family liked to heap on her shoulders wasn't normal. "You're telling me nobody in your family besides Bernardo gives you *the look*?"

"No," he said. "And no one would dare tell me or any of the other bigger members of my family what to do."

"At least you have backup," she said. "I'm the only overweight one in my family, and, trust me, I will be hearing about it every day from the moment I walk in the door until I fly home on Sunday. Every bite of every meal will be questioned, every morsel of food will be judged."

"Even on Thanksgiving Day?" he asked.

"*Especially*, on Thanksgiving Day." Cynthia rolled her eyes. "That's when they're at their worst. I won't be able to go near a bowl of nuts without being peppered with *tsks* and nasty looks."

Javi rubbed the pad of his thumb over the side of her hand. It was a small gesture, but an insanely comforting one, and Cynthia was grateful for it. So very grateful.

"So what do you eat?" he asked.

"Not much," she admitted. "Each year it seems like I'm in a contest to see if I can eat less than the year before. This year I'm down to a single thin slice of turkey and a lone broccoli stalk."

Javi smiled at her joke, but there was more sympathy than joy behind his eyes. "What about dessert?"

"Are you kidding me?" she said. "Dessert is definitely off the menu. My Aunt Carol would have a heart attack if I dared to take a bite of her pumpkin pie. I'm beginning to think she only brings the thing to taunt me."

Another smile. Another glimmer in his eyes that showed he understood better than anyone else she'd ever known.

"So why do you keep going back every year?"

Cynthia shrugged. "They're family. Where else would I go?"

"Somewhere where they accept you just as you are."

It was a beautiful thought. A really lovely one. But where ever that place was she hadn't found it yet.

"Maybe next year," she said.

Javi looked at her for a long moment. His warm brown gaze was becoming so familiar so fast.

"Screw next year," he said. "If you can't have Thanksgiving at your parents' house tomorrow, then we'll have it now."

"What?" There was no way she could have heard that right.

"We already have the drinks and the hors devours," he said, gesturing to the packets of peanuts and pretzels he'd brought back earlier. "Now all we need is..."

His voice trailed off as he rose from his seat. Cynthia's brows pulled together as she watched him pop open the overhead compartment and reach inside. A second later, he sat back down with a perfectly square cardboard box tucked close to his chest.

"What's that?" she asked.

"The dessert you should be having tomorrow night." He opened the lid and revealed a beautiful lattice crust apple pie.

"Where did you get that?"

"At the Auntie Apple's pie kiosk a few gates down from ours."

Cynthia shot him a look of disbelief. "We can't have that."

"You're right," he said. "We're going to need forks." He waved down one of the flight attendants passing in the aisle and asked her for a couple.

"No, I mean we can't have the pie you bought for your family."

"Why do you assume I bought it for them," he asked with a wink. "What makes you think I didn't pick it up for you?"

"Because you didn't know me two hours ago."

"Details." He waved off her practical answer before pulling down the tray table in front of him. He gently placed the pie tin on top. "Come on. Everybody loves a romantic gesture. Especially when that gesture includes fresh apple pie."

Cynthia sighed as Javier turned to accept a couple of white plastic forks from the flight attendant on her way back. He was right. She did love romantic gestures...and apple pie. But that still didn't take away all her guilt.

"I don't want to be the reason you show up to your family empty-handed."

Javier smile grew. He held a fork out in front of her, daring her to take it.

"You might have missed it growing up in the suburbs, but Chicago is home to a handful of bakeries. Maybe if I'm really lucky, I might pass one on my way home."

Cynthia pressed her lips together tight. Dammit. He was taking all her excuses away. It got even worse when Javier broke through the crust with his fork, and pulled up a gooey bite. Her mouth started to water at the scent of apples and sugar. The flecks of brown cinnamon suspended between slices of crisp apples made it even worse. Everything about the pie looked good. So good. Especially once Javier popped the bite into his mouth and closed his eyes, obviously relishing the taste. After he swallowed, he looked over at her.

"Trust me," he said. "You don't want to miss out on this."

And he was right. She didn't want to miss out. She wanted all the sweetness that was being offered to her. She leaned in, filled up her fork and brought it toward her lips...but she still couldn't quite make herself take the bite.

The smile Javier gave her crinkled the corners of his eyes.

"It's all right, Cynthia," he said. "You can enjoy yourself."

She popped the fork into her mouth. The sweet, crisp taste of apples and spice covered her tongue. Damn, it was a good pie. So good that it washed the last remaining bits of her guilt away.

Javier leaned against her. She leaned back against him. Their arms pressed together over the rest in a strangely intimate way as they dug into the dessert.

"So what do you think of our little makeshift Thanksgiving?" he asked.

"Honestly?" Cynthia looked down at the brightly-colored cocktail, packet of peanuts, and absolutely scrumptious pie. "It's the best I've had in a long time."

"That's pretty sad," he said with a laugh.

"Yeah, well, it's the truth."

"We need to do something about that."

Cynthia turned her head to face him. "Don't tell me you've stowed a turkey in your carry on."

"I'd like to take you out to dinner once we're back home." His voice dropped down low, making his words every bit as sexy as his smile. The combination of the two together was downright devastating. "One without tray tables or plastic forks."

Cynthia's heart pounded against her breastbone. He wasn't joking, was he? He didn't sound like he was kidding. He sounded serious.

She decided to test the waters. "How about canned drinks, or packets of peanuts?"

"I'd like to take you on a real date." His words came out slow and sexy. "At a real restaurant with tablecloths and waiters."

Oh my God.

She couldn't believe this. Just a hours ago she'd been in hell—shuffling onto a crowded plane and preparing herself for the worst weekend of her year. She'd been mentally preparing herself for all the nasty words and looks that her family would throw her way. But now she was facing the prospect of something else altogether. Something that filled her with joy, and hope, and a thrilling sense of longing that she hadn't felt in a good long time.

"I'd like that, Javi," she said.

Javi narrowed his gaze. He leaned in even closer across the armrest. "Good."

An electric sizzle ran up Cynthia's spine. She might have been out of the dating pool for a while, but she knew what was going to happen next. What's more, she wanted it. She started to close her eyes. She pressed deeper into his arm. She readied herself for the feel of his full lips against hers...but he stopped with his mouth just barely an inch away.

"Of course, there's a price."

Cynthia's eyes popped back open. "A what?"

"A price," he repeated, looking far too satisfied with himself.

"You're kidding me," she groaned. "We talked about this, Javi. You can't pull this on me again."

"Now that you know my tricks you should have been more prepared for them," he teased.

Cynthia glared at him, but it didn't seem to do much good. His brown gaze stayed steady on hers.

"All right, so what's your price?" she asked.

"You need to eat a slice of your aunt's pumpkin pie."

She blinked once. Then twice. "Are you crazy?" He had no idea what he was asking.

"Possibly," he admitted. "But it still doesn't change the price."

"Why in the world do you want me to do that?"

He looked at her as though the answer was obvious. "So you

can tell me how she reacted. How they all reacted when you started to live your own life instead of theirs."

A slow smile crept over Cynthia's face. She didn't believe in providence or fate, but she had to admit she was grateful for whatever happy accident had seen fit to give her and Javi these seats right next to each other.

"You've got yourself a deal." She held out her hand to shake on it.

Javi shook his head. "I prefer to seal my deals with a kiss."

Cynthia didn't even have time to blush before he wrapped his hand around the nape of her neck and pulled her in close. His lips pressed against hers, all apple-sweet and cinnamon-spiced.

At that moment, Cynthia knew this Thanksgiving wasn't going to be hell. After all, any man who kissed like that had to be from heaven.

Crazy Old Money by Kilby Blades

A HEXAGON UNIVERSE SHORT STORY

JADA

"You're cute when you're nervous."

Jada's lips set in amusement as her gaze shifted from Marsh to the scenery. Autumn must have been mild for all the russet and gamboge leaves that still clung to the trees. The sky had the look of snow, but forecasts had insisted it would hold off another day. Dry roads and mild November temperatures should have found them speeding up the Taconic Parkway.

"I'm not nervous." Marsh's smooth baritone held a calm she'd believed in when they'd first started dating. Marsh was the kind of man who could raise hell without ever raising his voice. Quiet control was his gambit, made more believable by his natural confidence. But she'd seen his game and knew every one of his tells.

"Oh, yeah?" Her sly gaze slid back to his face. "Then why are we doing forty in a fifty-five?"

"I like to obey traffic laws." His slow, cheeky smile copped to the ridiculousness of the lie.

"Do you also like blood flow in your extremities?" Jada jutted her chin toward the grip that white-knuckled the steering wheel, eyeing the speedometer again as she did. She didn't think she'd ever seen him take an A7 under sixty-five.

They had passed the point in their relationship that merited an out-loud answer to every question. Entire conversations were had with the slightest quirk of a lip, the precision of a gaze or the clever maneuver of a brow. And so should it have been for a couple who had been together for four years. The look he gave her then relented, admitting with the clarity of a church bell: "You caught me. I'm totally freaking out."

"Baby...these are your blood relatives, not a pit of vipers. Besides, you know I can hold my own."

Marsh did know that. Hell, *everyone* knew better than to go up against Jada Jones, titan of industry and one of the most successful venture capitalists on Sand Hill Road. Marsh was among the rare breed who actually meant it when he said that being with a powerful woman was a turn-on. It had happened that first time he'd seen her in her element and again every time since. His eyes smoldered when she put her bossy boots on.

"It's not you I'm worried about," he murmured.

"You forget that I've met them," she pointed out. "*More than once*. A bit non-traditional, maybe...but, babe, they're really nice."

"Correction. You've met my *parents*. The ones who rebelled. The ones who got out of the family."

"You make it sound like the mafia. You do realize that your family owns textile mills and isn't an old country crime syndicate, right?"

Marsh didn't share her humor. "My parents aren't as bad as the others. They're on the lovable end of the crackpot spectrum."

"So it's a spectrum, huh? What's on the opposite end?"

He took his eyes off of the road long enough to blink over at her.

"Unadulterated crazy."

"Please. The Bay Area is crackpot central. If I had a dollar for every chem-trails conspiracy theorist I had to dodge at Berkeley Bowl..." Jada shook her head.

His responding smile looked forced. For the better part of a day, she'd sensed his anxiety around returning home. Marsh never went to Connecticut for the holidays and Jada never asked why. She'd convinced herself that he must have his reasons.

For one, he had never relished the quarterly trips he made from San Francisco to Hartford, solo voyages in service of his position on the Brewster Textiles board. He never said much about it—only that he went out of love and duty to his grandmother, who exalted the value of having a lawyer from the family on the board. All Jada really knew about that part of his life was that his family had run a small but successful business milling wool for the better part of one hundred years, and that his octogenarian grandmother, the CEO, was still going strong.

Jada had been more-than-a-little curious to meet them, not that she'd ever said as much to Marsh. She never wanted to be *that girlfriend* who applied pressure to be brought into the family fold. The truth was, she'd been brought in already. The only family Marsh saw socially were his parents. They'd had some good times together over the years whenever his mom and dad had paid their separate visits to the bay.

"Do we need to review again?" he asked.

Jada rolled her eyes. She'd barely slept on the plane for Marsh's words of warning: half-primer, half-cautionary tale. The cast of characters she'd heard about only in snippets over the years were described to her in color. But they were the kinds of things she might have expected: what family didn't have a religious zealot? A jackass who became a loud mouth when he drank too much? A grandmother who said whatever the hell she wanted?

Then there was the *other thing* she expected—the thing that Marsh didn't have to say because they both understood: she was the black girlfriend coming home to meet the WASPy family. In the spirit of not bringing up ex-boyfriends, Jada hadn't mentioned how much bad behavior she'd dealt with over the years. She could write a dissertation on people who had too much class to be overtly rude but too little class to mask their disapproval.

"I passed your test, babe. Twice. Talk loud with Uncle Peter—he's loads of fun but hard of hearing. Don't take the bait when your cousin Jason wants to talk gun control. Keep your mom's new girlfriend away from your dad. And always let Maw Maw be right."

But her answer didn't appease him. If anything, Marsh seemed more on edge. Even his chiseled quad muscle that her hand rested upon seemed more-rock-hard-than-usual through his fitted slacks.

"Just...don't let anything anyone says offend you."

She moved her hand from his leg to stroke the back of his neck. "Baby. Don't worry about me. I think I can handle one dinner with your family."

Marsh

Jada is in no way prepared to handle dinner with my entire family.

Driving up the Taconic, the thought slapped Marsh like a spiteful hand. For years, he had avoided telling Jada the whole truth. Keeping secrets about the money meant keeping secrets about the business. And for the Brewsters, business and family were the same.

Marsh would have told her everything in his own time, but Maw Maw had summoned him home urgently, ruining his plans for a romantic Thanksgiving getaway in Whistler. *Supremely* romantic, actually. It was the weekend Marsh had planned to propose. It had taken him all day Monday to rework the trip when he'd received the insistent call from Maw Maw. Thursday to Monday in British Columbia would become Friday to Monday in Vermont. It was less important, the location of their winter wonderland than the single circumstance that would add to the magic: Jada absolutely loved snow.

But first, they had to endure a situation he'd been careful to avoid. It was only a day, but still... He loved his family, but opting out of holidays was a logical response for someone who didn't fit in.

Jada was anything but stupid. It went without saying that bringing his girlfriend home to his very white, very New England, very old money family would be met with shenanigans that summed up everything he'd tried to escape. Marsh had worked so hard to create a distinction between the way he lived now and the way he was raised that he'd never completely revealed to Jada what his family was like and how much money they really had.

Jada thought he'd grown up with moderate privilege, but figured that his family was just stuffy. Everything she knew about Connecticut she'd learned from *The Ice Storm* and *The Stepford Wives*. She didn't know what a shit show it would be with every last aunt, uncle and cousin in attendance this year, at Maw Maw's peculiar insistence.

Soon enough, Jada would see that his claims of crazy weren't an exaggeration. All crazy meant was being divorced from reality. Jada had dealt with her share of narcissists, but they tended to be of the new money, Silicon Valley variety. Marsh's family, on the other hand, was old money crazy. No one was more estranged from reality than people who had been so rich for so long.

He'd tried to convey the extent of it. His cousin Biff openly cheated on his wife, Krista, who waited on him like a servant, even though he was an enormous dick. Biff had cost the company millions in settlements for sexual harassment law suits and all manner of other legal problem. Marsh's cousin, Liz—currently in rehab—had gratefully accepted plastic surgery as a twenty-first birthday present from her mother, his Aunt Minnie, who had herself been under the knife more than a dozen times. His cousin Jason was congenial enough on the surface, but scratch just a little and his delusion showed. He genuinely believed that women should stand behind their men and that poor people were lazy. Yet no one was as fearsome or as feared as Maw Maw. She ran the family like she ran her companies: with an iron fist. She wasn't a cold woman, merely an exacting one.

Maw Maw was as hard on the people around her as she believed that life had been on her. The Brewsters may have been one of the wealthier families in New England, but their fortunes had been lost and regained twice. Every ounce of ambition, of perseverance, of sheer grit she had learned had come from she and her brother, Peter, falling with stockmarket crashes and recessions and clawing their way back to the top.

Marsh, luckily, had long-since been rubber-stamped with Maw Maw's seal of approval. A bright, quick-witted child with clear entrepreneurial sensibilities, Marsh had won his grandmother over with his first lemonade stand. His habit of melting her with a dimpled smile and a climb in her lap may have also helped. To say that others hadn't been as successful in earning Maw Maw's approval would be an understatement. Every expression of the woman's emotions felt as binary as code.

"Mom says she'll fix you a plate." Jada's voice broke Marsh from his thoughts.

He looked over just in time to see her slip her phone into her purse. He couldn't help but smile when he took in her utterly over-done but completely adorable get-up. California living made winter weather a novelty that Jada relished. Beneath her white padded parka with its oversized fur-rimmed hood, she wore a gray wrap dress of soft cashmere that fell just above her knees. Her slim leather boots were accented with a knit collar, and around her shoulders hung a completely unnecessary alpaca scarf.

Her fashion bug tendencies were among the many things he loved about his girlfriend. She was always pulled-together and sharp. And she was creative about it: classic couture one day and high-fashion avant garde the next. Today, no bold lipstick, dramatic eye shadow or bright shade of nail polish spiced up her look. Though, her naked brown skin seemed to radiate light. Her cropped cut was sleek—shaven in the back and curled in the front to soft, smooth waves. Jada's slim, diamond-jaw face really pulled it off.

"Don't tease." He gave her a mock-warning look. You know how I love your mother's cooking. I'll move our flights to a day earlier. We'll do a stopover in LA."

"Wow, really? You'd sell out our mountain getaway for a piece of sweet potato pie?"

When he pretended to think, she swatted his shoulder. Little did she know that he wouldn't be changing a single other one of their plans that weekend. The proposal could still be salvaged as long as the weather panned out.

"Oh, so it's like that..." she said.

"Uh-huh," he baited. "That's exactly how it is."

Between the two of them, banter always led to flirting, which always led to more. If he hadn't been driving, he'd have leaned over and kissed her. In fact, when they got out of this car, kissing her was exactly what he was going to do.

JADA

Marsh had that look in his eye—the one he got any time he was thinking about kissing her. Two-and-a-half-hours in the car without stopping was becoming a bit much. They had long-since turned off of main roads and hadn't seen other houses for at least a mile. When they crested a hill, Marsh's eyes brightened in a way that made Jada follow his gaze. Looming in the distance, a grand estate stood alone.

"Is *that it?*"

She hadn't meant to sound so astonished, but...could that really be where Maw Maw lived? Jada had expected something, well... smaller. Like a suburban mini-mansion or a really nice house. Spotlights illuminated what looked like a small castle. It had a lake and a guest house and acres and acres of forest. Deciduous trees stood leafless and bare, while evergreens had been decked out in small white lights. Gaslight posts lined the driveway and the space just below each light had been tied with red velvet bows.

"Nice place," she remarked when he didn't answer.

"My grandmother has champagne tastes."

But this was no $20 split of house sparkling—it was a

nebuchadnezzar of Taittinger. He said nothing for a moment and she thought he'd let it settle. His voice was quiet when he finally spoke.

"Like I said before...this is my family. Not me."

Marsh pulled the car to a crunchy stop behind a parked Suburban on the gravel driveway. Jada pulled her hood up as he came around to open the door. She was delighted to see her breath freeze in front of her face as he helped her stand in the cold air. After he'd closed her door, he didn't wait to pull her into his arms.

God, he smells good.

Even after airplanes and rental cars, Marsh still smelled like *him*. It seemed like ages ago that they'd showered together that morning, having so much fun they'd nearly missed their flight. Marsh brought the sexy times all right, but he always took time for the romance.

"I can't wait to get away with you," he murmured, touching their noses in an Eskimo kiss. "This time tomorrow, we'll be in Vermont."

"You promised me snow," she quipped softly as he brushed a stray lock of hair behind her ear. "I'm gonna hold you to that."

She liked the way his lips always melted into a smile as his blue gaze washed over her face, how he got his fill of drinking her in before he leaned in for a kiss. Marsh was a master kisser. A championship kisser. An Olympic gold medalist in kissing. He took his time even then, in the frigid cold, with a brisk wind stinging their faces, to devour her mouth deeply and right.

The heavy double-doors were three steps up from the gravel driveway. She and Marsh walked up hand-in-hand. Jada half-expected some sort of butler to swing them open—if a butler was even what you called the person who opened the door. Houses that looked like this seemed like they should be teeming with footmen and valets and lady's maids and every other hierarchy of servant she had learned on Downton Abbey.

Stepping a bit ahead of her, Marsh reached out to grasp the right-most door handle. One firm push and the brisk, refreshing cold was replaced by a wave of fragrant warm. Marsh's expression relaxed just as Jada stepped over the threshold to breathe the scent of evergreen sap and mulling spices and ancient, polished wood. He slid his arm into its rightful place around her waist as they walked farther inside.

A grand staircase drew Jada's gaze upward. It rose to stop at a mezzanine before splitting into two and rising to a second floor. Downstairs, two rooms flanked the staircase, which themselves were flanked by twin hallways with antique rugs that led in opposite directions. The house didn't exactly seem empty. Classical music floated from somewhere. Decorations from nature that brought the outdoors in made the entire space look festive. But it unnerved her that she couldn't hear anything. For a house that was supposed to be full of people, it sure seemed like no one was around.

"Come on," Marsh prodded, tugging her to the left. "Everyone will be in the big room."

"Maybe we're the first ones here?" She was still skeptical that any sort of crowd could be here at all.

He led her down a hall. "We're probably among the last. I'm sure they've all been drinking for hours."

An antique clock told her that the time was just past five. Dinner was scheduled for seven. Jada tried not to peer with too much interest through the halls. Her plan not to out herself was foiled when she stopped short at the site of a lit-up painting, done in oil. The man's suit was dated, but the set of his eyes, the curve of his slightly-plump lips, his roman nose...he was a facsimile of Marsh. Letting her eyes fall upon the name plate at the base of the painting, she read out loud: "Marshall Evan Brewster, Jr. - 1920 to 2008."

She looked up at Marsh. "Was this your grandfather?"

He nodded. "Paw Paw."

"I thought you were the only Junior. I didn't know his name was Marshall, too."

Marsh shrugged. "So your dad is the third, which makes you..."

"Marshall Evan Brewster IV," he admitted.

She narrowed her eyes. "Mmm-hmmm..."

As they approached a perpendicular hallway, a woman with Marsh's ash-blond hair and dark blue eyes came into view. An infant lay prone on her shoulder and she walked alongside the little girl. The girl spotted Marsh before the woman did.

"Uncle Marsh!" she exclaimed, dropping the woman's hand. He let his hair fall from Jada's waist just in time to absorb the shock of the small cannonball of a little girl.

"Hey, Jillybean..." His deep voice was a stark contrast to her juvenile one. "You're bigger than the last time I saw you. Are you six?"

"No..." she stretched it out into about three syllables in a way that only little girls could.

"Five?" he scratched his chin. She shook her head again. When she held out four fingers, he narrowed his eyes. "No, that can't be right. You're too much of a big girl to be four."

When she giggled again, Marsh let her down gently before introducing the suddenly-shy girl to Jada and turning to the smiling woman at his side.

"Suze." Marsh said warmly, capturing his cousin in a one-armed hug before reaching out to tickle the sleepy-looking infant's cheek. Jada hadn't seen him around kids, but she knew he wanted them. Seeing him with a baby made her ovaries quiver just a little.

"Jada, it's so nice to meet you. I'm Susie." The woman stepped forward and engulfed Jada in half a hug. "He talks about you all the time."

Jada smiled graciously. Because that's what one did when someone you knew barely anything about seemed to know a whole lot more about you. The first time Jada had heard of Susie was on the plane. Susie's grandfather, Peter, was Maw Maw's brother. Marsh had identified her as one of the "sane ones".

"We're on a walk," Jill informed Marsh.

"Uh-oh..." Marsh's glance at Susie was a question.

"Millie and Steven are at it already."

"What is it this time?"

Jada had also heard about Uncle Steven and Aunt Millie on the plane. Steven was the brother of Marsh's father.

"Liz checked herself out. Millie gave her money."

It dawned on Jada why they were talking in code. Liz was Marsh's cousin who was supposed to be in rehab. They clearly didn't want to say this in front of Jill.

Marsh just shook his head.

Susie continued. "I know. And the rest of her trust fund? Gone."

Trust fund?

Marsh had made the business sound small. If trust funds and inheritances were floating around, and this was how Maw Maw lived, Marsh's family was filthy rich.

Some of them, Jada corrected herself gently. Maybe that was what Marsh had meant about his parents getting out of the family. Marshall Senior was a self-made hotelier. His mother was fairly bohemian—a lifestyle Marshall claimed she could afford thanks to the alimony he paid. Marsh himself did well as a human rights attorney, and Jada did very well as a VC, but this...this was in a completely different league.

"She sold her shares a while back." Susie lowered her voice, as if the walls themselves were listening.

Marsh hissed, "To who?"

Susie pressed her hands over her daughter's ears long enough to utter a single syllable. "Biff."

Marsh had made his cousin, Biff, sound like a colossal jerk. Jada mainly knew that he was Steven's son and worked full-time in the family business. He was jockeying for the CEO position after Maw Maw passed, which no one thought would happen until the woman was at least 100.

"Do I wanna know how much?"

Susie shook her head. "A lot less than they were worth. And lot more than any addict should have."

She'd whispered it now that they were closing in on the others.

Jada could finally hear party chatter and make out a group of people through the double doors of the open room at the end of the hall. She did smell food now, though she wasn't sure whether it was food from the kitchen being prepared for the sit-down dinner, or things that had been set out as hors d'oeuvres.

Susie stepped into the room in front of them and Marsh slipped his arm around Jada. It was an enormous sitting room, with antique sofas and upholstered chairs. A long, narrow table on the far wall was laden with cheeses, wines and canapés, and a roaring fire burned off to the side. Marsh squeezed her waist a little and looked down at her with a reassuring smile. For hours—maybe for years—Jada had anticipated meeting the rest of his family. But things were already shaping up differently than she'd anticipated. It seemed the other person she'd be meeting for the first time today was Marsh.

MARSH

"She speaks so well!" Krista whispered excitedly to Marsh, cornering him at the hors d'oeuvres table. Refusal to talk with his mouth full made Marsh think twice about schooling her with a retort. Krista meant well. Marsh liked her. And he'd give her a break for now. Biff was already giving her shit about nothing.

"She's a gem," he responded, instead of gratifying her comment with praise. Then, "Hey, do you know what this business is with Maw Maw?"

Krista shook her head, her brow knitting in concern that echoed Marsh's worry.

"You don't think she's sick..." he prodded.

"I hope not," she said, beginning to pile a plate. Like all of the women in his family, Krista didn't eat much, which meant the plate was definitely for Biff.

After sliding another canapé into his mouth, Marsh ladled out two glasses and delivered the egg nog he'd been tasked to retrieve.

Jada had politely asked for a second glass. Aunt Minnie had requested a bit drunkenly that he make her a double. But she was drunk enough already. He'd done no such thing.

"Where do you summer?" Minnie was asking Jada when Marsh returned to the circle, smiling what Marsh like to call "the socialite smile"—whatever the hell some women did to their lips and their cheeks gave them a Jack-Nicholson-as-the-Joker kind of look. Minnie had blonde hair, a tiny nose and eyebrows that rose permanently in surprise. To save his life, Marsh couldn't remember the natural color of her hair.

"We travel throughout the year. Summer is sort of an East Coast thing," Jada replied.

Minnie laughed, with a mix of drunkenness and discomfort. She had no idea what Jada was saying.

"What I mean is," Jada said more slowly, "the lifestyle in California isn't really to go to a summer house."

"Well, you'll have to join us in the Vineyard one year. Have you been to Vineyard Haven?"

"No. I don't think I have.

"I think you'll like it," Uncle Steven popped in. He raised his glass and gave Jada a little wink. "It's becoming very diverse."

All right, Marsh thought. *Time to move on.* Jada had already been introduced around the room, without much incident, but it was still early. Jason had insulted her education, but she'd taken it in stride. Now they needed a safe haven. The room was a minefield of bad conversations, just waiting to be stepped on.

Wes scanned for his father—one of their safest bets—he and Jada shared mutual affection. Apart from his mother, his father's was the only familiar face that Jada had known coming in. They'd said their hellos a half an hour earlier, but his father was nowhere to be found.

"Is this you and Marsh?

Jada beat Marsh to the punch of choosing a conversation. She walked toward something on the mantel that caught her eye. Susie picked up the framed photo and studied it. "I think he was ten and

I was eight. That was the summer they were rebuilding the stables."

"The stables?" Jada directed her question to Susie, but shot a look at Marsh. Susie's husband, Josh stood beside, holding Jill's little brother, Dante. The infant liked Marsh. All babies did. Even as he lay on his father's chest sucking his thumb, he eyed Marsh with interest.

It'll definitely distract Jada if she sees me holding a baby.

"They're too far back to see from the driveway," Susie was telling Jada as Marsh held out his hands to Josh, who seemed relieved to hand off tiny Dante. Holding babies was precious, but even the little ones got heavy.

"Hey, buddy," Marsh whispered, smiling down into the clear brown eyes of the child . He really was a sweet little thing. Marsh remembered affectionately that Jill had looked the same when she was little. His future children with Jada would likely have brown eyes. He hoped they were dark and lovely, like Jada's.

"Just how far back does the property go?" Jada was asking.

"I'll take you on a walk tomorrow," Marsh interjected, not wanting Susie to say the number. Sixty-seven acres was an obscene amount of sparsely-developed land. Especially in this part of the country.

"Oh, here it is!" Susie exclaimed lightly, handing Jada another framed picture—one he couldn't see. "It's you and Chancellor. God, you loved that horse."

Keeping his eyes fixed on Jada, Marsh waited for another accusing look. But she studied the picture for a long time.

"You were really cute," she said finally, sincerely, in a way that made him sure she'd have loved to have seen this piece of him before. The betrayal in her eyes as she looked up from his childhood picture was worse than any accusing look.

"Do you mind if I steal my son a minute?" Marshall Senior came out of nowhere. "There are papers I've been wanting him to look over."

"Go," Susie put down her wine and motioned to take her baby back.

Jada's arms were crossed and she refused to let her gaze meet his. Marsh knew better than to push her. Maybe him getting out of her sight for awhile would help her cool down. At least there were no more photos on the mantel.

Marsh might have told his father of his own predicament. Over the years, they'd become close—the gradual reconciliation of an absentee father and his adult son. Marshall Senior had loved Marsh and his mother. There had never been any doubt of that. But running his company made it so that he was never around.

"Dad. What's up with Maw Maw?" he asked, remembering his other predicament. He asked only after they'd reached the privacy of the back stairs. "Why did she call us all here?"

Marshall Senior paused from climbing long enough to give his son a pointed look. "I thought *you* might know. I've been trying to pry it out of her since this morning. "

Marsh shook his head, disappointed. They kept walking.

"You meet this Ashley woman?" Marshall Senior asked, feigning casual interest in his ex-wife's girlfriend.

"Uh-uh, "Marsh confirmed. "This'll be the first time."

"You think they're serious?" his father pressed, a bit winded when he reached the top of the stairs.

"Honestly, Dad? I have no idea."

Marshall Senior chuffed out a humorless little laugh. "You're right," he said, as if his son had given him a solid "no" instead of a tentative "maybe". "...Last year it was that Sarah woman. They can't have been together for long. I mean, really, how serious could she and Ashley be?"

In the twenty years since their divorce, Marshall Senior had never remarried, never gotten serious about anybody, never even brought a date to any family event. But because Maw Maw ran things, and loved her ex-daughter-in-law dearly, Kate was a holiday guest every year.

Unlike his father, his mother had no qualms about bringing

whoever she was dating at the time. Marsh had speculated over the years that his mother's partners were either a little bit crazy or too rubbernecking for their own good. What kind of person agreed to spend the holidays with their girlfriend's ex-husband and ex-mother-in-law?

"Are you seeing anyone, Dad?" Marsh suspected that he knew the answer and that the answer would make him sad. His mother's relationships may not have been long, but at least she gave herself a chance.

"No one special," came his pat answer. They reached the bedroom that Marshall Senior always stayed in when he visited. Too distracted by the task at hand, any platitudes Marsh may have had for his father died on his tongue when the door closed.

"It's all ready." Marshall Senior said as he locked the door behind him and strode to retrieve a package from the dresser drawer.

Marsh's heart raced as he joined his father. The hexagonal ring box in fine, dark leather was new, but the ring was vintage. It had been his mother's, and Maw Maw's before that. It was the one heirloom that had survived the fall, then the revival of his family. The art deco band flared to contain twin butterflies that formed the setting for the stunning asscher cut center stone. Jada would love this ring. He'd always considered it a good omen that butterflies were her favorite animal. Now, all he had to get her to do was say yes.

The "business trip" Marsh had gone on the month before had been entirely made-up. He'd gone to New York to see the ring. His father had taken him to the jeweler the Brewsters had used for more than five decades to get it ready. He'd had it cleaned and resized the ring to fit the same as the one he'd stolen from Jada's jewelry box. After he'd left New York, Marsh had traveled to Los Angeles to pay a visit to Jada's family.

Because it was the 21st century, he didn't ask Jada's father for her hand in marriage. He did sit down with both of her parents and tell them he knew what happiness they had always wished for their daughter. He told them of his plans and promised that, if she accepted, he'd make her happy and treat her well.

"It's..." Words failed Marsh as he took in the sparkling ring. The room was dim but it glowed somehow, as if lit from within.

"Yeah," Marshall Senior agreed, captivated by the ring himself for a long moment before he looked back at his son. "I know it won't mean much coming from me, given how things turned out between mom and me...but that ring is special. We were very happy once."

Marsh remembered those days. For some reason, he'd been thinking about them a lot—his parents happy and in love.

"What was your secret to making it work? You know, until it didn't?" Marsh asked his dad.

Marshall Senior looked over with the saddest look he'd ever given Marsh. "Integrity, son. I lost everything that mattered to me the second I stopped being honest."

Jada

"Encinitas," Jada repeated for the fifth time to Uncle Peter. He cupped his hand behind his good ear and leaned in even closer.

"Say again?"

"Encinitas," she repeated, a bit louder.

"Costa Rica?" he asked. It was his fourth bad guess.

Peter turned to his nephew for clarification. In the hour since she'd been introduced to him, Jason hadn't once stopped thumbing the screen of his phone. He seemed to be browsing articles on Fox News.

"She's Spanish?" Peter asked loudly, by then thoroughly confused.

"She's from California."

"She's Mexican?"

"Los Angeles," Peter said loudly, and slowly.

"Ah, Los Angeles,!" Peter smiled as he turned his attention

back to Jada. "Great town. Back in the fifties, I spend a little time there. You ever stay at The Beverly Hills Hotel?"

Jada simply smiled and nodded.

"I lived there one summer. We did some business with the costume shops at the studios back then. It was like sleeping on a movie set." Jada's smile widened as he leaned in conspiratorially. His hearing may have been bad, but his eyes were sharp and it was plain to see that he had an active mind.

"Grace Kelly, Lauren Bacall...all the beautiful women were there," he proclaimed with a flourish of his hand. "You know how many times I drank with the Rat Pack? I can't get into the details, but I once helped Elizabeth Taylor out of a precarious situation."

Jada raised an eyebrow and nodded in approval.

"Telling cheeky stories again, are we, Uncle Peter?" came an English-accented voice from the direction of the doorway. The dull roar of all other talking stopped. Jason stopped thumbing. Minnie glared openly at the new arrival, who ignored her completely in favor of beaming Uncle Peter a warm, playful look.

Marsh's mother was as chic as ever in crocodile pants and obscenely impractical shoes. Her hair had been expertly colored from its usual silver to stunning ombre layers of purples and blues. The dramatic bow on her plum-colored woolen coat made her look like Christmas had just come early. Jada guessed it sort of had —things were always more interesting with Marsh's mother around.

Placing her cup down, Jada stood, eager to greet the woman and relieved to see a familiar face. Genuine smiles and hugs confirmed that Kate was loved by all. All except for Minnie, who received a kiss so perfunctory that Jada might have been embarrassed for her if Minnie herself hadn't seemed displeased to be on the receiving end.

Second to last in line was Uncle Peter, who Kate gently commanded to keep his seat. "Looking better every year, old chap," she said affectionately as she clasped his hands.

When Kate finally turned her attention to Jada, her smile

widened by degrees and she enveloped Jada into a long, swaying hug.

"Radiant as ever, darling," Kate murmured as they hugged, then pulled back and kept Jada's hands in hers. "Is it any wonder that my son is in love with you?"

"I'm glad to see you," Jada smiled just as Kate took her arm and began walking her toward the hors d'oeuvre table.

"I'll just bet you are..." Kate murmured too low for the others to hear over conversations that had picked back up. "First time meeting Maw Maw?"

Jada nodded. "She hasn't made an appearance yet."

Kate hummed in understanding. "Don't let her smell fear. Stand your ground early on and she'll respect you for a lifetime."

Jada must have looked miffed for the look that crossed Kate's features then. She stopped short. "Don't tell me Marsh didn't warn you..."

"No, he did," Jada insisted quickly, before quietly admitting, "I'm just...not sure I believed him."

Kate picked up a cracker and chewed thoughtfully, as if there were something she were working out to say. Words seemed more on the tip of her tongue as she swallowed. Jada waited in anticipation for more advice at the same moment as Marsh's elated voice sounded from just next to them.

"Mom."

Kate had saved her warmest of hugs for her only child. Marsh's expression relaxed as he breathed his mother in and Jada forgot for a moment that she was annoyed. Few things were sweeter than a grown-ass-man who loved his mom.

"Unicorn's a good look on you." He complimented her hair.

"Of course it is, darling. I'm made of magic."

"Apparently she's made of modesty, too," Marshall Senior chimed in.

Jada watched the ensuing silent exchange with interest. Kate and Marshall Senior couldn't take their eyes off of one another. It was fascinating to watch—the mute conversation that felt so intimate Jada almost thought she should leave the room. Was this how she and Marsh would be after they'd known each other for thirty years? You know, except for the part where they'd be divorced? Marsh looked over his mother's shoulder, breaking up their stare.

"I thought you were gonna bring Ashley..." he said.

Kate slipped her coat off of her shoulders and waved a hand toward the door.

"Oh, Ash is getting our bags out of the car...He should be here any minute."

"He?" Marsh and Marshall Senior said in unison just as a tall, bespectacled man with a bohemian look about him appeared just outside of the double-doors. He sported a tan, and bright blond hair that was pulled back into a disorganized man bun. Layered beneath his fine gray jacket was a wheat-colored vest that might have been suede. It buttoned once over a strategically-wrinkled white linen shirt. The sleeves of the jacket itself were rolled up, revealing a silk pinstripe lining in lighter browns and beiges that matched his vest. Full ink on both forearms snaked down toward his hands, where he easily held two heavy-looking Louis Vuitton duffles.

"Evening, everyone," Ashley said in a voice a bit like velvet. Everything about him emanated peace. Perhaps that was why he took his time, making eye contact, one by one, with everyone in the room, including the baby. His gaze became warmer when it fell upon Kate. "Where can I take these?"

"Set them down for now. Come in, love. I want you to meet everybody."

Three things happened quickly, then: Susie shot Kate a look of approval. Marsh poured his father a double, and Minnie's face went from pink to red.

Kate did the same with Ashley as she had done for herself moments before: started with the family closest to the door and made her way around. By the time she and Ashley made it back to where she had been, Marshall Senior had poured his father another.

Standard pleasantries were exchanged, though it was clear from Ashley's comfort that he'd been primed with far more information about them than they had about him. He complemented Jade's social justice work, mentioned to Marshall Senior that he'd stayed at one of the resorts his hospitality group managed. He even asked Marsh whether he might talk to him later about legal advice.

"What kind of advice?"

"I live on a farm, but I've had some troubles with my neighbors. I'd like to understand my goats' rights."

Marsh blinked in astonishment. Jada nearly spit out a sip of her drink.

"And what exactly do you do?" Marsh pressed.

"I'm a shaman."

By then, no one else in the room was pretending not to listen. Conversation had quieted, and the other occupants had inched even closer.

"He's a Brahmin?" Peter asked Jason, not nearly as quietly as he might have imagined.

"He teaches yoga," Jason hollered.

"I'm a human rights attorney," Marsh interjected, the expression on his face having gone from annoyed to perturbed. "I don't think I can help with your goat situation."

"Human rights...goat's rights...they're all the same."

Ashley cast Kate a glowing look. "We're all people, right, my love?"

March's jaw was clenched as he asked his next question. "I'm in the market for a new shaman. How much does a good one run?"

"Ignore him, darling." Kate was speaking to Ashley but looking at Marsh. "Sometimes he loses track of his manners. I'm confident he'll find them again by dinner."

A minute later, Kate had led Ashley to the hors d'oeuvres table, Marshall Senior had excused himself from the room, and Marsh approached Jada with caution. She didn't know whether to feel more sorry for him or for herself. All those years, she'd taken every piece of information he'd given her about his family—about his upbringing—at face value, but he'd hidden half of it and forced her to find out like this.

But he looked run through the wringer, and not just because he was in the dog house with her. He hadn't been wrong about his family. Half of them really did seem unstable, and, even as a newcomer, she could see some ugly things were going on.

"Anything else you want to tell me?" She put down her glass. All the better to cross her arms. She shot him her moderately-fierce look, wanting to make sure he knew she had his number. It was an act of mercy. He couldn't handle full fierce right now.

As he sighed, his face etched in repent. "This weekend. I promise we'll talk. Can we just..." He swept his hand over his face. "...get through tonight?"

Jada still had questions, but this wasn't the place or the time. She'd give him a break—for now.

"It'll keep," she said quietly.

Hope flickered in his eyes from beyond the fatigue. She remembered their early flight. She led him to an empty sofa next to the roaring fire. She sat down first and held her hand up in invitation. Mild relief washed over his face and he took it, and sat. When she leaned into him a little, he did that magic he knew how to and tucked her into the perfect spot beneath his arm.

MARSH

Jada's totally giving me a break right now.

It was better than he deserved and he would take what he could get. The later it got, the more chaotic things became. Fur flew as his mother pushed Minnie's buttons for sport. Krista had taken an interest in what shamanism was and had peppered Ashley with questions until a very drunk Biff's shaming her for her "stupid questions" chastened her into silence. Marshall Senior, already irritated and listening intently to get a read on Ashley, had forcefully told Biff to knock it off. Ashley had put his hand on Biff's shoulder and said "You can't fix yourself by breaking someone else." That hadn't gone over well at all.

It didn't help that the weekend weather forecast still said that Vermont wouldn't snow, or that he had no more information about why Maw Maw had insisted they all come together. The downside to living in California was feeling out of the loop. But he'd asked nearly everybody. It unnerved him that no one seemed to have figured Maw Maw's reasons out.

For the moment, things were quiet. Jada looked thoughtful as she stared at the fire and settled into his arms. Part of him was relieved. She'd had to find out sooner or later. Ripping the band aid off had hurt. But maybe after this, they could go back to their normal lives.

Speaking of normal...Marsh let himself mourn what they were missing. Jada's family traditions were ones he'd come to love. Right now, they'd all be at her parents' house in Encinitas, camped in front of the TV watching football. Uncle Lou would have made Brandy Alexanders and Jada's far-more-rational grandmother, Nana, would be waiting to be topped off. The sideboard in the entertainment room would be teeming with everything from crab dip, to jalapeño artichoke spread, to salmon paté. He liked that Jada's family worked with flavors with a bit of a bite. Jada's brother, Eric, made a mean cornbread stuffing. Her sister, Kara killed the sweet potato pie every year. Jada herself made an incredible cranberry chutney.

Yes, Marsh thought longingly. Thanksgiving in Jada's family was the way God had always intended: with family actually thankful for their many blessings and any occasion to be together. At Jada's house, the only screaming and yelling came whenever the Rams fumbled the ball.

"Can I take our bags upstairs?" Marsh looked up when he heard Ashley's question.

Kate stood talking to Susie. "Up the left staircase, darling. Down the hall to the right and third door on the left."

Marsh may have gagged a little when this Ashley character held his mother's shoulders from behind and kissed her before floating out the door. But what was he going to do? His mother was a grown woman. She wasn't in any danger and even if this was bad judgment, she was still of sound mind. Marsh supposed she could keep company with as many shamans as she wanted.

"I thought you were a lesbian."

Minnie's faced had been etched with judgment since Kate had introduced Ashley to the rest of the room. Somebody saying it was only a matter of time. Kate hummed and dipped her fingers into a pile of marcona almonds. Marshall Senior leaned in.

"You did?" Kate feigned confusion. "What would make you think that?"

Among her own friends, Marsh's mother wasn't a cruel person, but she and Minnie had history. Kate had a not-so-nice habit of putting their different life choices on display. Minnie's embracing of the trophy wife, socialite lifestyle stood in stark relief to Kate's free-spirited don't give a fuck. In fairness, Minnie had never treated Kate particularly well either, half from jealousy, half from disapproval.

Minnie lowered her voice. "You've been bring your girlfriends to Mom's house for the past ten years," Minnie's whisper-hiss was punctuated with the crossing of her arms. When talking to Kate, Minnie never referred to Maw Maw's as home.

"Okay..." Kate replied slowly.

"You left Marshall for another woman." Minnie was indignant.

"Is that why I left him?" Kate's voice was as smooth and measured as the sideways glance she shot her ex, who wilted a little under her gaze.

"So you're..,*bisexual* now?"

Marsh put his hand over his face to cover his smile. Jada gave him a discreet "Is this woman for real?" look. Minnie had a way of making things she knew nothing about sound like she'd gotten what little she did know from a USA Today article written in the early '90s.

"I don't use that term," Kate replied easily.

"What term *do* you use?" Minnie demanded.

"Pansexual."

Jason stopped thumbing the screen of his phone and looked up at Kate with interest.

"Pan...*what*?" Minnie's bitch face faded long enough for her to look genuinely confused.

Kate picked up a dried apricot, looking a bit bored as she dipped the fruit in chestnut honey. "Just Google the phrase, *gender is a construct.*"

Minnie stood frozen and staring at Kate, her jaw slacked more than a little. Her surgically-lifted eyes finally closed in a labored blink.

"What's that?" Uncle Peter asked loudly. He appeared to be messing with his hearing aid.

"Kate switched back to liking boys," Jason intoned slowly and loudly enough for Peter to hear, though, he was thumbing his screen so incessantly, Marsh was sure he was Googling the term.

"She gonna get back together with Marshall?" Peter asked at full volume. He glared openly at his nephew for a long moment before regarding Kate with softer eyes. "Never should've divorced that woman in the first place," he muttered.

"Do you really think it's appropriate to parade your latest girl-friends or boyfriends or...whatever...in front of your ex-husband, in your ex-mother-in-law's house?"

Kate smiled smugly at Minnie even as he chewed a mouthful of apricot. If Marsh knew his mother, she wouldn't gratify the question with a response. It turned out she didn't need to. An unmistakable voice rang from the grand entryway of the salon.

The lady of the house stood regally, her presence overshadowing even that of the much taller and extraordinarily well-built Ashley, who had taken her arm and was presently escorting her inside. She wore a smart, timeless evening suit—a pale cream with gold brocade. Maw Maw had just arrived.

"Millicent," she scolded sharply. "You're being rude. Ashley is a lovely man and, most importantly, he is my guest." She turned her glare to Marshall Senior, but raised the volume of her voice, stepping toward her brother, Peter. "And, no—Marshall never should have divorced our Kate." When she shifted her gaze a third time, her eyes warmed as her gaze met his mother. "You and your friends will always be welcome here."

Releasing herself from Ashley's elbow, she stepped farther into the room, toward Jada, who sensed what was about to happen, and stood.

"And this must be the elusive Jada. I've been waiting a very long time to meet you, dear."

JADA

"Tell me, dear. Are you expecting?"

Jada had been busy throwing a "your grandmother seems lovely!" look over her shoulder to Marsh when Maw Maw posed the question. It was issued in the same casual tone she might have used to ask whether Jada had ever been to Connecticut before. Maw Maw had taken her elbow and and insisted that they walk together to the dining room to be seated. They led the entire party back up the long hall, toward the front. Her visit to the salon had been brief—she'd stopped only to greet her guests, put Minnie in her place and give Jada a rather keen once-over. One which had led her to a baffling hypothesis: that Jada was with child.

"Maw Maw..." Marsh chided, hastening to fall into step next to them. "This is Jada's first time meeting everyone. Let's try not to scare her away."

"It's a legitimate question." Maw Maw turned toward Marsh briefly before looking back to Jada with sharp eyes and a half-smile. "She has a glow." She turned back to Marsh. "Maw Maw's not getting any younger. I need more great-grands. Lord knows I can't count on Krista and Liz. Susie did her part. Now it's your turn. Jada's my only hope."

Before Jada could answer (and what did you even say to that?),

Maw Maw inspected Jada's left hand, a feat she could easily achieve owing to their hooked elbows.

"Are you the kind of woman who doesn't believe in marriage?" Maw Maw grilled. Jada had yet to get a word in edgewise.

Marsh chimed in. "You don't have to answer that."

"Hush, child. I'm asking the woman a question." Maw Maw took her free hand and swatted at her grandson's arm, as if to shoo him away from walking with the pair. She turned her attention back to Jada. "What's your position on pre-nuptial agreements?"

"No, no and no," Jada said definitively. "No, I'm not pregnant, though I do want children one day. No I'm not the kind of woman who doesn't believe in marriage. No, I don't believe in pre-nups. I think the psychology behind them messes everything up."

Maw Maw gave no reaction as to whether Jada's answers were satisfactory. Instead, she turned a gimlet eye on Minnie. "You want to talk messed-up psychology? A lot of people could be happily divorced if no one was holding them for ransom.

"Anyway, dear..." She turned her attention back to Jada. "I was beginning to think I'd have to send an engraved invitation. I've been wanting to meat you for years."

"Well I'm grateful to be with you here now," Jada answered with a smile that belied her returning anger. This was her second reminder that Marsh had never given her any inkling that his extended family had wanted to meet her.

"The circumstances aren't ideal, of course. It's not often that there are pressing matters of family. I hear that being here today cut into your weekend plans."

"Family first," Jada said, even as she knew the smile didn't reach her eyes.

Maw Maw patted her hand just as they entered an enormous formal dining room. The table was set for exactly thirteen. Jada was certain that it could be extended to accommodate a party twice as large, if ever necessary. Crystal ceiling chandeliers and candelabras that sat on sideboards and sconces were wick-lit with actual candles. If Jada wasn't mistaken, not a single inch of the room was illuminated with electric light.

The table was unclothed, yet laden with so many flowers, such an array of plates and cutlery, that no further adornment was needed. Glasses in the heaviest crystal Jada had ever seen were arranged in front of each place setting awaiting water, with separate chalices for red and white wine. A steaming feast sat waiting on bone china rimmed in gold. There was a turkey, of course, mashed potatoes, green beans and a few more things she couldn't make out at the other end. It was lavish, set for exactly the sort of occasion this room had been built to host.

Jada jumped a little when she felt Marsh's hand on her back. He shot her an "Are you okay?" look as he stepped past, pulling out the chair at the head of the table to help Maw Maw sit. She shook her head, not so much with a "no" vibe as with a "not now" one. His brows knitted in a combination of dread and concern when she mouthed, "Later."

Good, you should be afraid, she thought indignantly as she stepped closer to the table. Most everyone else had walked past her and was looking at the place cards to see where they were meant to sit. She didn't have to look far. A place card bearing her name was seated to the right of Maw Maw, corroborating what nearly everyone had insinuated by then: that Meeting Maw Maw was some sort of test.

Kate was across from Jada, with Marsh next to his mother and Marshall Senior on his son's other side. Ashley sat calmly next to Jada herself. Biff and Krista sat at the far end of the table with Biff's parents, Minnie and Steven. On the opposite side were Susie and her family.

By the time everyone was seated, Marsh was openly looking at Jada with concern. Jada, meanwhile, was trying to immerse herself in a conversation with Ashley. Just as he was exalting the joys of living off the grid, Maw Maw instructed the group to quiet for their prayer. Perhaps it was because Steven was her first born that she asked him to do the honors. It was nothing spectacular, but he was articulate about gratitude for their health, wealth and the company of their guests. He spoke more words in that brief prayer than she'd heard him speak all day.

"So, Jada, you work in finance?" Susie inquired good-naturedly, the first to interrupt the sound of knives cutting on china. Despite the warmth of the candle glow, something in the air had turned cold. Maw Maw's sharp admonition of Minnie had found her sulking. A nanny had long since swept up the children and taken them to another room. Jason looked a bit bereft without his phone in his hand.

"Venture capital," Jada nodded after swallowing a bite of turkey that was a bit bland for her tastes.

"Software and biotech," Biff chimed in. "That's where you ought to focus."

"A lot of upside, yes, but also a lot of risk." Jada took a sip of her wine.

"So what are your typical returns on a Series A?" Biff referred to the riskiest round of funding. If a company failed to thrive, Series A investors may never see a return. For that reason, VCs tended to charge enormous fees in these rounds—requiring interest of anywhere from 30%-50%.

"15%," Jada revealed calmly, as she'd done to many others before. "It's half the industry standard, but my firm has an alternative model."

Biff blinked. "An alternative to making money?"

"We focus on women and minority-owned businesses. We help them maintain a strong financial position, even after our exit."

"If they can't be profitable on their own, they deserve to fail," Jason chimed in.

Jada cast an even glance in his direction. "I didn't say we keep them from failing. I said we have an alternative model that helps their profitability by allowing them to retain more of their earnings."

"So, what, it's like Affirmative Action for investing?" Biff asked. His distaste for the idea was clear.

Marsh looked like he was bursting to say something.

"Every VC fund has a space it likes to play in. The space we like to play in is equality."

"How is it equal to only fund women and minorities? That sounds racist," Minnie chimed in.

Marsh put his face in his hands.

"Racism is a system of disadvantage," Ashley said calmly, leaning in toward the table until he was in the perfect position to smile serenely at Biff. "Since minorities don't hold the power to exact disadvantage on the objects of their bigotry, black people can't be racist."

"Kanye West sure is," Jason chimed in.

Biff looked between Jada and Ashley like both of them were crazy and scoffed. "Like hell they can't."

"How is it legal to favor women and minorities?" Minnie still seemed put out by the notion.

How it legal for all the traditional VC firms to keep them out? Jada thought.

But she'd anticipated coming into this that she might have to use the voice she reserved only for the embarrassingly un-woke. "Less than five percent of VC funding goes to companies led by women and minorities. My firm is staffed with employees who understand the market potential of a range of businesses."

"So you only hire black people? That's straight-up against the law," Jason complained.

"Jada is talking about women and minorities." Kate threw Jason a sharp look. "You're the only one talking about black people, you idiot."

Kate turned to Maw Maw, who was at her side, and patted the woman's arm. "And I think we've all seen how much money there is to be made when a strong woman runs a business."

Biff and Jason had the decency to look chagrined, if only for their fear of insulting Maw Maw. The matriarch hadn't uttered a word throughout the exchange. Jada went back to eating, sampling mashed potatoes that could have used a lot more butter and a little more garlic. Maybe the stuffing would be a win, she tried to convince herself.

"What Jada's too modest to tell you..." She looked up at the sound of Marsh's voice. He was not-at-all-shyly glaring at his cousin. "Is that hers has the highest revenue of any firm in its size in Silicon Valley. She's so good at picking superstar companies that 100% of them have hit their return. And what she doesn't do in margin, she makes up in volume."

Marsh shifted his gaze to Jada long enough to give her a small smile. From the corner of her eye, she saw Kate raise her glass in concurrence at the same time as Marshall Senior nodded his head in agreement.

"And giving everyone a fair shot isn't racist, Aunt Minnie," Marsh continued a minute later. "It's standing up to an establishment that has favored people who look like you and me for way too long. It shouldn't be a room full of white guys deciding that the only companies have merit are ones that are run by a team full of white guys. "

Biff scoffed. Marsh shifted his gaze. "You got something to say to me?"

"Like you're one to talk," Biff spat with venom.

"Excuse me?"

"Playing the part of the California liberal...looking down your nose like you're so different than us."

"I *am* different from you."

"Oh, yeah? How?"

Marsh shook his head and raised his hands in frustration.

But Biff didn't stop there. He kept provoking Marsh, his voice dripping with sarcasm. "Do we get to hear again about all the *important work you do*? Since you're a *human rights attorney*?"

Marsh stared at Biff darkly.

"I'm different from you because my life is about people. Not about money and power," he growled.

Biff swirled scotch in his glass. He was the only one to have made the long journey to the dining room without leaving his drink from the big room behind.

"I don't remember you saying no to your trust fund, or to the money you got when Paw Paw died," Biff challenged.

Marsh's teeth were clenched now. "At least I didn't piss it away on stupid shit. I took it because I knew I'd put it to a good cause."

"What cause would that be? Last I checked, it wasn't so easy to give away $250 Million."

Marsh's eye twitched at the same moment that Jada dropped her glass. She'd only had it lifted a few inches off of the table and it was made of such heavy crystal that the glass was no worse for wear. It rocked a bit on its base before settling to a stop. Jada, on the other hand, *was* worse for wear. Because trumping the litany of things it was now clear he'd never told her was the fact that he was heir to an unfathomable fortune.

"Jada..." Marsh stood, every muscle in his face etched in regret, every fathom of his eyes washed in guilt. The warning he had to have seen in her eyes must have given him pause.

"Mrs. Brewster," Jada eked out in a controlled voice and tried her best at a gracious smile. "Thank you for a lovely dinner. I'm sorry to excuse myself early, but I think I'd like some air."

Jada barely waited for a response before pushing herself back from the table. Her composure had its limits and the way things were going, it might not matter after all what Maw Maw thought. Marsh made it halfway to following her, to where, she still didn't know. One sharp look as he approached to fall into step with her, and he stopped in his tracks.

Many things crossed Jada's mind in that moment:

Do I have cell phone reception all the way out here?

Do they even have Uber in Connecticut?

Then, *Screw Uber, I'll take the car and let him fend for himself.*

By the time she remembered she didn't know how to drive in winter weather and thought about their ruined weekend in the snow, tears had begun to fall. She didn't know where her coat had been taken, but she did remember how to get back to the den next to the kitchens. She also remembered that a very warm-looking blanket had been folded on one of the back of the chairs.

MARSH

"*You* are an *arse-hole*," Kate informed Biff with so much ice in her voice even Marsh got a chill. Marsh wasn't a violent man. Yet, as he turned slowly, fists clenched, to face the room, he honestly wasn't sure that he wouldn't obey every reptilian inclination to punch Biff. God, he had it coming. Biff had taken pleasure in provoking Marsh since they were kids. He'd always bet—and bet correctly—that Marsh had too much respect for Maw Maw, to ever give Biff his comeuppance.

"The first thing you're going to do is apologize to Maw Maw." Marsh felt out of breath. He walked slowly toward Biff, his temper barely contained. "After that..." Marsh's lips trembled and he could feel subtle vibrations in his chest. "You'd better go apologize to Jada."

Biff snorted a bit drunkenly. "Apologize? For what? Telling her the truth about St. Marsh? You're the one who should apologize." When Biff lifted his glass and waved his hand dismissively, Marsh felt a hand pull back on his arm.

His father's eyes, when he met them then, didn't hold an ounce of "It's not worth it". More like, "I've got your back, son." Or, even, "Let me know when it's my turn." Marsh took a look around the room. This was Thanksgiving dinner. And all of them were Maw Maw's guests. He would kick Biff's ass one day. But not today.

"You're right." Marsh turned back to Biff, then extended his glare to Minnie, to Mark and to Jason, too. "I do owe her an apology. For going against my better judgment for the past four years and exposing her to you. "

Marsh turned to his aunt Minnie. "All your name-dropping socialite bullshit? Seriously, who are you trying to impress? She's got a lot more going for her than day-drinking at the yacht club. Believe me—she's not interested in joining your clique."

Minnie's face reddened. "I didn't...I wasn't..."

"You did. And you definitely were. And do me a favor: don't try to cause drama between my mother and my girlfriend just because *you* don't get along with *your* mother-in-law."

Next was Biff. "And you..debating investment strategy with one of the most successful VCs in Silicon Valley? Jada doesn't need you, or anyone, mansplaining how to do her job."

Not waiting for a response, Marsh shifted his gaze to Jase.

"What'd I do?"

"That comment about her going to a state school. What cave do you live in? UCLA is nationally ranked. And even if it wasn't, there's no shame in getting a good price on a good education."

"And Krista..." Marsh had to soften his voice, because his cousin-in-law really was sweet. "Do you comment on how well your white friends speak?"

Seeing where he was going with this, she sighed sheepishly. "No."

"Next time, could you try not to sound quite so surprised?"

Krista nodded in vigorous solidarity. "Yes."

Marsh sighed. He was angry with his family, yes. But he was also angry with himself. He should have told her the truth about the money long before.

"I'm sorry, Maw Maw," he said, turning to his grandmother and taking steps toward her. "I tried. I really did. But I don't think—"

"I'm retiring," Maw Maw cut him off cleanly, her words slicing a shock through the room.

"Well, don't act surprised," she said. "I'm not getting any younger. I brought all of you here to talk about my succession plan."

Many eyes shifted to Biff, and he straightened a little in his seat.

"That's why I called you here this weekend. I wanted you to hear it directly from me. No rumors. No triangulation. I wanted to face you, and for all of you to face each other. Just like I've had to take a hard look and face what the company's up against." Maw Maw looked around the room. "Rising workforce costs. Offshore competition. Differentiated demand in consumer markets. And do you know what my biggest risk is?"

No one answered. She looked at Biff.

"You."

Every pair of eyes at the table watched as the color drained from his face. By then, Biff had been gearing up to rise from his seat. He had buttoned his jacket, and his chair was pushed halfway back.

"You know all the technicalities. You know how to crunch the numbers. You know how to get things done. What you don't know is how to do it with heart."

"Maw Maw—" he began, but she raised her hand, in a gesture for him to stop.

"And that's just the good parts. I may be old, but I'm not stupid. No more law suits. No more creative accounting. These past two years have been a disaster. I'm done."

The room was deadly silent. Biff's face changed yet again. Its red that had faded to white now rose to green.

"So, Biff, you're fired. I've already put Miguel in place as the acting COO. You're no longer welcome on company property."

Maw Maw stopped looking at Biff and looked around the table. "And I'm not stupid enough to wait until I die for the rest. Why? So everyone can contest the will? I'll die a poor woman, but at least I'll be sure everything is where it belongs. No will and testament. If I've left you something, you'll leave here with it tomorrow. I have folders in my office about the smaller bequests."

Maw Maw turned to Susie. "Welcome to your new house. I know you've always loved this place."

Susie's eyes were wide, and blinked in surprise. Maw Maw didn't wait for a response.

"Marsh, I'm leaving my company shares to you."

Upon hearing Maw Maw's words, Kate choked on her wine. It

even dribbled down her chin a little. It was the least elegant thing Marshall ever seen his mother do.

"What?" Marsh said, at the same time as someone gasped and someone else let out a low, "Wowwww."

Maw Maw turned to Marsh then. "I don't expect you to run it. Just to reorganize and figure things out. Get Jada to help once she's speaking to you again."

Unable to process what this meant for him, Marsh looked over at Biff, who swayed in his seat while glaring intermittently between Maw Maw and Marsh. He looked like he was building up to say something. Probably not a good idea. But instead of words, he vomited into the blessedly empty chair at his side.

Millie covered her nose dramatically and pushed back a little from the table, even though she was two seats away. Ashley looked with passive curiosity but maintained the same calm he had throughout.

"I want a divorce," Krista announced. She pushed herself back from the table and threw her napkin into Biff's lap. "You can clean up your own messes now."

"Good girl," Maw Maw winked and praised a furious Krista as she stormed out of the room.

Marshall Senior stood and looked at his ex-wife intently. "And I want to get back together." He looked at Kate meaningfully, and for a long time. "No disrespect intended."

Marsh couldn't tell whether it was meant for his mother or Ashley. He supposed it didn't matter, judging from the fact that, throughout the exchange, his mother hadn't looked at Ashley once.

"And you..." Marshall Senior tore himself way from looking at his ex wife long enough to send a pointed look at Marsh. "Don't make the same mistake I did. Don't let secrets get between you and woman you love. Go get your girl. Before it's too late."

❄

Jada

Jada might have been content to stay in the gazebo she'd found down the hill behind the house, inhaling the smell of wood burning in the fireplace for hours. There was something splendid about chimneys and fires. Snow covered the ground, and the lake looked made of ice, and treetops moved in the wind. If she hadn't been so busy doubting everything she thought she knew about her relationship with Marsh, all of this would have been splendid.

She tightened the blanket around her. Yes, coming outside might have been hasty. Her knees were freezing. The blanket wasn't quite warm enough but it felt right that she should suffer the sting of the cold.

"Stay mad or make peace?"

She hadn't heard his approach. But she'd known he would show up, sooner or later. This was their code—the way they told one another whether they needed more time, or whether they were ready to talk.

"I want to make peace, but..." She let out a shuddering sigh.

Knowing this had to happen, she turned to face him squarely. "This is my family...not me."

She repeated his own words back to him, words he'd said to her not three-and-a-half-hours before.

He took a step closer, kept his gaze on hers as he shook his head.

"I didn't ask for any of it. And I *am* different from them. Inheriting money like that doesn't define who I am."

She sniffled. Because he was right. But there were still too many unanswered questions. "I don't understand...did you spend it or something?"

His eyes were clear and his voice was honest.

"Some of it, yes."

"How much of it?" Suddenly, she had to know every detail of every dollar.

"Around a hundred million."

"On *what*?"

Even though Jada dealt in huge sums of money every day, $100 million was a lot of money. And Biff had been right—having that much money wasn't easy to hide.

"Causes," he said simply. "Some I find myself; sometimes Kendrick brings me things."

Kendrick was Marsh's friend who worked for The Loxley Foundation. She'd met Kendrick twice when he'd been in town from New York. She loved the work the foundation did and she, herself, had become a donor.

"How much do you have left?"

"A little under two-hundred million."

"I just don't understand how you hid it all from me. We share bank accounts, for cripe's sake. I see who sends you things in the mail."

He shrugged. "Paperless statements."

Tears pooled in her eyes as she heard this information and she knew she would cry again. Because no woman wanted to find out that her boyfriend was such a smooth liar. Worst of all, it struck her as odd that he'd give up comforts he could easily afford. If he was so rich, why was he so cheap?

"So was it all an act?"

"Baby, nothing I feel about you is an act."

"Not that. Pretending you were working class. I mean, Jesus, Marsh...you go bananas every time that protein powder you like goes on sale at Costco. You spent an hour on the phone last weekend optimizing our cell phone data plan. And you'd better have a bulletproof explanation for why the hell we fly coach."

His eyebrows shot to his hairline and for a second he looked surprised. Then, astonishment melted into humor. She could tell from the way that his eyes twinkled and his lips twitched that he was trying not to smile.

"I live on my salary, Jada. It might not sound like a big deal to most people. But living on my own money is important to me."

"Who else knows?"

"Kendrick. People who knew me when...it's been a long time since I decided to distance myself from this."

"Why didn't you just *tell me*?" It was the most obvious question. "Did you think I wouldn't understand?"

Tears welled in her eyes when something in his face told her he did.

"You're this...social-justice-fighting, punch-the-patriarchy, disassemble-the-system badass. It didn't take long to figure out how you felt about this kind of money." His eyes held no guile, though they did hold sadness. "I still don't think you understand how hard I fell in love with you. The first year we were together, I lived in constant fear that you'd figure it out."

"About the money?"

He chuckled, sad and deep.

"That you were way out of my league...that you're this jugger-naut of change, and that the least interesting person you could ever choose to be with would be some privileged white guy like me."

Oh, baby.

Jada's breath caught in her throat. Had she really made him feel like that?

"I know it wasn't right, but...I didn't know what I'd do if you left."

"Where you ever going to tell me?"

"Eventually. When it became inevitable for you to know."

"What did you think would happen, bringing me here?"

"I sure as shit didn't think Biff would figure it out and throw me into hot water. Though, come to think of it, I probably should have anticipated that."

She sighed. "I just don't understand. Bringing me here to meet your family...why now, after so long? It's obvious you've been keeping me away from all of this. Is it just because you couldn't get out of Maw Maw calling you home for Thanksgiving?"

He sighed. "For a lot of reasons...it was just...time."

"Time for what?" she wanted to shout. Instead it came out as a strangled whisper.

"Time you saw it all for yourself."

Something complicated came into his eyes as they washed over her face. She shook her head helplessly. He took a step toward her, covering her hands in his. Casting his gaze downward, he rubbed her fingers between his palms before raising them slowly, to warm them with his hot breath. She'd forgotten that they were cold.

There was something he wasn't telling her. She was halfway to pointing out that it was in his own best interests to come completely clean when his gaze shifted beyond her shoulder. He blinked in disbelief and muttered, "No fucking way…"

Turning to see what was so interesting behind her, she saw that it had begun to snow, slow, thick flakes floating by the light of the moon down from the sky. Jada couldn't help the smile that erupted from her heart to her face. Not in her coziest wintertime fantasies had she imagined a snowfall as beautiful as this—the house lit and splendid, the frozen lake at their side, and the forest all around them.

"I'm sorry, baby. For every sideways choice I made that made it happen like this. I never should have put you in this position."

He looked duly repentant, and strangely nervous—perhaps anxious for her forgiveness?—as he peered to study the reaction on her face.

"No, you shouldn't have," she agreed. "But I can see why you were worried. I've never made it a secret that this isn't really my scene…"

He sighed, looking past her shoulder again, frowning a little as he did. When he caught her gaze again, his eyes were intense.

"You know…I can't really do anything about my family."

"Who's asking you to?" She shook her head.

He brought his hand to her cheek and smoothed back a lock of hair.

"If you marry me, they'll be your family, too."

Jada stopped breathing. Because…*what?*

"If—" She stammered a single word and cut herself off, still shaking her head to comprehend. Was he asking her to marry him or speaking in hypotheticals? He gazed down at her intensely, gauging her reaction.

"Just in case you wanted a big wedding or anything. They're the kind of family that makes you want to elope…"

His tone was flip but his eyes were serious and she could see then that he was really nervous. But she couldn't answer what he hadn't asked.

"Not funny." The pounding of her heart thrummed through her cheeks.

"Who's joking?"

The world tilted on its axis as he reached into his pocket.

"If I were, what would I be doing walking around with this?"

He got down on one knee.

"And just so you know, this isn't how it was supposed to happen. We would have had our turkey dinner there, and I would have taken you for a night-time forest walk.

"What else would have happened?"

"It would have snowed, even though I've been watching the forecasts like a hawk and now they're saying it's gonna be warm. I would have told you that what I was most thankful for every day, every week, and every year, is getting to share my life with you. "

"What would I have said? You know…if it had happened the right way?"

"You would have said yes."

MARSH

"What did I miss?" Jayda yawned as she asked the question. Marsh didn't miss that she covered her mouth with her left hand and smiled subtly when her eye caught sight of the ring. He could tell that she'd been delighted and stunned by the gorgeous piece of jewelry, and a bit awed to know that he'd been warned by so many Brewster women before.

He'd insisted they go in when he saw how cold she was getting. He, too, would have prolonged the moment. Though what had passed, he would not soon forget. The look in her eyes when she said yes. The glow of her skin under the moonlight in the snow. The vow they seemed to have silently spoken to one another in that moment. Months ahead of standing at the altar, it somehow felt that they had already spoken the words.

He'd been so busy seeking her forgiveness, that he'd forgotten about the others and the fact that she'd missed quite a bit.

"Maw Maw is retiring. She just fired Biff. She's giving me her shares in the company. Everyone's getting their inheritances early, and Susie's getting the house. Krista's divorcing Biff. My dad's finally admitted he still in love with my mom. And I think she's still in love with him, too."

"Wow." Jada stomped the snow off of her boots as they walked into the rear entrance. "I was only out there for, like, half an hour."

"Like I said. Unadulterated crazy."

Marsh took her blanket and held her hand as he navigated to the staircase that would take them to their room. But they were intercepted by Maw Maw.

"Are you feeling better, dear?" she asked Jada.

"Yes. Thank you."

Stepping up to Jada, Maw Maw reached again to lift her left hand. For a long moment, she admired the ring that she herself had worn for so many years before smiling up at Jada. "It looks better on you than it ever did in me," She praised. "I wish you every happiness. I know my grandson will do right by you."

"Thank you, Mrs. Brewster."

"Now go make some babies. None of that shit about keeping yourself pure for your wedding night. And, Jada... You can call me Maw Maw."

Stealing Christmas by Kari Lemor

A WILD CARD UNDERCOVER SHORT STORY

"WHO THE HELL STEALS CHRISTMAS PRESENTS ON CHRISTMAS Eve?"

Dave Johnston clenched his fists as he surveyed the jimmied lock on the back of his SUV. His girlfriend, Tina Washington, placed her hand on his arm, the calming effect immediate.

"The Grinch does," Tina's brother, Tommy said, his thumbs whipping across his new phone on some game. "Good thing you gave me this before all our stuff got taken."

"Isn't this supposed to be the City of Brotherly Love?" Tina glanced around, her eyes narrowed.

"Supposed to be," he muttered, stuffing clothes back into the suitcases. Luckily the thieves hadn't rummaged too deeply into them. His service weapon was still hidden under the panel in his bag. "Let's get to the hotel and see what's missing other than the presents." The dinner they'd just had at a fast food place was threatening to revolt.

As they piled in his vehicle, Dave grumbled softly. Some kind of Christmas reunion this would be. It had been over two years since he'd spent *any* holiday with his family and this one was already a shit storm.

"Dave," Tina said, her fingers rubbing back and forth on his thigh. "Your mom and grandma will be thrilled to see you. I doubt they'll be looking for gifts."

"And this is why I love you, gorgeous." Pulling her hand to his lip, he kissed her knuckles. The sound of gagging from the back seat reminded him they had a chaperon.

Tina twisted in her seat, her brown curls bouncing on her head. "You could have stayed at Great Aunt Mildred's for the holiday, Tommy. Be grateful Dave decided not to subject you to that torture."

"Fine. Go kiss. Just don't drive us off the road. I'd like to see my thirteenth birthday, thanks."

"Keep up the sarcasm and you won't make it until the New Year."

Dave chuckled as the beautiful lady next to him settled down. He wished it were closer. Damn bucket seats. Tommy became absorbed back into his game and Tina ran her hand over his thigh again.

"Totally teasing me, gorgeous. Not fair when we can't really do anything about it." Placing his hand over hers, he caressed her silky, mocha skin, trying to keep her hand from getting him too worked up.

Her deep brown eyes turned mischievous but she remained silent. They'd taken some time to drive up from Miami and the last few days in motels had been torture. The fact that Tina was raising her little brother had certainly put a crimp in their romance. But he'd made it a point to book a nice hotel here in Philly with adjoining rooms. Though Tina would still be sharing one with her brother. Not wanting to instill any immorality in him at a young age, she said. Once they were married though, all bets were off. He'd have Tina in his bed every night. Now all he had to do was ask her.

The little box with the diamond ring blazed a hole in his denim jacket. When would be the perfect moment to give it to her?

Thankfully he hadn't left it in the car. He put the vehicle in gear and drove.

When they got to the hotel, Tommy dawdled outside staring up at the fat white flakes floating in the sky.

"This is so cool. Literally," he said scooping up a handful of the stuff.

"Yes, it is." Dave chuckled. "It's frozen water. Come on, let's get inside. I promise we'll try and get you out in the snow more in the next few days. My sister, Renata, has a little girl who's only a few years younger than you. She'll teach you how to build a snowman or something."

After checking in and hauling their bags to their rooms, Dave texted his mom and let her know they'd gotten there safely.

"You didn't mention the robbery, did you?" Tina asked, walking through the connecting door and perching on the arm of the chair he was in.

"No, no sense in worrying her."

"How did she get through for the two years you were under-cover at Surf?"

Dave wanted to forget the high-class nightclub he'd dedicated so much of his life to. Except it was where he'd met Tina, who was waitressing at the time, trying to get money to go back to school. Last month they'd put Salazar Moreno behind bars for a long time. Dave had spent the days since getting closer to the woman who'd stolen his heart.

"She knew what my job was. And I'd call her every now and then when I was certain I wasn't being monitored."

"And you haven't visited her once since Moreno was arrested. That was the end of August."

Pulling her into his lap, he ran his fingers down the side of her face. "For the same reason you were in protective custody. So Moreno didn't try and influence our testimony. And the last month, well, I've been hanging out with you."

"And Tommy," Her gaze slid to the open doorway.

"And Tommy," he growled then pressed his lips to hers. Never did he think he'd be saddled with a pre-teen. Though Tommy was a great kid, his presence certainly caused a ton of sexual frustration on Dave's part. Damn, Tina heated his blood like no other. How he'd been able to go two years without making any kind of move on her must make him eligible for sainthood.

"Gross," the one they'd just mentioned said from the doorway.

Tina scrambled off his lap but Dave stayed where he was. Standing would give away the boner having Tina's beautiful ass on his crotch had given him. Tommy didn't need anatomy lessons right now. But, man, this was getting tiresome.

"Uh, I'm gonna go to bed," Tommy said, his thumb pointing toward the other room. "And I'll be using my ear buds so I can listen to music. This way I won't hear you in case you wanted to," his fingers moved up to do air quotes, "*watch a movie*."

Pursing his lips, Dave tried to keep his laugh contained. Tina's eyes widened. The kid was twelve and he'd lived in Miami his whole life. Doubtful he was as innocent as his sister wanted him to be.

"We might check out the news for a bit, but I'll be in shortly," she assured her brother. "Good night."

"Sure." Tommy rolled his eyes then closed the door behind him.

Tina gazed his way. "Do you think he—"

"Knows what we're doing? Yeah. He's not a little kid anymore, gorgeous." Dave moved to the door and twisted the lock. Turning back to the love of his life, he pulled her into his arms.

"But..."

"The only butt I want right now is your gorgeous ass, in my hands." He proceeded to show her. Damn, her assets were fine.

"You know, you're lucky I forgave you for lying to me for two years." Her soft voice purred with delight, so she couldn't be that upset. He thought they'd settled all this months ago.

"I was undercover, gorgeous. I couldn't tell you I was Miami PD. You know that. I'll make it up to you, I promise. My Gram is the best cook you'll ever meet."

Tina's eyes twinkled and her lips quirked. "You did lock the door. And the new phone with all those apps was brilliant. He barely said a word the whole trip up here."

"Kind of my intent. Now let's say we watch that movie."

After turning on the TV and finding an actual movie to drown out any sound they might make, he slipped her sweater over her head and tossed it on the floor. The pastel pink bra against her warmer skin tone bedazzled him.

"What kind of movie is this?" she said as her hands undid the buttons on his shirt, her eyes on him and not the program.

Gently pushing her onto the bed, he bent and yanked off her shoes and socks then reached for the button on her jeans. "R rated for sure." Yes, the panties matched the bra. He was all but salivating at the sight after dragging the jeans off her long, lean legs.

"Mmm, I may have seen this movie before." His snap popped open and Tina pulled the denim material down his legs, her fingers burning a line across his skin. When he stepped out of his shoes and pants, she skimmed her fingertips over his erection. "And if I remember correctly, there are a few parts that could be considered X-rated."

"Definitely X-rated." He rolled onto the bed, tugging her on top of him and pushing the straps off her shoulders. "And I may have already seen it too. But I don't think I'd ever get tired of this movie. I really like the ending."

THE WARMTH AT HER BACK FELT LOVELY. DAMN, SHE COULD STAY here all day. But it was Christmas and they needed to get to Dave's mom's house.

"Shit." Jumping up, Tina glanced at the clock then at the man whose kissable lips were smiling at her. "I wasn't supposed to stay here all night. What will Tommy think?"

"He'd think you were happy," Dave replied tugging on the sheet she held to her chest. "If he's even awake. It's barely six. That kid never wakes up before noon if it isn't a school day."

Glancing at the door between the two rooms, she nodded. "True, but today's Christmas. He could be up early."

"Excited for Santa? Pretty sure he learned that truth a while ago. My mom said to come by for brunch but I don't think she expected us quite this early. You can relax for a bit."

As she snuggled down onto his chest, he ran his fingers over her back. Her naked back. She'd never even put her clothes back on the night before, which worked out now as her skin touched that of the man she loved. Her hand decided to get in on the action, too. Down his chest of warm mahogany then to the muscled shoulders he'd allowed her to cry on at times.

"I like relaxing with you. Thanks for being so good to me. And Tommy." Dave had been there for them when they'd been placed in protective custody. Not that she hadn't fought him on it, but with a broken arm and beaten face, courtesy of their employer, she'd feared for her life as well as that of her brother.

Dave gazed at her with his chocolate eyes and she lifted her hand to touch his face. The well-trimmed goatee he wore tickled her fingers then his lips nipped at them. Pulling her closer, their mouths met. Nothing else mattered for at least an hour.

Tina didn't allow herself to linger too long in Dave's arms though. Slipping back into the adjoining room, thankful Tommy was still asleep, she grabbed her things and jumped in the shower. She wanted to make a good impression on Dave's mom and grandmother. If their relationship was heading in the direction she thought it was, then they could be her family soon also.

They did need to wake up her brother, and he grumbled accordingly, until Dave reminded him of all the food that would be at their destination.

"And we'll need to stick together," Dave said to him. "The women will outnumber us five to two."

Thirty minutes later they were pulling up to a row house in a middle-class neighborhood.

"Is this where you grew up?" Tina asked. It was far nicer than where she and Tommy had been living in Miami. Though the weather was considerably colder.

"No. My sister and I got Mom and Gram to move after my dad died. He'd been in an accident and the insurance and settlement was enough to help them buy this place."

"I'm sorry about your dad." Snuggling into his arm, Tina walked beside him up to the front door. Tommy trailed behind, his face glued to the damn screen. Maybe it wasn't the best gift for him. Though he'd probably complain all day he was bored if not for the device.

"You haven't exactly had it easy either, gorgeous. You've been raising your little brother since you were twenty."

"Which was only a few years ago," she said, winking at the handsome man at her side. Closer to eight. It had been challenging having a new little brother when you were sixteen, especially when your mom wasn't sure who the father was and took off four years later leaving you with a young kid to raise. But she loved Tommy and would never have wanted him to go to foster care. She'd certainly raised him better than their mother ever had. And now, hopefully, he had Dave as a role model too.

"You keep telling yourself that, gorgeous." Dave was mid-way through his thirties so he shouldn't be one to talk. He gave a quick rap on the door then turned the knob. "Mom, Gram, we're here."

"David Einstein Johnston. Well, it's about time." The feminine voice boomed from a back room.

"Einstein?" Her gaze went to Dave's face, which seemed to have a bit of red it in it.

His lips pursed as he pulled her through the front hall. "She thought it would make me smarter."

"You picked me so you must have some brains."

"Best thing I ever did," he whispered, then looked at the two women rushing through the doorway.

After giving the younger of the two a warm hug, Dave turned

and pulled Tina forward. "Mom, I want you to meet a very special lady. Tina Washington. And this is her brother, Tommy."

"It's lovely to meet you, Mrs. Johnston. Thank you for inviting us for Christmas."

The tall, slim woman pulled her in for a hug then shook her head. "Oh, honey, please, it's Delores. And I can't thank you enough for finally getting my son to come for a visit. We're so happy to meet you, Tina. We've heard so much about you in the past few months."

Her pretty face, surrounded by fashionable short dark hair sprinkled with some gray, softened. "Tommy, thanks for coming along too."

Her brother had the good manners to lower his phone and smile with a clipped, "You're welcome."

Dave was currently enveloped in the arms of his grandmother. His tall body stooped over to accommodate the tiny woman. Tiny is height but not in girth. Her gray curls hugged her head tight in a 50's style while her festive pale green dress looked like she was heading to church.

"Now it's your turn, darling, and you just call me Grandma." Tina found herself wrapped in soft arms that smelled of Jean Naté and cinnamon.

To his credit, Tommy didn't protest when it was his turn for Grandma's hug, though his expression certainly wasn't one of delight. Until she said, "I bet this young man could use some food. He looks near starved to death."

True, Tommy was thin, but it sure wasn't for lack of sustenance. The kid could shovel more food in than anyone else she'd seen. Five or six bowls of cereal in the morning was typical. Dave had said all teen boys ate that way but darn, if it didn't put a dent in her budget.

"She's stunning, David," Delores said under her breath as they walked toward the kitchen. Tina still heard and let out a sigh. Making a good first impression was important. The new knee-high boots she'd purchased, and luckily had been wearing last night when the SUV had been broken into, were something she'd never needed living in the heat of Miami. Too bad the adorable red sweater Dave had insisted looked great on her hadn't been so fortunate. She'd had to settle for a white blouse to go with the floral skirt she'd paired with the boots.

The kitchen was a hive of activity. A younger version of Delores, along with a little girl, were busy rolling dough onto a cutting board. Grandma already had Tommy sitting at the table with a plate of cinnamon rolls in front of him.

"It's a shame he's so shy," Dave murmured, slinging his arm around her shoulder. "Come on, before it's all gone."

"Oh, there's plenty where that came from," Grandma said, grabbing a pan of scrambled eggs and sliding them into a large bowl. "Give me a hand getting these dishes on the table."

Tina rushed over to take a large platter of bacon while Dave managed the eggs and pancakes.

"Renata, this is Tina and her brother, Tommy." Dave brought over a stack of plates and cutlery. "Tina, my sister, Renata, and her daughter, Mallory. How are you, munchkin?"

The child tilted her head and ducked behind her mother's legs. Dave's mouth turned down but he shrugged and sat next to Tina at the table.

"She hasn't seen you in a few years, big bro. Give her time."

"Sure, where's your better half?"

"Is that me, Mama?" Mallory asked and her mother chuckled as she slid the cut dough onto a cookie sheet and into the oven.

"He's working a twelve-hour shift at the hospital. Double overtime, plus he gets the next few holidays completely off."

"Ren's husband, Will, is a nurse at Jefferson." Dave explained. He'd already told Tina this, plus that his sister was an accountant. Their parents had wanted them to be more successful than they'd been. He'd made it sound like his career as a Miami police officer didn't count.

After forking up a few mouthfuls of food, Dave glanced around the kitchen. "Grandma, how'd you get so much of the dessert done? I thought your old mixer died a noble death?"

Was he going to explain that they'd bought her a brand-new Kitchen Aid to replace her old one but that it had been stolen? Wiggling her hand into his, she squeezed his fingers. He'd wanted to make a good impression since he hadn't been around in so long.

"It did," she said, frowning. "But we just had to do it the old-fashioned way."

Renata shook her head. "Brute strength. Too bad you hadn't been here earlier, bro, you might have been helpful."

Was that a snipe or just sisterly badgering? Dave's expression told Tina it had hit a soft spot with him.

"I'm sorry I wasn't around much the last few years. The undercover assignment had to be solid. I'll try and take on a bit more from now on."

"Don't you even worry, David," his mom responded. "We've been just fine. Don't need a man to take care of things. Your grandmother and I are perfectly capable of dealing with anything that comes along."

It sounded great but somehow that didn't seem to relieve the guilt she saw on Dave's face.

"THE TREE LOOKS GREAT, MOM," DAVE SAID AS THEY ALL MOVED to the living room after cleaning up the breakfast dishes and food. There should have been more presents underneath it, though. Damn, why hadn't he found a place to eat where he could park the SUV in his view? Because Tommy had started grumbling about dying of starvation and he'd wanted to shut the kid up. He really was great, but when he got hungry, or *hangry* as Tina called it, you didn't want to be around him.

"Now, we got you some gifts, though we didn't exactly know what you liked," his grandmother said, settling herself in her upholstered rocking chair. "But you can always return anything you don't want."

"You didn't need to get us anything," Tina insisted. "We're just happy to be here."

"Are you kidding me?" Mom said, smiling. "My son finally decides to bring a woman home with him. We are definitely doing everything in our power to make her feel welcome."

Renata's mouth was more of a smirk. "Yeah, kind of like a bribe so you won't notice what a mistake you made choosing him."

"Love you, too, Ren."

Mallory poked her head from behind his sister and asked, "Did you get me a present, Uncle Dave?"

Those puppy eyes killed him. Especially because of the answer he needed to give his niece. "We did buy gifts for everyone, sweetheart, but unfortunately we had a little mishap and we don't have them right now. We'll make sure to go out and replace them real soon."

"Nonsense," Gram said, "Christmas doesn't come from a store. Christmas perhaps means a little bit more."

Had his grandmother just quoted the Grinch? After he was deGrinchified, of course.

The front door opened with a bang and "Ho, Ho, Ho!" boomed from the hallway.

His mom's eyes widened then focused on Gram. "Mom, you didn't invite them, did you?"

Gram's face tightened and her eyes narrowed. "He's your brother, Delores. And your nephew."

His mother's brother. Shit. His uncle and cousin walked into the living room, the older one carrying a large sack, like freakin' Santa. Renata's expression turned sour as well and she pulled Mallory close to her side.

"Uncle Lonnie?"

"Davey, yo, heard you might be here today!" The bag dropped at his uncle's feet and he shook the snow from his greasy ball cap.

Dave took a deep breath and held it. This was the last thing he'd expected. He thought his uncle was still doing time. "When'd you get out?"

"Couple weeks ago. Good behavior, you know. Calvin was waiting right there for me. He got out last month."

Calvin, a few years younger than Dave, leaned against the doorway, his Ray Bans lowered on his nose and his slimy gaze on Tina. How the hell did a man just out of prison afford those? Like he had to ask.

"Whoa, cuz, who's the babe? She got a fine set of—"

"My girlfriend," Dave interrupted, standing. He threw a harsh look at the younger man, not that is would matter. Calvin never took hints very well.

"Well, hello there." Uncle Lonnie oozed his own brand of charisma. Like Fagin. And Calvin pictured himself the Artful Dodger. "Come give your old Uncle Lonnie a kiss."

Dave moved in front of Tina. "You're not her uncle and there's no way she's kissing you."

"I'm simply trying to welcome her to the family, boy. Now where's my little sister."

His mom stood with her hip cocked and her arms folded. "Why are you here, Lonnie?"

"I invited him," Gram said, her eyes like steel. "This is my house too. He called the other day and said they didn't have anywhere to go." His grandmother had always been too kind-hearted, as well as stubborn. Probably figured she could get Lonnie and Calvin to mend their ways with one quick visit. Dave hoped it was quick.

"I'd tell them where to go," Mom muttered then sighed. "Fine, but no funny business, you understand."

"Sure, sis, we'll be perfect angels, like on the top of that Christmas tree." Lonnie gave Mom a quick peck on the cheek then leaned over Gram for the typical get-the-stuffing-squeezed-out-of-you hug. Calvin followed suit, jingling along the way with all his chains, around his neck, out of his pocket and on his wrist. How much of that had he actually paid for?

"Tina," Dave said putting his arm around her possessively. "This is my mom's brother, Lonnie, and his son, Calvin."

"Guess that makes us kissing cousins," Calvin crooned, reaching out for Tina with puckered lips.

Raising his fist, Dave said, "You're gonna be kissing this if you keep it up. And Tina's not related to you." Not yet, he wanted to add, but the ring was a surprise and he certainly didn't want to give either Calvin or Lonnie reason to touch her. Hopefully having these two here wouldn't make her refuse to marry him.

"This is her brother, Tommy." He indicated the boy who had barely looked up from his phone. This was one time Dave was glad the kid was distracted. Lonnie and Calvin weren't the best role models.

"Well, let's get some presents opened," Lonnie shouted. "The day's a wasting."

"If you've got someplace to be, don't let us hold you up." Dave hoped they'd take the hint and skedaddle sooner rather than later. But knowing these two, they'd linger as long as they could if they'd get something out of it. For once he actually wished his grandmother wasn't such a great cook.

"Renny, we got something for you and the kid, here." Calvin pulled a few boxes out of the bag and tossed them at Dave's sister. She looked about as pleased as he was.

Renata carefully slit the paper and opened the box. Her surprised look was followed by, "Oh, it's very pretty."

The red sweater was pretty and also familiar. Glancing at Tina, he knew she also had recognized the garment. The one he'd bought her yesterday to wear for today. It couldn't possibly be a coincidence, could it? When Mallory tore the wrapping paper off her gift and it was an Easy Bake Oven, Dave's blood began to boil. Shit, had they seriously been robbed by his own family?

"Great presents," he growled, wanting to reach behind him and pull his Glock from its belt holster. Maybe he'd give them a chance to explain first.

"Yeah," Lonnie grinned, the metal in his front teeth gleaming.

"I figured the kid here could learn to be as great a cook as Mom."
He reached into the bag again.

Dave clenched his fists but remained vigilant. Tina sat at his side glancing at him every few seconds.

"Here's a little something for that nurse husband of yours. Got him a bottle of that fancy wine. Since he's got a girly job, figured he liked girly drinks too." Lonnie shoved a bottle into Ren's hands.

"Are you supposed to be buying alcohol while on probation, Lonnie?" Mom asked, her face still set in stone.

"We didn't buy it," Calvin said, tapping on his pocket. Probably where he had his own concealed weapon.

"Cause that's so much better," Dave muttered. "Tell me you didn't hurt anyone."

"I ain't never hurt no one." Lonnie scowled searching in the bag again. "Not physically. Not anyone who didn't deserve it, anyway."

Calvin helped his father get two big boxes and brought them to Mom and Gram. Dave studied the shape and had a really bad feeling he already knew what was in them."

"Where'd you two go shopping for all this stuff?"

Calvin chuckled. "Great little place over near tenth street. They were practically giving the stuff away."

"I'll bet they were."

"Oh, my, you certainly didn't need to do this," Grandma exclaimed, her eyes bright. The replacement for her Kitchen Aid mixer. Yeah, he'd known she'd love it.

Dave crossed his arms. Mostly so he wouldn't strangle Lonnie and Calvin. "Let me take a guess what that is, Mom? A computer? Maybe a Dell Inspiron 7000 series. Lightweight and has touch screen and camera also. You know, so you can face time with your children when they aren't nearby."

His mom finished removing the paper, looked at the side of the box, and frowned. "That's exactly what it is. How did you know, David?" Her gaze rested on her brother and nephew though.

Lonnie looked around and saw Tina and Tommy staring at him also with disbelief in their eyes.

"Because those are the exact presents we got for you, but had stolen from my car last night."

Lonnie scrubbed his hand over the stubble on his thin face. "No need to feel embarrassed because you didn't bring any gifts."

"We didn't have any thanks to you two. I can't believe you stole from your own family."

"Oh, Florida plates?" His uncle grimaced and shrugged. "Didn't make the connection."

Calvin readjusted the black beanie on his head and smirked. "You should take better care of your things."

Heat rose in Dave's entire body and the control he usually had was ready to snap. When Tina touched his arm and smiled at him, some of the anger started to dissipate. Not all though.

"What does it matter how the gifts got here," his uncle said dramatically, "Gram got her mixer and Delores her new computer. No harm done, right."

"Except that sweater was Tina's."

Renata pulled the garment from the box and held it up.

"No, that's fine," Tina said. "I'm sure it looks better on you."

"I can't believe you stole presents from my car," Dave grumbled, not wanting to start a fight on Christmas but still incredibly pissed.

Calvin actually looked embarrassed. "We didn't know it was you. Never would have grabbed them if we did."

"We got you something too." Lonnie held up a gaily wrapped box.

"Don't even bother. I don't want it."

Walking closer, Renata cocked her head. "So, what'd you get me, Dave, if it wasn't the sweater?" Her eyes flickered across the room to where Tommy was helping Mallory read the directions for her oven, keeping the little girl busy.

He eyed his uncle and cousin. "Got you an iPad, so you can still do work when you're hauling Mallory around to dance lessons and stuff."

"That would have been real nice to have." Her voice dripped sarcasm while her gaze speared Calvin. "Where did that go?"

Their cousin looked away like he was interested in the decorated tree.

"Calvin kept it and gave her the sweater," Lonnie said, then, at the daggers they sent his way, added, "What? It's a really nice sweater."

"It's back at my place," Calvin muttered. "I'll get the fucking thing later."

Ren glared at him. "There are kids present. Watch your mouth."

"I'd rather watch hers." He smirked staring at Tina. The heat came back, and not the good kind Dave got when he and Tina were alone.

THE SLIMY COUSIN WALKED TOWARD HER. IT WAS HARD TO imagine that these two men and Dave were related. Where Dave was tall and trim with lean muscles, his cousin was short and stout, like their grandmother. And even with the extra weight it didn't seem like he could hold his pants up. They bagged on him something awful and hung halfway down his ass. The uncle was scrawny and looked far older than he probably was.

"If you ever feel like walking on the wild side, bitch, come see me. Cousin Dave can be drawlin at times. I can show you a real good time."

"Think I'll pass, thanks." Moving toward Mallory and Tommy, she helped them set up the small oven. Dave strolled over a few minutes later.

"Sorry about all this. You okay?"

Nodding, she ran her hand down Dave's arm. Her touch had a calming effect on him. So many times when they'd been working, she'd patted his hand or touched his arm to have physical contact with him. Only recently had she learned why he'd never responded the way she'd wanted him to.

"Hey, Dave," Tommy said quietly. "At least now we've got four guys so it's better odds."

"You like playing the odds, kid?" Of course Lonnie had heard that. "I can teach you how to beat the odds in a bunch of games."

"I don't think so," Dave warned and slung his arm over her shoulder. Was he trying to protect her? She'd certainly held her own against all the scummy creeps who'd hit on her for years while working as a cocktail waitress in Miami.

"So, what do you do for a living, Tina," Delores asked.

Tina told them how she'd saved to go back to school and Dave joined in at how proud he was of her. For the next few hours Dave talked about his life in Miami and what it had been like to be undercover. He was keeping it clean, no doubt. No need to worry the mom or grandma.

When Lonnie and Calvin started talking about what prison had been like and the guys they knew who were planning to help get them set up, Renata asked Tina if she and Tommy wanted to help her get the meal ready in the kitchen.

"Yes, of course, I'd love to help somehow." Best get away from the two deadbeats. They reminded her too much of her life in the nightclub.

Dave stood in the doorway between the kitchen and living room, his eyes still locked on his two male relatives.

When they'd gotten the food in serving dishes and on the table, Renata leaned in close. "Don't judge my brother on Lonnie and Calvin. I think part of the reason Dave became a cop was because he hated seeing men like them tearing a family apart."

"I love Dave and there's not much he could do to change how I feel. But don't tell him that. I don't want him thinking he can take advantage of me and go partying with the boys all the time." She winked at Renata, making sure the woman knew she was only kidding.

"Where's the food?" Calvin bellowed from the other room then Lonnie walked in with Gram on his arm, like he was escorting the queen. At least he had manners where some were concerned.

Once settled, Delores said grace and they dug in.

"Oh, Gram, I missed your food. This is fucking unbelievable. The stuff in the joint makes you gag."

"Language, Calvin." Delores scowled.

Luckily both Lonnie and Calvin spent the next hour shoveling food in their mouth so they didn't have a chance to say much.

"Hey, Rennie," Uncle Lonnie said after he'd cleaned his plate a second time and reached for more. "I got a friend who could use a good accountant like you." Food spilled from the corners of his mouth and flakes of it flew across the table. "Fat Louie pays big bucks. He needs someone who's got a good creative streak in them. You know what I mean?" His wink was exaggerated.

Renata only glared. "I've got a job."

"But this one," Calvin interrupted, juice running down his chin, "will get you so much fucking money you can buy your own damn iPad."

Delores cleared her throat muttering, "Language."

"Like the kids ain't never heard this shit before," Lonnie mumbled, taking a huge bite of an overly buttered roll.

Gram started talking about a few of her friends and what children and grandchildren they were with this holiday. Her gaze stayed on her son and grandson, giving them a glare every time it seemed they were going to open their mouths. And not for shoving food into.

When dinner was done, Tina offered to help clean up.

"You're our guest today," Delores stated. "You should sit back and enjoy yourself."

"Really, I'd like to help. I feel comfortable in a kitchen." Which wasn't exactly the truth. Sure, she could cook, but mostly she wanted to stay out of the living room where Lonnie and Calvin had gone.

Delores looked to where Tina's gaze had gone and nodded. "Well, then, I'd love to get to know you better. Thank you."

Mallory begged Tommy to play a game with her while Gram settled back in her rocking chair talking to Lonnie and Calvin about her church group. Good luck there. If those two ever managed to go to church they'd probably rob the collection basket.

"Sorry about the presents, Mom," Dave said taking a dish from her and loading it in the dishwasher.

"Certainly not your fault, sweetie. I hope those two didn't ruin your day."

"It could have been worse."

Tina tubbed his back then leaned in for a kiss. Dave obliged though kept it chaste.

As Dave looked around the kitchen, he said, "Hey Ren, I was wondering if maybe you could keep an eye on Tommy for a bit. I was hoping to show Tina around town. You know, alone."

Renata's eyes gleamed. "Alone? I'm not sure I know what that means any more. But, sure."

"Maybe I'll wait until those two clowns take off. God knows what they'll get up to if they aren't kept in check."

When the kitchen was cleaned up, Tina hated to go back into the living room. His uncle and cousin had been leering at her since they'd gotten here and Calvin had groped her a few times as he passed by. Since she didn't want any bloodshed, she hadn't mentioned it to Dave. Pummeling your cousin wasn't the best way to reconnect with your family after two years away.

When the doorbell rang, she peeked into the hallway as Delores answered. Did they have other relatives dropping by? Please make them better than Lonnie and Calvin.

"Do you mind if we come in, ma'am? We have a few questions."

Standing in the doorway were two policemen.

❄

Police? What the hell were they doing here? Glancing in at his uncle and cousin, Dave had a good idea.

"Did you seriously rat us out?" Calvin glared his way, jostling him shoulder to shoulder.

Shit, he needed to avoid anyone being hurt. Shaking his head, he said, "Why don't we see what they want."

But Lonnie and Calvin started sweating, apparently already aware of why the cops were here. His mom opened the door and led them into the living room, her mouth tight, her eyes narrowed.

"What can we help you with, officers?" Gram asked politely. God, he loved his grandmother but she honestly had no clue at times.

"I'm Officer Suarez and this is Officer McKenna. The black Audi out front, who does it belong to?"

"Isn't that the car you drove here in?" Renata asked her uncle, arms crossed over her chest. She'd sent Tommy and Mallory down the hall to Gram's bedroom. Quick thinking. Who knew how volatile this situation could get.

"Nah, we took a taxi. Must be yours," Lonnie said looking at Dave.

"My vehicle is the SUV, officer. What seems to be the problem?"

"The Audi was reported stolen this morning."

Heat rose to his face as he stared at his relatives. "You stole a car and brought it to Gram's? Are you nuts?"

"You ain't got no right to come in here accusing us of anything," Lonnie yelled.

Calvin joined in, waving his arms in the air then he reached in his pocket. When Dave took a step forward, one of the cops moved closer, hand on his sidearm.

"Everyone stay where you are until we get to the bottom of this. The SUV has got lots of bags in the back seat. We'll need the keys to search that also. There's been a rash of thefts lately with items being stolen from vehicles."

Dave dug in the front pocket for his keys as Calvin pulled out a small leather square and flipped it open. "Maybe you could back off and let me handle this. I'm a cop too."

"You're a cop?" McKenna asked, checking out Calvin's baggy pants and chains. Where had his cousin gotten the badge?

Calvin lifted his index finger to his lips. "Deep undercover."

The cop glanced at the badge. "Sergeant in Miami?"

"Why you..." Dave said, feeling for his back pocket which was now empty. The little prick has lifted his badge.

"Hold it right there!" Both cops drew their weapons and aimed at him. What the fuck? As he felt to see if Calvin had stolen anything else, Suarez shoved him to the floor, his knee connecting with Dave's back.

"We'll take this," he said pulling Dave's Glock from his belt holster.

"I'm a cop."

"Yeah, you're all cops. With a stolen vehicle sitting outside." His arm was twisted back and a metal cuff clinked on his wrist then his other hand.

"Dave?" Tina's anxious voice floated over.

"Don't worry, gorgeous. We'll get this cleared up." After being pulled roughly to his feet, he addressed the officers. "You can check my wallet in my back, right pocket. My license gives you my Miami address which should corroborate the Miami police badge."

Hands groped but Dave could tell the wallet wasn't there either. He'd had it at dinner. One look at Calvin and he knew where it was. Freakin' little weasel.

"Check those two," Dave insisted lifting his chin toward Lonnie and Calvin. He wasn't going through all this hassle for them to walk free. "And while you're at it, you might want to check with their parole officers."

"Parole, huh? Turn around, we're taking you in too."

"Taking us in?" Lonnie growled. "On what charges?"

"Possession of a deadly weapon," McKenna said, pulling a knife from the depth of Calvin's pocket.

Tina walked closer, her expression worried but determined.

"This man here is David Johnston. I've known him for over two years and he's a police officer in Miami."

"Except he doesn't have any identification on him at the moment. We'll clear this up as soon as we can. A tow truck will be picking up the stolen vehicle shortly. And we're getting a warrant to search the SUV. Please don't tamper with either of them."

"You have my permission to search the SUV. The keys are on the floor." Where they'd fallen when the guy had body slammed him. The little aches right now told him just how hard.

Dave saw another police car pull up as he headed to the door. Calvin and Lonnie were escorted outside. Tina hovered nearby, Tommy tucked behind her, for once not focused on his phone.

"Tina, call Shaunessy. Tell him what happened. See if he can vouch for me and get this settled faster. He should be in Pennsylvania also, at Meg's house."

Tommy ran over and hugged him around the waist. Damn, not exactly the shining example he'd wanted to be for the kid.

"They taught me how to pick a lock," he whispered as Dave leaned into the hug. "Want me to help you?"

Fuck. Those two had managed to corrupt the kid in one afternoon. "No. Stay here with your sister. I'll be back soon." He hoped.

Luckily, they stuck him in the back of a different car from the other two losers. Losers he happened to be related to. Of all the fucking timing. Why couldn't they have gotten out of prison a few months from now when Tina had already agreed to marry him? And they were back in Miami.

At the precinct, as Dave emptied what was left in his pockets, the Booking Officer jotted down what he had. When he got to the ring box, he opened it and whistled.

"Nice. Where'd you lift this from?"

"It's not stolen. I was planning to ask my girlfriend to marry me today, before the shit hit the fan."

Suarez chuckled. "Does she know what you do for a living?"

Gritting his teeth, Dave said, "Yes, she's knows I'm a cop. I met her while undercover."

"Deep undercover?" Suarez teased, his eye gleaming. "Like your friend with the badge."

"It's *my* fucking badge. He lifted it from me."

And since Calvin had also take his wallet, though obviously hadn't kept it on him, Dave ended up getting fingerprints done as well. Not that those would confirm his place in the Miami PD. Due to being undercover, they'd made sure to wipe any link to him being a cop from all records.

He got why they wouldn't take his word for it but it was pissing him off. When he got his hands on Lonnie and Calvin... maybe then they'd have a reason to lock him up.

As the officer closed the envelope with his possessions and headed to the inventory locker, Dave yelled over, "Don't lose that ring."

The guy laughed. "Think I might be able to get out of the dog house with my old lady if I showed up with that rock?"

Suarez grinned and led him down the hallway to an interrogation room. Didn't look much different from the ones they had in the Miami precinct where he'd worked.

"Okay, let's cut to the chase. We got the vehicle back so if you don't have any priors, you might get off with community service and probation. First, what's your name? Really?"

"David Einstein Johnston." At the cop's smirk, the words *fuck off* came to mind. But as someone who'd been on the other side of the table, he knew that wasn't a good response. "Yeah, my mother had a sense of humor. I grew up in Philly but spent the last eight years working Miami PD. The last two were undercover attempting to put Salazar Moreno away."

"Hey, I heard about that one. Guy just got some heavy time. So how come you don't have i.d. with you?"

"My cousin, the one waving the badge around, guessing he took my wallet at the same time."

"Your cousin, huh? That sucks."

He was ready to throw both Calvin and Lonnie under the bus by mentioning the gifts lifted from his SUV, but his Gram would never forgive him. They'd find out about those clowns soon enough anyway. He assumed they were getting the same treatment he was.

The interrogation didn't take long as he had nothing new to say other than giving the name of his direct supervisor in Miami. But it was Christmas Day and there'd be a skeleton crew in the precinct. Hopefully Tina could get in touch with Shaunessy and the FBI agent could pull some strings to get this cleaned up faster. For now he was led to a room with several holding cells. And unfortunately, they were full.

"At least you won't be alone for Christmas," Suarez joked as he closed the cell door behind Dave.

Each cell had three or four guys inside, many of them curled on the floor or benches, shivering. Addicts? Drunks? Great, exactly where he wanted to be instead of curled up next to Tina, being thanked for the diamond he'd planned to give her.

"Hey, Davey, didn't expect to see you in here." His cousin's voice floated over from two cells down.

Narrowing his eyes, he glared at Calvin. "Well, after you stole my...i.d, they didn't believe any of us." Best not to mention being a cop in this place.

"You don't got no cop friends who can help you?" Lonnie laughed, knowing just what he'd done by announcing that tidbit of information.

Turning his back on his relatives, he surveyed the occupants of his cell. One obvious junkie, curled on the floor twitching, one very large dude who eyed him suspiciously, and a kid who looked like he could barely be eighteen. Settling on the bench on the right, Dave crossed his arms, puffing up his muscles. Mostly to disabuse anyone of thoughts they might have of messing with him.

As the clock on the wall ticked by and curses flung around the space, he kept his eyes peeled for any trouble. The big dude leaning against the bars on the other side of the cell kept glaring at him. Unfortunately, the guy in the cell right behind him reeked of alcohol and pot. Damn, he felt like he could get high on the fumes alone.

Lonnie and Calvin were having a blast in their cell though. Taking bets and discussing how much Fat Louie could make them if they wanted to go into the delivery business. As Dave stared at them, shaking his head, he felt warm breath from above. The big dude towered over him.

Standing, Dave shoved his fists on his hips and frowned. He didn't want any trouble but he wouldn't sit around waiting for a beating either.

"You got friends that are cops?" Big dude growled.

"What's it to you?" No sense answering if he could scare the guy off.

Unfortunately the man stepped closer and got his face right up in Dave's. Shit. This didn't bode well. He could defend himself fine but this dude looked like he ate steel for breakfast.

Shifting so his back was to the others, big dude cornered Dave against the bars. "I was hoping your cop friends could help me." His voice was low and soft. "I was in the wrong place at the wrong time and got pulled in here with a few guys who were holding up a convenience store. My girlfriend's probably freaked by now that I haven't come back with her soda."

Was this guy for real? Or playing him? As he looked deeper into the guy's expression, he felt it was genuine.

The outside door opened and Suarez walked in pointing. "Okay, you two, and you, need you for a line up. Witnesses to the car theft are here."

Dave sighed, but it was one way to clear things up fast. He looked nothing like his uncle and cousin, except perhaps the color of their skin.

The big dude near him let out a breath of air in defeat.

"If I can clean up my own shit storm, I'll see what I can do for you."

It took almost a half hour to get things set up and five men to stand for the line-up. One of them was the janitor, as Dave had seen him emptying wastebaskets when he'd first come in. The witnesses were behind a dark window with a faceless cop who every now and then instructed them through a speaker to turn left, right or step forward and back. Seriously, this was taking forever. Lonnie and Calvin weren't that easy to forget. He'd been trying for years.

After another twenty minutes of dancing left and right, Suarez came in.

"What the hell's taking so long?" Dave muttered.

"The witnesses say you all look alike and they can't tell. Even thought it could have been me if I hadn't been wearing the uniform."

Yeah, cause the only thing that mattered was they all had darker skin. Lonnie had to be eight inches shorter than him while Calvin was twice as wide.

"So, what's happening?"

Another officer came in and motioned for Lonnie and Calvin to follow him. Two more walked behind. The other two line-ups left through the other door. Suarez motioned for Dave to exit the room then steered him down the hall to an office.

"You're all clear. You've got someone here to vouch for you."

"Thanks." He put a word in for Suarez to check on the big dude's background then walked through the doorway. A tall blond man waited in the office. "Shaunessy."

Chris Shaunessy, the FBI agent he'd worked with on the Moreno case, strolled across the room and shook his hand. "Just so you know, Dave, you owe me. A big one."

"Yeah, sorry, but things got a little complicated with my badge and wallet being taken. I'll buy you a beer."

"Oh, no, my friend, you owe me way more than that. Meg and I just got engaged a few hours ago. It took me this long to finally pry her away from her three big, overprotective brothers. We were about to leave for my place in Maryland and be alone for the first time in months."

Dave winced. "Yeah, I get that. Sorry. Try a twelve-year-old. I was planning a Christmas engagement as well."

"You and Tina?" Chris grinned. "Meg's catching up with her in the waiting room right now, showing off the hardware."

"I'm hoping I can still get Tina to marry me. With the shit that went down with my family today, I'm surprised she hasn't jumped on a bus back to Miami."

"She loves you, man. I could tell that even when you were still undercover and she thought you were only a bartender."

"I need to get the ring back first. They confiscated it when I got here. I hope to God they haven't closed the inventory locker yet. With my luck, I won't be able to get it back until after the new year."

"I CAN'T BELIEVE CHRIS PUT YOUR ENGAGEMENT RING ON A snowman? How cute is that?" Tina admired the diamond glittering on her friend, Meg's finger. It was great they were both in a much better place right now. Well, maybe not at this exact moment, in a police station, waiting for her guy to be sprung from jail. But much better than waitressing at the nightclub for that slime.

"Yeah, I'm still getting used to the cold after almost two years in Florida. I've totally lost my tan."

Tina chuckled. The usual blond highlights were also missing from the pretty brunette's long hair.

"You're lucky you caught us when you did. We had just gotten in the car and were heading to Chris' place. The engagement ring was the only thing keeping my brothers from pummeling Chris when I said we were staying at his place tonight. They've been a bit overprotective since I've gotten back."

That wasn't surprising. Poor Meg had been basically trapped in Miami working for that slug, while her family had no idea where she was. Being a little overprotective now was expected.

"I'm so happy for you two," Tina said, giving her a hug. "Dave and I are working things out too."

"You'll get there." Meg looked up as the two men strolled down the hall toward them.

"Dave." Tina rushed to him and was enveloped in his arms. "Are you all right?"

Kissing the top of her head, he said, "A little pissed at some of my family members but it's cleared up now. Justice will prevail. Where's Tommy?"

"With your sister." Tina grinned and stroked his arm. "She's taking him overnight to her place since she wasn't sure how long it would take to clean up this mess."

Dave's gaze roamed over her and he pulled her close. "He's gone all night? Maybe we can finally have some alone time."

"I was kind of hoping for some of that myself," Chris said, his arm around Meg's shoulder. Tina had seen the feelings the agent had for Meg, and vice versa, and was thrilled things were working out for them.

"We have an extra hotel room." Dave smirked. "You're welcome to use it."

"I think we'll head to my place. More privacy there." Chris threw Meg a steamy look. "Meg can get loud."

"Oh, you..." Meg slapped at her fiancé, but laughed. "We appreciate the offer but this way Chris can cook something for me."

"This woman never stops eating." Chris kissed her to stop her from objecting. "I'll have to make sure she works off all the food somehow."

"Thanks again for stopping here first to help me out," Dave said thrusting his hand out to shake his friend's. "I'd hate to have spent Christmas night in handcuffs."

"I don't know," Tina said, her eyes twinkling. "Handcuffs could be fun."

"All right, woman. Maybe I can arrange something. Let's get out of here. I need to get my possessions."

Picking up a large envelope from a nearby desk, Tina said, "It's right here. Suarez got it for us when Chris vouched for you and who you were."

She handed it to him, watching his face as he opened it and took out the items.

"Are you fucking kidding me? The damn cops ripped me off."

"What's the matter, Dave?" She sidled closer and ran her fingers down his back. His strong muscled back. She couldn't wait to have some serious time alone with this man.

"I had something important in here and it's gone."

"I have the keys to the SUV. After searching it, they let me take it to follow you here. I also have your wallet and badge. The wallet was under the cushions in the living room."

Dave smiled weakly. "That's great but there was something else." His disappointed expression almost killed her.

"You mean this?" She held up the ring box and opened it.

"You...already looked inside."

Nodding, she got down on one knee and held up the ring box. "David Johnston, will you marry me?"

He laughed and pulled her to standing. "After everything that happened today, meeting my notorious relatives, and having to come bail me out of jail, you'd still want to marry me?"

"I love you, Dave Johnston, for better or worse. Today was one of those worse days. Let's hope they get better from here."

"God, I love you, Tina. Last chance to get out of it. Meg and Chris are here as witnesses to your insanity."

"Crazy in love with you. Yes, I still want to marry you."

Kissing him with everything she had inside her, she stroked his cheek. "But maybe it would be best if we did holiday celebrations from now on down in Miami. That way we can control the guest list."

Touched by Fate by Preslaysa Williams

❦

ANALYN RICHARDS STOOD ON THE STEPS OF CHARLESTON Community Church, shook.

Yeah, she'd planned plenty of weddings for other blissful couples, but plan her own wedding? That put a whole lot of extra into an already extra event.

First, it had to be perfect. No questions.

Second, it had to be perfect. No questions.

And third, it had to be perfect. No questions.

No big deal.

Yes, it was a big deal. A very big deal. After her first failed attempt at a marriage, she didn't want any screw-ups this time around. Second time was the charm, right?

Or was it third time? No third times! Analyn pushed the possibility out of her mind.

She hefted her 220-page wedding plan in the crook of her elbow and pried open the mahogany doors of the church. The sanctuary charged her pulse into a frenzied rat-a-tat-tat. She ignored the sensation and fished her iPhone from her clutch. Miranda, her maid of honor, was late. Surprise, surprise.

Miranda had promised to help her with figuring out the proper layout for the wedding party, but Miranda had her own relation-ship drama to deal with. So much for her promises.

Analyn trudged to the marble altar and candelabra. Three pillared candles emitted a burnt odor and evoked memories of wasted wedding vows from her first, unraveled union.

She swallowed the ashen taste in her mouth, set the thick binder on the oak podium, and rested. Review the logistics and leave. Simple.

Holding her breath, she surveyed the suffocating space, a stark contrast to Charleston's welcoming, cool December weather. Pews flanked the narrow aisle. No more than one hundred guests could squeeze into this house of worship. She'd kept her guest list short for this very reason.

Everybody in her family, except Analyn's parents, had jumped the broom. Until Analyn, everybody in her family had done so on the first day of Kwanzaa, the day of unity, also known as *Umoja*. Grandma Edel said *Umoja* weddings were good juju. Analyn's first marriage had been on Valentine's Day, long after the Kwanzaa festivities. Was that why her first marriage failed?

Whatever. Analyn wasn't into superstition. All she had to do was make everything go according to plan for her wedding on Saturday.

Footfalls echoed from outside the door. Seconds later, a mass of curly brown hair accompanied by an electric smile lit the door-way. Miranda. The woman could've doubled for Beyoncé.

"Morning, blushing bride!"

Miranda's sugary sweet twang brought a curve to Analyn's mouth. "Black girls don't blush."

"They do if they're getting married to Corey Marks. He's fine, rich, and fine. Girl, you got lucky. He's the kind of guy who could—"

"Whoa. Whoa. Whoa, Miranda. That's way inappropriate."

"Inappropriate? Why?"

Analyn's cheeks warmed. She was gonna do it right this time, and for her, that meant being a second-time virgin.

Analyn had one conversation with Miranda about her choice to wait until marriage, and now Miranda wasn't gonna let Analyn live it down. No matter. Analyn was still waiting until her wedding night.

Sure, Analyn and Corey had plenty of make-out sessions, but they never went all the way. Thankfully, Corey was patient with all her hang-ups and misgivings. She wanted to do things the old-fashioned way this time around. It was the only way she could ensure Corey loved her for her, and not for any other reason.

A huge wooden cross loomed over her. Probing. *Corey's The One, right God?*

Her stomach knotted. No answer from the Upper Room. "Let's get started." She flipped to the wedding plan section entitled "Bridal Party". "We should have—"

"Doves!"

"Doves?"

"For your big send-off."

"When did we discuss doves?"

"We didn't, but a hundred doves released from their cages on your wedding day will mark your freedom from the prison of your chastity belt." Miranda laughed. She closed her fan and tossed it in her oversized bag.

"I made my choice for good reasons."

"It's still a dumb reason. You should've made love to Corey by now. What if you find you're not compatible?"

I thought of that, but it doesn't matter to me. I want Corey to love me for me, not for my skills in the bedroom. "Why are we having this discussion?"

"You're such a prude." Miranda rolled her eyes. "The doves weren't my idea, by the way. On my way over here, your grandmother Edel texted me. She said she had misplaced your number. Wanted to let you know she special-ordered not one hundred doves, but five hundred doves from Florida."

Analyn stilled, and salty sweat dotted her upper lip. "You're kidding."

"Nope," Miranda said.

"Every time my clients have doves at their wedding, it turns into a disaster. Once, the doves crapped all over the guests. At a different wedding, a flock circled around the bride and groom. They nearly plucked all the hair out of the bride's head. She was bald and bleeding afterwards."

Miranda's eyes widened. "For real?"

"For real."

"Ah, don't worry about all of that," Miranda said. "I'm sure those were fluke events. It won't happen at your wedding."

The air in the room increased a couple thousand degrees, just enough for Analyn's rib cage to squeeze too tight, her throat to slam-bam shut, and her lungs to recoil and constrict. This was her thirty-sixth panic attack since she'd said yes to Corey's proposal six months before. The closer they got to the wedding date, the more frequent the attacks. They were weekly at first, but now they were every few days. Perhaps it was just nerves, something that would go away after she said "I do."

"You don't look right. Are you okay, Analyn?" Miranda leaned closer than close. Too close.

Analyn forced out a showgirl smile. No way would anyone see her weakness. "I'm fine."

"This Charleston humidity can do a number on a gal. Makes our noses shiny. Want some oil blotting paper?" Miranda lifted her shoulder in a half shrug.

Analyn's chest tightened. She needed to get out of there. Quick. "Be right back." Lungs ready to explode, Analyn ran from the sanctuary, into the foyer, snatched her inhaler, and took two puffs. Her breathing slowed to normal. Much better. Analyn pressed her palm against her forehead. Yep, she was clammy. Blotting paper could get rid of the clamminess.

Her cell phone rang, and she reached for it. *Caller unknown.*

"Hello?"

"Is this Analyn Richards?"

The deep baritone voice gave her pause. For a millisecond, her pulse thrummed. Analyn pushed aside the sensation. "Are you calling about those damn juju doves?"

"Yep. I'm Derrick, the delivery guy. I'll be there on Wednesday. Driving them over from North Carolina."

Who gets doves from North Carolina? Grandma Edel. That's who. "You'll be early for my wedding. How will you keep the doves in the meantime?"

"Don't worry. I'm a professional. I always give myself a few days cushion, especially with these rowdy fellas. All seven-hundred of them are right here in the back of my truck."

"Seven hundred?" Analyn pulled the phone away from her ear, resisting the urge to scream. "Who's gonna clean up after them?"

"I am."

She was silent. "You're joking."

"No, ma'am. It's part of my job as the dove delivery guy."

Analyn scrunched her nose. How'd he gotten that job? "As long as you're willing to clean up the mess. The last thing I need to think about is bird poop."

"I've done this gig for a long time. I keep the doves under control. There's nothing to worry about. I wanted to meet with you and your fiancé before your wedding to discuss the logistics. Would you be available when I get in town?"

Why did his voice sound so yummy?

"Your schedule must be packed," he said.

"My rehearsal dinner is on Friday night."

A pause. "No worries, Ms. Richards. I'll figure it out."

Figure it out? Her wedding wasn't the day to figure it out. "You can stop by at the dinner to discuss."

"Good thinking. Some of these doves are kind of jumpy."

I should just cancel the order. Cancel. Cancel. Cancel.

"Does six o'clock work?"

"Yes. That's perfect." The words spilled from her mouth, but it was too late to mop them up.

Why did I say yes?

"Great," Derrick said. "I'll text you my email, and you can send me the location details. Sound good?"

"Sure."

Why am I agreeing to this stupidity?

After they hung up, Analyn slumped against the paneled wall. "Just go along with it, Analyn," she whispered to herself. Grandma Edel had always mentioned her disappointment in never having seen Analyn's parents married. Maybe this was Grandma's way of living out the dreams she missed with her now-deceased daughter, and again with her granddaughter. Analyn had eloped at a courthouse the first time around.

Analyn waited until she believed her little pep talk but believing didn't happen. OMG. She was not ready.

Not ready for the doves that her grandmother ordered for the wedding. Not ready for the second-time-around, virginal anxieties thrumming in the back of her...or was it at the bottom of her...

Never mind.

Analyn thrummed.

And she definitely was not ready for any of her well-laid plans to go to waste.

Memories of her first marriage fail hovered and taunted. Maybe her first husband wouldn't have divorced her if she hadn't been so nitpicky and anxious. But Analyn couldn't help it. She was a planner by nature. It was part of the package.

Good thing Corey didn't mind her quirks. Whenever she got into Type A mode about something, he stepped aside so she could do her thing. It didn't matter the issue—triple-checking an appointment time or running through the daily schedule. One. More. Time. Corey went with the flow and never hassled her about her worries.

Analyn shoved aside her concerns of a wedding disaster, determined to pull this off. She always completed everything she planned, even when it quietly killed her.

❄

"Ooooh my goooosh!" Miranda's face puffed, and mascara ran down her cheeks. "I'm so sorry, Analyn. So, so sorry. I was going to hold in my emotions, but Rick just called. He dumped me."

Analyn's stomach knotted, and it wasn't because of Miranda's love emergency. The rehearsal dinner was in twenty minutes. The dove delivery guy was due to arrive at any minute, and Corey... where was Corey? Analyn glanced outside the restaurant window, looking for her fiancé.

"Rick said he was feeling too much pressure to get married. I asked that man about marriage one time. Okay, more than one time. I didn't know it would scare him off." Miranda sniffled.

"If it scared him off, then he wasn't the man for you." Analyn sat next to Miranda at the teakwood head table. Corey had booked the entire restaurant for dinner. She wasn't even gonna ask how much it cost.

"You're right. If a conversation scared him off, he wasn't worth it." Miranda wiped a tear from her cheek, and a dribble of snot stretched from her nostril. Gross. That was not very Beyoncé-ish.

"Lemme get you some tissues."

"My life is ruined. You're so lucky to have someone who loves you and wants to make that lifetime commitment." Miranda rested her head on the linen tablecloth.

Had Corey ever actually said he loved her?

Hmm. Not that she remembered. Didn't matter. He loved her, or else he wouldn't have proposed. "I'll be back with those napkins."

She headed to the entrance of the restaurant as a black Mercedes pulled into view. Analyn exhaled. Corey. Analyn stepped through the door to meet him. His side windows were tinted, but she could tell he was on the phone. She stood outside the passenger door and waved.

No response. Must've not seen her. Analyn waved harder.

Corey did a double take, hung up, and rolled down the automatic window. "Hey, babe." His electric smile thrummed through her.

"Hey. Glad to see you. It's just me, you, and Miranda. Still waiting on the others."

"Your grandmothers aren't here to run the show yet?"

Analyn laughed. "No. I'm running the show."

He stepped outside the car and stood tall, like a warm cup of cider on a freezing cold day. When Corey walked into a room, every single body warmed up.

Dark, thick lashes framed eyes the color of the amber earrings he'd given Analyn as an engagement gift. The tailor-made pinstripe suit hung perfectly on his long athletic body. Ebony skin. Chiseled cheekbones. L.L. Cool J lips. But it was the tense set of his jawline —as subtle as a shadow cast in a dimly lit room—that gave her pause.

"You okay?" she asked.

"Sure am." He pulled her close, and Analyn inhaled his scent, a divine mixture of soap and musk.

"How about you?" Corey asked. "How are you feeling?"

"We're getting married, so I'm feeling great," Analyn said. "But you seem nervous. What's up?"

"Nothing." He gently cupped her chin in his hand. "You know I'm committed to you, right?" His tone sounded off.

"Of course." They walked inside the warm foyer of the high-end bistro, and Analyn told him about the doves.

"I knew your grandmother Edel was gonna do something." He chuckled. "Don't worry. It'll all work out."

"Think so?"

"I know so." A worry line crinkled his smooth forehead. "Is something else bothering you?"

He knew her so well. Analyn told him about Miranda's outburst.

"I don't know about Miranda." A shadow crossed his face, and he glanced away. "She seems unstable."

His last word sounded bitter. "I wouldn't peg her that way."

Corey shrugged. "Suit yourself. Just my observation."

The ceiling fan in the restaurant whirred a steady *da-dum, da-dum, da-dum*, but it did little to cool the worry rising from her neck and spreading to her cheeks. Corey's observations meant everything to her. He knew this. Since Corey was always forgiving of Analyn's Type A ways, she lent an ear on the rare occasions when he offered his opinion.

And Analyn wasn't gonna lie to herself. Her first husband had been verbally abusive. His harsh words left invisible bruises that still lingered on her heart. Good thing she was working all that out in therapy, but the after-effects made her sensitive to any critical feedback, especially when it came from Corey.

Just as she was about to inquire further, the faint sound of a motorcycle grew louder and louder. Analyn looked over her shoulder. Her grandmothers Edel and Maria rolled into the parking lot on Harleys. Her scalp turned tingly. "Why are they on motorcycles?"

Corey chuckled and stepped back. "I'll let you handle them."

They stepped outside, and her grandmothers parked right next to Corey's car. Grandma Edel's tire touched the rim of the Mercedes. They pulled off their helmets in sync, as if they were spunky Las Vegas showgirls.

"*Kumusta magandang.*"

"*Mabuti naman ako*," Analyn replied to the greeting in Grandma Maria's native tongue, Tagalog.

"How you doing, girlfriend?" Grandma Edel asked.

"Chillin'."

Analyn had been raised speaking English, Tagalog, and Black folks talk, and being fluent in all three was second nature. Being called girlfriend by her eighty-year-old grandmother wasn't. Grandma Edel had changed after returning from her trip to Nigeria. She was more laid-back and weirder, always talking about this African history stuff. Made Analyn's brain hurt.

"And there's my future son-in-law." Edel tucked her bike helmet under her arm and squeezed Corey's bicep. "Ooh, hey now. You got some firm meat on them bones. If I was sixty years younger, I'd—"

"Grandma!"

"You better keep this man, Analyn. He's foine!" Edel looked him up and down like he was a juicy steak.

"He sure is. Too bad I'm married," Grandma Maria said.

Married to her grandfather! What the hell? "Where's *lolo?* I thought Grandpa would arrive with you two."

"He wanted to finish watching his western on television." Grandma Maria winked at Corey. "*Diyos ko.* I wish I was a young thing too."

Now she was calling on God in Tagalog. Grandma Edel nudged Maria, and they laughed.

"Your man makes me wanna press pause on my menopause and make some Kwanzaa babies." Grandma Edel thrust her hips at Corey, and his eyes rounded.

Analyn's lips twitched as though they were undergoing a miniature cardiac arrest. "Grandma Edel, this is my fiancé. How you gonna do me like that?"

"The last I heard y'all wasn't doing nothing." Grandma Edel rolled her eyes. "You on this second-time virginity nonsense. I might as well get in on the action."

Had she been talking to Miranda? "That's enough."

"Aw, come on, Analyn. You embarrassed by your horny grandmas?"

"Yes." She wound her finger around the thin gold chain resting on her collarbone. Analyn glanced at her necklace, at her fingertip blooming red. One more twist, and the necklace could snap.

Correction: one more embarrassing comment, and Analyn would snap.

"I'll be inside with Miranda. Corey gestured towards the door. "It's getting chilly out here."

"The hell it ain't." Grandma Maria tossed her keys in her purse. "You warm up the coldest of winters, son. Handsome as you are."

Corey gave a half-smile and left—quickly. Analyn faced them.

"Look, you can't be acting like this around Corey. It's bad enough this is my second marriage."

"Hey, don't fault us for your inability to keep a husband. You weren't pulling your weight the first time, and you sure ain't pulling your weight this time." Grandma Edel waved her finger at Analyn. "I ain't just talking 'bout conjugal relations. You always so tense 'bout stuff. Nobody can relax around you because you're afraid to be you. Don't scare this one off, Analyn. You hear me?"

All her memories bubbled to the surface. Memories of heartbreak and rejection and regret. Like the time when Analyn was self-conscious about her curly-frizzy hair as a high school freshman. She bought a relaxer at the local drugstore and ended up going bald. She would've been better off if she had learned to be comfortable with her hair, as is. But embracing her difference was a lifelong struggle.

"Don't go there." Her syllables shivered, and her pinky twitched.

Maria looked at Analyn's trembling finger. Self-conscious, Analyn shoved her hand in her pocket. "If it's causing you that much strain, *apong babae*, granddaughter, you should see a therapist."

"I do see a therapist."

"You need to get a better one." Grandma Edel crossed her arms. "Or some of my African roots and herbs. They can cure all that bad energy you got."

"Bad energy? I don't have no bad energy."

"You sure do." Edel nodded. "I found out this morning through my cowrie shells. The divination don't lie."

Those divination shells were something else she'd brought back from her trip to Nigeria. She carried them around like they were golden nuggets. Analyn rolled her eyes.

"Look, Analyn." Grandma Edel pointed inside the restaurant at Corey and Miranda. She was giggling at something Corey was saying.

"Why is she giggling?" Analyn squinted at them. "She was wailing at me just a few minutes ago. Her boyfriend dumped her."

"See? That's what I mean. The divination don't lie." Edel said to Maria. "A man likes to see a woman laugh. It makes them feel important and young. You need to smile more."

What was this? Some relationship advice from a 1952 issue of Good Housekeeping magazine? "Is that so?" Analyn's lashes fluttered triple time.

"*Oo*," Maria said. "Listen to your *lolas*. We know best."

Analyn's lashes stopped fluttering. Her grandmothers were a trip. "Whatever."

Edel cupped her hands around her face and pressed against the restaurant window. "That don't look right."

And gyrating at my fiancé was a-okay? Whatever.

Miranda and Corey stood next to one another, and she had her hand on Corey's back. Corey didn't push her away or nothing. Analyn's ribcage tightened, and she pressed out a slow, steady breath. *No panic attack today, Analyn. They're just being friendly. That's all.*

"You know what, granddaughter?" Puffs of Edel's breath steamed up the glass pane. "Your little friend Miranda ain't right. She needs a good hexing."

"What?!" Analyn asked.

"She needs a good hexing to keep her away from your man. She is rubbing up on Corey way too much. I need to hex her skinny butt. Stop her from causing trouble."

Analyn wasn't fooling with that magic nonsense. "Y'all two were just out here hitting on Corey. How you gonna complain about Miranda?"

"First of all, we were joking around with Corey. Miranda isn't joking. She's on the hunt," Maria said.

"I don't fool with magic. Mess around with them spirits in the wrong way, and my life could get tore up quick. I've had enough drama to last me a lifetime. And I don't believe in hurting other folks, especially my friend."

"Girl, Miranda is hurting you." Edel pointed to the two. Miranda placed her hand on her ample cleavage and gave Corey a Kool Aid smile. "Your friend got a small butt, but she got big boobies to make up for it. What are you, Analyn? An A-cup?"

Analyn cringed. She was small chested, but that wasn't the point. She'd had extra gel pads sewn into her dress for this reason.

"These modern girls don't understand our old ways, Edel." Maria turned her focus on Analyn. "Your *lola* Edel is only suggesting she use magic to put your situation in a divine, peaceful order. Her spell will make things sound and right and good. It won't hurt anyone."

"Hey, I ain't said I wasn't gonna hurt nobody," Edel said to them. "Miranda could use a good butt kicking from Spirit. I'll be glad to deliver one."

Oh, Lord. Her magical grannies took this way too far. "This is nonsense talk. No. No. No." Analyn tugged on the lapel of her peacoat.

"My *lola* was an *albularyo*, a powerful healer. She did herbal and spiritual remedies all the time in the Philippines. It provided a lot of good for our village." Maria stepped towards Analyn and gently brushed a piece of lint from her shoulder. "I know you are in pain, *apong babae*. You've forgotten that the healing power is in you, too. It can heal your hurt. That's why we help."

Analyn's eyes stung. "I'm not hurting. I just want a perfect wedding day. All this magic talk is not in the plan."

"What about planning the marriage?"

Analyn's mind blanked. "What about the marriage?"

"Never mind." Maria's lipped thinned, and her eyes seemed to probe Analyn's soul. Uncomfortable, Analyn glanced away.

"I think our granddaughter could use a love spell, so Corey will only have eyes for her," Maria said. "You do love spells, Edel?"

"I sure do." She stepped away from the glass. "Corey needs to stay faithful to our baby girl. I can fix a love spell up right quick."

Unease snaked down Analyn's back. *He loves me already. He loves me. He loves me. He loves me.* "Stop all this talk! I don't need your spells and healings. I don't need to force fate. Corey loves me already, or he wouldn't have proposed."

Her grandmothers glanced at Analyn, both looking unconvinced. Deep down inside, Analyn was equally unconvinced.

The sound of boots scuffing against the sidewalk cut into her thoughts. A short, muscular brown-skinned man in a navy uniform headed their way. He smiled.

"I'm Derrick, the dove delivery guy. I'm here to meet a couple for their wedding."

Analyn's blood pressure shot up. She rubbed her temples. This was gonna be an entire mess. "I'm Analyn. We spoke on the phone." The words scraped her throat.

Derrick's empathetic eyes flitted to Analyn, then to Analyn's grandmothers, and back again. "Where's your fiancé?"

At least this guy knew what was up. "He's inside."

"He's also busy," Grandma Edel said.

Busy? Wasn't she just telling Analyn she needed to keep an eye on Corey?

"I placed the order," Grandma Edel said. "And I paid for it. What you need? I thought we already had this squared away."

Oh, brother.

Derrick tipped his hat to Edel. What a gentleman. "I understand. I spoke to Analyn the other day. I wanted to meet with her and her husband-to-be to discuss the logistics."

A pause. A very long pause.

"Eegg-cellent. Simply eegg-cellent." Grandma Edel piled on an extra helping of Lowcountry drawl. This was her professional, job interview voice. She flipped personalities when needed. "We're going for a modern, elegant wedding with touches of West African and Filipino inspiration. The doves are the modern part. What else do you need to know?"

Seven hundred doves were elegant? Seven hundred doves were more like disastrous. "I don't think—"

"We got this, Analyn." Maria waved her off. "You go in there and see to your man and Miranda."

Analyn didn't budge, even though now her brain was split in two—did she attend to Corey or attend to the meddling grandmas? Decisions, decisions. "I'll bring Corey out here. Be right back."

When she returned with Corey, the dove man was gone. "Where'd he go?"

"We sent him away," Maria said. "You don't need to worry about all that. We have it under control."

"Can I go back in now?" Corey gestured to the dining area—and Miranda.

Corey's apparent preoccupation with Miranda knifed into Analyn. The feeling twisted and twisted until she ached from the incision. Both grandmas tilted their heads to the left, in sync and on cue, as if to say "I told you so".

"The guests will be here in half an hour. We'll all go inside," Analyn said. Corey led the way, and they followed. Once inside the dining area, Corey sat next to Miranda, but Analyn didn't say a word. *Way to put your foot down, Analyn.*

No. She was imagining things. He was just being friendly, that's all.

"He's the kind of guy who could . . ." Miranda had said at the church the other day.

A thick, suffocating blanket hovered over Analyn. Corey wouldn't. Miranda couldn't.

Yet the doubt lingered. Why'd Analyn's grandmothers make her doubt?

But still, she cared about what they'd said. Did she need to smile more? Did she need their magic?

Whatever. They were meddling. Last time she considered her grandmothers' machinations, she got burned. Analyn and her first husband were trying for their first child with no success, and the doctor said her husband was sterile. So her grandmothers suggested he take some homemade herbal drink which caused a bacterial infection. He was out of work for weeks in recovery. Her ex-husband couldn't stand them afterwards.

Yep. She didn't need her grandmothers' opinions and advice. The only thing on her mind should be tomorrow's wedding.

Nothing more.

THE DAY OF THE WEDDING, SUNLIGHT WARMED ANALYN'S BACK as she arrived at the church two hours early. Thankfully, her bridal party—her cousins Jamila and Darlene—arrived to help. Then Grandma Edel showed up. Where was Miranda? She'd be late again. Analyn gathered her bridal team for a pep talk.

"I've got assignments for everyone. If we each do our part, we'll pull this off. Here are your instructions." She handed out copies of a detailed spreadsheet. The corners of the pages fluttered as a cool, wintry breeze wafted through the half-opened windows.

The team read through Analyn's complex plan. As they did, the vendors trailed in and gathered by the fountain inside the church. Waiters outfitted in white button-down shirts and pressed black pants stood at attention, ready to serve pre-wedding appetizers to the guests.

The appetizers were Analyn's idea. She'd always wanted to have special touches like that on her wedding day. She felt blessed to be able to do so, even if this was the second time around.

Yet Analyn wasn't here to celebrate. She was here to get married. Her sole mission was to ensure this big day went off without a hitch.

"I don't need no task sheet." Edel crumpled the paper in her hand. "Been on this planet longer than you. I got a strong memory."

"I know, but we can't have any hiccups." Analyn's eyebrows knitted.

"Granny, it's only for today," Jamila said.

"Harrumph." Edel rolled her eyes and patted her twisted locks. "We starting with the lighting of the Kwanzaa candle?"

"Of course," Analyn said. "I'll get dressed in a minute. I wanna see if Miranda is here yet."

She left the sanctuary through the rear exit and trekked across a wide expanse of grass lightly dusted with snow. Miranda was in the distance, talking to Corey. Analyn's steps slowed, not wanting Corey to see her before the wedding. What were they talking about?

Analyn hid behind a crepe myrtle and craned her head to eavesdrop, but she couldn't hear a thing.

Her grandmothers' advice filtered through her conscience. Corey and Miranda weren't an item. Were they?

I promised myself I wasn't gonna worry about this anymore. Yet Corey had said Miranda was unstable. The only thing Miranda could be unstable about was her recent breakup. Was that why she'd clung to Corey last night?

Miranda's laughter carried over the blustery air, and Analyn's chest tightened. Crap.

"No. No. No. I'm imagining things. There's nothing going on," she whispered to herself. Memories of her last conversation with her ex-husband bubbled to the surface.

This marriage isn't working for me anymore, Analyn. I'm sorry, he had said.

She pressed her hand against the trunk of the crepe myrtle tree. "If there's a God in this world, please don't let me go through that heartache again."

Corey walked away with a blissful look on his face. Why? He never looked that way with Analyn. Miranda headed in Analyn's direction. She took a deep breath, smoothed the front of her taupe sheath dress, and met her maid of honor.

Surprise flitted across Miranda's features. "What are you doing here?"

"Looking for you."

"Oh," Miranda said.

"Oh."

A bird cawed in the distance, warning.

"The vendors are here." Analyn tucked her black ringlet behind her ear. "I didn't see your dress in our dressing area. Did you leave it in the car?"

"It should've been there." Miranda shrugged. "I'll find it."

Analyn held up her task sheet. "I emailed this to you last week. Says here all dresses should be in the dressing area the night before the wedding at the latest."

"Oh, well. I forgot that part. Sorry."

"This is not the time for sorry, Miranda." Her voice tightened. "The rest of the wedding party is in the fellowship hall inside the church." Analyn pointed her French-manicured hand to a walking path behind her lined with snow-covered cobblestones. "Follow that walkway. It'll lead you to a yellow door with white trim."

Moments later, Jamila, Darlene, and Edel headed their way. What were they doing out here? They were supposed to be getting dressed.

Edel crossed her arms. "We're waiting to help you get ready, Analyn. What are y'all doing?"

Worrying about seeing Corey and Miranda in a private conversation. "Don't worry about us." Analyn held up the task sheet, agitated. "What does my document say?"

Edel held out her task sheet, still crumpled in hand.

"Grandma!"

Edel huffed and uncrumpled the paper. "It says: 'You're the dress guard. Guard the dresses with your very life.'" She grimaced. "Oh."

Why was everyone oh-ing today? "Okay, gang, let's go." Analyn clapped, and a rush of energy zipped through her. Or maybe it was the December chill.

Everyone returned to the dressing area, except for Grandma Edel. She glanced down at the grass, then at Analyn. "I know I was hard on you last night at the rehearsal dinner, but you're going to do great. I believe in you."

Analyn stepped back and tugged on one of her curls. "I hope so. I worked hard on planning this wedding."

"That's why it'll be great. You worked *very* hard." Edel adjusted her bifocals. "But you never answered your *lola's* question last night. What about your plans for your marriage?"

"The marriage will be great." Analyn's voice squeaked.

Edel stared at her for a long moment, then dug in the pocket of her quilted jacket. "This is for you. I put it together late last night, after the rehearsal dinner. Then I spent some time praying my intentions over it and over your life. Heartfelt prayers." She held out a small flannel pouch. "It's a love mojo bag, specially created to bring you a lifetime of bliss with your one and only. It's not a hex to cause trouble, and it's not a love spell to control anyone. I promise."

Analyn stilled. Grandma was doing her magical juju things again, and Analyn wasn't into it.

"When you emailed me in Nigeria to tell me you were getting married again, I visited a Yoruba priestess. I told her the story of your first marriage, and she gave me the herbs in this bag." Grandma smiled. "Keep it on your person at all times, and you'll attract your heart's desire. You'll also repel the people and situations that don't deserve you."

"I don't know, Grandma." Analyn shrugged. "I ain't into all that stuff."

"It's not 'all that stuff', baby girl. Folks can't prepackage this and buy it in a store. It's your homeland. It's your people. It's you."

She twisted her mouth. Grandma meant well. "I know all about my heritage. That's why I'm getting married today, on the day of *Umoja*."

A complex symphony of emotions played over Grandma's features, but Analyn couldn't capture all of the muted notes.

"You're a grown woman. You can take this mojo bag, or not. If not, I'll keep it for myself. I need a good lover in my life."

Grandma was also a master of guilt-tripping folks. "Fine." Analyn took the mojo bag. "I'll tuck it in my wedding dress. It has pockets."

"Wonderful." Grandma's cell phone buzzed. "Welp, that's Maria. She needs assistance with the dove guy."

Analyn froze. "What's the problem?"

"Ain't no problem, baby. Go on and get ready for your wedding. We got this under control."

"But what about my plan?" Analyn gestured to the uncrumpled piece of paper in Granny's hand.

"You got that mojo, Analyn. Don't need to worry about no plans. Everything will work out in the end." Grandma pressed the Talk button on her cell phone. "Be right there." Grandma Edel mouthed good-bye to Analyn and drifted to the front entrance of the church.

Analyn went to the fellowship hall to get ready, but her mind was on the doves. What happened? Did the birds already doo-doo all over the place?

Or worse, did they get in a bloodied feeding frenzy? Did doves fight? Analyn groaned. Once inside the fellowship hall, she dressed, and her cousins helped her with her hair and makeup. Miranda was nowhere to be found. Forty-five minutes later, Edel returned, her expression grim.

Analyn's stomach twisted. "What's the problem?"

"Look." Grandma Edel gestured to Miranda, who followed slowly behind. Disappointment colored Miranda's golden-brown face.

"What happened?" Analyn asked, uneasy.

Miranda showed her the evidence: her maid-of-honor gown was splotched with huge grass stains and had a rip at the back.

A fist of panic gripped Analyn so tightly she forgot to breathe. The sight cut her into tiny little pieces. "Oh my gosh." She studied the torn seam, hands trembling.

"I'm so sorry. I tried. When I thought of putting this gown on, it didn't feel right. I was angry, sad, confused. Everything. I thought I could ruin this dress, say it was an accident, and then get out of being in your wedding. But that would be deceitful too. I can't be your maid of honor because . . ." Miranda's shoulders slumped. "I love Corey. That's why my boyfriend broke up with me."

Analyn's palms tingled. Her worst fears materialized. "You love him? Corey? What do you mean?"

"I love him in a my-soul-will-be-forever-shattered-if-I-lose-him sort of way."

Analyn thought back to all the instances they'd hung out together. Had Miranda and Corey spent lots of time alone together, or was this a one-sided attraction? "How did this happen?"

"It wasn't anything that I sought out. I promise it wasn't," Miranda said. "Sometimes Corey and I would have these long talks. I'd share my misgivings about my future, and he'd always give me the best advice and encouragement. Over time, I grew to love him."

So they were homey-lover-friends? And when did they have these talks? "Did you two—"

"No," Miranda said. "We haven't had sex or made out or anything physical. I remembered your vow, and I wanted to at least control the physical part. But my feelings for Corey became too overwhelming. It's more of an emotional relationship than anything. Now you're getting married to him, and I'm the maid of honor and—"

"How could you let this happen? You know all I've been through."

Miranda looked away. "Love can't be contained. It's the one thing you can't plan."

Analyn's pulse went into overdrive, and anger burned from head to toe. This was why she'd had this unsettled feeling all this time. Did Corey feel the same about Miranda? Did he love her?

And what the hell did Miranda mean about not being able to plan love? She should've kept her feelings in check, for Analyn's sake. What a backstabbing, conniving man thief. "Get out. Get out!"

Miranda scooted out, and Analyn's eyes watered. Vision blurry,

Analyn pulled on the loose threads of the gown, trying to put the ripped pieces back into place. It was no use. It didn't matter anyway. Miranda wasn't going to wear it—no one was.

"It'll be all right, honey." Edel placed her arm around Analyn. "We'll get this mess with Corey fixed. I won't let that woman ruin your big day."

"How? A spell ain't gonna fix this. We have to get lined up for the processional in forty-five minutes. This can't be fixed in forty-five minutes."

Analyn's chest convulsed in short, belabored breaths. She brushed her hands over the clipboard, scanning her wedding plan spreadsheet, grabbing for some sense of stability. More tears trickled down her face. She studied the dress. Honey-colored threads were woven into the hem. It was beautiful, despite the stains. Too bad she couldn't say the same thing for herself.

"This isn't your fault. Be grateful for the magic," Edel said.

The magic? That mojo bag could have caused this disaster. What kind of mess did Grandma Edel put in it? Analyn felt the tiny lump in the pocket of her wedding dress. This thing was bad luck. Why would Grandma Edel want Analyn's life turned upside down on her wedding day?

Grandma Edel reached over and held Analyn's hand, but she pulled away. "I need to think."

"And you need to talk to Corey. If he was fooling around with that gal, then you best know now, before you get caught up in another failed marriage."

Her words pummeled Analyn's ears. Not the conversation she wanted. "I can also bury myself in a hole and wait this disaster out for twenty years until people forget who I am. Then I can live life working as a waitress in a nameless small town with a population of ninety-eight."

"That ain't happening. You gonna face this one. It's the only way."

Too bad Grandma was right.

✳

ANALYN STOOD BEFORE COREY IN HER WEDDING DRESS. BUT they were in the fellowship hall, not the church. He was handsome as ever in his tailored tuxedo. He offered a lopsided smile, and Analyn's pulse somersaulted. His smile carried the same forty-five degree angle, the same glossy-white shine, that used to make her feel she could conquer anything.

Anything except this moment.

She stood before him in her wedding dress, and they hadn't even exchanged vows yet. Would they get to tie their engagement into a perfect marriage knot?

Seemed like all of her wedding plans were trashed. "Corey, do you love Miranda?"

The fellowship hall emptied out. Only Analyn and Corey stood in the dimly lit room.

Corey exhaled. "This is our wedding day, Analyn."

Analyn remembered how happy he seemed with Miranda in the parking lot one short hour ago. And at this moment, she noted his deflected response, his pseudo-calm tone, the gentle downturn of his lips, the soft tensing of his jaw. He had feelings for Miranda. For certain.

How long had he shoveled away his disappointment with Analyn? Hushed his discontent with their relationship? From her estimation, too long. "Do. You. Love. Miranda?" Her voice turned to steel.

Her fiancé didn't answer. Analyn buried her face in her hands and wiped another tear from her cheek. For some reason, he was comfortable with blazing forward with this marriage, even though she wasn't. "I poured the last ounce of myself into this wedding. I thought this would be a new start. A fresh start, but now it's flushed down the toilet."

"Your plans aren't flushed down the toilet, Analyn. Don't let Miranda's outburst hold us back. I should've never given her any indication I could've been interested, because I'm not." Corey's voice trembled. "I told you Miranda was unstable, and I thought I was being a friend by listening to her. I want you, Analyn. I want to spend the rest of my life with you." Corey stepped closer, and the mojo bag felt heavier, more burdensome.

"I have questions."

"And I have all the answers, Analyn."

She faced him and didn't flinch. "First question is this. Do you love me?"

Corey clamped his lips together.

Great. Analyn took a deep breath and blinked back the urge to cry and scream and cry again.

"You should know the answer to that question," Corey said.

"Why should I know the answer when you never said it, not once? Sure, you said you wanted to marry me. You said you wanted to spend the rest of your life with me. You've never said you love me." She shook her head. "How could I have been so dense? This was right in front of my face all along. I should've known."

"Should've known what? Analyn, I went out of my way to ease all your worries about us, about this second marriage. I listened to your stories. I never failed you. I never cheated."

And you never loved me. "Why can't you say it?"

"I'm not marrying you for love, Analyn," Corey said. "My parents married for love, and when the passion ran out, so did their vows. I'm marrying you for stability. For commitment. And you are the most stable woman I know."

Stable woman? He made her sound like she was a mule. "Maybe I was too quick to believe another marriage, a more perfect marriage would be the answer. When—"

"It's your homeland. It's your people. It's you." Grandma's words nestled into her soul.

"When what?" Corey's voice slid into sadness.

A picture of Analyn's past heartache floated up, up, up. The failure of her last marriage had nothing to do with her quirks getting in the way of a relationship. It had to do with Analyn's refusal to embrace her unique self. Her obsessive list-making, frizzy-haired self. Analyn chose perfection over herself.

She had breezed over the fact that Corey didn't love her because she wanted another marriage, a perfect marriage, but perfect *hurt*. Corey said Miranda was unstable, but he seemed more at home with the emotional maid of honor than with the composed bride. "Um, I have— no. I can't."

"Can't what?"

"I can't get married to you. Not like this."

He barked out a laugh. "You aren't serious. People are sitting in that church, waiting for the two of us to exchange vows. There's a man out there ready to release all these doves into the sky. You will not embarrass me, Analyn. I swear, you won't."

"Embarrass you? You won't even say whether you love me."

His face turned red. When a Black man's face turned red, that meant he was pissed. "I swear to God, Analyn. You will regret leaving me. You'll never live it down. I promise."

Oh, so he was threatening her now? A cold fear swept over her. What happened to the handsome, smooth-talking man who wined and dined her with promises of happily-ever-after?

"I'll tell the guests that the wedding is off since I'm the one who made the decision. You can spare yourself the embarrassment." Analyn left the fellowship hall, and Corey's footsteps did not follow. Yet having him by her side no longer mattered. Releasing this false façade of perfection mattered more. All she had wanted was someone who loved her. Just her. But she'd been looking for the wrong thing, chasing the wrong thing, finding the wrong thing.

She needed to find who she really was and learn to love herself. Analyn grasped the mojo bag. *Can you help me learn?* Analyn took a deep breath. Perhaps she wasn't meant to have a Prince Charming ending.

A bittersweet yearning swelled. Analyn glanced at the clear sunless sky and wondered how she would let go of her desire for perfection. If she focused on the sky, perhaps a solution on how to move on would float into her brain. She looked. And looked. And looked.

No answer.

A headache pulsed at her temples. She'd never get married again, not until she figured herself out. Yet the notion of figuring herself out left her nauseated.

A tap on her shoulder jerked her from her stress-induced haze. Derrick, the dove guy, stood before her. He gestured to a bazillion birds in a huge truck parked near the black lamp post. "Ready to get married today, ma'am?"

She burst into tears.

"Oh, I'm sorry. Did I upset you?"

Analyn shook her head and tried to feign calm, tried to produce a fake smile, then she caught herself. No need to mask her true feelings. "I'm not getting married today." Saying those words was like chewing nails.

Compassion flitted over his features. "Sorry to hear that. Guess it's better to know today than later on down the road when you're in divorce court."

"I've been married before."

"Oh." Derrick surveyed her barely there bouquet, her barely there gown, her barely there self. "If you need anything, I can—"

"I don't need a savior," she said.

The doves cried in the distance. They must've agreed. Analyn brushed her hair from her forehead.

Derrick was gazing at her. Analyn shifted. Then, as if suddenly uncomfortable, Derrick walked the perimeter of the truck. Analyn stewed, thinking of how to break the news to the guests.

"Those doves are antsy," he said. "They've been cooped up in there for a while. Our company can refund the money to your grandmother, but now I'll have to drive them back to North Carolina. Boss will want them returned for another event. That's gonna be some ride, seeing they haven't had a chance to stretch their wings."

"Neither have I," she said without thinking.

Derrick stopped walking. "Hey, I hate to see you like this on what was supposed to be your big day. I have an idea."

"What?"

"These doves need some freedom, and it looks like you need to let some things go too. How about you do the honors?" He motioned to the truck filled with doves. "Release them. Let them fly away."

"Won't your boss get mad?"

Derrick waved her off. "Yeah, but this is more important. What do you say?"

Miranda's ironic words from earlier this week floated into her head. *"A hundred doves released from their cages on your wedding day will mark your freedom from the prison of . . . your chastity belt."*

Analyn needed more than freedom from her self-imposed chastity belt. She needed freedom to be herself. Perhaps doves would help. "Sounds like a plan."

A smile danced across his features, open and light and free. "Come on over here and release the latch."

She gathered her heavy tulle skirt in her hands to lift it a tad. Then she walked over to the rear of the truck "Eew! These things smell disgusting."

"The smell of God's creatures, Analyn. The smell of good living."

She stood on her tippy toes and peered inside the truck. There was loads of poopy crap in there all right.

"Ain't they beautiful?" Derrick crossed his arms. "The loveliest birds in the world."

Analyn studied them. He had a point. They needed to be set free. "Where's the latch?"

He pointed, and she released the birds into the sky. Their wings swished gently in the cool air, flying high. One flew near her head, and she ducked.

Derrick laughed. "They won't bite. They're well trained."

That dove flew gracefully away, and a heaviness lifted from her chest. Her gown danced around her like a tethered kite, flapping at her calves as if straining for something else.

She unhitched her tulle skirt, revealing a white A-line skirt underneath. This was supposed to be her reception garb, but why not celebrate now? Celebrate her first steps to being herself.

Life wasn't all about magazine-ready weddings and well-executed plans. Life also consisted of the mundane and the messes and the mistakes, the heartaches and the headaches. Life was this sentiment now pulsing in her veins, saying that she'd be okay as long as she stayed true to herself.

Derrick hummed a melody, and his voice soothed away Analyn's tensions.

After the last dove flew away, Derrick tipped his baseball cap to her. "How you feeling now, Analyn?"

"Feeling good."

He smiled. "As you should be."

Ringing in the Reefer by Marie Booth

A STEAMY BITES SERIES SHORT STORY

RAFE

"MIXING YOUR FAMILY WITH MY FAMILY IS A REALLY BAD IDEA." A stiff breeze ruffled my hair as I watched the dark road for an approaching car.

"Don't be silly, Rafe." Mai gave my arm an affectionate squeeze. "Your cousins Michaela and Uri have invited us for Christmas Eve dinner every year since we've been together. You always say no, even though I've told you I want to meet them. I was so disappointed when they didn't attend the wedding."

"They don't get out much."

Mai and I turned our heads at the same time. The run-down Victorian owned by the Angelson family was perched on the edge of a cliff, as if a tsunami had washed it up and over the precipice, then spit it out again. We'd parked as close as possible, but the muddy cliffside path leading to the decrepit house seemed a hundred yards long.

"It looks deserted. Are you sure they're in? Maybe we should call," Mai said.

"Michaela and Uri don't have a landline or a cell phone." I rubbed my temples and closed my eyes, allowing the extraordinary energy pulsing in Podunk to wash over me. For the first time in years, my body sang with power, connecting to familiar minds, bringing up familiar feelings. None of them peaceful.

"Is that headache back?" Mai touched my arm. "You look anxious."

Mai was a natural sleuth. "I'm great. And don't worry about a thing. They're in the kitchen cookin' up a storm for my honeybun."

Mai squinted in the direction of the house. "How can you tell?"

"They wouldn't miss meetin' you for anything in the world." But meeting and sharing a meal wasn't all they had in mind. A family crisis had called me here.

"You'd think on such a gray day, they'd have a few lights on."

"They mostly use candles and oil lamps. Back-to-nature types."

Mai buttoned the last two buttons on her coat. A cold wind had picked up but she was being a good sport. "Now that we're here in Podunk, I'll have a chance to see a bit of your hometown. I know practically nothing about your childhood."

"It isn't somethin' most people want to hear about."

Not exactly a lie. The Department of Defense or the FBI might love an earful, not that they'd believe a word.

Mai poked playfully at my belly. "Your childhood secrets are not safe from me."

I jerked her close, snaking my arms around her small, perfect body and leaning down to whisper in her ear. "You're not safe from me either."

She giggled and clutched at my shoulders, nuzzling my neck. "Trying to distract me?"

"Maybe."

"It won't work. I'll discover the truth, no matter how much you torture me."

"Nosybody." I could forgive my sweet, sexy bride anything, but would she forgive *me* when she found out the truth?

"Mmm. I love the salty scent of the ocean." Mai moved closer to the edge but I pulled her back with a violent jerk. Large waves pounded wildly against the side of the cliff, looking to crush anything that might have the bad luck to fall into their destructive path. Humans included. Even large sea creatures had been trapped in the swirling eddies of the quick-changing tides.

"Sorry. The edge crumbles in a storm."

"Oh." She turned in my arms, rising on tiptoe to kiss my cheek. "My hero. You know you can tell me anything. No matter how horrible."

"Mmm hmm." My early life had been far from horrible. That was part of the problem. I loved Michaela and Uri and owed them everything. They'd taught me respect and loyalty, the value of a life with purpose. Michaela and Uri had set me free to make my own choices.

Now something was up and I couldn't turn my back on them, even if it meant losing Mai.

I closed my eyes as I held her close to my body. "I love you, sweetcakes."

"Thank you for agreeing to bring me." Mai kissed my chin and wiggled closer. Even with our coats between us, Mai could get me hard faster than any female on earth. "You're going to show me your room, aren't you?" she asked in a sultry tone.

"If we can get away from the party."

"Have they left your room the same? Like when you were in high school?"

"Um. Probably." I hadn't actually gone to high school. I closed my eyes and sent a message. Uri replied. He'd do his best.

"I want to do dirty things to you in that room."

Visions sprang up of Mai spread-eagled on an old double bed, moaning and sighing. "Done." Somehow, I'd get my smokin' wife into whatever bedroom they fixed up to look like it could have been mine.

"You won't be sorry," she said, slipping her hand inside my coat, snaking it around to squeeze my ass.

"Neither will you."

Despite the cold wind and sprinkling rain, we kissed, our

mouths curling up at the corners as the breeze blew her long dark hair around to tickle our faces.

I'd discovered the love of my life in the men's room during a tribute band concert for Exile. She and a group of women had taken it over in protest, saying the venue didn't have enough stalls. They'd turned it into a gender-neutral facility and forced burly males to wait their turn like women had to. Right then, I knew she was the one.

I'd asked if she'd rather go out for coffee than see the rest of the show.

Two weeks later, we were engaged.

Two months later, we were married.

Two years later, we were standing on a cliff in the small town of Podunk, a divorce probably looming in my future. Or maybe not. As long as Michaela and Uri kept their hippie habits in check, their feet on solid ground, and hadn't invited Lucas, I might have a chance to convince her this was a normal human family.

I fixed my gaze on the SUV hybrid. We could still get away.

"Look. A dolphin! It's on the rocks."

Mai wasn't wearing her distance glasses, thank god. My eyesight was exceptional.

Shit. Shit. Shit.

"Looks like some of that refuse you hear about on the environmental news. Do I hear your parents' car?"

Excited, Mai turned and trotted closer to the road. I closed my eyes and rubbed my temples, hissing out a slow breath. When I opened my eyes, the sea had claimed the human body in the gray coverall. He'd been left there as a warning. Only one creature would blatantly break the rules on such an important night for me, Mai and our families.

Lucas. Lucas had made life difficult for ages, all because of a silly grudge. So my twin, Raphael, had ratted him out. No biggie.

Anger roiled in my gut as lightning flashed in the distance and the sky opened up. Icy rain battered my cheeks and slid inside my collar. Thunder rumbled above. Mai shrieked and ran into my arms, so I ushered her back into the SUV. She laughed as she dabbed her hair and face with the paper towels I kept in the door pocket.

"The clouds weren't all that dark a minute ago."

I scowled. "Podunk's in a moody part of the state. You never know what kind of storm might suddenly blow in." This particular inopportune storm stank of a slimy sea god. Was he working with Lucas again?

"Loosen up. A little rain can't put a damper on our Christmas." Mai leaned closer and kissed my soggy cheek. "As long as I'm with my big cutie, nothing can go wrong."

Wrapping an arm around my sweet love, I groaned on the inside. Mai's *big cutie* was kicking himself for agreeing to this. "Your mom and dad don't know the area. I'm a little worried about them getting here in the storm."

Dr. Tsin Lee McGillicuddy and Dr. Franklin McGillicuddy had traveled the world, staying in luxury hotels or onboard five-star cruise ships. I was fairly certain they'd never shared a Christmas Eve dinner in a run-down house in the middle of a freezing rainstorm with creatures of questionable character.

The wind blew across the water, battering the car with horizontal sheets of rain. Mai shivered, so I unbuttoned my coat, pulled her closer and wrapped it around both of us. I tugged her knit hat over her ears and kissed her cold nose, then started the car and blasted the heater.

"We'll wait another few minutes, then we're jogging to the house. I'll come back for your parents. We don't both have to catch pneumonia."

Headlights blinded us for a moment as a car turned down the narrow road and parked.

"Look! There they are." Mai opened the door and jumped out, falling into a large puddle.

"Mai. Are you okay?"

"I'm fine. I'm fine." She got back to her feet and jumped up and down, waving her arms so her parents would see her.

"You're perfect." She was too busy running toward her parents to hear me. "Just give me a chance to explain."

MAI

I hadn't seen my parents since last summer when Mom had insisted we attend some modern art show in Manhattan put on by an artist she knew. We'd caught a Broadway show together the next day, then that was it. Rafe and I had only been married a year at the time, and we were more interested in the luxury hotel's king sized bed and enormous Jacuzzi bath tub than the Big Apple.

I already had tonight's amorous evening planned out. First backed against the door. Then sitting on his childhood desk. Eventually, we'd get to the bed. I'd brought a few toys to make it interesting. Even though Rafe had amazing stamina, I hadn't gotten pregnant yet. I grinned despite the rain and the worry. My family was together and it was Christmas Eve. What could go wrong?

Mom and I hugged, then I moved on to Dad, but a tremendous gust tore the large umbrella out of his hand and flung it off the cliff. Mom screamed and covered her hair, always her first concern. Rafe and I tugged up our hoods, but the wind kept trying to snatch them off, almost as if the storm wanted the four of us soaked to the skin.

We gave up the fight and moved toward the path to the house. Rafe suggested everyone hold hands to stay safe as we traversed the slippery trail along the cliff. After fifteen horrible freezing minutes of battling gusty winds, horizontal rain and soggy shoes that kept sticking in the mud, we climbed the few steps to the porch. A cheerful looking woman opened the door. A slightly older man stood behind her.

"Hi all! I'm Michaela. Merry Christmas Eve." She didn't look a day over thirty in her peasant style, ankle length dress, a headband decorated with California poppies, and strappy sandals right off the muddy plains of Woodstock. "Come in."

Rafe urged me forward and my parents followed.

"Rafe!"

"Hi, Cousin Michaela."

His cousin delivered a two-cheek kiss and a hug to everyone down the line. "I'm so glad you, Mai and the McGillicuddys made it. The weather's kickin' up. Take off your wet jackets. This is Cousin Uri."

Mom and I exchanged a glance after giving Uri the long once-over. A silver fox to the nth degree. I mean, totally fuck-able. Rafe definitely got his looks from that side of the family. Dark bedroom eyes. Silver-gray hair with a few streaks of dark brown still evident on top. Olive-toned skin. He had the kind of yummy mouth a woman might want to spend a lot of time enjoying.

Uri snatched up the laundry basket sitting near the wall and we handed over the dripping jackets, making another puddle in the foyer while we were at it.

"Shoes on that rack in the corner. I have plenty of slippers. Everything else goes in the second basket," Michaela said.

"Excuse me?" Mom wasn't thrilled with that idea. But then she'd never been one to go with the flow. Oddly, our clothes were completely drenched, despite the protection of our weather proof coats.

I smiled to reassure her. "I'm sure we'll dry, Cousin Michaela. We can stand around the fireplace."

"Just Michaela is fine, dear. If you stay in wet clothes, you'll catch a cold."

Mom shook her head. "Frank and I are doctors and that's just an old wives'..."

Dad sneezed. Rafe sneezed. I felt the urge to cough up phlegm. Michaela handed me a box of tissues. Dad sneezed again. Snot flew. I passed him the box.

Mom looked at us as if we were playing a joke on her, only Dad wasn't looking that great. "Fine. Do you have a room we can use while our clothing dries?"

"Girls, take the downstairs bathroom; boys, in the laundry room. I'll get you some clothes to put on."

Mom and I stripped to our bras and panties and waited in the tiny room. Mom sat on the closed toilet seat and I leaned against the sink. "You okay, Mom? You look kind of shell-shocked."

"We had the flight from hell." She glanced in the mirror. "Oh my god. Is there a brush or something in this closet?"

"Mom, you look fine."

She sagged. "There's something I have to tell you."

"You mean about you and Dad splitting up two months ago?"

"How did you find out?" Mom poked at her hair.

"Do you really think Grandma McGillicuddy wouldn't call me?"

"That bitch."

"She wants you back together. So do I."

"It's just that we're both so busy. We hardly say good morning or good night anymore. It's not a real marriage."

"You could cut back on your hours."

"We have patients who need us."

We were interrupted by a quick rap on the door. "It's me." Michaela opened our door without waiting. "Here you go, dears. Do what you will with them." Rafe's cousin handed me a plastic bag and closed the door again.

I peeked. "Plaid pajamas or an orange parachute."

"What?"

I shook out the overly large ankle length cotton gown. Mom's horrified expression was matched only by my resigned one. "I'll wear the parachute."

"I believe it's one of those caftans popular in the sixties. A muumuu." Mom scowled, then snatched it away. "I can make it work. You look better in plaid." She slipped it over her head and we stared at the result in the mirror.

"I look like a fucking pumpkin."

"But you look great in that bright color."

"I wouldn't be cremated in this outfit." Mom flapped the voluminous skirt. "I'd take off like a helium balloon with the first gust."

"We're in the house, Mom."

I hunted around in one of the vanity drawers, pulling out a container of safety pins. "Eureka!" Using skills I'd learned in fashion school, I shaped the gown from the inside, pinning it tighter on the sides and in the back. The pins were hidden.

Meanwhile, Mom had unfastened a few buttons in the front so she was showing a bit of cleavage. She frowned at the hem of the gown. "I don't suppose you can..." I fished out a roll of duct tape and a pair of scissors, carefully opening one of the side seams to make a slit, then taping it shorter.

"My daughter, the fashion designer."

"I wish I'd stuck with that. The start-up I work for is going under."

"You get job offers all the time."

"Yeah, but it isn't what I wanted to do with my life."

"I know. How's the baby-making going?"

"No luck so far."

"Rafe shooting blanks?"

"Mom!"

"Okay, okay." She turned, surveying her appearance from every angle. "Maybe Michaela has a sash."

"And a flower for your hair." I giggled. "Look at you. You're wearing a muumuu and smiling."

"The plague is going around." She handed me the pajama top. "Now you."

I slipped on the men's cotton pajama top and rolled up the sleeves. It was five sizes too large but well-worn and very comfy. "I love this."

"Where are the pants?"

"She didn't give me the pants." I stood on tiptoe to see the length in the mirror. "The top's plenty long enough." I was five foot two and the hem hit a few inches above the knee. I took a minute to pin my outfit so it fit more snugly, then opened a few buttons.

Like mother like daughter.

"Rafe will like it."

"Rafe and I have plans for later." I glanced at the ceiling. "He's going to show me his room." I winked and Mom laughed.

We walked into the foyer. Mom sighed. "Might as well meet the other guests, even though we look ridiculous."

"Not as ridiculous as we do," Dad said. He and Rafe were waiting for us in the foyer. Both wore long robes right out of the Regency period.

"Those are antique dressing gowns." I was so jealous. I smoothed a hand over the brocade work on the collar. It was in pristine condition. "Exquisite."

"Michaela said she found them in a trunk in the attic," Dad said.

Mom sniffed Dad's robe twice. "Smells like pipe tobacco." She leaned closer. "Mmm. Remember when you used to smoke a pipe? You'd read the evening paper and puff away."

"You used to enjoy it." Dad smiled, but Mom turned aside, adjusting her pumpkin dress. "I like you in that color."

At least he was making an effort. I leaned against Rafe. "Yum. Dark chocolate. My fave. What did they do, spray the fabric?"

"Not exactly." Rafe slid his large hand around my waist, sending wicked ideas to my body. "You look pretty hot yourself, honeybun."

Michaela entered the foyer through a side door. "How is everyone doing? Oh, you look wonderful." Michaela's eyes sparkled with good humor. She was the light to her husband's darker appearance. Golden blonde hair, pale blue eyes, cupid bow lips. They were both tall and beautiful, like Rafe. I was the only shrimpy one in the room.

Michaela turned toward an archway that seemed to lead into a living room. "Cousin Gabe! Get our family some slippers. Their feet are blue. Uri, brew some of your special tea. The poor dears need warming up. Cousin Abby! Throw their wet things in the dryer."

A voluptuous young woman dressed in a toga picked up the

basket of soggy clothing and danced off toward the back of the house.

"Wait!" Dad called out. "My suit's a Brioni."

"I didn't know this was a costume party," Mom said watching the toga-clad woman bounce away.

"Oh, no. Cousin Gabe and Cousin Abby are wearing their bedsheets to protect your human sensibilities. They live in the nudist camp down the road. You passed it on the way here."

"I saw the sign," Dad said. "Bare All at Beaverbrook."

"That's the place." Michaela grinned. "Rafe used to hang out there when he was a teen."

"I bet he did." Abby's curvy figure jiggled around enticingly. I was on the slim side. "But what did you mean by human sensibilities?"

Before I got an answer, we were ushered into the living room. The scent of yummy food drew me toward the kitchen. My stomach growled loudly enough to make curvy Abby laugh. "We didn't have time for lunch," I explained.

"Food's on the way," Uri said.

Rafe scanned the occupants of the room as if he expected someone to pop out from behind the curtains. "Who are you looking for?" I asked.

"No one."

"Let me introduce you around," Michaela offered.

The toga-clad pair poured drinks at a portable bar. "This is Rafe's Cousin Gabe and his partner, Abby. They work in the entertainment industry."

"We make movies," Abby said.

"I don't believe I can place you in any of the films I've seen recently. What was your latest?" Mom asked.

"*Bumkirk*. It won five AVNs."

"Abby was nominated for Best Actress in a Drama." Gabe beamed with pride.

"One of those shoot-em-up kinda movies." Abby winked at my dad, who'd turned a little pale.

Mom sidled closer to Dad. "Have you by any chance seen that movie?"

Dad ignored the question. "Scotch, please. A double."

Gabe poured Dad's scotch, then wine for the rest of us.

Rafe suddenly tensed, as did his cousins, but other than the pounding rain, I hadn't heard anything unusual. "Michaela. You promised."

"He wasn't invited. I swear."

The front door opened and closed and another tall, handsome man entered the room with a beautiful woman on his arm. He gestured toward the couch and she sat.

They were bone dry. Even their shoes.

"Do something or I will." Rafe scowled at Uri.

"What's wrong?" I asked.

The newest guest pushed his way between Mom and me. "You two lovelies are a delicious sight. I'll have a double single malt like the gentleman and malbac for my donor." He nodded toward Dad, Mom, then turned to me, glancing at my glass of cabernet. "You must be Rafe's attempt at normalcy." He pointed toward my glass. "Wouldn't you prefer sex on the beach?"

"Um..." I should have told him to use his line on someone who gave a crap, but his presence, his scent, his strangely green eyes... I was tongue-tied for the first time in years. "I... I like wine."

"The blood of life, they say." He gazed at my neck.

Rafe grabbed my arm and yanked me beside him. "Lucas." He practically growled the word.

Lucas, huh? I leaned closer to catch another delicious whiff and a pleasant shiver tickled my spine.

Lucas gave me the sleazy once over. "Your hubby's such a goodie-goodie. Has been for ages." Lucas scanned Rafe's outfit with eyes the color of AstroTurf. "Still living in the past, *Cuz?*"

"Still living a dead-end life, *Cuz?*"

Rafe kept stepping in front of me but I wanted closer to Lucas. That scent... Jeez.

"You smell sooo good."

Rafe dragged me to the couch, sat me down and handed me my wine. He was angry. I hadn't touched the guy or anything, only... Why had I wanted to?

RAFE

My father-in-law shook hands with Lucas and his pretty donor, Ambrosia. Of course, her name was Ambrosia. Food of the Gods. Lucas always thought of himself as top dog, but Michaela and Uri could wipe him off the face of the planet if they wanted to. So could I, only they'd taught me violence wasn't the answer and family was family and all that other crap, and I'd believed it.

But Lucas had come on to Mai. This dude was going down.

"Your name is really Sin?" Lucas had turned his attentions elsewhere.

"T-s-i-n."

Lucas rolled his gaze over my mother-in-law's body. She took in a breath and trembled. I strode in that direction, intending to punch the asshole, but luckily for him, Uri showed up.

"Appetizers!" He set down a tray of mini quiches. Mini pizzas, crackers with a cheesy looking spread— *please don't let it be cheese whiz,*—tiny hotdogs wrapped in baked dough, and mozzarella sticks. The cousins snatched up plates and started to dig in.

I'd warned Mai that the food wouldn't be fancy, but what had me gasping in horror were the little flags labeling each grouping: *Skip These. Mild. Medium. Strong,* and finally, *Mind Blowing.*

"Pick up the tray," I ordered. "Make something else."

Uri slumped in defeat. "It's Christmas."

"Exactly."

Tsin had already snatched up one of the mozzarella sticks marked *mild.* She lifted it closer for examination but it flopped over limply.

"Is that a sign of things to come?" Lucas directed his question to Frank, but Tsin was too engrossed in the appetizer to notice and Frank was classy enough not to rise to the bait.

"Is the spice in the breading?" Tsin asked.

"Nothing is spicy except the wings." Uri pointed to a second platter.

"What are the flags for?" Tsin sniffed at the stick.

I lowered my body into a chair and covered my head with my hands. "Go ahead and tell them."

"Uri and I cook with weed on special occasions," Michaela bounced up and down with enthusiasm.

Tsin's eyes widened. "Weed? Like—"

"Reefer. Pot. Ganja. Herb." Uri rattled them off.

"Marijuana?" My mother-in-law narrowed her eyes.

"Just the appetizers," Michaela said. I groaned. Michaela smacked me, laughing. "This will be fine."

I stood, hoping to save the evening. "I'm sorry. I asked them not to..."

Tsin sniffed at the breaded stick. "This one is mild?"

Michaela nodded and sat beside her on the couch. "Go for it, dear. Christmas is a magical time. I promise you won't regret it." Tsin stole a meaningful glance at Frank, but he was watching Abby pile the items labeled *Strong* on her plate.

"This shit is great." Abby laughed and jiggled beneath the Egyptian cotton.

Ambrosia had filled a plate with *Strong* hot dogs and *Mind Blowing* mini quiches. Uri had already set aside a heaping plate of equally lethal tidbits.

"Michaela and I share, Uri explained.

"I don't think it's a good idea, Mom." Mai glanced at her dad for support and the look of horror on her face told me everything I needed to know. Frank had swallowed down a *Mind Blowing* mini quiche and was about to have another.

"Nooooo!"

But Mai was too late. He was already chewing. "This is great. Compliments to the chef," Frank said.

Mai stood. "We should leave."

Thunder rattled the windows. The wind howled.

And Tsin was enjoying her limp stick. "This is so good. What's inside the breading?"

"Mozzarella." Abby said, smiling.

"What is that exactly?

"Cheese."

"Cheese? I've never... I didn't know..."

"Mom! You're vegan!"

"But I didn't know..."

"They'll be fine," I said, giving up and pulling Mai closer. "My cousins will make sure they don't overdo it." I glared at Michaela and Uri, who were looking kind of sheepish. "Let's head upstairs and talk this out."

I urged Mai up the stairs, then peeked into several rooms before I found the right one.

"You don't remember where your room is?" Her mouth was pinched with anger, her knuckles white as they rested against her hips.

"It's been a while." I finally found a room with a double bed and an old-fashioned quilt. One lone trophy sat on a shelf. Most likely to Stay Single. Pictures of dogs and cats that looked like they'd been ripped out of magazines were pinned to a cork board. I stood in front of the bookcase. *The Story of A* wasn't exactly high school reading, although I liked the wings on the cover.

Mai glanced around. "This is your room?"

"They must have changed things around."

"I'm glad to hear it, because that quilt is covered with symbols of female sexuality."

"No it isn't."

She pointed to a picture of an orchid. "What does that look like?"

I shrugged. "I was a teenaged boy."

Mai kicked the door closed.

"What happened to your Southern accent?" Her hands were on her hips, her dark eyes narrowed in anger.

"What da ya mean, sugar?"

"You aren't even from Podunk, are you?"

"I am, in a roundabout way. I mean, I spent time in Podunk, but in other places too."

"How old were you when you moved here?"

"I can't say. Other areas draw us, but Podunk is our favorite."

"Draw you? What does that mean?"

"Sit down. Please."

"Fine." She sat on the bed.

Best to ease in smoothly. "The storm outside isn't natural. One of Lucas's seagoing buddies is controlling it."

"Like with magnets?"

Mai did snarky so well. "Ooookay, I don't expect you to believe me. But Lucas is bad news and we're not going to be able to leave this house until things are straightened out. My cousins called me in to help."

"What exactly is real about tonight? Nudists in costumes. Strange storms. Clothes that get soaked underneath waterproof coats. A man who smells so good I want to..." She stared at her lap.

"Everything's real. Just not in the way you're used to seeing things." She shook her head and wrapped her arms around her body. "I should have told you who I was before I married you. Before we ever made love." I lifted her chin. "I love you, Mai. I've loved you from our first coffee date. I don't want to lose you, but this is going to be a shock."

I kissed her hard. She didn't pull away, but she didn't kiss me back either.

I cleared my throat. "I've never shown my true self to a human."

"But you're human too." It was a plea.

"No, sweetcakes. I'm not." I removed my robe. My body wasn't overly muscled but I had nothing to be ashamed of either.

Mai shook her head. "You only had boxers on under that robe?"

"It was hot."

I rubbed my temples and closed my eyes, calling out to the Power of Podunk to change me into my real form. The old house rattled a bit, an okay effect, but I didn't feel like pulling out the really big guns.

Anyone watching would have been disappointed in the transition. No wings. No halo. No groups of incredibly annoying naked cherubs strumming off-key on harps they were forced to play.

The life of a cherub sucked. They were naturally musical, but many would have preferred lessons on the sackbutt or even the lute, but noooo. Had to be the fucking harp.

And manna gave them gas. That's why they looked bloated.

My change began. What was most noticeable was the sheen and the glow. My skin glistened like one of those oiled-up cover models decorating spicy romance novels. An aura thingy kind of framed my body with a constant radiance. I glanced in the mirror. Lookin' good.

"You're sweating."

"It's not sweat."

"Oh." She leaned closer. "You're so shiny. And not just your skin." She touched my bare arm, stroking it slowly, warming my heart. A hopeful sign. "This is so nice. Silky smooth." She glanced at my face, saw my smile, then snatched her hand away.

"You're a demon."

"No! Do I look like a demon?"

"I've only hung out with humans so I don't know."

"I'm an angel."

"Oooo. The Christmas Angel?"

"That was my stuck up twin. I'm a fallen angel."

"Dropped out of angel school?"

"You're not taking this seriously."

Mai filled her lungs then huffed it out. "Okay. You say you're an angel. Could be worse. But where are your wings? I've seen the paintings."

"The artists didn't exactly have angels flying in to sit for portraits."

"You said flying."

"Fallen angels don't need wings to fly."

"You *can* fly."

"I'm not supposed to say." This was not going well.

"Too late. You're probably not supposed to tell people you're an angel either."

"You're my mate. It's allowed."

"I'm not your mate. I'm your wife." She froze in place. "Can we even have a baby? Have you been pretending all this time that it was possible?"

"Yes, we can. It's rare, but it happens." She turned aside, her fists covering her eyes. I pulled her against me, hoping to soothe the only woman I've ever loved. "I adore you, Mai. A mate is a stronger bond than husband and wife. Like a soul mate."

"Right now our bond... needs... needs some crazy glue."

It killed me when she cried. "You don't mean that, love."

"How could you marry me and not tell me?" She pushed away and paced the room.

I had to fix this. "Would you have stayed with a male who told you he wasn't human?"

"I don't know. You didn't give me a chance to decide."

"I was afraid to lose you."

"Why do you think I'll stay now?"

"To be honest, I don't. But I was wrong not to tell you." She deserved to know I heard her pain. "I'm sorry."

Mai turned her back. My eyes burned. I couldn't lose her. Her voice was shaky. "Don't they need you...you know, upstairs? You should take me home and...and head back where you belong."

"We're *fallen* angels, twins of the angels you've heard about. The difference is, we've chosen the pleasures of the Mortal Plane over the perfection of the Upper Reaches."

"Your family are all fallen angels?" I nodded. She scowled. "I guess that explains Lucas."

"He's recently turned vampire. Lucas is always looking for some kind of excitement."

"Are any of you really related?"

"We call ourselves cousins. Makes it easier."

"For us mere humans. You mentioned the pleasures of the Mortal Plane. What..." Mai glanced at my groin. "Um..."

I tried out a smile. "I can adjust my body as necessary."

Mai lost some color, so I sat her down next to me on the bed. "I warned you about Podunk."

"You told me Podunk was a supernatural hotbed with vampires and stuff. But you left out the part about you and your family being members of Hotties Anonymous."

"You think I'm a hottie?"

A pillow smashed into my face.

MAI

I took a few moments to digest the most important item of information. "You can adjust your body like an anatomically-correct Gumby?"

"Only key parts. I can't make my head swell," Rafe said.

"Too late for that. Have you been...*adjusting* key parts all along?"

Rafe's slow grin transformed his face into a work of art and my body into a puddle of paint. God, he was beautiful. "I like it when you scream," he whispered.

He sure knew how to find the bull's-eye with that cock. Still, I wasn't ready to forgive him. "I can see your head swelling."

Rafe laughed. "That's not the only thing swelling. I want you all the time, Mai. I'll never get enough."

"So..."

"If you're going to ask about my tongue, then—"

I walked to the door.

"Wait. We haven't finished talking."

I locked it, turned in place and leaned back. The buttons on my PJ shirt were easy to slip through the well-worn holes. I unbuttoned the next two.

"I'm forgiven?" He was looking way too smug.

"No. You've lied to me since we met."

"So, then, what are you doing?"

"Torturing you."

I squeezed my breast through the so-soft fabric and his gaze followed my every move. "You and your big reveal are not going to ruin my plans for tonight." I pulled the shoulder of the shirt down and stroked my nipple, making it poke out beneath the silk of my bra.

Someone knocked on the door. I moved toward the bed where I wouldn't be seen. Rafe threw on his robe and answered it. Uri held a tray of food and a bottle of wine. "Your honeybun's hungry. No weed in this batch."

"Thanks, Uri."

"Everything okay?"

"It might be if you'd leave us alone."

"Won't see me again unless you come downstairs for dinner in an hour or so."

Rafe closed the door and locked it again, then placed the tray on the dresser. "How hungry are you?" He backed me toward the door.

"It can wait. I'm not done torturing you."

He placed his hands flat against the door on either side of my head and pressed his large body into mine. I was trapped. *Yay.*

"You're mine, Mai."

"Yeah? You're mine too." I grabbed his cock through his boxers and squeezed. "*My* Gumby angel."

He hissed out a breath and covered my lips with two fingers. "No more talking."

I grasped his wrist and sucked a finger into my mouth, pulling hard in a rhythm we'd be working later, his cock growing larger under my other hand.

"You're asking for trouble." The robe flew across the room, landing on the floor near his desk. His boxers followed while I pulled off my PJ top. Rafe kissed a wet, hot trail down my neck, over my chest, pulling my bra down and using his tongue on the tips of my breasts.

I arched against his sweet-smelling skin, his body firm and extraordinarily ready. He pinched my nipple. "Again. Harder. Oh. Yes."

"Tell me your fantasy." His thigh split my legs, his knee shoving into my core.

"The door."

"Already here." He nibbled my ear.

"On the desk." I panted in his chocolatey scent. Oh my god. I wanted to lick him everywhere.

"Desk. Got it."

I moaned when he sucked in my nipple. "Maybe... Maybe th... the closet?"

He stopped. "Anything could be in there."

"Uh, okay. How about the dresser?"

"Great."

He clutched my ass and lifted me. I wrapped my legs around his waist and he snaked his hand between us to slip his wide fingers through the folds of my sex. I gasped, my breath coming faster. "I'm so ready."

But he drew it out to torture me back, using his fingers to urge me closer, then slowing down. When he finally thrust his perfectly-shaped and adjustable cock inside me, I cried out, my strong orgasm rocking both our worlds. My back and ass banged against the door loud enough to wake the dead. Only my parents and Ambrosia were kicking around in the normal way downstairs. The rest of them might have looked alive, but I wasn't too sure.

He slowed and held me closer for a moment, pressing his forehead into mine. "I should have trusted you." His kiss was heartfelt and perfect. "God, I love you, Mai."

My heart warmed. Rafe was mine as much as I was his. Good or bad. "Say that again, caveman."

"I love you." He bit my shoulder and I gasped. So good. "You. Are. Mine."

I bit his chest. "Ditto. Is this room soundproof?" I asked.

"No."

"Oh well." Our rhythm grew wild, and a minute later we were both crying out. The banging slowed.

Someone downstairs clapped.

RAFE

Lucas spent the entire dinner staring at Mai's breasts. Not that they weren't gorgeous breasts, but they were my fucking mate's breasts. When she got up to help in the kitchen, Lucas spoke to me for the first time.

"Heard you and your little sticky bun banging around up there, Rafe."

"Abby and I clapped all three times. Did you hear?" Gabe sat across from me with Abby on his lap. They were drunk or stoned. Or both.

Lucas chuckled. "They heard. Impressive. Bet Mai is sweet and syrupy in all the right places. You think she's got anything left for me?"

"Shut your mouth."

"Or?"

"I'll throw you into the sun." I was ready to do it now, except it was the middle of the night.

"In case you haven't noticed it's always raining here."

"Weather didn't used to be like this," Michaela said, coming in from the kitchen. "Started when you showed up, asshat."

Seated at the head of the table, Uri shook his head. "He's been living with us for five mortal months."

"I enjoy the sea air." Lucas sucked in a deep breath.

I met Uri's gaze. "You should have contacted me sooner."

"The magic is stronger on Christmas Eve, but you'll need some local help." Uri looked worried.

"I've taken care of it," I said.

Uri smiled. "Good boy."

Lucas laughed and sipped his wine. "I'll leave when I'm ready."

I scowled at the world class tool. "You paying off Neptune again? Getting him to whip up a coastal storm?"

"He likes his little games."

"Was that why that body was stuffed onto the rocks?"

"Wasn't that a dolphin?" Mai had been dozing against my shoulder, but our argument had woken her. "Did you say Neptune?"

"Arrangements I make with my associates are none of your damn business." Lucas sneered.

I glanced at Mai, my perfect mate. Twenty minutes ago she was sated and smiling. Now she was anxious. But Lucas and I had a score to settle. "You went vamp. Left your people behind."

"I chose to turn vampire for the perks." He winked at Mai but she flipped him off.

"Perks like not being able to go out in the sunshine," I said.

"Who needs the sun when I've got connections?"

"You and that jerk are going to flood the whole town."

"It needed a good cleaning out." Lucas shrugged.

"The sheriff and the mayor are two of Maurice's donors."

"Yeah, so? They have no power." Except Lucas didn't look quite so confident.

Fallen angels and vampires did not get along, but when necessary would work together. Angels liked to keep to themselves, where vampires enjoyed lording it over everyone. Maurice, Nate and their new partner, Estelle, were three of the more prominent vampires in Podunk and had recently helped wipe out two violent nests who were wreaking havoc with the population. The sheriff and the mayor now worked closely with the powerful trio on vampire-related cases.

"When Maurice finds out what you've done to his town, he will hang you up by your—"

Michaela raised a hand. "Dears, this is not an appropriate dinner conversation."

Stumbling in from the kitchen, Tsin had a bag of chips under her arm and carried a plate with an enormous mound of macaroni and cheese.

"I could eat this cheesy deliciousness every day for the next six months." A splotch of cheese sauce dribbled down her cheek. She may have already eaten six months' worth.

Mai handed her mom a napkin. "Do you even remember being vegan?"

Tsin put the napkin in her lap but didn't wipe up the cheese on her face. "Where did you get that idea?"

"Since forever."

"Well I'm a cheeser now." Tsin flung out her arms and knocked over Frank's glass of scotch.

"Cheese eater," Frank said, righting it and smiling at his wife.

"Whatever."

Lucas laughed at the pair. "I'd like to drain that one. Make her a vamp. Start a nest. Then I could enjoy watching her drain her lover."

Frank lifted his glass and Abby sauntered over with the bottle, refilling it. "I am her husband and you will not touch her. I'm a former middleweight champion."

"No you're not, Dad." Mai rolled her eyes.

"I could've been a contender."

I rose to my feet. "Get out, Lucas."

"Or?"

"I'll find a way to end you."

"I'm Immortal, like you, dumbass."

Mai smacked my ass. "You're immortal? What the fuck. What's next? Don't tell me. You're Hercules in disguise." Mai's voice had risen in pitch, her words flying out of her mouth at turbo speed.

"Uch. Hercules was only a demigod." Gabe waved a hand in front of his face like something smelled bad.

Abby giggled. "He was a pretty boy, but when he started to make demands, I kicked his ass."

Gabe nodded after swallowing a large forkful of string beans with almonds. He pointed toward the ceiling. "Abby's twin is Abaddon, The Destroyer. Ass kicking runs in her family."

Mai whimpered so I rubbed her back. "It's okay. We're leaving as soon as I take care of Lucas."

"It's not okay. Nothing is okay."

Lucas leaned back in his chair and grinned at Mai. "Hard to take it all in, isn't it? Rafe will never grow old, but you will. He'll dump you when your tits start to sag."

I needed to get her alone and explain. "Don't listen to him. I've taken care of everything."

"Are my tits going to sag?"

"Honeybun..."

"Don't fucking 'honeybun' me. He's threatening my parents. And you're not even Southern so you should call me angel ass or something like that."

"Love it!" Michaela dabbed at her eyes.

"Why did you two get thrown out, anyway?" Mai asked.

Michaela clasped hands with Uri. "We fell in love," Uri said, smiling.

"That isn't a bad thing."

"Angels aren't allowed to express love in a physical way." Micaela kissed Uri's cheek.

"Yeah, they couldn't fuck," Lucas said.

"Oh. Yeah, I get it." Mai's cheeks pinked up.

"Right?" Michaela spread her arms.

"Ridiculous rule." Tsin crawled into Frank's lap.

"Mom!"

"It's okay, sweetie. I've got her." Frank grinned like he'd been given his Christmas present early.

"What about you two?" Mai pointed toward Abby and Gabe.

"We're über vain," Abby explained.

"And distracting to our celibate companions." Gabe winked.

Mai turned to Lucas. "You're not hard to figure out."

"Au contraire. I'm very hard right now."

"Uch. You have the worst pickup lines." She turned to me. "And you were the best liar I suppose?"

I winced. "I'm a healer. That's why we got the invitation to come. Lucas is a virus that needs wiping out."

"This was the best invitation ever." Tsin licked her fingers.

"Where's your fork, Mother?"

Tsin lifted the table cloth and everyone snatched up their glasses. No reason to waste mediocre wine. "I think I dropped it somewhere." She shoved the bag of chips toward Mai. "Have you ever eaten these? They're so fucking good."

"Those are nacho cheese chips. Everyone eats them."

"Before tonight, I was a cheesy chip version."

"Virgin," Frank corrected.

Mai glared at Uri. "What have you done to my mother?"

"Your parents will be fine in a few hours," Michaela said.

Mai rose wearing a determined expression. "No matter how bad the weather is, we have to leave."

A clap of thunder rattled the dishes on the shelves. Tree branches pounded against the house. Bullets of rain battered the outside walls.

"It's not safe, honey...um, angelface. Your parents can't drive in this condition."

Mai stormed to the door and ripped it open. Wind blew her backwards and onto her ass. The door slammed shut. I jumped up to help. Tsin crawled under the table in search of her fork. Frank landed face down in his plate and started snoring.

Abby cheered, "Party!"

"Don't worry. We'll wake him up," Michaela said.

"He didn't used to be a pooper party."

"Party pooper," Frank mumbled in the pasta.

Tsin stood and gently lifted her husband's head, wiping his face and scooting the plate out of the way so he wouldn't drown in the cheesy gravy. She kissed the top of his head, then licked a splash of sauce from his cheek. "Still love you."

"Uri's going to play." Michaela pointed toward the living room.

"Not the harp," Tsin pleaded.

Everyone shuddered. "No, dear. The piano."

"Oooh, I looove to sing."

"Mother. You don't sing," Mai called from the foyer.

"I sing when no one is home."

Lucas leaned forward. "Let's hear it, babe."

"I'm Frank's babe!" Tsin lifted her plate of macaroni and cheese, squinted and threw. Her aim was dead on. Not one to be outdone, Lucas picked up Gabe's plate and threw it at Tsin, only she'd ducked down to search for her fork again and the plate hit Frank.

"Best Christmas Eve ever!" Abby snatched up the string beans and turned them into little green missiles while Gabe pelted Lucas with ice cubes from the portable bar.

Mai sank onto the bottom step. "We're stuck with these crazy angels forever, aren't we?"

"It's not even midnight yet. I promise we'll get this straightened out."

Glasses and plates shattered. Shrieks of outrage were joined by howls of laughter. I rose to my feet and faced my family. "Okay, stop! Now!" As one, the food fighters turned to face me. As expected, they reacted badly. "Duck!" I jumped on Mai, covering her with my body as every available platter of food landed on my head, my back, my ass and my legs.

Mai was laughing beneath me.

"Damn it." Macaroni plopped to the ground as I straightened. "I liked this robe."

"I'm not cleaning this shit up," Michaela announced. Abby and Gabe giggled.

"Success!" Tsin stood with fork in hand. "Where did the food go?"

"I'll clean it." I closed my eyes, rubbed my temples and pulled in the Power of Podunk once more. When I opened my eyes again, everything was as clean as... Well, it was better.

"I thought you said you were a healer." Mai said, still laughing.

"Healer is a general term."

"How is healing like cleaning?"

"I healed the house, okay?" Uri nodded at me in thanks, then sat down to play. "Let's dance." I pulled Mai to her feet and urged her forward.

"Dance?" Mai swayed, the spell of the music drawing her to the space in the living room Michaela had cleared.

Mai usually wore heels when we danced, since I was so much taller. I lifted her up a little, resting her slippered feet on mine. We danced to Uri's music in the way of all angels, above the floor and floating on air. Uri played the song we'd fallen in love to, sitting in a coffee shop while the Exile wannabees played on and other women ensured the men's room stayed open to all.

"You dance, hot stuff?" Lucas asked Tsin.

"I looove to dance."

"Good."

Lucas didn't pick her up, but there was very little of her body that wasn't touching his while they were moving across the floor. He stared down her dress and quietly unbuttoned her third button. His fangs were showing. Tsin was completely oblivious, lost in the spell of the music and the handsome male.

Frank stormed over, tore Tsin out of Lucas's arms and signaled to Uri. How Uri knew to play a tango was beyond my understanding, but then Uri had a way of keying into people's needs, especially when it came to music.

Lucas made a move to interrupt the proceedings but the other three angels stood in his way. He might be powerful, but Christmas Eve magic wasn't something even a vampire would mess with.

Tsin and Frank's tango was exquisite and when it was over, everyone cheered. Tsin and Frank bowed like professionals, then stole away somewhere private. Maybe this would be the beginning of a reconciliation.

I was about to take Mai upstairs for a different sort of tango when I heard our visitor arrive.

MAI

Bam. Bam. Bam. Bam. Bam.

"What's that noise?" We'd moved our dancing to the foyer so my parents could do their Tango without bumping into us. Rafe had tried to take us higher, but he hit his head on one of the beams. Instead we'd drifted to the only other open space.

"Maurice."

The banging was drowning out the beautiful music. I continued to nuzzle Rafe's neck, rubbing my achy body against his firm one. He held me so tightly I could barely breathe, but that was fine. Who needed breath?

"Isn't anyone going to let him in? This is irritating," I said

"He can let himself in."

"He made it through the storm?" I nibbled Rafe's earlobe, not really caring about the guy at the door.

Unless it was pizza. Pizza would be great.

"Maurice is a master vampire. He can survive just about anything as long as he's not exposed to the sun."

"He's the vampire they always ask to come." Uri said over the soft jazzy music he'd switched to. "Clean-up detail."

Hope he wasn't as sleazy as Lucas.

Bam. Bam. Bam. Bam. Bam.

"I'll go." Rafe lowered us to the floor. "You sit on the steps." Rafe pointed halfway up. "It's dry there."

Rafe opened the door and a gorgeous blonde guy blew into the room and into Rafe's widespread arms. The door slammed shut behind him as the duo slid across the now soaked floor, both of them still managing to remain standing. They came to a stop in a romantic embrace, the sultry music rising to a crescendo. After a tension filled moment, the two males separated, took proper manly stances and stared at each other. Neither moved as they spoke.

"Maurice."

"Raphael."

"It's just Rafe. Raphael is my twin."

"Your parents weren't exactly original."

"The parent thing is still a mystery, so let's not go there."

They were about the same height, but that was the only similarity. Maurice had fine features and was dressed like a Dom right out of a BDSM club, even carrying a whip coiled across one of his shoulders. His expression was so fierce I thought about scooting all the way upstairs, but my strong, determined angel was every bit Maurice's match.

Uri stopped playing and Gabe, Abby and Michaela moved forward, glowing slightly. Maurice ignored them.

"*Où est-il?*" Maurice asked.

"He's hiding. You're the only vampire I know who freaks him out."

"Lucas!" Maurice had sharpened, not raised his voice, but Lucas showed up a minute later.

"What do *you* want?"

"You will follow me." Maurice spoke in an old-fashioned way with a beautiful accent. Bet he smelled good too.

"You're not my master. I have no master."

"Your maker has sold your skinny ass to me." He held up a document that looked like a printed out PDF.

"My maker doesn't own me."

"Did you not read the manual before agreeing to share blood on the solstice?"

Lucas laughed. "There's no manual."

"It is available online." Maurice shrugged with one shoulder, waving his hand in dismissal.

"But why? I haven't bugged him or the other vamps in the nest."

"You are killing donors, our precious source of blood. We bargain for blood, and the arrangement is more than satisfying for both parties. But because you have murdered their regular donors, some vampires have been placed on waiting lists and must glamour occasional tourists."

Every angel shuddered.

"Tourists come to Podunk?" I asked Rafe.

"It's the restaurant. Three months to get a reservation."

"His restaurant?" I tilted my head in Maurice's direction.

Rafe nodded.

"Is this your mate?" Maurice asked, suddenly smiling.

"Maurice, I'd like to introduce Mai. Mai, this is Maurice."

He took my hand and kissed my knuckles, meeting my gaze with his clear blue eyes. "You are lovely."

"Thank you."

"She's mine." Rafe said, taking my hand and pulling me closer.

"Nate and I are pleased to have recently welcomed a female into our family who surpasses all others, however, one is quite enough for me. I prefer dealing with males."

Lucas had sneaked closer to the kitchen and the back door, but with a flick of his wrist, Maurice encircled Lucas's neck with the whip, then dragged him across the floor, head first. When Lucas tried to squirm away, the coil tightened.

Rafe grinned and threw up a bubble around the captive, so when Lucas tried to attack Maurice with his magic, it ricocheted inside the shield and didn't hurt anyone else in the room.

Maurice nodded to my handsome angel. "*Merci*. This prick and his storm forced me to close my restaurant. It will take more than a week to do the necessary repairs. How will I occupy my time?" He grinned at Lucas's crumpled form before turning back to Rafe. "If your family is still in town, please come by on the night we reopen. I will hold a large table in the back for you."

Michaela walked forward. "Would you like to stay for a glass of wine. Or brandy?"

"*Merci*, madame, but I have work to do."

"I understand. Thank you, Maurice."

"Rafe made the call. You should thank him as well."

"'Scuse me." It was Ambrosia, Lucas's donor.

"Yes?"

"I'm...I'm with him." She pointed at the sorry-assed vampire.

"No longer, mademoiselle. You are now with me." Maurice helped her on with her coat and they turned to leave. "Type A positive?"

"How did you know?"

"Many years of experience."

Our group followed them to the door, and the minute Maurice dragged Lucas across the threshold, the sky cleared and thousands of stars became visible. A crescent moon shone in the glistening sky, the entire firmament reflected in the now-calm ocean.

"I have one more jerk to deal with." Rafe walked to the edge of the cliff. "Come forth, you slimy asshole."

An enormous merman rose from the waves. He tossed his golden blonde and silver hair so it would catch the light of the night sky. No trident or beard. No overly muscled body. His nose was pierced. My fantasies were being crushed left and right.

"No reason to be rude." His voice was high pitched. "I would have bargained with you instead. I can't stand that arrogant ass."

"You trapped us in the house with a dangerous maniac. My mate and her parents were vulnerable."

"C'mon. It was only gonna last a mortal year. He gets bored pretty fast."

"A year?" Rafe clenched his hands and took a step forward.

"Don't even. I saw you sneaking out to contact Maurice. You could have gotten everyone out of that house."

"You left me with the dangerous maniac?" I whacked his shoulder.

"You were sleeping."

"Ooo. Spicy."

Rafe's voice boomed out and the earth trembled. *Cool.* "You will swear on the waves that rise and fall, on the hidden mountains that erupt into islands, on the deepest trenches that swallow life. You will swear on the life of every sea creature in your kingdom that you will not have dealings with Lucas again."

Neptune stared at the sky and stroked his chin.

Rafe huffed in exasperation. "Maybe I'll heal the sea by swallowing it down then spitting it out again. You'd have to start from scratch. It would give me indigestion for sure. I've never even liked seafood, but I'll do it if you try to fuck me over again."

"Can I pick the creatures I like best, 'cause jellyfish are a real pain."

"I'll give you extra."

"But..."

"I have etched out a life I love with a mate I adore. No one is allowed to fuck with us or any member of our families, including those misanthropes on the porch. You will stick to your sea shenanigans and stay the hell away from us."

"Fine." Whiny Neptune tossed his head and disappeared under the waves.

"We're free to leave now." The angel who'd changed my life stroked my hair and kissed my cheek. Rafe wasn't glowing anymore, but I liked him better in this form.

I slid my arms around Rafe's waist and snuggled my head into his shoulder. I also had a life I loved with a mate I adored. Scanning the perfect night sky, I sighed. One star seemed a tiny bit shinier than usual, but then that might have been my imagination.

"It's Christmas. Let's spend tonight with your family. We can leave in the morning when Mom and Dad are feeling better."

"I was hoping you'd say that." His kiss was sweet and yummy.

Everyone danced while Uri played his smoky music, the other two males taking turns partnering Michaela. She served dessert— apple pie from the supermarket that we heated in the oven and whatever vanilla ice cream had been on sale—and it was the best dessert I could ever remember eating.

At two in the morning, we wished each other a Merry Christmas with hopes for a good night's sleep. Rafe and I made love again, this time on his bed, a slow and gentle burn to shattering releases that made me weep with happiness. I was in the arms of the guy I loved—angel or human, who cared? Nothing could ever take away the happiness I'd found on this perfect night.

Thankfully, nobody clapped.

The next morning, we discovered Mom and Dad curled up together on the couch, looking happier than I'd seen them in years. I was shocked to find a tree in the middle of the large foyer, decorated with colorful ornaments, tinsel and lights. The two beautiful plastic angels holding hands at the top of tree, resembled Michaela and Uri exactly.

We weren't going to stay for dinner as we had flights to catch. Mom and Dad to Boston and Rafe and I to Philly. But our family brunch together was perfect, our conversation filled with laughter and friendship.

Mom was happy to see the eggs had been scrambled with cheese.

Michaela hugged me extra hard before we left, then took me aside. "I'll expect a thank you letter in a few months."

"Why a few months?"

She patted my belly. "Congratulations."

"You're sure?"

"Angels know these things. Even fallen angels." I threw my arms around her, tears streaming down my face. "Don't tell anyone but Rafe. And see a doctor as soon as you can."

"Yes. I will. Do you know..."

"With all the fancy equipment in doctors' offices, you'll find out soon enough."

"But will I live a human life while Rafe and my child go on?"

"Ask him."

As Rafe and I walked hand in hand to the SUV, I did.

"I gave you my magic and my heart with our first kiss. Our lives will be long and perfect."

Mom joined us. "Rafe."

"Yes, Mom?"

She liked it when he called her Mom. "Do you think your angel family will invite us back next year?"

"I can guarantee it."

"Good." Dad slipped his arm around Mom's shoulder. "But I'm bringing an extra set of clothes. I was sweating in that robe."

We were wearing the clothes we'd come in. They were wrinkled and shrunken, but serviceable until we got to the hotel and could change.

Dad stopped when we reached the car. "We don't really have to go back just yet, do we? How about a trip to Hawaii? I can use my points."

Rafe picked me up and spun me around. "I'm in."

"Me too." I giggled.

"I might get myself one of those muumuus," Mom said.

I looked back at the house, but it had disappeared. "What happened?"

"It'll be there when we need it. You're all family now."

"Family." I placed one hand on my belly and the other in Rafe's. "There's nothing like it."

The Thanksgiving Parade from Hell by R.L. Merrill

10:45 A.M., THANKSGIVING DAY
The Palo Alto home of Dalton Bishop and Orrie Jones

"BABY, WE SHOULD STAY AT THE RITZ NEXT YEAR AND WATCH the parade from the balcony of a suite." Dalton moaned as he ran his fingers through Orrie's silky black hair. The enormous flat screen Dalton had insisted on having in their bedroom showed the holiday festivities live from New York City, but the real celebration was taking place a little...lower...

"*God.*" Dalton gasped. "I love it when you lick me right...there."

"I must not be doing a thorough enough job if you can concentrate on the damn parade," Orrie complained. He'd awakened Dalton with the remote and the best hands-and-mouth-on wake-up call Dalton had ever had.

"I'm not, I swear. I just—*ohhhhhhh.*"

"That's better," Orrie said with a smile. He licked his lips and changed positions so Dalton could see exactly where his tongue was headed.

Dalton recalled some giant balloons floating by on the screen and the shouts from cheerleaders, but who the hell cared when you were getting serviced by a god? That's what Orrie was. A deity who frequently brought Dalton to his knees. He had a voice that made his fans swoon, talented hands that played *all* instruments with precision and style, and eyes that mesmerized, as if Orrie was some sort of hypnotist. Not that Dalton minded one bit.

Orrie's head reappeared and Dalton smiled at the relaxed expression on his face. His boyfriend's chin-length hair was always slicked back and neatly styled, only falling into his eyes when he was lost in one of his passions—music or Dalton. Dalton made it his mission to put a look of sublime ecstasy and bliss on Orrie's face. In fact...

"Come on, baby. You know I won't last if you keep that up."

"You can't last too long this morning anyway. *We have places to be*," Orrie sneered like a teenage girl revving up for a rant.

"We have time." Dalton held his arms out and wiggled his fingers, coaxing Orrie to snuggle with him. There would be time to finish what Orrie so expertly started, but first he knew Orrie needed something else this morning.

"I know you hate this day," he began, pressing a kiss to Orrie's temple. "But our schedule should provide for just enough time at each place that we'll be off the hook for visits for a while—"

"Yeah, until Christmas." Orrie sulked, but he surrendered into Dalton's full-bodied embrace. It wasn't often that he allowed his vulnerability to show, other than when not on stage.

Dalton let out a sigh of his own, cherishing the intimacy he'd missed while Orrie was on tour. "I'm sorry this isn't your favorite time of year."

"The Thanksgiving parade is the one thing I like about this day. Once it's over, the holidays begin for real and life becomes a nightmare." Orrie fingered the collar of Dalton's t-shirt. "Why are you still wearing a shirt?"

"Because I was cold." Dalton jerked slightly as Orrie ran his fingers over his chest. "I think you and I should host Christmas this year," Dalton said, changing the subject. "It would cut down on all the traveling, that's for sure."

"God, are you high?" Orrie sat up and stared at Dalton like he'd lost his last brain cell. "You'd actually try to bring all of those people together under one roof?"

"Absolutely," Dalton shot back with a confident grin. "We could charge admission. It could be the next big thing in entertainment. The Live Bishop-Jones Holiday Gathering, where the alcohol flows and pretentiousness reigns. It would be better than reality TV! We'd make millions."

Orrie rolled his eyes and flopped back down next to Dalton, a reluctant chuckle escaping his lips. "You already have millions."

"So? We can give it all to charity. Use the money to build low-income housing smack-dab in the middle of Palo Alto. Piss off all the old-money folks." He slid down to drop kisses on Orrie's tattooed torso, along his ribs, down the line of his pelvic bone to that spot at the crease of his thighs that made him jump and squeal.

"You are such an instigator." Orrie tried to scoot away, but Dalton had a good grip on his hips now. He nuzzled the satiny hair on Orrie's stomach and blew into his belly button, which made Orrie squirm even more.

It wasn't until Dalton swallowed him down that Orrie stopped fighting.

It was a long time before either of them spoke coherently again, not until they were both panting and covered in sweat. They reclined against the padded headboard of their king-size bed and tried to recover while watching a bit of the Macy's Thanksgiving Day Parade. At this moment, a group of strange clown-like dancers in afro wigs danced their way up 34th Avenue waving some kind of sparkly tree branches to the tune of a gospel singer.

"It's like Pride and Christmas had a baby," Dalton said, his brow furrowed in confusion.

"It's like my worst high school nightmare mixed with a little nostalgia. You don't know what it's like marching with the band in a parade. Pure torture, and yet the trips were a blast."

"Aw, you were one of those adorable band geeks, weren't you? I bet you were hot even then."

Orrie rolled his eyes. "I was a string bean with greasy hair. You never would have noticed me. You would have been too busy in student council or, like, debate club."

Dalton snorted. "Please. Student council was for the brainiacs who faded out once they got to college and realized they weren't head of the class anymore. It was all about marketing for me. That and whatever tech classes I could fit in my schedule. I wanted to learn it all yesterday."

Orrie placed a finger under Dalton's chin and turned him to face him. "And look where that got you."

Dalton knew he meant on top of Silicon Valley's most successful tech empire, but that's not what made him feel like king of the world.

"Yeah. It got me you." He leaned forward and kissed Orrie before he could pull away. Orrie eventually gave in and let Dalton kiss him with lots of tongue and teeth, and Dalton was grateful. "*You're* the best thing to ever happen to me." *And I intend to prove it to you tonight.*

Orrie frowned and turned to sit on the side of the bed.

Dalton loved and hated the sight of Orrie's back. He never really saw it with the exception of times like these, when Orrie went to that place Dalton couldn't reach.

"Yeah, well." He rested his elbows on his knees and ran his hands through his hair, and then he stared at them. He picked at a piece of skin that must have broken loose from the calluses he'd built up playing guitar.

He'd only come home yesterday and would be heading back out tomorrow to play shows until just before Christmas, and then Dalton got Orrie all to himself for two whole weeks. Orrie would be off tour, Dalton was closing the company offices for his employees to enjoy a nice long break with their families, and the two of them could use that time to start making arrangements.

If all went as he'd planned. It *had* to.

"I'm going to shower," Orrie said, standing from the bed. He walked over to his dresser and took out the diamond studs Dalton bought him last Christmas. The moment he'd opened Dalton's gift was the only time Orrie had smiled that day.

Orrie walked into the bathroom and shut the door. The lack of invitation to join him in the shower told Dalton that he needed some time to collect himself. He'd mostly learned to not take it personally.

The holidays were difficult for Orrie. Some of his family's most heartbreaking moments had occurred either on Thanksgiving or Christmas, like the physical fight that ended his parents' marriage and his stepmother's drunken outbursts which eventually turned into sobriety inspired meltdowns. There was also the fact that being around his father's family provided ample opportunity for them to criticize his every move. Dalton wanted this holiday to be a good memory for Orrie for once and hoped that everyone would just behave.

Both Orrie and Dalton were children of divorced parents. Around the holiday that meant making the rounds to various family members' homes. Dalton looked at it like a carefully orchestrated military campaign. Hit the targets with maximum impact, get out without any casualties. Dalton Bishop may not be a military strategist, but he *was* the CEO of Bishop Tech, and his company was currently sitting atop the NASDAQ. The value of its shares more than doubled this past year and continued to climb, and Dalton had even bigger plans for 2019, only some of which were business-related.

His greatest conquest would be winning the hand of the man he'd come to love ferociously over the past year.

When he'd planned last year's company-wide End of Summer Bash, he never thought hiring alt-rock sensation Orrie Jones would change his life. He'd heard the guy's music after receiving his album in his vinyl subscription pack from Jack White's record label and knew he'd be great for the party. A local band opened for him, and when he took the stage, Dalton had been gobsmacked, dumbstruck, and instantly infatuated. Orrie's hands made his guitar weep soulfully one moment and then growl predatorily the next, and his voice blasted Dalton's skin like the heat from a bonfire.

The moment he'd hit the last note, Dalton raced to shake his hand, bring him a drink, and invite him to a more private party. Orrie had rocked his world that night—and every night since, whether in person or on FaceTime when he was on tour or Dalton was traveling for business.

Orrie'd given him such happiness. Dalton intended to return it for the rest of their lives.

ORRIE WANTED TO KICK AND SCREAM, BUT THAT WAS A TERRIBLE idea in the shower. He was exhausted from being on the road for the past six weeks, and all he wanted to do was wrap himself around Dalton and hide out here in the house Dalton had moved him into six months ago.

Orrie snorted. Dalton always got what he wanted, and thankfully, he wanted Orrie. For some damn reason. Orrie still couldn't understand why Dalton had chosen him. He could have anyone. He was smart, funny, rich...beautiful. He had a heart of gold and a drive to achieve that Orrie could only hope to apply to his own career. Dalton had fought hard to build his startup into a tech empire, and at the tender age of thirty was a much sought-after genius.

Orrie, on the other hand, had been toiling in obscurity for years until a pass through Nashville caught the attention of his idol, Jack White. When his manager told him the music mogul had seen his show at a small club and wanted him to pay a visit to Third Man Records the next day, he never dreamed two years later, he'd have a hit record and be playing *The Tonight Show*, the Billboard Music Awards, and corporate gigs like the one he'd played at Bishop Tech.

Dalton Bishop... He was everything to Orrie; a best friend and lover, a muse, a cheerleader, and an anchor. Because sometimes Orrie thought in all this madness he just might drift away.

He let the shower wash over him and tried to let his foul mood swirl down the drain. Unfortunately, some of his confidence went right along with it. He knew this day was going to suck. Not only did he have his father and grandparents to deal with, but Dalton's brothers? Disaster. And Dalton's mom? He liked her, he really did, but she was yet another person who frequently made Orrie feel like he wasn't good enough for Dalton. Thankfully they'd be ending this horrific day at his sister's with *his* mom.

Orrie truly had the best mom in the world. She'd fought through a difficult life to provide everything for Orrie and his sister, Olive. Orrie was now in a position to take care of his entire family. They'd supported his dreams of a career in music, and the best thing about him succeeding was that he made them proud. He hadn't seen them since she and Olive had come to his show in San Francisco at the start of the tour. She'd cried. Orrie shook his head at the memory; his cute little mom, Ava Donaldson, rocking out at his show.

"That's my boy!" she'd told everyone she'd met that night with pride in her voice. No matter what he did or didn't do, she never lost faith in him. Even when he'd dropped out of college; even when he'd lost his apartment because his boyfriend at the time had been taking his money rather than paying the rent; and even when his first manager pocketed his funds from his first tour and he'd had to call his mom to ask for a flight home from New York.

These past two years had been beyond his wildest dreams, and his mom was there to tell him that every hard knock had been part of his journey. And that she was proud.

His father, on the other hand...

Better not to think about him this morning. Otherwise he'd

never have the courage to leave the house. He'd played crowds in the tens of thousands, performed for millions on TV, but Percy Jones made him feel about as talented as a rock.

He stepped out of the bathroom and saw Dalton on his phone, a smile on his face.

"Someone looks like they're up to something."

Dalton dropped his phone on the floor and stood from the bed, still in just his t-shirt.

"You done? Uh, I'll hop in and we can get this road on the show!"

He scurried over to his dresser, grabbed boxers and a white t-shirt, neatly folded, and grinned mischievously at Orrie before entering the bathroom.

Orrie enjoyed the view of Dalton's tight ass dusted with strawberry-blond hair peeking out from underneath the t-shirt.

Just as cute as the rest of him.

Orrie dressed in layers, as the Bay Area weather could be unpredictable. Black jeans, black boots, and his worn David Bowie t-shirt under a maroon cashmere V-neck sweater, an early birthday gift from Dalton. It was a blessing to his skin, so soft it caressed his every move. It reminded him of how affectionate Dalton was, always touching him, soothing him. It was just one of the many reasons Dalton had made Orrie blissfully happy.

Orrie was a private guy, but he craved the physical touch of a loved one to bring him down when he perseverated or to lift him out of the darkness when he couldn't do it himself. He'd always been uncomfortable asking previous partners for affection, but he'd never needed to ask Dalton. He could read Orrie almost from the beginning of their relationship.

After meeting Dalton at the Bishop Tech gig, they'd gone back to Dalton's apartment in Menlo Park and hadn't come up for air for days. It had felt too good to be true. Dalton was convinced he was in love, told Orrie he was all in. Orrie had wanted to believe him, but after the initial high had worn off, Orrie had almost thrown it all away. He'd given Dalton some excuse, said he'd be in touch, that he was going back on tour soon and needed to rehearse, and he'd left. Thankfully Dalton hadn't been convinced by his act. He'd pursued him and broken down every last one of his walls.

Just over a year later, they were as comfortable as a couple who'd been together for decades. Mostly. Orrie was still waiting for it to go south. Today would actually be a perfect occasion for that to happen.

As Orrie applied pomade to slick his hair neatly out of his face and put his studs back in, he prayed one last time that today wouldn't be a total clusterfuck. All he'd need is his father to make a snide comment about Orrie being prepared for when the music career dried up, or Deborah to point out one of his odd behaviors and he'd lose his shit. His grandmother loved him, but even she was frequently critical of whatever Orrie was passionate about. Dalton being there was the only thing that would make it bearable.

Dalton opened the door to the bathroom to let the steam out and Orrie was disappointed to see he was already dressed. He looked adorably edible in khakis and a mint-green button-down with a gray sweater vest and a pale yellow bow tie. Chucks the color of his tie rounded out his very hipster outfit. The two of them looked like polar opposites, and in many ways they were. But in the ways that counted, they were perfectly complementary.

"You look dashing in that sweater," Dalton said as he tried to tame his thick, wavy strawberry-blond hair. It stuck up in various places from cowlicks that he could never manage to tame no matter how much product he used.

"Thanks," Orrie said, wrapping his arms around Dalton from behind. He rested his chin on Dalton's shoulder, gazing at the picture the two of them made in their large mirror. Opposites. Complementary. Totally in love.

He squeezed and Dalton turned for a kiss. Orrie moaned as their lips touched, once again swept away by the soothing balm that was Dalton. His enthusiasm for life and generosity combined to make Orrie feel heady whenever they kissed. It was an innocent sort of sexiness. While Dalton had loads of experience in business by the time they'd met, he hadn't had much experience with other men. He'd been so busy taking over the tech world, he hadn't had time to *get* busy. He'd more than made up for it since.

"Can we grab some donuts, oh please oh please?" Dalton asked. "We can stop at your favorite spot on the way to Gloria's."

Orrie laughed and kissed him once more. "If that's what you want."

"After the breakfast we had, I'm ready for dessert,' Dalton said, his hand wandering to Orrie's fly. "Unless you think we have time—"

"We're going to be late to my grandma's," Orrie said, disappointment thick in his voice. He'd love to forget all about their responsibilities.

Dalton gave a little squeeze that made Orrie gasp. "We can't have that. I promise I'll make it up to you tonight. We'll have all the time in the world to cele— I mean to, well, you know."

Orrie let his hand drop down to cup Dalton's ass in the buttery-soft khakis. "I'm going to need this tonight," he whispered against Dalton's ear.

Dalton's voice cracked like a pubescent boy's when he spoke, bringing a smile to Orrie's lips. "I'm all yours, baby."

But not even the donuts could cheer Orrie up. He sat quietly in the passenger seat of Dalton's Tesla Model S, clutching the pink box of donuts like a life preserver. The scent of sugar, chocolate, coffee and roses filled the car, making Orrie's nose twitch. It had been Dalton's idea to pick up roses for Orrie's grandmother, Gloria Silver-Wrona. She was the mother of Orrie's stepmom, Deborah, and one of the most loving, if not opinionated, women in the world when it came to her only grandson. Orrie's father hadn't wanted any more children after Orrie and his older sister Olive, and Deborah had agreed. Instead, he opted to trot out his biological children and use them like trophies when necessary, and then in private, deride them for not being the children he'd have made sure they were if he'd stayed married to Ava.

"Too bad I couldn't have had an emergency C-section like Olive and missed this circus," Orrie said.

"Or too bad she couldn't have popped that kid out a month sooner so they could be there. I miss Clapton and Hendrix," Dalton said, speaking of Orrie's nephews. "I can't wait to see the baby."

"Yeah, the kids being there really helps. Watching my grand-mother attempt to protect her valuables from their little boy energy is highly entertaining."

"At least we'll get to see them tonight. I brought surprises."

Dalton loved spoiling his nephews almost more than he did. They'd talked about having their own kids someday, but at this point, they'd decided it would be best to just be the super-cool uncles since they both traveled so much. Olive was grateful for them, especially now that she had Janis to contend with. For all Orrie knew, she and her husband Patrick would create enough offspring for their own band, and he and Dalton would have plenty of kids to share their love with.

Dalton flipped stations on his Sirius radio until he got to Alt-Nation and, as if on cue, Orrie's latest single from his sophomore album played. It was a cover of k.d. lang's "Constant Craving."

"I remember when you played it for me on our first official date." Dalton reached over to squeeze Orrie's thigh. "When you sang it to me..." He trailed off as his fingers walked their way up his leg and into the box of donuts. He pulled out a rainbow sprinkle and took a big bite. "Mmmm, I love what you did with the song," he said with a full mouth. "Got you into my pants."

"Got you *out* of your pants." Orrie couldn't help but chuckle thinking about that night. It was three nights after they'd met, and they'd finally left Dalton's apartment to get pizza. Orrie had driven them to his old neighborhood in Niles and parked at the end of a dark street. He led Dalton down a path to the Alameda Creek and they'd sat on a park bench. Orrie had brought his guitar and sere-naded him. Sappy, true, but then that was just the kind of relation-ship they'd fallen comfortably into.

Dalton pulled off Highway 238 and took the windy canyon roads up into the Castro Valley hills as the clock turned over one o'clock. Making them late. One strike against him already. When Orrie had spoken to his grandmother two days prior, asking what they could bring, she'd told him "just that handsome man of yours." Maybe the roses would help?

"I'm so glad you're bringing Dalton. He's such a nice man. You're sooooo lucky to have found him, darling."

Orrie was sure he would hear that a lot today. And while he agreed, there was nothing like being repeatedly reminded by your beloved grandmother that you might not be quite the catch yourself. She probably didn't mean it that way, but with all of the criticism of his shortcomings, that's how he took it.

"Boys! I'm so glad to see you! Come in, come in. The neighbors are here, and Orrie, your great aunt Marvel and your great uncle John. They brought an exchange student with them. She's come all the way from Germany, can you believe that?"

"I can't believe it. Can you believe it?" Dalton said with a wink as he hugged Gloria.

"Oh, you brat," she said, patting him on the cheek. "You've found such a cheeky one, Orrie. It's a good thing he's so handsome and charming."

"That he is." Orrie shook his head. "Where's Dad?"

Gloria stopped walking. "He didn't tell you? He and Deborah had to stop in Washington D.C. for a meeting with upper management. You know your father is very important. They send their love."

Orrie felt a familiar pang of disappointment. No, Percy Jones wouldn't think of calling his son to tell him he wouldn't be there for the holiday. He wouldn't consider it. That's how much Orrie factored into his plans.

Gloria took Dalton's arm and ushered them into the living room. Orrie steeled himself for all of the comments as they entered the room and greeted his family:

"Don't you two look adorable."

"Yes, Dalton is the CEO of Bishop Tech, isn't that wonderful?"

"Orrie, are you still playing that music?"

"Our Orrie is *sooooo* lucky he found Dalton."

"I know, I know," he finally said. "I'm *sooo* lucky." He said the last with a smile for Dalton.

"I'm the lucky one," Dalton answered.

"Well, you boys are late. Orrie, I swear, I keep hoping someday you'll learn how to be punctual. Go ahead and take your seats. I've already got all of the food out on the table. Mimosas?"

"I'll make one, Grandma. You sit down," Orrie said, walking her over to her seat at the table. He knew Dalton wouldn't want one, but he needed liquid courage if he was going to get through this meal. Dalton had already given him absolution from any consumption necessary to get through the day. Dalton himself was a teetotaler, a choice he'd made after a lifetime dealing with alcoholism in his family. Since the holidays were really the only time Orrie imbibed, Dalton hadn't taken issue.

As he walked into the kitchen, he could hear Gloria start in.

"We're so glad you boys could make it. I wasn't sure, since Orrie's been running around all over the place."

"This tour has been a great opportunity for him." That was his Dalton, always standing up for him.

"Well, it's just a matter of time before he has to settle down—"

"Gloria, he's doing what he's meant to do, and he's amazing. You should see him sometime."

Gloria didn't respond, which meant she was trying hard to follow the "if you don't have anything nice to say" rule. Orrie appreciated her attempt.

Orrie took a deep breath before rejoining the party, a mimosa in his shaky hand.

Dalton was sitting next to a pretty blonde and carrying on a conversation with her in German. Because of course he spoke German *and* Spanish.

"Orrie, dear," Gloria said. "Meet Elke. She's a German exchange student staying with Marvel and John this semester while she takes courses at East Bay. Elke, this is my grandson, Orrie Jones."

Dalton put an arm around Orrie. "He's a famous singer, did you know that?"

Orrie shook hands with the slight woman. She didn't smile and looked as if she felt a bit out of place. Orrie could relate. He'd been a member of this family for twenty-five years and he still felt out of place.

"Orrie was enrolled there for a while," Gloria said. "Until he decided to drop out and give this music business a shot."

Dalton squeaked when Orrie squeezed his thigh with a tighter grip.

"Well thank goodness he's got talent," Howard said, raising his glass. "If I'd have had a voice like his, and the looks to go along with it, I'd have done the same thing." He winked and Orrie felt the tightness in his chest ease a bit. *Grandpa for the save.*

"So, Dalton," Gloria said to change the subject. "How's your mother? Is she almost finished with her treatments?"

Orrie squeezed Dalton's thigh again, gently this time. Dalton and his mother might frequently find themselves at odds, but he loved her dearly, and her diagnosis of breast cancer four months ago had been tough on him. Thankfully, she was handling the chemo very well and would be finished, with a great prognosis, in two more months.

"She's just as ornery as ever, Gloria. Thank you."

"How's your sister, Orrie?" Howard sat at the head of the table and smiled kindly. "I can't wait to see the new baby."

"It was a tough delivery, but she's doing okay. Her and Patrick are in love with their new little girl and the boys are just as wild as ever."

"That's wonderful. Gloria and I will be going to see them just as soon as Olive is ready to receive guests."

"I'm sure she'll love that," Orrie said, knowing that, while she'd be happy to see them, she'd get just as much of the disapproval treatment that Orrie did. Grandma couldn't go five minutes without telling her she'd gained weight or her hair looked awful dyed whichever color of the rainbow Olive had chosen. And then she'd turn around and brag about what a great author she was and how wonderful that she'd made a bestseller list. Loving...and opinionated. That was Grandma.

The guests made small talk while serving themselves from various quiches and a large fruit salad. There was also a cheesecake, a carrot cake, and a carafe of pumpkin soup, served cold. Orrie couldn't stand any of it. He remembered the first time Percy had prepared a "gourmet" dinner for them. His dad had been on a culinary kick for a few months and he tried out his newly found skills. Orrie had been sitting at the end of table next to Howard, who took one slurp of the soup and spit it out. "Looks like baby shit to me." He and Orrie had shared a secret laugh about it. Memories like that helped him survive these gatherings that took so much out of him emotionally.

Dalton served him a heap of fruit salad and a small slice of carrot cake, knowing if he didn't look like he was eating he'd get even more negative attention. They shared a smile that gave Orrie hope. He knew soon they'd be on their way and he could relax. A bit.

Aunt Marvel placed a hand on Orrie's arm. "Tell me, Orrie. Do you have any more television performances planned? We loved seeing you on Jimmy Fallon."

Orrie smiled. He'd always loved Marvel. She was much more accepting of his career choice. "Actually, I might be on—"

"Your father told us he'll be going to Greece for work after the holidays," Gloria interrupted. "He said he would try to call you later. Isn't it amazing they get to go to Greece? Dalton, honey, has your business ever taken you to Greece?"

Dalton wiped his mouth with a napkin. "Yes, ma'am." He shot a sorrowful glance at Orrie. "Twice, actually."

"Orrie, dear, you're so lucky to have found such a handsome man who's so successful! Perhaps he'll take you to Greece on business someday."

"Yeah, maybe," Orrie said. He looked at his phone under the table. By Dalton's calculations, they needed to stay at least 90 minutes. It had only been 30 so far. *Damn.*

"Orrie, son, are you going to be around this weekend?" Howard asked. "I could really use some help with those boxes in the garage."

Orrie swallowed hard and folded his hands in his lap. "I'm leaving for more tour dates tomorrow night, Grandpa. I'm sorry."

"Again? All this running around isn't good for you, you know. And I'm sure Dalton would like for you—"

Dalton reached for her hand. "I'm ecstatic that Orrie has this opportunity. He's really in demand, you know."

Gloria sighed and took a bite of her quiche.

Orrie picked at his finger, the smell of the quiche turning his stomach.

"I'd be happy to come over," Dalton said, placing his arm around the back of Orrie's chair for support.

"Oh, no, dear. We know you're far too busy to come help with something as silly as those boxes. Howard, come on. You know the boys are too busy."

"Grandma, I'd be happy to help, I just—"

"Gloria, it's no problem."

Dalton was so good with Orrie's family. *I really am lucky to have him.*

"I'll grab my good-for-nothing brothers and be over Saturday," he said with a triumphant grin.

Orrie shot him a grateful look.

"You are such a good man, Dalton. Orrie, you are so—" "Lucky. Right. I know."

DALTON HUGGED GLORIA AND HOWARD BEFORE HE AND ORRIE waved goodbye and headed on to stop number two. His least favorite of the day. As much as Orrie dreaded spending time at his grandparents' home, their next stop was likely to be even more eventful. Dalton rubbed a hand gently over the sore spot on his chest and sighed. *Just a few more hours.*

Once they were in the car, Orrie put his head in his hands.

"You hardly ate anything." Dalton rubbed Orrie's back. He'd suggested the donuts because he knew Orrie would be too stressed out to eat.

"I don't know why she insists on serving quiche at these things. Who the hell eats quiche, anyway?" Orrie picked at the spot on his finger.

Dalton shook his head. "Only old people. And hipsters."

Orrie laughed humorlessly and leaned back in the seat. "You don't have to do the boxes this weekend. I can do it tomorrow before I leave."

"Forget it," Dalton said as he started the car. "I get you to myself tomorrow until I take you to the airport, and I'm not losing a single minute of time with you." He leaned over and kissed Orrie sweetly. "It's been a long six weeks, baby."

"Too long. I missed you." Orrie closed his eyes and Dalton took that as a good sign. He hoped that meant Orrie would be able to relax at their next stop. Because *he* sure the hell wouldn't.

Ahhhh, Casa de Bishop. The eternal bachelor pad. The house where Bishop men went to lick their wounds and drink. A lot. And today being Thanksgiving and the holy day of the pigskin, Dalton had prepared his defense. He just had to get past this next two hours, and then he and Orrie would move on to...his mom's.

Okay, make that the next four hours.

He pulled the car out of the pretentious neighborhood where Orrie's grandmother lived and drove down the hill to the more blue-collar area of Castro Valley. It was a funny town in that way. You had these newer, expensive developments up in the hills and canyons, but a lot of old neighborhoods from the forties and fifties that remained affordable for the low- to middle-income folks in the East Bay.

Peter Bishop, Dalton's father, lived in such a home, one he'd inherited from his parents. The boys had grown up there, and currently, Dalton's brothers Terrence and Stanley lived there with him. Both had broken up with their significant others in the past year and now, with their divorced father, they lived the life of swingin' singles. Dalton just hoped the house was in better shape than it had been the last time he was here.

"Hey, doll," Orrie said, reaching for his leg. "I know how much you worry about them. You don't have to do anything you don't want to. If you want to go..."

And that was just one of the many reasons Dalton loved this man more than anything. He looked over and Orrie was smiling at him in that way that made Dalton feel like any second he was going to be a weeping mess on the floor, but in a good way. Not in the way he'd grown up experiencing.

"I want to see them. I do. We're supposed to be thankful on Thanksgiving, right?"

Orrie nodded, frowning. "You are the most thankful person I've ever known. You see the positive in everything. Sometimes to your own detriment."

Dalton barked out a laugh and his eyes burned. He was tired of fretting over a situation that was never going to change.

Orrie got out of the car and walked around to Dalton's door, which he promptly opened, pulling Dalton in for an embrace that felt more supportive than seductive, and yet it had both effects. Dalton may have been the one to pursue Orrie, but Orrie had seduced Dalton with his compassion as much as his passion, with his love as much as his loving.

"If you promise not to take any shit from your brothers, I'll promise not to cause any bodily injury."

Dalton snorted and dropped his forehead onto Orrie's shoulder. "You know they're going to give me shit, and I know you're going to give it right back. Just don't hit anyone this time. You don't have that luxury, you know? You can't afford any injuries." He thought about Orrie picking at his finger and hoped it wouldn't get worse as the day wore on.

Orrie sighed and kissed Dalton's head. "I'm insured," he said against Dalton's hair. "If I happen to have an injury, they'll find some other poor schmuck to play guitar for me. Shouldn't be too hard. Any adolescent boy could play—"

"Stop it right there. You're as full of shit as a Thanksgiving turkey." Dalton put a finger against Orrie's lips. "I'm serious, baby. Please."

Orrie laughed. "We have an audience. Should we give them a show?"

Orrie just loved to be demonstrative in front of Dalton's brothers. They couldn't contain their disgust, not so much because Dalton was gay, but because the thought of their oldest sibling being sexually active with *anyone* made them want to hurl. Since Dalton had been more of a father to Terrence and Stanley than dear old Dad, they tended to treat him that way.

"I'd say we should give them a show, but honestly, that's not playing fair. If I want them to behave, I can't exactly go sinking to their level."

"So I shouldn't fondle you right here?" Orrie slid his hand down Dalton's chest.

Dalton winced and sucked in a breath.

"Did I hurt you? I'm sorry."

Dalton pressed his lips together firmly and pulled back from Orrie. "I'm fine. Really." *Was that my voice coming out sounding like a little girl's?*

Before Orrie could interrogate him, which would really ruin the surprise Dalton had worked so hard to make happen, Peter Bishop slammed open the front door.

"Hurry up, you two, before Terry burns the damn turkey!"

Dalton stared wide-eyed at Orrie. "Did he just say turkey?"

Orrie nodded, his brow furrowed once more. "Are your brother's actually cooking?"

"Come on, you two. I gotta get in the backyard."

The screen door slammed shut and Dalton jumped at the sound.

"Have your phone ready to call the fire department," he said to Orrie as he sprinted up the walk. *Dear God, don't let those idiots burn the place down.*

He ran straight for the kitchen, his nose working overtime trying to detect any smoke. All he smelled was mouthwateringly delicious turkey, and it wasn't coming from inside. He moved through the galley kitchen toward the patio slider—and grabbed his chest with one hand.

"Holy shit. Is that a—"

"Deep-fried turkey, coming right up," Stanley shouted from the backyard. "It's time to take this baby out!"

Dalton stepped out onto the patio to find his two brothers and his father, all dressed in khakis, dressy-ish shirts, and naked-lady aprons, preparing to remove their bird from the fryer. Orrie stopped at his side and cursed quite colorfully under his breath.

"You got the thing to put in the hole, right?" Terry asked, his hands covered with heavy-duty gloves.

"That's what she said," Stanley said, cracking himself up.

"I'm serious, dickwad! Where's the bar?"

"Uh, son?" Peter asked, scratching his head. "You're missing the hole."

"That's what she said," Stanley repeated, holding his stomach as he howled with laughter.

"Shut the hell up, dumbass. What do you mean I'm missing a hole? The thing's supposed to be sticking up out of the turkey." Terrence walked around the fryer that stood in the middle of the vast concrete patio in the backyard. It doubled as a driveaway to the detached garage, which housed Peter's refurbished classic cars and was far enough away from the house, Dalton prayed there'd be no structural damage.

"Did you put the hook through the turkey?" Orrie asked, crossing his arms over his chest. He covered his mouth with his hand after he spoke, and Dalton could see the pain of fighting back laughter in his face.

"What hook?" Terrence asked. "There was no hook in the box. Was there a hook in the box, Dad?"

"Hell if I know," Peter said. "I borrowed it from my buddy George at work."

"How the hell do we get it out of the fryer?" Terrence cried.

Stanley continued to laugh and was therefore no help.

"We'll just have to use some of them barbecue forks," Peter said. He trotted into the house, and Dalton was once again flabbergasted by his wardrobe.

"You guys go shopping? All your football jerseys in the wash? What's up with the clothes?"

Stanley stopped laughing and shrugged. "We were trying to do a nice holiday for you. Terence got us these shirts off Amazon. We got this turkey and everything. Even all the rest of the fixins."

Dalton felt Orrie leave his side, but he was too stunned to move. The oil was bubbling and crackling around the bird and the heat coming off the fryer could be felt all the way on the steps where Dalton stood, still frozen.

"Here, I got it. Hey dumbass, grab the big bowl for us to put this sucker in." Peter stood at the ready with his giant forks. "I'm going to spear this sucker and drop it in the bowl. Got it?"

"Got it," Stanley said. He held a large salad bowl, but Dalton had the sneaking suspicion it still wasn't going to be big enough. From where Dalton was standing, it appeared the turkey filled up most of the fryer.

Dalton wanted to cover his eyes to avoid seeing the train wreck about to occur.

Peter skewered the bird with both of the tools and planted his feet with his legs bent. "You ready, son?"

"Don't you drop that bird, Dad," Terence pleaded. "I paid a lot of money for that peanut oil. I want to eat fried turkey."

"Shut up," Peter said. "Piece of cake. Alright. Here we go, Stanley. Ready? One..."

Dalton sucked in a breath and held it.

"Two..."

Dalton squeezed his eyes shut, but morbid curiosity popped one open.

"Three!"

Peter heaved his big shoulders and flexed his strong arms and lifted what appeared to be at least a twenty-five-pound-plus bird out of the fryer.

"Take a look at this baby, would ya?" Peter let out a maniacal victory laugh.

The brothers cheered him on as he lifted the bird inch by inch out of the oil.

"That's it! Come to papa!"

The bird now hovered six inches over the fryer and Peter adjusted his grip, ready to turn toward a waiting Stanley with the bowl.

And that's when the Bishop Jinx was unleashed.

As Stanley moved the bowl closer, Peter lifted the turkey toward him.

The forks slipped.

The bird hit the edge of the fryer.

The bird ripped the rest of the way free of the tongs and splatted onto the ground.

The fryer tipped just enough to spill boiling-hot peanut oil onto the flames, which ignited the bird.

Dalton shrieked for them to get back.

Stanley fell on his ass, still holding the bowl.

Terrence managed to right the fryer before the entire contents spilled on the ground.

Orrie brushed past Dalton with the fire extinguisher and shouted for them to back up.

"Hold-it-hold-it-hold-it!" Peter shouted. He reached for the lid of his Weber barbeque and dropped it on top of the turkey, smothering most of the flames.

Orrie used the extinguisher to cover the fryer in white foam.

It was over in a matter of seconds...and then they all stood there breathing heavy.

Terrence spoke first.

"D-d-did you...save it?"

Dalton looked at his middle brother incredulously.

Terence used the gloves to carefully lift the Weber lid off of the bird. Underneath was a blackened mound that used to be a turkey.

Stanley stood and looked down at his precious bird. "You think we can save any of it?"

Peter took the bowl from Stanley and used the tongs to try to scoop the carcass into it. "There. We'll just take this inside, scrape off all the burnt stuff and any extinguisher bits that got on it, and maybe we'll have enough to eat, huh?"

He carried it inside, continuing to mutter optimistically to himself. Stanley followed, not looking as upbeat.

Orrie bumped Dalton with his elbow. "I'll just clean this up," he said, gesturing to the extinguisher, which was old and had mostly only sprayed itself and Orrie's pants.

"I'm sorry, baby" Dalton said.

Orrie grinned as though he wanted to burst out laughing, but the situation was still too fresh. "It's fine. I'll be back." He glanced at Terrence, and then gestured with his chin for Dalton to see to his distraught brother.

"You okay?" Dalton finally asked Terrence.

Terrence stood staring down at the mess with his gloved hands on his hips. He'd managed to splatter oil on his pants, likely ruining them, but he didn't seem hurt.

"I wanted to make today nice for you," he said. Finally, he looked up at his older brother. "Mom told me about your plans and, well, I know we always give you guys a bunch of shit, but I want you to be happy."

"You did this for us?" Dalton asked as he was about to turn into that weepy mess again. "You didn't have to do that. We're fine with your usual finger-food selections."

"Shut up," said Terrence. An embarrassed grin broke across his face. "I know. It was *mostly* for you guys. That, and Stanley whining about how he'd never had fried turkey before." He pulled off the gloves, which Dalton noticed had holes in them, and he tossed them on the ground.

"The clothes sure were a shock. The aprons are a nice touch," Dalton teased. "You got some newspaper?"

The brothers got to work trying to blot up the globules of grease with newspaper from the garage and Dalton hosed down the rest, praying there would be no showdowns with local wildlife this evening. All this day needed now was one of his brothers to get injured in a row with a rabid raccoon.

"Thanks, bro," Terrence said. "So, you going to do it?"

Dalton's cheeks flushed, a dead giveaway he was nervous. One of the many curses of his Irish heritage—and one of the many reasons he sucked at poker.

"Yeah, but don't say anything, please? Mom shouldn't have told you."

Terrence frowned. "Look, just because I'm not all perfect and shit like you, it doesn't mean I can't keep a secret. I'm not a complete idiot."

Dalton sighed. Once again he'd managed to hurt his younger brother's feelings. Terrence was three years younger than him at 27, and Stanley was turning 26 this weekend. When their parents split up, the boys were passed back and forth. It became Dalton's responsibility to keep his brothers in line, and they resented him for it. His role meant they could never just be brothers. He had little hope that would ever change.

"I know. I'm sorry, Terry."

Terry nodded and looked down at the damage done to his outfit.

"Sonofa—I was going to wear these pants to a job interview next week! And look at my shoes."

There were dark splatters from the oil all over his dress shoes that looked a size too small for his six-foot-three brother. Terrence and Stanley had gotten all the height in the Bishop family. Dalton claimed he was six feet, but that was while wearing shoes, sadly.

"You got an interview? That's great! Where at?"

"Remember that guy at Tesla you introduced me to?" "You mean Barry? He called you?"

Terry frowned. "Did you set this up, Dalton?"

"No! I swear. We had lunch last week, and I gave him your number because he was looking for a new service manager, but I swear I didn't—"

"Doesn't matter." Terrence walked away from him. "It's not like I'll get the job anyway."

You won't if you keep drinking so much.

It was amazing how Dalton could run his successful company, but he couldn't seem to get his family together. He'd tried so hard to teach his brothers the life skills they'd need, but they had preferred he do everything for them, and like an idiot, he had for many years. Now he couldn't even have a conversation with them without a fight. Somewhere in his mind a phrase from his psychology courses surfaced. *Codependency.*

He kept his mouth shut to avoid any more drama and followed Terrence into the kitchen. Which smelled like burned ass.

"I thought you thawed out the rolls?" Peter shouted at Stanley.

"I figured they'd be fine in the oven. I didn't know—"

Orrie moved swiftly between them, stirring the instant mashed potatoes, heating up gravy from a can, and scooping some cranberry sauce out of another can while they argued.

"You guys go sit. Dalton, give me a hand here."

Terrence cursed under his breath and opened the fridge, grabbing three bottles of beer before slamming it shut. A foul stench wafted out as it closed.

Peter yelled at Stanley all the way out to the table, which had been cleared by some miracle and was set with their grandmother's china.

"Man, they tried so hard." Orrie picked up a piece of turkey from the platter and tried it. "Mmm. At least it's cooked. It's pretty good."

Dalton swallowed back his tears and focused on Orrie's ruby-red lips as he smiled around the piece of turkey.

"I love you."

Orrie's grin fell. "Don't...don't cry. I love you, too." He had Dalton in an embrace in two beats and held on long enough for him to get himself together, and for his brothers to start yelling for the food.

"They're getting restless. Grab me a beer? Please? And meet me at the table. I've got this." Orrie winked at him.

"And open that pungent fridge again? No, thank you. You can have water."

Orrie laughed all the way out to the dining room.

Dalton's brothers sat sullenly at the table while Peter continued to bitch at them.

"Here we go." Orrie set the platter down and backed away as the three other Bishop men dove in. By the time they were done, Orrie and Dalton were able to snag a sliver each of dark meat and some mashed potatoes, forgoing the gravy and cranberry sauce.

"Here's to the Bishops' first fried turkey," Peter said, holding up his beer. They all clinked glasses, and then Peter, Terrence and Stanley picked up their plates and walked over to the couch. "Which game we got next?"

"Redskins and Cowboys."

"Fuck the Cowboys," Terrence said. He kicked back the last drop of his second beer and then cracked open the third.

Dalton and Orrie finished their small portions in silence then moved to the kitchen to assess the damage. Orrie turned around and leaned against the counter. "Leave the mess."

Dalton sighed. "I know I should, but they were trying to be civilized."

Orrie snorted and they both laughed for a moment, probably a little harder than the situation called for, but that's stress for you.

"They're going to be wrapped up in that game for a while. They won't even notice we're gone."

Dalton nodded. "I'll just go say goodbye." Orrie slipped his hand into Dalton's. "*We'll* go say goodbye."

And that was the best part of this disaster. Dalton didn't have to do this alone anymore. He had someone on his side now.

They strolled into the living room, taking care not to block the view of the flat-screen.

"We're headed out," Dalton said. "We've got to go to Mom's and then we're going to go see Olive and the new baby."

Terrence waved from the couch. "Tell Mom we'll be over later." Which they wouldn't because they'd drink too much. Like usual.

"See ya, Dalton. Bye, Orrie." Stanley raised his beer, his eyes never leaving the screen.

Peter frowned at his youngest sons and stood stiffly from the couch. "I'll walk you guys out."

"It's okay, Dad. You looked comfortable."

Peter waved off his comments. "I gotta move around anyway otherwise my damn arthritis freezes everything up."

Peter Bishop was in pretty good shape for a guy in his late fifties, but manual labor took its toll on his body. Dalton had finally convinced him to go see a chiropractor, massage therapist and acupuncturist, which he'd paid for, to help ease his pain. Dalton had also offered to supplement his retirement so he could just take it easy, but his father wanted to keep working, too ashamed to live off of his celebrity son.

"You still driving that Tesla, huh?"

Dalton turned to hug him, ready for the next part.

"I'd sure miss hearing that rumble from the tail pipes. You know what I'm talking about, Orrie?"

Orrie shook hands with him, an evil grin on his face. "I love a good rumble in the tail pipes."

Peter's cheeks darkened beneath the red lines denoting years of alcohol abuse, and he shook his head. "Well, you boys enjoy the rest of your night. Cong— Uh, Happy Thanksgiving. Glad you came over." He shoved his hands in his pockets and nodded at Dalton.

"Love you, Dad. Thanks for the turkey." Dalton climbed into the car and shut the door before Orrie even had his open.

"Thanks, Peter."

Peter Bishop waved without looking as he returned to the home he'd lived in his entire life. It looked shabbier as Dalton grew older, kind of like the man inside.

"That was a weird experience," Orrie said. "I'm not sure what's more disturbing, their unusually low level of testosterone poisoning or their attempt at civility."

Dalton slid his left hand into his pocket and fingered the chain he'd hidden there this morning. It held a very prized possession, one that he couldn't wait to pass on.

His phone buzzed.

Not feeling great. Thank you for the food delivery. I'll try to eat some of it later. You boys have a good time with Orrie's family. Love you.

Dalton exhaled. "Mom's not up to a visit tonight."

Orrie turned sharply. "But we can't leave her alone. I know she's...well... It's Thanksgiving. I'd hate for anyone to be alone."

"If we go over there right now, she's liable to lock the doors or sick her psycho mutt Friendly on us."

"Shit. Did she get the food at least?"

Dalton had insisted on having a meal delivered to her so she wouldn't have to cook. She'd had a chemo treatment two days ago and the first few days after were always tough.

"She did, along with the loaf of Wonder bread you recommended. She'll love having the sandwiches when she feels better."

Orrie touched his shoulder. "You're a good son."

Dalton put the car in gear and turned to kiss Orrie's hand. "It's your turn. Want to call your dad from the road? Get it over with?"

Orrie let his hand drop. "It can wait."

ORRIE FELT GUILTY THAT HE DIDN'T WANT TO SPEAK TO HIS father today, but he only had this one night with Dalton and he wanted it to be special. He'd spoken to his father three days ago from Portland. Percy hadn't said anything about not being there for Thanksgiving.

"*Now you'll be at Gloria's for brunch?*"

"*Yeah, Dad. Of course.*"

"*I just know now that living with your friend, you two want to spend time together, and I understand that—*"

"*Dad, I'm in love with Dalton. He's my boyfriend. We're going to get married someday. You need to be prepared that that's where this is going.*"

"*Well, at least you'll have some stability with him. You know your music career could be gone in the blink of an eye, and since you didn't finish college—*"

Deborah had gotten on the phone then. "*Your father just wants to make sure you're making good decisions...*"

Orrie hadn't even told Dalton about that phone call. Even thinking about it now still hurt, though he'd had much worse conversations with them in the past. He felt a sting in his finger and looked down to see that he'd managed to make himself bleed.

"Hey, can you pull over? I need something out of the back." Orrie grabbed a napkin from the center console and held it over his finger so he wouldn't get blood on Dalton's seats.

Dalton swerved sharply on Mission Boulevard in Hayward before pulling into the McDonald's parking lot down the hill from the place of Orrie's failed education, California State University, East Bay.

"Is it your finger?" Dalton unbuckled his seat belt and climbed out of the car.

"How'd you know?" Orrie asked when he returned with the first-aid kit.

Dalton smiled and opened up the box. He took out a cleansing wipe and a Band-Aid, along with a tube of bacitracin.

"I saw you picking at it this morning and I just figured... I'm sorry, I know this is a stressful day."

Orrie let Dalton play doctor and fix him up, wishing once again that he was good enough for him.

"I'm sorry. It hasn't been bad like this in a while."

Dalton touched his thigh. "Don't apologize. It's always worse when you have to deal with your family. I just wish..."

But there wasn't anything more Dalton could do, and he shouldn't have to.

"They're right, you know. My family. I am *soooo* lucky to have you," Orrie said, looking down at the Band-Aid. He smiled to see SpongeBob's goofy face looking back at him.

"Like it? I thought that one might make you giggle."

"You always make my boo boos all better." Orrie snaked a hand behind Dalton's neck and pulled him in for a kiss. Their tongues brushed together in soft sweeps of simmering lust and a touch of sorrow. The pain of the day made itself known and then drifted away as their mouths became greedy.

Dalton moaned his desire into Orrie's mouth, and he gripped Orrie's biceps tightly. Orrie wished once more they'd stayed home as he desperately needed to touch Dalton's skin. He grasped the front of Dalton's shirt roughly—and Dalton gasped.

"What's going on? Why do I keep hurting you?" Orrie reached for the buttons on Dalton's shirt, fearing the worst.

"It's nothing." Dalton grabbed for his hands to impede their process.

Orrie pulled back and his dark brows nearly touched in the middle of his frowning forehead. "Dalton, what is it?"

Dalton's blue eyes were wide. "Nothing, I swear. I just, uh, have a big pimple there. You know? I get those big ones sometimes. Nasty one. I was hoping it would go away before today, but it's not quite gone." His smile was kinda freaky, like he was embarrassed... but almost as if he was hiding something.

Orrie knew better than to let his mind wander to dark places. They were beyond that. Orrie had been clear early on that he had real trust issues after the fiasco with his ex, and Dalton had done everything to assure him he had no reason to worry.

He sucked in a breath. *It's just a zit. Dalton's embarrassed about his acne. That's all it is. Cool your jets, Orrie.*

Orrie let his arms relax, and he smiled. This called for a little

reveal of his own. "I want to play you something." Orrie comman-
deered the USB cord from Dalton's phone and plugged it into
his own.

"What is it?" Dalton's creepy grin eased into his naturally
cheerful expression, though he seemed tired after this last visit.
Hopefully this would keep them both smiling through the rest of
their day.

Orrie searched through his demos for the one that would eventually become his love song—his proposal to Dalton, if he ever got
up the nerve to ask him. He'd titled the tune "Check This Box," a
joke from their first date. He hoped Dalton would understand.

"I don't have the vocal tracks down yet, but I laid down the
basics on the bus between gigs. I hope you like it."

Orrie had played songs he was working on before, but this time
he was particularly concerned about Dalton's reaction. The first
chords echoed through the car and Orrie reached to turn the
volume down.

"Go ahead and drive. I promise not to bleed on your seats."

Dalton frowned. "No, I want to listen. Shhhh."

Orrie paused the song.

"What are you doing? Turn it on." Dalton laughed at him as
though he were being ridiculous.

"We should go. Just drive." A twinge from his finger let him
know he'd tried to pick at it again. *Shit.* Good thing it had a
Band-Aid on it. The last thing he needed was to have a big sore
before leaving again tomorrow, his earlier joke notwithstanding.
His leg shook as he waited for Dalton to drive away. "Go!
It's fine."

"Fine, okay. But put it back on."

Dalton pulled the Tesla back out into traffic on Mission and
sped off towards Orrie's sister's house in Niles. His mom had
decided to bring their meal over there since Olive and the baby
weren't ready to travel.

"Can you start it again?" Dalton asked as they pulled up to the
next stoplight.

Orrie realized they'd been driving in silence for some time. In the meantime, he'd found a string on a frayed part of his jeans.

"Let's just wait 'til later," Orrie said, taking the cord out and putting it back into Dalton's phone. His palms were sweating and at the rate his leg was shaking, Dalton was going to think they were having an earthquake.

"But baby—"

"It's fine. I'll play it later. It's really rough anyway." The string on his pants came off in his hand and he went to work on another one.

"Okay, but you know I love to hear—"

"I know. It's fine."

But he wasn't fine. Another string came off in Orrie's hand and he cursed. By the time they got to his sister's, he was going to have a gaping hole in the knee of his jeans. His mom used to get so mad at him back in school for wrecking his clothes. Money had been tight and hand-me-downs from his older cousins only came once in a blue moon. But once he started, he couldn't stop, and the more he tried, the more of a mess he became.

Dalton didn't say anything as he drove. Eventually he turned on Alt-Nation again, and once more Orrie's voice spilled out of the speakers and into their space, this time singing "Do," a song he wrote shortly before meeting Dalton.

Many of Orrie's lyrics were openly gay, which was becoming more commonplace, with artists like Troye Sivan and Tyler Glenn putting out pop albums and finding mainstream success, but Orrie Jones also played balls-out dirty guitar, which set him apart. He'd always done as he pleased lyrically, but since he'd gotten together with Dalton, he'd taken more risks and been extremely blunt.

He couldn't wait to play the completed song for him. He shouldn't have even brought it up today. It wasn't ready, wasn't perfect enough to say what he really wanted to say.

Another string, and Orrie could now see his pale skin through the black material. Some things never changed.

Dalton had turned onto Nursery Avenue in Fremont and was

on Niles Boulevard before Orrie realized they were so close. He suddenly needed to see his mom and his sister desperately. They'd give him the shot of bravery he'd need to have a very serious conversation with Dalton tonight. Or they'd tell him to wait until his emotions weren't so raw.

Either way, he intended to let Dalton know that he wanted more than just living together. He wanted to make a commitment to the man he loved in front of the people who mattered, and he wanted to do it soon. If Dalton's mom's cancer or Olive's difficult delivery of little Janis had taught him anything, it was that life was incredibly precious, and he wanted Dalton to know how serious he felt about them.

"Hey, baby? You okay over there?"

Dalton turned onto G Street and the car rolled slowly past Orrie's mom's home toward Olive's house just down the street. As the sky darkened, a faint, dusky-blue and purple hue could be seen through the canopy of sycamore trees along the quaint street. Orrie knew Dalton needed to live on the other side of the Bay so traffic wouldn't be such a hassle for him, but Orrie missed the old neighborhood. He fantasized about him and Dalton buying one of these old Victorians so that when he was home, he could walk over to see his nephews. He hadn't said as much to Dalton. He'd already done so much for Orrie, he didn't want to ask for more.

"I love this neighborhood," Dalton mused as he pulled the car to a stop.

Orrie worried he'd spoken his thoughts out loud. "It's pretty great. I loved growing up here. All of this history hidden right under the nose of the rat race."

Dalton got out and smiled across the roof of the car at him. "Maybe we should keep an eye on the listings over here." He waggled his eyebrows.

"Forget it," Orrie said, closing his door. "Your commute would be a nightmare."

Dalton shut his door. "One of the perks of being the boss is flexible hours, baby. Traffic's no big deal."

Orrie stopped at the foot of the walkway and paused to stare at Olive's house. He could already hear his nephews. Any minute they'd come racing out to their favorite uncle, which already was Dalton. Orrie's whole family loved him. He couldn't bear it if he screwed this up, not just because of his stupid heart, but he would be letting everyone down again.

"Doll, you've already given so much," Orrie said quietly as he felt Dalton press against his side. "If you give up any more, you're going to wish—" "What are you even saying?" Dalton gave a humorless laugh. "I haven't given up anything to be with you. Where is this coming from?"

Orrie groaned. "Maybe I just don't want to be a drain on you, you know? You've already got your whole family depending on you—"

"Oh please, Orrie. Come on, you're not making any sense. Let's just go inside—"

"I'm making perfect sense! Look at this day. You came with me to my family's crazy brunch, you volunteered to move shit for my grandparents, which probably contains buckets and buckets of Grandpa Howard's coins he's collected that will break your fucking back, and then—"

"Yeah, then you held me up when my crazy brothers tried to burn down the house! You held me when my mom got sick, you called me every night when I thought—"

"Dalton, doll, I'm sorry. Please."

But by now, Dalton was fired up. He stepped back and pulled at his wild hair, his blue eyes wide. "Stop apologizing! Dammit, Orrie! This isn't how I wanted to do this, okay?"

Orrie staggered on his feet. "Wh-wh-what? *What?* Dalton?"

Dalton growled. He pulled off his sweater vest and threw it on the ground. "I'll tell you what, Mister Orrie Jones. I've about had it with this day!" He pulled off his bow tie and yanked his shirt out of his pants before Orrie could stop him.

"You can't just undress right here! What are you doing?" Had

Orrie's insanity finally rubbed off on his love? What was happening?

"Just listen to me," Dalton shouted, his adorable face completely flushed. "I have been waiting all day to do this, but I can't wait anymore. Orrie—goddammit, I can't get this stupid shirt off—there! Okay? Do you see now?"

Orrie thought for sure Dalton had lost it. *Why is he showing me his zit?*

And then he saw it.

It was only about three quarters of an inch tall, but it was letters, it was black...

"Is that a tattoo?" Dalton had said he was too nervous to get tattooed, that he didn't handle pain very well. Why would he—

"So, what is it?" Dalton said.

"Uncle Dalton, why you got your shirt off? It's cold outside!"

Five-year-old Hendrix came running down the walkway with a blanket. "Take my woobie so you don't freeze your balls off!"

"Hendrix!" Ava shouted from the door. "Where did you— Orrie? Honey, what are you guys doing out here? It's freezing."

Ava Donaldson stood all of about five foot nothing, but she still knew how to project her voice. The whole street was going to be out here in a minute.

Orrie stepped forward. "Doll, let's go inside. Let me fix your shir—"

His breath left his lungs in a rush. Up close, he could make out the words on Dalton's chest.

Yes

No

Each had a box next to it. Just like the night they'd spent at the park a couple of blocks from here. After Orrie sang to Dalton, they hung out next to the water until the sun went down. Orrie started doodling on his jeans, and then Dalton's, and then he was writing on Dalton's hand...

"Check this box," he whispered. His eyes instantly filled with tears. "Check this box?"

Dalton covered Orrie's hands with his and his voice cracked when he spoke. "What do you say?"

Orrie's knees wobbled ominously, as though they couldn't handle the weight of his feelings. "What do I say?"

Dalton squeezed his fingers then let go with his left hand. He reached into his pocket and pulled out a silver chain...with a ring suspended from it.

"You can wear it like this until you decide, you know, if you aren't ready, but I want you to have this. I got it from Gloria. It was the original wedding band she bought for Howard. They've since upgraded, but they wanted me to have this."

Orrie swallowed hard. "You talked to my grandmother?"

Tiny hands pulled at his jeans to grab his attention, but he couldn't tear his eyes from Dalton.

"And your mom. And Olive. I was going to propose all normal-like, you know, with the knee and everything, and then I was going to show you this when we got home, but you were being so pigheaded in the car—"

"Pigheaded?" Orrie snorted and the sound finally broke the tension. The boys ran circles around them, snorting and making pig sounds while Orrie and Dalton held each other, laughing and crying, though Orrie couldn't tell which they did more.

"I figured when you were ready, you could fill in the box of your choice, and eventually we could make it permanent, you know, if you wanted—"

"If I wanted?" Orrie picked Dalton up off the ground and squeezed him so tight, he gasped. "Doll, I love you. Of course my answer is yes!"

Dalton's eyes went wide and he collapsed against Orrie. "Thank God." He sighed loudly. "I've been questioning my sanity in getting this done for a week now!"

"A week? And it still hurts? Is it okay? I mean, have you been taking care of it?"

Orrie started to pull out his phone and turn on the flashlight but Dalton pushed his hands away.

"I told you I was a wimp. There was a woman getting her whole lower abdomen tattooed when I was in there, in this giant Celtic wedding band, laughing and carrying on, and I was trying not to pee my pants or pass out, it hurt so bad."

Orrie hugged him again and kissed him.

"Ew," Hendrix and Clapton shouted, running back toward the house. "They're kissing!"

They hid behind Ava, who was also crying. "Will you two come here already and hug me?"

"Wait," Dalton said. He unhooked the clasp on the chain and held it out. "Can I put this on you?"

Orrie shook his head. "Not on the chain."

Dalton frowned. "But then what will I put on your finger when we share our vows?"

Orrie leaned forward and kissed him. "We'll think of something."

Dalton paused then he slid the ring off of the chain into the palm of his hand. He lowered himself to one knee and cleared his throat. "Orrie Percival Jones, will you please—"

"Yes! I said yes, now put the damn thing on me!"

Poor Dalton. Orrie appreciated that he was trying to be all romantic, but Orrie needed the weight of the ring on his finger, and he needed Dalton in his arms, close enough to breathe him in. He barely let Dalton get to his feet and get the ring on him before he swooped him up in a kiss that had them both clutching at each other as though they couldn't get close enough. Orrie pulled Dalton's hair, Dalton scratched Orrie's neck and nearly sucked Orrie's lip off in his excitement. Orrie's belt buckle dug painfully into his skin as Dalton pressed even closer, and if they didn't get horizontal right now—

"That's enough, you two! Dalton Henry Bishop, if you don't let me hug you both right now, I'm going to hose you both down and I won't even care if you freeze to death out here!" Sure enough, Ava had the garden hose in one hand, the other on the faucet.

"Sorry, Mom. We just...he just... Mom, we're getting married!"

"I figured that out, and so did the whole neighborhood! Now get your skinny asses over here!" Dalton and Orrie rushed her and picked her up, despite her protests. They carried her into the living room, where Patrick was helping Olive get off of the bed they'd moved in there for her. She was on bedrest while her sutures healed and was not very happy about it.

"Did I just miss it, Dalton? Dammit! I wanted to see, too!"

Olive was a mess. Her green mohawk lay limply on her head and she had a boob hanging out of her cow-print nursing night-gown. Orrie had bought it for her when she had Clapton. He thought it was hysterical.

"Sorry, sis. It kind of couldn't wait anymore."

"Well, let me see! Get over here."

"Okay, but I'm not hugging you with your breast exposed. While I fully support a woman's right to breastfeed in public or wherever the hell she wants to, I don't want your cooties."

"Shut up, fucker," she said, righting herself. She handed Janis to Ava and hugged Orrie while the boys ran in circles chanting "fucker, fucker, fuuuuuuuucker."

And no one corrected them.

"ARE YOU COLD? YOU WANT TO GET OUT OF HERE?"

Dalton sat on Orrie's lap on the park bench where they'd spent their first date so long ago. After enjoying a lovely dinner prepared by Orrie's mom, they'd called Orrie's dad, who gave them perfunc-tory congratulations, and they'd called Dalton's mom. She hadn't cried, but she'd come pretty close for such a tough woman. Dalton told her they wanted to come by before he had to take Orrie to the airport the next day if she was feeling up to it, and she said she'd try. He didn't want to push it. It was enough that Orrie's family had gone totally insane over their engagement. There'd been enough hugs and snuggles with the boys and baby Janis to tide him over.

How could Orrie think he had given up a damn thing to be with him? Dalton had gained a very loving family that appreciated him. Everybody gained in this situation.

"You know what this means, don't you?" Orrie asked.

Dalton had been lazily kissing Orrie's neck, enjoying their closeness despite the cold, but he really wanted to get home to their bed.

"What? That I get to marry you? That I get to grow old with you? That we'll someday have to pluck each other's ear hairs and, like, give each other sitz baths when the hemorrhoids—"

Orrie gave a belly laugh that vibrated through Dalton. "You have a very vivid picture of where this is going. I, for one, swear I'm not going to have ear hairs or hemorrhoids."

"You say that now," Dalton teased, nibbling on his earlobe. "Seriously, what does it mean?"

Orrie sighed. "It means your wacky plan for the Bishop-Jones Live Holiday just might become a reality."

Dalton sat up and grinned down at his fiancé. "It also means a wedding and reception."

Orrie's eyes bugged out. "Are you kidding? No way. Doll. We've got to elope. We can't—"

"We can decide later." He leaned down and licked teasingly at Orrie's lips.

Orrie growled and gripped his hips, pulling him closer and crushing him with his kiss.

"God, I love you."

"And I you. I can't wait 'til you come home from tour. We can decide then what we want to do, when we want to do it..."

Orrie brought his hands up to cup Dalton's jaw. "Thank you for today. For everything. The boys are so excited."

Dalton's surprise for Hendrix and Clapton had been tickets to Disneyland. Dalton had already cleared it with Olive that he and Orrie could take the boys when Orrie got home. She was thrilled for them, and thrilled to have the break to just spend a few days with her precious baby girl and her husband.

"I'm so excited," Dalton said. "I've never been to Disneyland with kids."

They held each other for a little while longer when Orrie suddenly sat up.

"What's wrong?"

"Nothing, I just need my phone."

Dalton shifted so Orrie could grab his phone from his back pocket.

"I figured I could play that song for you." He scrolled through his apps until he found the one he used to save his demos and pressed play.

Dalton leaned against his chest and sighed. How amazing was his life? He not only had a fantastic career and his family hadn't completely self-destructed yet, but he was in love with one of a wonderful and talented man. From Orrie's phone poured the most beautiful melody he was sure he'd ever heard. The rhythm was slow and the effects Orrie'd used were a little less squealy and growly than usual. The chords sounded the way Orrie made him feel when they were alone together, like this, just holding on, sometimes for dear life.

"It's beautiful," he whispered, turning to kiss Orrie's jaw, loving the feel of his stubble against his lips. "What's it called?"

Orrie turned to gaze at him with a mischievous smile.

"Check This Box."

Dalton's eyes bugged out—and he laughed so hard, he finally felt the last of the stress from the day completely bleed away.

Orrie shushed him. "You're going to get the cops called on us."

Dalton caught his breath and stood, holding out his hand. "Then let me take you home, baby, before I give them something to really call the cops for."

Dalton pulled Orrie to stand and they kissed once more before walking arm in arm back to the Tesla they'd left parked in front of Olive's. As they climbed in, they heard Ava shouting at the boys.

"If you two don't stop saying 'fuckers,' I'm going to call Uncle Dalton and tell you you can't go to Disneyland!"

All shouts ceased.

Dalton pulled his door shut and turned to Orrie with a smile.

"Uncle Dalton. I'll never get enough of hearing that."

Orrie rolled his eyes. "Yeah, well, get used to it, Mr. Jones."

Dalton's eyebrows nearly disappeared into his hairline. "Mr. Jones? I think I like that. But we might have to hyphenate, you know, for business purposes—"

"Just take me home, doll." Orrie dropped his head against the headrest and closed his eyes. He slid his hand onto Dalton's thigh, his long fingers dipping between his legs.

Dalton swallowed hard, his oversensitive cock twitching under Orrie's caress. "That sounds like the best way to end this parade from hell."

Orrie chuckled and leaned over, his lips brushing Dalton's ear. "I'll make sure this day has a happy ending."

The Tesla jerked as Dalton pulled away from the curb. They made it across the Bay in record time and were naked before they reached their second-floor bedroom.

Orrie admired Dalton's cute tattoo, so tiny compared to the miles of ink that covered his own skin. It was such a sweet reminder of their beginning and a promise for the future.

"Hey, doll? How about you don't get the box filled in?"

Dalton frowned from his position on his back, his legs draped over Orrie's thighs. "What do you mean?"

Orrie ran a hand down Dalton's chest and abs until he reached his happy place.

"I want to be able to check that box every day. 'Yes, Dalton, I want your mouth on me. Yes, Dalton, I want you bent over that couch. Yes, Dalton, I'll give you my big—"

Dalton rolled his eyes. "Whatever you want, baby. I'm all yours."

Orrie bent to kiss his soon-to-be-husband. "That's exactly what I want. All of you."

Thankful in Perdition by Erin St. Charles

❦

ALMOST THANKSGIVING DAY

"You know the first thing I noticed about you?" AJ traced a finger down Jasmine's spine to the cleft of her ass cheeks, watching goosebumps form on the smooth expanse of her deep brown skin. She'd slept restlessly the night before, and as a result, had lost her satin bonnet so that her hair stood straight up in an unruly tangle, and she was gently working her fingers through it while he applied teasing strokes to her skin.

"My rent checks?" She asked.

He rolled his eyes and chuckled, thinking of the first time they'd met. Jasmine rented the guest house behind his rambling Tudor, but through his business manager. As a result, he had not actually met Jasmine until several months after she'd moved in and knocked on his kitchen door to borrow an egg.

He pushed the sheets down, revealing her plump, round ass cheeks. He palmed one and gave it a squeeze. Her ass twitched under his hand.

"No, mouthy girl. I mean, besides the rent checks," he said. "After we actually met in person."

"Hm, let me see...maybe my cookies?" She teased. She rolled

over on her back and he was treated to the sight of her large, soft breasts, softly rounded belly, and her sparsely haired mound. She propped herself up against the pile of white pillows at the headboard, and continued to detangle her hair. He crawled over to her, moved her legs apart, exposing her sex to him.

"Your eyes," he told her, sliding one hand up her thigh as he spoke. "You were looking at me with your big, Bambi eyes, begging me for eggs."

"I was not begging you for eggs," she said, feigning indignation. "And I did pay you back. In cookies."

"Yes, and then, nookies," he slid his hand further up her thigh, his target the vee of her thighs. She shook her leg, trying to discourage him, but he held fast.

She tilted her head to one side and smirked at him.

"We don't have time for this," she said. But her eyes told him she might be willing to *make* time.

"When your parents and my parents get here, we won't have time to get our groove on," he pointed out. "We need to make the most of our time before they get here."

"We'll have time when they leave," she said. Her brows wrinkled into a frown and she sat up abruptly, trying to tuck her legs underneath her bottom. "What time is it, anyway?"

"Oh, no you don't," he said, grabbing her by the ankle and yanking her towards him. She stared at him hard, then put up a token resistance.

"Oh no I don't what?" she asked, stifling a giggle..

"Stop trying to seduce me. We don't have that much time before we need to go pick up the parents," she said, trying, and failing, to look annoyed.

"I'm not trying to seduce you. I'm trying to make love to you." And to illustrate his point, he began to kiss her, starting with the instep of her foot, and continuing up the length of her legs. Jasmine was not an overly tall woman, maybe five feet eight inches, but she was all legs. Truth be told, it was one of the first things he'd noticed about her, along with her big doe eyes and the exaggerated Cupid's bow of her lips.

"As excuses go, you gotta admit, borrowing eggs was a pretty thin one," he told her, in between light kisses to her skin.

After she'd borrowed the eggs, he was treated to the sight of her round ass cheek, clad only in the skin-tight fabric of her leggings, and it was all he could do not to follow her out to the guest house. Looking back, he realized that part of him had decided to pursue her the moment he'd looked at her— even if he didn't realize it at the time. She'd piqued his interest when nothing else could penetrate the lingering cloud of sorrow that had hung over him since he witnessed the terrorist attack at a shifter-human wedding dissipated, his depression started to lift, and he was once again ready for whatever life had to offer.

She shivered as he kissed up the length of her leg. He paused at the juncture of her thighs, lingering over her mound but not touching it. He scented her musky arousal and could almost taste her sweetness, but stopped short of touching her there with his tongue. Instead, he skipped her heated core and trailed kisses down the other leg, from thigh to instep. When he sat back on his haunches to look at her, his dick pointing at her core with the precision of a homing beacon. Her eyes held a dreamy expression, her hands gripping the pure white sheets, her legs wide open to his gaze. Her pussy glistened with her desire. Despite her protests to the contrary, he was certain she could be persuaded to indulge in a little nookie.

He hooked his elbows under her knees and was preparing to pull her down the bed to better position her for sexy times, when a loud buzzing sounded from the other room.

He raised his head to peer at her. He frowned. "What's that sound?" He said, cringing inside, knowing in his heart that whatever the sound turned out to be, it would be the death knell this interlude.

Jasmine frowned as well. She pursed her lips, knit her brows together, and then realized what the sound was.

"Move!" She said urgently, swinging her legs over his head, planting your feet on the floor, and moved so fast for the door that all AJ saw was her brown butt cheeks disappearing through the doorway. He sat on the bed and had a good sulk before following his woman, and his penis, out of the bedroom.

He found her at the kitchen sink, emptying a pot into the sink. As he grew closer, he noticed that she was actually pouring the contents of the pipe into a colander in the sink. Steam billowed up from the sink and bathed her face.

He crept up behind her, slid his hands around her waist, then ground his still – erect dick into her ass cheeks.

"Hey now, I need to work on this," she told him, pushing at him. "We have a lot of people coming in for Thanksgiving, and I want it to go well."

He ignored her objection and nuzzled her neck. The colander in the sink held a steaming pile of sweet potatoes — what appeared to be enough to make candied yams to feed a small village. Jasmine was an early riser, as he had learned over the past few months. She must have gotten up early to start the food prep.

"What still needs to be done?" He asked, undaunted by her rejection. He nuzzled her neck and his hands crept up from her waist to her breasts.

She had turned on the water and was rinsing the sweet potatoes. He could still scent her arousal, and it was driving him nuts. His dick remained hard and eager.

"The pie crusts, the turkey brining, the cranberries..." he tuned out the litany of tasks yet to be completed, reached around her, and switched off the water faucet. Ignoring her sputtering protests, he hefted her up easily, and planted her bare butt on the kitchen counter. He plunged into her swiftly and they both hissed with the pleasurable sensation of being connected.

"Cooking makes you hot?" he whispered in her ear. She was as warm and steamy as a sauna, and he closed his eyes to savor the sensation.

"Ohhhhh..." she said, clenching around him. Food preparations forgotten, she threaded her fingers in his hair, and opened her legs wider for him.

"Baby, you feel so good..." he crooned in her ear. His lips brushed the shell of her ear — something he knew always got to her — and his fingers splayed out over her ass cheeks as he gave himself over to the sensation of being surrounded by her warm flesh. Fully seated, he began to grind his groin into her with circular motions.

"Stop playing," she said, impatiently, and he chuckled. He lifted her off the kitchen counter, and, still connected, carried her over to the leather ottoman in the family room. He repositioned the two of them for maximum penetration, draped her legs over his shoulders, and began to fuck her in earnest.

He watched her eyes roll back in her head as he pounded into her wetness.

"Does it seem like I'm playing, baby?" He bit out between thrusts. He tilted her hips back slightly, the better to hit the roof of her pussy, and thus, her g-spot. This had the desired effect, sending Jasmine over the cliff of orgasm with a speed that never ceased to amaze him.

"Ughhhh...." she wailed, as her pussy pulsed around him. She looked dazed, her eyes heavy lidded and glazed over.

"No, baby, I'm not playing," he could keep going, bringing her to orgasm again, but she herself had said they were in a hurry.

He gave himself over to the sensation of being with her, being inside her. The familiar tingling sensation began in his balls as his own release built, and when it began to unspool, he didn't try to stop it. He came in a flash of electric pleasure, emptying himself into her pussy, stars exploding behind his eyes. His body went slack and as he tried to avoid collapsing on Jasmine, he put out an elbow to break his fall, he missed the edge of the ottoman and hit the floor, hard, and he saw stars again.

He winced at the pain, and when he opened his eyes, Jasmine looked over the edge of the ottoman, eyes wide with alarm, her hair standing out from her head like a halo in the early morning sunlight.

"Are you okay?"

He groaned dramatically. "I don't think I can feel my legs."

Jasmine gasped, scrambled off the ottoman and cradled his face in her hands. Her eyes darted around his face. She looked frantic with worry.

"AJ, oh baby! Oh shit! Don't try to move!"

He made a hissing sound from the back of his throat. He beckoned her closer. "Come closer," he hissed.

She placed her ear close to his mouth, the better to hear him.

"Closer..." he whispered.

She obeyed instantly. It was something he really loved about her ... she was so trusting and sweet, and ...

She was in no way anticipating that he would grab her, then roll her under him to begin tickling and ruthlessly nuzzling her neck.

Jasmine screamed and giggled. "You asshole!" she exclaimed, trying to get away from him. They rolled around on the floor for a bit, when another alarm sounded. She had a sudden burst of adrenaline and managed to push him off.

"The macaroni!" she yelled, and he was once again looking at her bare bottom as she dashed for the kitchen.

It was going to be an interesting weekend.

Autumn in Perdition

Jasmine wanted to keep an open mind about the upcoming weekend. AJ's parents would stay in the very nice guest room, and her parents, who had been more or less amicably divorced for more than a decade. Her father would stay in the smaller of the two guest rooms in the main house, and her mother would spend the weekend in the guest house, which Jasmine had temporarily vacated in order to keep her parents separated and make things easier for her mother, who had persistent knee problems. As they drove into town on that beautiful crisp fall day, Jasmine was optimistic about how the weekend would turn out.

This weekend had been AJ's idea, a way to bring the families together for the first time. The subtext was clear, and always came back to one thing: AJ wanted Jasmine to move in with him. Never mind that they practically lived together as it was...he wanted to wake up to her every morning, to rent out the guest house and bring some permanence to their relationship.

AJ had brought up moving in with him several times in the past few months, and had made a number of persuasive arguments. They got along quite well, and had from the beginning (completely true — they rarely argued). They had fantastic chemistry (indeed, they'd had passionate, hair-pulling sex the night before, followed by a quickie in the family room that morning). They had the same approach to finances (live a little, but plan for the future. All indicators pointed to relationship longevity for the two of them.

And yet...

It somehow wasn't enough for her to be able to commit to him. AJ was a good "catch." She moved forward in the relationship to the extent she could, but something kept her from throwing caution to the wind and giving herself to this man.

"What time does the train come in?" AJ said, breaking into Jasmine's thoughts.

"A little after two, same as the last time you asked me," she said, lifting an eyebrow at him. He knew full well what time their parents would be arriving.

"When did I last ask you!" His face reflected genuine confusion.

"Honey, you asked me this about four times in the last couple of days," she teased him. "I'm starting to think you're more invested in this weekend than you're letting on."

He gave her a sidelong glance.

"Baby..." he started, only to be interrupted by Jasmine.

"I already told you that we can talk about me moving in after the holidays," she said. "Holidays. As in after Thanksgiving. After Christmas."

"You might as well make it official, you're at my place so often," he said, sparing her a quick glance, his green eyes sparkling with good humor.

"You think?" She asked. Irritated, she shifted in her seat, wondering how he could be so presumptuous.

"I don't think. I know." He gave her a smug look.

"I haven't given you an answer yet," she pointed out. "Don't get ahead of yourself."

They came to a stop in front of Richard's Hardware. AJ planned to purchase a replacement thermometer for the oven, as his had been on the fritz for a while. They still had time before they were to pick up their parents.

Still annoyed by their earlier exchange, Jasmine told AJ that she would meet him at the Perdition Glide Depot. He started to follow her, but she put a hand up to stop him.

"Just go ahead and get the thermometer," she barked, her patience at an end. "I'm going down to Auntie's place. I'll meet you at the Glide, okay?" He started to speak, and she glared at him. He twisted his lips into an impatient pout.

"Is this what you plan to do whenever we have a disagreement?" He asked. Before she could respond, AJ gave her a glowering frown, then turned on his heel to go into the hardware store. Jasmine watched him go, admiring the attractiveness of his broad shoulders and tight ass, then reminding herself she was mad at him.

This.

This drama was the reason why she didn't want to move in with him. She wanted to get away from him, whenever she got mad at him, without a fuss. She could never get away from her ex, Jesse, when she needed space — he wouldn't allow it. Before her parents divorced, they never took a break from one another, and she and her younger sister were subjected to their constant bickering. She didn't want to go there again, and potentially ruin a great relationship with too much...togetherness.

With a frustrated sigh, she turned away from AJ and the hardware store, and headed down the street to Auntie's apothecary.

WE ARE FAMILY

"Were you able to find that part you needed?" Jasmine asked when AJ arrived at the Glide depot. His expression tensed, and she wondered whether he was still annoyed about their earlier disagreement.

"Yeah, about that," he started, looking a little sheepish, his dark green eyes watching her intently. "I ran into Mr. Richards."

"Well, it's his hardware store," she quipped, "so that hardly seems surprising." She smiled at him, hoping to lighten the mood. She glanced down the train tracks to look for the Glide car.

He smiled back at her, his tense expression easing a bit. He looked good enough to eat in a forest green sweater that set off his beautiful eyes, and a pair of faded jeans.

"You know how Mr. Richards is..." he looked on the verge of a confession and it was her turn to go tense. Everyone in Perdition knew how Mr. Richards was. Nosy. Meddling. Often lacking a brain-to-mouth filter.

"What about him?" she asked, cocking her head at AJ.

"Well, he sort of hinted that his video screen was on the fritz...and he was going to miss the Dallas and D.C. game..."

"And then what?" she prodded, moving close enough to wrap her arms around his abdomen. It was near impossible to stay annoyed with this man, who was so sweet to her, and way too adorable to resist. She laid her cheek against his chest, enjoying his manly scent.

"I told him he and his wife could swing by after dinner and watch the game with us," he admitted.

She tensed for a moment, then relaxed against him.

Shrugging, she said, "Could be worse."

He set her away from him and looked at her, his brows creased with worry. "You don't mind?"

"Hey, at least my parents will have to be on their best behavior," she quipped.

He smiled at her. "You have no idea how relieved that makes me."

She snuggled into his sweater-clad chest again. He smelled so *good*.

"It's not a big deal. I know this weekend is important to you," she told him. AJ's commitment to family was one of the things she loved about him.

When the Glide pulled into the station, Jasmine was more relaxed and was actually looking forward to meeting AJ's parents in person. She just needed her parents to behave.

As he drove his and Jasmine's families home from the Glide depot, AJ wondered what it would take to get Jasmine's parents to behave. First, they brought with them Jasmine's younger sister, Petunia, whom AJ knew existed, but wasn't expecting.

Jasmine's mother, Dahlia, had simply waved a hand dismissively and stated that they couldn't leave her alone for the holiday. Luckily, the house was large and built in an era when families had many children, so they had space for "Tutu," as her sister was known. And on the subject of nicknames, he was surprised to find his beloved also had a nickname, "Jazzy," which made a lot of sense, but which had oddly enough, never occurred to him as a nickname.

Jasmine, who had not exactly been on board with this holiday weekend idea, was even less happy with the addition of her sister. She had pulled her sister and mother aside and engaged in a whisper-screaming match while AJ helped his parents get their bags into his Suburban. Once he got his parents settled, along with

Jasmine's father Edward, AJ returned to the women, who were hissing like a herd of cats.

"Mom! You can't just show up with a whole extra person and expect us to be okay with that!"Jasmine told her mother, waving her arms in irritation.

"Jazzy, where else am I supposed to go?" asked Tutu, who appeared to be a younger, shorter version of her sister.

Jasmine glared at her sister. "You should go where you are invited. And don't call me 'Jazzy.'"

AJ stood a discreet distance away, wondering what hornet's nest he'd stepped into with these women. How had his sweet girlfriend morphed into a shrieking harpy?

"Honey, it's okay," AJ stepped into the conversation, cautiously, hoping to defuse the situation. "We have plenty of room."

AJ ended with a confident smile. He stroked her back, which was oddly stiff under his touch. He turned curious eyes on her, and saw Jasmine's glare now directed at him. It was kind of cute, actually, because she looked like an angry wet kitten. Cute...but also unnerving.

"Sweetie—" he started, only to be interrupted by Jasmine's snappish reply.

"Fine," said Jasmine, stomping off toward the suburban. AJ flashed his most charming smile at Petunia and Dahlia. He swept an arm in front of the two women in and "after you" gesture and follow the women to the car. Jasmine sat in the passenger seat, brows knit and arms crossed, fuming. She would not look at AJ as he settled behind the wheel and turned the car on.

Definitely, this was going to be a long weekend.

Sweet Potato Pie

While AJ got their guests settled, Jasmine slammed around the kitchen, yanking open drawers, setting pots on the stove with a bang, and generally letting everyone within earshot know that she was preparing the Thanksgiving feast.

Not that anyone cares that I'm doing all the work...

Jasmine's parents at on successful real estate company throughout her childhood, and devoted much of their off hours time to client demands. As a result, the Greenes did not have regular sit-down dinners. Holiday meals were generally purchased from restaurants, delivered to their home, and arranged on the dining room table by their housekeeper. Of the four Greenes, only Jasmine enjoyed cooking. When she was old enough to prepare Holiday meals, she did all the planning, all the food purchases, and all the preparation. Her parents merely paid for the groceries and showed up at the appointed time.

Jasmine long since accepted that her family had a light touch when it came to holiday preparations. She knew that when she agreed to Host everyone at their house for the holiday, that she would have to do all of the food preparation. She agreed to it anyway, because she knew that AJ was keen for their families to meet before she moved into the main house with him.

If. If I move in...

She also knew that even as an only child, AJ had had an idyllic childhood, with two doting parents, a close-knit extended family, and all the childhood milestones usually only encountered in family-friendly films. When Jasmine decided to leave Jesse, she'd made an effort to find a story book town to live in.

Perdition, a pack town founded by wolf shifters more than 200 years ago, fit the bill. Everyone knew shifters were family oriented. And even though Jasmine and AJ were full humans, the town considered all its residents to be pack members. The fact that her aunt had already moved to Perdition several years ago made the decision to settle there easy. She reminded herself that the irritation of the next few days was a small price to pay for AJ's happiness. He'd wanted her to move in for months, and she had more or less decided to take the plunge. Yet, she could not bring herself to say the words she knew he wanted to hear: *yes I'll move in with you.*

Jasmine gave the small pot of fresh cranberries and sugar boiling in a small saucepan a stir, added orange peel zest, then turned down the heat to a simmer. She took out flour, yeast, and all the ingredients needed for tomorrow's fresh baked rolls and set them on the counter. As she prepared to make bread dough, their guests started trickling into the kitchen area.

"Let me help you, dear," said Anne Cotter, AJ's mother. She was a tall, attractive woman with strawberry blonde hair that was similar to AJ's. She and Jasmine had been planning the meal in advance of the Cotter's travel from their retirement home in Belize, first flying into Dallas, then taking the Glide train into Perdition.

Jasmine offered Anne a tremulous smile. "Thanks," she said, handing the older woman an apron. Anne took over the bread making and was measuring ingredients into the mixer when Dahlia and Petunia appeared at the breakfast bar.

"How's everything coming?" Petunia asked brightly. She smiled and watched Jasmine and Anne as they continued with meal prep.

"So far so good," Jasmine said, giving her sister or brother pointed look. "You know, you're welcome to help out with the meal prep." Jasmine already knew what the answer to this would be, but after her sister had simply invited herself for the holiday weekend, she was feeling churlish and wanted to put Tutu on the spot.

Jasmine's sister and her mother's eyes went wide. They both looked at each other, and burst out laughing.

"You know your sister can even boil water," Dahlia said, wiping tears from her eyes. She gave AJ's mother a sheepish look. "I don't know if my daughter told you, but we never cooked big meals like this when she was growing up. I tried, but I didn't get the cooking gene."

Anne smiled at the other woman. "No worries. Jasmine and I have been working on the menu for while, so I think we have it under control. Why don't you two go get some fresh air? The weather is beautiful today."

Jasmine gave Anne a curious look. The older woman's gracious-
ness made Jasmine feel small and mean. She really did not seem to
care that the Greene women weren't going to help out with
preparing the holiday meal.

"I think we'll do that," said Dahlia, giving her younger daughter
a quick hug. "After all that travel, I'd like to stretch my legs a
little."

Mother and daughter left the house at the kitchen door, and
Jasmine was relieved. It was better than having the two women
there, doing nothing more than watching Jasmine and Anne make
dinner.

Right on their heels of the women's back-door exit, AJ, his
father DJ, and Edward entered the kitchen. AJ walked up to
Jasmine to hug her from behind, slipping his arms around her
waist. By then, Jasmine had forgotten her earlier annoyance with
him and offered her cheek for a kiss.

"Y'all just missed the ladies," Jasmine said, and nodding at the
back door.

Jasmine's father chuckled. "My daughter is only been here a
year, and already she speaks Texan."

Jasmine beamed at her dad. "You have to admit, 'y'all' is more
efficient than 'you all' or 'you guys.' "

Edward Greene walked up to his daughter and gave her a quick
kiss on the cheek.

"It already smells good in here. I hope your grandmother's
sweet potato pie is on the menu for tomorrow," said Jasmine's
father, looking around the kitchen for evidence of pie making.

"Oh, Daddy, of course it is. It wouldn't be Thanksgiving
without Grandma's sweet potato pie."

Jasmine lips trembled with emotion, thinking about the
Saturday afternoons spent at her grandmother's house. While her
parents focused on showing houses to clients on the weekends,
Jasmine spent that time at Grandma Sadie's house, learning how to
cook. Petunia had no interest in learning any of Sadie's famous
dishes and was content to let others cook for her. Saturday after-

noons were her special time with Grandma Sadie, who had passed away eight years before.

AJ kept his arms around Jasmine, nuzzling her neck in a PG-rated sort of way. "I'll have you know, your daughter was up before dawn boiling sweet potatoes."

Jasmine smiled and shrugged her shoulders in a "what can I say?" gesture.

"My daughter is just like her mother," Edward said. Jasmine tensed, wondering what dig her father would have against her mother.

AJ, perhaps sensing Jasmine's tension, gave a noncommittal, "Really?"

"Son, Dahlia is a terrible sleeper. Jasmine stopped taking naps when she was eighteen months old. Just an FYI."

Jasmine was relieved that her father had nothing negative to say about her moth, and also warmed at Edward's use of "son" when addressing AJ. She let out a small, contented sigh. AJ again nuzzled her neck, then whispered in her ear softly enough that anyone not blessed with shifter senses would not be able to hear.

"It's going to be a great weekend." His lips brushed her earlobe and she had to restrain herself from shivering in response.

It was by then late afternoon. Once they set the bread out to rise overnight, and the cranberry sauce to chill in the refrigerator, they were done with meal prep for the day. AJ had been brining the turkey in the garage refrigerator all day. In the morning, he would flay and barbecue the turkey. In addition to everyone already gathered, Auntie would be by for dinner the following day. Mr. and Mrs. Richards were invited to watch the football game after dinner.

AJ, Jasmine, his parents and her father chatted about holiday, their plans for Christmas and the new year, until Petunia and Dahlia returned from their walk. They all shared a simple dinner of Chinese take-out, popped popcorn over a crackling fire, and watched holiday films.

Jasmine was surprised and pleased at how well her parents were

getting along, and chalked it up to the holiday spirit and maybe —
just maybe – a desire to make a good impression on AJ's family.
Even the unexpected presence of Tutu couldn't detract from
Jasmine's warm feelings and mellow mood.

At about 10 o'clock everyone went to their separate quarters:
Edward to the smaller guest room that had once been AJ's nursery,
Petunia to the loft space above the game room, DJ and Anne to
the larger of the guest rooms. Jasmine's mother had had knee
issues for the past several years and was given the guesthouse to
save her the trauma of climbing stairs.

Jasmine felt her optimism rebounding as she said goodnight to
everyone. She had her family all together under one roof, and a
man she was crazy about to keep her warm at night.

Life truly didn't get much better than this.

THANKSGIVING DAY

The moment AJ opened the garage cooler Thanksgiving morning, he knew something was wrong. A blast of cold air greeted him
as he swung the door open. Very cold air. Colder than a refrigerator. About as cold as a freezer.

Icicles hung like miniature stalactites from the wire shelves. A
giant stock pot, which he had been using over the past several days
to gradually thaw the turkey in the brining solution made with his
mother's recipe, had telltale signs of frost clinging to its sides.

Dread gathered in the pit of his stomach.

Please don't be frozen. Please don't be frozen.

This was his fervent prayer as he slid the stockpot out of the
cooler. The turkey sloshed around in the pot, and he thought
perhaps his prayers have been answered. However, a peek inside
revealed a layer of ice had formed in the brine covering the turkey,
in much the same way as a pond freezes over in winter.

He set the pot down on the garage floor, closed the cooler,
then looked at the stockpot warily, as he might eye a rattlesnake in

his path. He leaned over, poked two fingers into the pot. They punched through the membrane of ice and came into contact with the turkey. While the skin seemed pliable, the bird's underlying meat had none of the slack one would expect of a thawed turkey. It was beyond firm. It was frozen. Definitely frozen.

Shit. Shit. Shit.

He stepped away from the pot in horror, wiped a hand down the side of his face, and tried not to swear out loud.

How has this happened?

He no sooner had the thought when he realized exactly how it had happened. Garages were where refrigerators retired, when the owner invested in a newer model. His had to be at least thirty years old, and while it was usually fine for keeping beer cold in the summer, it's demise had been inevitable for at least a decade.

Shit. Shit. Shit.

His thoughts immediately went Jasmine. He could just imagine the look on her face when he told her that the turkey wouldn't be ready in time for dinner.

Shit. Shit. Shit.

AJ stood there, looking at the turkey as if wishing it were thawed would magically make it so.

What was he going to do?

The garage door swung open, and there stood his father, looking at him with puzzlement in his eyes.

"Son?" DJ strode into the garage, concern written across his face. "Everything okay?

Thought about assuring his father that all was well, then decided against it. He dragged a hand through his hair and scrubbed his scalp with frustration.

"It's frozen dad."

JASMINE WAS PLEASED WITH THE PROGRESS WITH DINNER. SHE congratulated herself for having the foresight to make many of the side dishes well before Thanksgiving. The green beans had been washed, cut, and seasoned the night before. All that remained was to make the bacon that would add flavor and color to the green bean side dish.

The sweet potato pies had also been put together the night before, and only needed to be extracted from the garage cooler and placed in the oven in a few hours, to bake. Anne had prepared potato salad the night before, and it too chilled in the garage overnight. The candied yams would be easy to put together, since she already had the cooked sweet potatoes.

Jasmine had planned so well that she didn't have much to do, so she decided to go have a little quiet time in the master bedroom. AJ would be getting the turkey ready, and his father and mother had plans to visit with friends in town. Her father had decided to join Dahlia and Tutu for a walk in the country. Jasmine looked forward to the opportunity to stretch out and relax before was time to finish up dinner and entertain guests.

THREE HOURS LATER...

Jasmine awoke to a darkened room, with no idea how long she'd been asleep. She noticed with a smile that the blinds had been pulled closed while she was asleep. AJ must have crept into the room, and closed the blinds while she was asleep.

He's always thinking about me....

Jasmine stretched like a kitten who had fallen asleep at her mother's nipple. She couldn't remember ever feeling so rested and content. She sat up, swung her legs over the side of the bed, and went through the mental checklist of what she still needed to do before it was time for the Thanksgiving feast.

Using a voice command she asked the local Omni network the time, and was surprised to find it was just two hours before they were to sit down for the meal. She calculated in her mind what still needed to be done, and realized that she had plenty of time to finish cooking, even with her impromptu nap.

She rolled her shoulders, stretched her neck, and rose to her feet.

Time to get the side dishes in the garage refrigerator warmed up...

in the garage, she found an odd sight. There was an old wooden table to the right of the refrigerator, covered in what appeared to be bits and pieces of turkey flesh. On the table were several kitchen knives.

Weird.

She opened the refrigerator and frowned at the tiny icicles hanging from the shelves.

What the hell?

She didn't have much time to think about what this meant, because with the sinking heart she pulled out one of the pies, unbaked, with frost covering them. And it wasn't just a light dusting of frost, but hoary crystals of ice all around the edge of the pies crust and the top. She tapped the bottom of the pie experimentally, and realized to her horror that it was frozen solid.

"I can still make this work," she muttered under her breath. She had never tried to freeze Grandma Sadie's pies, but they sold frozen pies all the time, right? She thought they would still be okay if they were baked from a frozen state.

It then occurred to her that all of the overflow dishes, including the string beans, the potato salad, and the green salads they had prepared the night before would not fare as well. Extracting the items from the refrigerator proved her instincts correct. The salads were a frozen mess, covered in frost. Some of the leaves were transparent. Totally inedible.

The green beans were also covered in frost. The potato salad was a solid, frozen mass. It looked like the fake food that comes with a child's cooking playset.

As Jasmine stood in front of the open refrigerator, wondering what she could do to salvage the meal, she heard chopping sounds coming from outside. Brows wrinkled in confusion, she opened the garage door and followed what sounded like someone wielding an axe. A few yards away from the house, she found AJ holding a red-handled axe, a frozen turkey perched carefully on the stump she knew AJ used to cut wood. His parents stood at a safe distance, watching him whack away at a still frozen turkey with a vengeance. She stood there in stunned silence, trying to parse the meaning of it all.

The turkey resisted attempts to cleave it in two. AJ would give it a whack, and it would remain stubbornly whole. He tried hitting it harder, only to see axe bounce off the bird, which would then simply slide off the stump.

"AJ... honey ... what are you doing?" He whirled around and his gaze landed on her. He looked oh, so guilty.

She actually had an idea of what he was doing, and what had happened to bring him to this point. She knew because this was the man she had come to love over the past nine months. She realized in that moment that not only did she love this man, but she was *in love* with him.

She was so, so screwed. No matter how flawed the logic that brought him to this point of absurdity, where hacking a frozen turkey seemed like a good idea, she was in love with this man, and this bizarre display would do nothing to stop the inevitability of their union.

Jasmine could see in her mind's eye how the scenario played out: the discovery of the broken refrigerator via the frozen state of their turkey. The resulting panic must have led him to create a workable solution. Once that failed, feeling he had nothing to lose, he'd resorted to an act of desperation involving a frozen turkey with no hope of being thawed. Maybe he thought cutting it would make it cook faster? In any event, the turkey, which had already sacrificed its life for their meal, now suffered the indignity of having its hapless corpse mutilated.

His eyes on her looked concerned. Serious. And a little sheepish. His parents looked at him, then at each other, then at her. The all had the look of a child being caught with his hand in the cookie jar. He put the axe down and walked towards her. He raised a hand, placed it on her shoulder, and began to speak...

Only to be interrupted by Jasmine's mother, father and younger sister stumbling out of the wooded area some distance away from the house, and into the clearing. They looked befuddled, and Jasmine had a distant thought that now everyone who mattered would be on-hand to witness what would surely be a Thanksgiving tale for the ages.

"What's going on here?" Dahlia sputtered, eyeing the turkey, the axe, and AJ's purposeful walk towards her older daughter. "What are you doing?" Dahlia demanded.

Something about how her family was so useless when it came to celebrating the holidays most people pulled out all the stops on, while AJ would apparently do anything to make Jasmine's holiday special, really touched Jasmine.

"Mom, it's okay," Jasmine said, smiling at AJ. "It's all under control."

AJ pulled Jasmine into his arms and began to explain the situation, but she leaned back and placed two fingers over his lips.

"It doesn't matter," she told him.

His eyes went warm and tender when they connected with hers. He leaned in to whisper into her ear.

"You're in love with me," he told her as if she hadn't just said those words to him.

She shrugged nonchalantly. "Yeah, I know."

He put an arm around her waist and led her away from the house. Behind them, they heard Jasmine's parents bickering about what to do with the turkey. She knew their truce wouldn't last long. Good thing she put them in rooms far, far away from one another.

"I was wondering when you were going to get around to telling me that," he traced a finger up her spine and chuckled. "I'm in love with you too, in case that wasn't already obvious..."

"I figured as much," she said.

"And all I had to do was ruin dinner to get you to admit it," he teased.

She chuckled. "You know, maybe we should just keep walking and let them fend for themselves," she suggested. She looked up at him, raising an eyebrow. Then she gave him a saucy little hip bump, not caring who might see them.

"Tempting," he admitted. "Probably not a good idea."

He steered them back toward the house, where their guests stood around the turkey, now covered in specks of grass. They all looked at the bird as if it were a meteor fallen from the heavens.

"Since you said yourself that you're in love with me, perhaps we should seal the deal and move you into the main house?" His face reflected the hope that her answer would be "yes."

She disengaged and looked him in the eye.

"After the holidays," she reminded him.

FAMILY BUSINESS

Dinner consisted of cornbread dressing for the turkey, grits and cheese (Anne Cotter's last-minute contribution to the meal), cornbread muffins, along with the dinner rolls Anne and Jasmine had made the night before. The turkey, which had already suffered so much, was wrapped neatly and placed in a sealed trash bag, and discarded, the better to discourage discovery by wild animals. After some debate, the hosts and guests settled on breakfast sausage as the main course. It wasn't exactly a twenty-pound grilled turkey, but it would do.

AJ thought this disaster dinner would discourage their families from showing up for the holidays, and expecting something fancy.

The frozen pies took took their sweet time baking all the way through. Jasmine set the frozen non-dairy topping on the kitchen counter to thaw while they waited for the pies to bake. AJ tuned into the pregame programming before the Dallas-Washington game, which was held every year on Thanksgiving. Edward, Tutu,

Dahlia, along with DJ and Anne gathered on the massive sectional to watch the game. DJ poked popcorn in the fireplace — like the pilgrims once did — and they settled in for the game while Jasmine and AJ cleaned up after dinner. Since there weren't many dishes that edible, there wasn't much to the cleanup afterwards.

Richards and his wife showed up around halftime, bearing freshly baked oatmeal cookies. The Greenes and the Cotters fell upon the treats like a herd of ravenous javelinas. Not long after that, the sweet potato pies were at last baked through enough to eat.

Although the evening hadn't gone the way AJ had hoped, things seem to be falling into place again. Everyone's spirits were high, thanks to the hot toddies, liberally laced with Hennessy and honey. They all agreed they'd have a funny Thanksgiving story to tell for years to come.

Jasmine's parents were the early to bed types. Dahlia announced, after dessert and boozed up hot chocolate, that she was more than ready for bed. She swayed toward the back door, headed for the guest house. Not long after, Edward stated he was going out for some fresh air before turning in for the evening.

Jasmine sat on the couch, snuggled up with AJ's arms around her. When she seemed close to nodding off, he nudged her.

"Ready for bed?" He asked her softly in her ear.

She nodded, gave him one of her sweet smiles, and stretched like a cat. "Yeah, I should get to bed. After I check on mom. Need to make sure she doesn't need anything.

AJ stood up, reach for her hands, and pulled her to her feet.

"Need any help out there?" He asked her.

"Nah, I'll just check on her and go to bed. Be back in a few minutes."

He watched her walk out the back door.

Barely a minute later, she was back. She closed the back door, leaned against it. Their eyes connected. Her eyes were big as saucers as she stared into space.

He met her at the back door, a little concerned.

"You okay?"

She managed a slight smile, and nodded. "I'm fine," she said.

"I love you," he said, enjoying the way the phrase rolled off his tongue.

"I love you too," she said, her dark eyes shining.

Jasmine said good night to the guests and headed to bed. When he joined her hours later she was still awake, one brown leg poking out from the white duvet. It was unlike her to still be awake. While she was a restless sleeper, she usually had no problems falling asleep when she needed to. He got ready for bed, undressed, and joined her, pulling her body into his in a spooning position.

She cleared her throat, and with her back still to AJ, and spoke.

"I went out to check on my mother, and walked in on my parents fucking on the kitchen counter."

He sat up quickly and looked at her. "They're divorced," he stated, knowing the moment he said it that divorced couples did sometimes have sex.

"I know they're divorced," she said. "And you know what? I'm ready to move in with you."

That caught him completely off guard.

"Really?" Elation swept over him at her words. "Is it because you said you love me?"

"Well, that's part of it," she admitted.

She stopped talking. He waited for her to continue, and was about to prompt her to go on, when she spoke again.

"The other part is that I don't think there's enough bleach in the world to disinfect that counter," she said with a sigh. "And I will never be able to look at that kitchen the same way again. It is a vision that I cannot unsee."

He lay down again, pulled her into his body, and kissed her shoulder. He smiled against her skin.

"At this point, I'll take what I can get," he told her.

❄

7/8 HOME 1000

Sunday afternoon, Jasmine and AJ shuttled their families to the Perdition Glide depot to see them off. Hugs were exchanged, well wishes were given, and everyone had a good laugh remembering the Great Thanksgiving Debacle of 2080.

As the Glide pulled away from the station, AJ gave Jasmine a hug, then bit his head to kiss her. He was *really* looking forward to having the house to themselves after four days of entertaining relatives.

"So," Jasmine began, as they drove back to AJ's house. "That didn't go as poorly as I thought it would."

"Yes," he agreed. "Even your parents managed to put aside their differences for the sake of family unity and peace."

"Don't get me started," she said. Jasmine hadn't mentioned anything further about her parents since the "incident" on Thanksgiving night.

"You aren't happy to see your parents getting along so much better these days?" He gave her a sidelong smirk.

"I really could have gone to my grave with seeing my dad's pants around his ankles, his brown butt cheeks, and my mother's come face," said Jasmine, rolling her eyes.

She hadn't mentioned those details before. Now AJ wished she hadn't, because whenever he saw her parents in the future, them having sex would be what his mind returned to over and over. And over.

He let out an involuntary shudder. She chuckled at his reaction.

"So I've been thinking of how we should handle this move," she said, before launching into a to-do list related to her moving her things a few yards from the guest house to his house. She went on and on, until AJ couldn't take any more.

"Jasmine, baby, you're not moving cross-country here," he told her. "Just pack your stuff, and move it to my place. If there's something you can't move by yourself, I'll move it."

This took the wind out of her sails for a moment, but then she recovered and went into a spiel about a change of address form at the Perdition post office, notifying her job of her change in relationship status. Because moving in together entitled her man to health and dental benefits, which might work out to be cheaper than what he was currently paying for health care.

She chattered on all the way out of town, and during the ten minute ride home. They pulled to a stop in the driveway, and he turned to give her his full attention.

"Jasmine?"

She looked at him, puzzled? "Huh? What's wrong?"

"Nothing."

He took a deep breath, reached across her to open the glove box. Her eyes followed his movements, especially when he removed a midnight blue velvet jewelry box and closed his glove box. He opened it to show it to her. Inside was a beautiful ruby, surrounded by a halo of brilliant diamonds.

She gasped, held her fingers to cover her mouth. Her eyes moved from the engagement ring, to his eyes, then back again. Her big brown eyes shone with tears.

"Jasmine Greene, will you marry me?"

She reached over to give him a hug.

"I...take it that's a yes?" he mumbled against her shoulder, enjoying her scent, thinking about how wonderful their life together would be.

She looked at him again, brows wrinkled and eyes wide.

"It's....a yes. A big huge yes!"

Feliz Chanukah! by Meg Bellamy

✿❀✿

"I UNDERSTAND THAT YOU VISITED SANTA AT THE SHOPPING center and you have a photo of yourself with the big man," Ana Maria Flores said to her adorable patient.

Tiny seven-year-old Emma Mallory—far smaller than most children her age because of the cardiac problems that brought her to Ana Maria's clinic—proudly brandished the glossy portraits and flashed a grin missing a few key teeth.

"Santa said that, this year, I'm going to get all better."

Ana Maria squeezed Emma's hand. "That would be the present I'd ask Santa for too," she said softly.

Emma giggled. "That's silly. You're too big to sit on Santa's lap."

They both laughed together, and Emma gave Ana Maria a copy of the special photo.

If only all it took to bring healing to Emma and the other patients in her pediatric cardiology practice was a chat with Santa...

Fortunately, Ana Maria was able to help many of the little people who came to her. Exhausting and, at times, discouraging as this work could be, knowing how much healing she brought to many children kept her enthusiastic about her daily work.

And, speaking of enthusiasm, Ana Maria treasured stepping
out of her office in downtown San Francisco and breathing in the
special scents and joy of the holiday season. Winter might be a bit
of a bear to get through, but at least the light-filled holidays were a
great way to ring in the special season.

She especially treasured this particular time because her loved
ones made it a point to spend more time together than usual. Ana
Maria adored her family. And she loved Chanukah, which her large
and boisterous family celebrated with as much gusto as Christmas,
Passover, Easter, and Cinco de Mayo, along with every other
holiday they could find the slightest excuse to celebrate. It was one
of the joys of being part of a mixed family. No single faith could
suffice to contain the Flores-Guzmán-López-García clan's joy for
living.

But Chanukah was one of her favorites. There was something
she loved about the ancient foundations of the holiday, which celebrated the independent spirit of the Maccabees in their revolt
against the dominant Hellenic culture of their time. Not to
mention the joys of latkes and sour cream. With or without
jalapeños and applesauce fragrant with cinnamon.

This year, there was someone new to heighten the excitement
of the holidays: Carlo Fiori, an attorney she had met at her
friend Monica's housewarming. Carlo had handled the complicated legal maneuverings that made Monica a happy first-time
homeowner. Ana Maria and Carlo had been on several dates, and
she found herself looking forward with joy at getting to know
him more. Though it might have been early to introduce Carlo
to her family, Ana Maria couldn't imagine not including him in
their holiday.

When they met for a quick drink after work, she issued her
invitation. "Your family celebrates Chanukah?" Carlo Fiori's raised
eyebrow accentuated the surprised element in his question.

Ana Maria expected the question. This wasn't the first time
she'd heard it, and it wouldn't be the last. "Of course. My family
loves celebrations. Doesn't yours?"

He looked taken aback. "My family loves celebrations too but—"

Good to know. Granted, Carlo and I are new to being together, but a family who doesn't love celebrations...that would be a deal breaker.

"But what, Carlo?"

He shrugged. "But Chanukah isn't one we've tried—yet." She melted when he smiled, and she liked that he'd added that *yet*. Carlo was one of the hottest, fastest-rising young attorneys in San Francisco. Ana Maria liked to think that she wasn't biased, but usually she avoided lawyers like the plague. Maybe because her least-favorite cousin, Madlyn Guzmán, was a member of that profession. But charming, elegant Carlo might be the one to challenge her bias.

Carlo set down the martini he'd been sipping. The man dripped elegance. Despite living and working in dress-down-everyday San Francisco, Carlo always wore precisely-tailored Italian suits and wore a fresh flower in his lapel. He was the picture of tall, dark, and handsome; his intelligence and generosity of spirit were even more impressive than his sparkling brown eyes, chiseled features, and imposing Roman nose. "I did not know that Chicano families celebrated Jewish holidays," he pointed out.

She looked him square in the eyes. "What? You never heard of Mexican Jews? You never saw the movie *The Mexican Shiva*?"

Carlo Fiori didn't do sheepish, Ana Maria was sure. But the grin he flashed probably came as close as he might ever have done to being sheepish.

"*Mexican Shiva*? That was a movie?" He shook his head. "I sure would have lost the bet if anyone asked me if such a title existed. Sounds intriguing. I know shiva to be the practice of Jews who are mourning the deaths of family and friends. Isn't that right?"

"Yes. As you know, Jews come from many traditions. Shiva practices are one of the areas of commonality. Amongst other elements, there is always abundant food. Friends provide loads of food for the grieving folk and the people who come to support them. In fact, you might have seen a funny online video about people of many different communities using the death notices of shiva schedules as a guide of good places to go for free food. Stoners, foodies, starving students..."

Carlo laughed. "My tradition also pays attention to food, but I can't say I saw the video."

"Not to be missed. My whole family watched it multiple times, and we still laugh."

"Your family sounds even more intriguing. Tell me more."

Where to start? Granted, everyone's family had some weirdness. Hers could probably win an Olympic medal.

"When it comes to inclusivity, my family wrote the book. Mom's family may have been traditional Mexican-Catholic, but Dad's clan includes Jews, Buddhists, Hindus, and several Muslims... even an agnostic or two. So we decided: why pick and choose among holidays when we can celebrate them all?"

"Kind of like a United Nations of families?" he asked.

"More like the European Union, with a Brexit referendum every other day."

He laughed again, which she took to be a good sign. Ana Maria had lost count of how many guys hit the exit once they heard about her family—and that was before the guys even met any of them. And then there were the guys who couldn't handle Ana Maria being a pediatric cardiologist. For far too long, her social life had been sparse to non-existent. With Carlo, she was feeling some warmth and optimism that had, lately, been absent from her life.

He'd agreed to go with her to her family's Chanukah celebration on the first night of the holiday. First hurdle cleared. Next would come actually spending the evening with her loved ones. Would Carlo still be around after lighting the candles and spinning the dreidel with her clan?

ANA MARIA TRIED TO STILL THE BUTTERFLIES IN HER BELLY AS she and Carlo went into her parents' elegant Society Hill house.

The delicious smells of roasted chicken and latkes fried in peanut oil filled the air, complemented by the sweet fragrance of holly. One side table bore ten menorahs, all with beeswax candles in primary colors waiting to be lit. Full, gorgeous poinsettias lent spots of color to other side tables. And a magnificently-decorated Christmas tree bloomed in one corner.

"Ana Maria," Mamá crooned. "So wonderful that you're here. It's been too long."

"Mamá, I saw you last week," Ana Maria reminded her.

"What I said. Too long."

"I agree," Papá said, pulling her into a big hug.

"Who is your friend?" Mamá asked.

Ana Maria did the honors, introducing Carlo to her parents.

"Thank you so much for including me in your celebration," Carlo said. "From what Ana Maria tells me, this is a very special time for your family, and I'm honored to be able to share this with you." He handed her the elegant box of chocolates he'd brought as a hostess gift. Ana Maria's mother accepted it with pleasure.

"What a lovely gift. We all love chocolates. Thank you." Mamá positioned her hands on her ample bosom and got the slightest bit teary. "We are the ones who are honored to have you with us." Papá nodded, though Ana Maria could see he wasn't quite as easily won over as Mamá had been.

"Please also accept this gift, from my family to yours." He handed Papá a bottle of wine from the Fiori vineyards in Italy. Papá loved Italian wine. It looked as if Papá might be won over after all.

"What the fuck are you doing here?" a harsh, ugly voice screeched out, instantly corrupting the warm, inviting atmosphere. It was Cousin Madlyn, once again butting herself in where she didn't belong.

"Madlyn!" Both Mamá and Papá admonished in chorus.

"Carlo is a welcome guest in our home. Your language is not acceptable," Mamá said in her most scolding voice. "Please apologize and speak to us all with respect and affection."

"Apologize? Respect? Affection? Carlo Fiori a welcome guest in the bosom of my family?" Madlyn spluttered like an incoherent bovine choking on cud. Ana Maria had never seen her verbose cousin at such a loss for words and wasn't the only one apparently struck wordless. An eddy of shocked silence swirled around them. Madlyn recovered first and geared herself up to resume hurling spite.

"*Dios mío*," Madlyn began, invoking the seldom-summoned deity in the language she used only when strategically effective. "That man may appear to be an elegant professional, but in reality he is the sharkiest of shark lawyers. He's the kind that gives us all a bad reputation. Widows and orphans abandon all hope when he shows up."

When Madlyn paused to take a much-needed breath, Ana Maria took a quick visual survey of the others in the room. Carlo's face bore a neutral expression, as if he were taking in what happened as a casual bystander. *Just gathering the facts, ma'am.* Ana Maria admired his ability to keep calm in the face of her cousin's onslaught, though she couldn't help noticing that the tiniest of smiles appeared to be quirking up a corner of his very sensuous lips.

Carlo was calm, but the same could not be said for Mamá and Papá. Madlyn's loud voice would soon attract more attention, and Ana Maria dreaded having a circle of relatives form around them.

In an effort to defuse the situation, in the calmest voice she could assume, Ana Maria said, "Carlo is my invited guest in my parents' home. Both for the sake of hospitality and to ensure we all really celebrate tonight, please speak quietly and, if you really can't bring yourself to wait for a more appropriate time, briefly state what your concerns are."

Madlyn snorted and then glared equally hard at both Ana Maria and Carlo, but at least, when she spoke, it was in a slightly more reasonable tone of voice. Maybe they could still manage to keep the evening from turning into a disaster—or, really, *more* of a disaster. Though when she mentally reviewed other family events that she and Madlyn had attended, Ana Maria had to admit that brawls and other fighting were becoming more common. What was Madlyn's problem—and what could they do to fix it?

"Count on you, little cousin—the big-shot cardiologist— instead of a lowly lawyer like me, to find the worst-of-the-worst to bring as a date to your family party. Just after I broke up with my long-time boyfriend, you have to show up with a date guaranteed to make me puke up the few latkes and sour cream I can force myself to eat."

Ana Maria could barely refrain from rolling her eyes. She suspected that Carlo could match her, eye roll for eye roll, after that onslaught. It would be bad form to give Madlyn any real ammunition to fuel her snit, so Ana Maria needed to restrain herself and listen to what Madlyn had to say.

"Please, Madlyn, I think we all can agree that we want this evening to be a success. My Mamá and yours have worked very hard on the food, the décor, and the gifts. It would be a shame to ruin everyone's time, including yours and mine. So please, tell me in a calm, cool voice, why you are so upset to see my date. Let's see what we can do to make this better for everyone."

Madlyn swallowed hard and appeared to be giving herself a strong dose of self-talk. Then she began her story. "He pulled every dirty trick in the book when I came up against him in court, just last month. It was a divorce case. He and I were opposing counsel. He was unfair. Manipulative. Unethical. He demolished my poor client." She threw up her hands. "This is who you invite into your parents' home? I might have known that this is the kind of bottom-feeder you would bring. Having the brains to be a cardiologist doesn't mean you have any social sense when it comes to men."

Ana Maria had to bite her lip at that. Everyone in the family had been relieved when Madlyn finally broke up with Gunnar Gunderson the III. Or, rather, when Gunnar had finally walked out on Madlyn after they'd lived together for five years and disappeared with no forwarding address. Then there was Madlyn's jealousy over the respect that Ana Maria got for her profession.

Madlyn had been a jealous type since childhood, and Ana Maria had come to dread the inevitable confrontations. Ana Maria had lots of respect for Madlyn, both for the profession she'd chosen and the way she performed that role. Sadly, Madlyn didn't seem to respect herself in that way.

Before Ana Maria could come up with a response, Carlo began to talk. "Madlyn, I would never want to disrupt your family celebration. I cherish being with my own family, and I want to extend that same possibility to other families. So, if we really can't find a way for you to be comfortable with my being here, I will reluctantly take my leave tonight. Even if I did so, I would still hope to get to know Ana Maria better in the future, and maybe your family as well. So I'd like to make a start in resolving your concerns if we can do that sufficiently for this celebration to continue as planned."

Madlyn actually sniffled, sounding about as glamorous as a horse headed to the glue factory. "Why are you hanging out with a damned cardiologist anyway?" she spat out. "It's not like you've got anything in the place where there should be a heart. And any way, her practice is limited to pediatric cardiology."

By then, they had a circle around them, and Madlyn's last comment drew shocked gasps. Tía Margarita, Madlyn's Mamá, clutched her own heart in a gesture that might have frightened Ana Maria had she not known this was one of her aunt's stock moves.

Carlo, still looking impossibly hot and elegant, merely sighed. "You're not the first to make that accusation, and you probably won't be the last. I'll merely say, much as I admire Ana Maria's professional achievements, my interest in her is not professional, but personal."

At these words, Ana Maria—to her eternal consternation—blushed. Madlyn also turned bright red, but it was not from a blush.

Mamá wiped a tear from her eye. "Carlo, that was beautiful.

Please, you and everyone else, come to the table. It's time to light the candles, raise our glasses in a toast, and eat latkes."

"What? No, we can't eat yet. We haven't dealt with my issues. I won't sit down at the same table with that...that...*law fiend*." Madlyn folded her arms across her scrawny chest.

Everyone around them groaned. The latkes, as always, smelled amazing. Tummies grumbled. Ana Maria's was one. In view of the night's feast, she'd skipped lunch.

Papá nodded. "Madlyn, we all care about you and your concerns, but we also want to enjoy the feast before us. How about we do this: before we eat, let's have you and Carlo here spin the dreidel. Depending on which letter comes up, that person can speak first. And whoever speaks first, the other person will get last dibs on talking. What do you say?"

Madlyn knew when she'd been given an offer she couldn't refuse. She snorted, nodded, and went sit at the table with the rest of them. The evening would proceed with the spin of the wooden dreidel they'd last played with as children.

As they made their way to the beautifully-set table, with places set for Ana Maria's parents, Tía Margarita and her husband, Tío Luís, Madlyn (who'd come once again with no date), Ana Maria's brother Jorge, his wife—the grandly pregnant Blanca—and her parents, Patricia and Pedro, and, of course, Carlo and herself.

"While I am sad that not everyone in our family could be here tonight to celebrate the first night of Chanukah with us, I am grateful for those who are here," Mamá said. "We will start by lighting the first candle and, of course, the helper candle, the *shamesh*, tonight. Then we can have the dreidel game."

Ana Maria looked questioningly at Carlo, who nodded to her. "I have had the good fortune to attend other Chanukah celebrations," he said, "so it is not a total mystery to me. Though I will admit that I've seen other dreidels but have never seen the game played before."

"It's been a number of years for us since we played," Ana Maria said. "Usually, the dreidel is regarded as a toy for children."

Madlyn actually stuck out her tongue at her cousin, strengthening the association of playing the dreidel game with childhood.

"Madlyn," Tía Margarita chided, adding words in Spanish that brought a blush to her daughter's cheeks.

"Though I've seen other dreidels, I've never understood the significance of the Hebrew letters on each of the four sides. Please tell me what they mean," Carlo said in an even voice that served to defuse the tension Madlyn inspired.

Mamá held up a hand. "All in good time, Carlo. Now it is time to light the candles and say the prayers. Then we will toast each other with the special traditional Chanukah wine."

Ana Maria, Madlyn, and Jorge all rolled their eyes at this. "The special traditional Chanukah wine is vintage last Tuesday," Ana Maria warned Carlo.

"Or it could be from a hundred years ago," Jorge added. "It wouldn't matter. It all tastes exactly the same, Carlo. You look like a man who enjoys good wine."

Carlo nodded. "My family has an award-winning winery in Italy. We all have grown up with an appreciation of a good vintage."

Jorge joined the others in laughing. "Abandon any hopes of a good vintage in what you're about to drink. Our traditional wine has been unfavorably-compared to the sweet cough medicines people give their children."

Carlo raised a brow then shrugged. "I'm here for the total experience. I can always get good wine, but being in such company to experience a Chanukah celebration? That's unique."

Murmurs of approval all around, except for Madlyn, who rolled her eyes again. Jorge gave Carlo two thumbs up.

Mamá and Tía Margarita lit all the menorahs and candles. Those who knew the prayers recited them quickly, and then it was time for the threatened toast. Ana Maria sipped decorously and watched in amused surprise as Carlo took a healthy swig of the stuff. And refrained from making a face.

"Dreidel spin and talk," Madlyn insisted once it was clear everyone had drunk their fill of the wine.

Papá shook his head. "I changed my mind. Or my stomach changed my mind. First we eat, then we play and talk."

Madlyn protested that she had waited long enough to say her piece, but she quickly discovered she had no support.

Jorge said, "Blanca is starving. You know she's eating for two."

"Looks more like she's eating for herself and an elephant or two," Madlyn muttered, her words still clear enough for everyone to understand. Blanca's eyes filled with tears, and she laboriously pushed herself away from the table. Moving with whatever speed and grace were available to her, she left the room. After shooting a murderous glare at Madlyn, Jorge quickly followed, as did Blanca's parents. Tía Margarita directed some more Spanish admonitions at her daughter.

I've never seen Madlyn in such a bad mood. I wonder what's going on with her? Is it just Carlo being present that's having such an effect on her? I'd like to be nice to her because I feel a bit sorry for her, but she's being such a bitch. Making poor pregnant Blanca cry on Chanukah.

Mamá shook her head. "I'll go see what's happening. Maybe they'll be able to come back to the table in a few minutes, and we'll eat."

Papá stood. "You wait here. I'll go."

This negotiation was interrupted when Jorge returned to the room. "Blanca's water broke. We're taking her to the hospital."

"Oh, *Dios mío*. Marco, we're going to be grandparents. Forget the latkes, we're going to the hospital with you."

Jorge shook his head. "No, Mamá. Blanca insists that you all have your feast. It could be hours until anything happens. I'll phone you in plenty of time to be there for your grandbaby's arrival."

Ana Maria added her voice. "Listen to Jorge. Let's do this the way Blanca has requested."

Mamá hit her hand on her head. "How am I supposed to concentrate on feeding everyone when Blanca's in labor?" Though Mamá was usually the sweetest-tempered, gentlest of women, she darted an angry glare at Madlyn.

"Hey, it's not my fault her water broke," she protested. "I get blamed for everything, and here I am, the injured party."

Tía Margarita shook her head and shook her fist at her daughter. "Ignore her, Rosa. I'll help you with dinner. Let's feed this lot, and then we'll be ready to keep vigil with Blanca."

Mamá and Tía Margarita trooped into the kitchen. Papá and Tío Luís decided now would be a good time to get a fire going in the fireplace. That left the three of us sitting awkwardly at the table: Madlyn, Carlo, and me, with what was left of the pretty awful wine. Wow. Carlo was still hanging in, a kind expression on his handsome face. What must he be thinking? He probably wondered how the hell he'd wound up in this looney bin excuse for a Chanukah meal. Could any latke be worth going through what he already had? Ana Maria would probably never see him again after tonight.

Can't say I'd blame him for making tracks the first chance he had.

IN WHAT SEEMED LIKE MERE MOMENTS, MAMÁ AND TÍA Margarita brought in bowls of sour cream and guacamole. Then came olives, salsas, and chiles. And then came turkey roasted with corn meal and jalapeños, and latkes, both regular potato and sweet potatoes. Meal on!

Papá dug in first. "Rosa, with a feast like this, who needs gifts from Mighty Menorah Man?"

Mamá fluttered her lashes. "*Gracias*, Marco. But nothing sweet you can say will distract me from worrying about what's going on with Blanca now."

"Of course," Papá said. "You wouldn't be my Rosa if you didn't worry. But there's plenty here. Later, when we go to the hospital, when Jorge tells us to come, we can bring food for the family. There's probably enough here to feed the staff in the maternity ward."

Mamá nodded.

"Mighty Menorah Man?" Carlo asked. "Can't say I've ever heard of him before."

Ana Maria laughed. "Not surprising. Mighty Menorah Man is one of the exclusive gang that hangs out with Santa, the Tooth Fairy, and Mighty Matzo Man. Given the important, secret nature of their various missions, the Mighty Men guard their identities carefully. It was only through amazing powers of investigation that our clan was able to learn of their super secret existence. Menorah Man brings candles and gifts for Chanukah. Matzo Man shows up for Passover."

Carlo shook his head in wonderment. "When I came here tonight, I expected a feast, though not as grand as this, I must admit. But I never expected the night would be educational! When I go home tonight, I'll be both well-fed and wiser."

Ana Maria smiled to herself. She was liking Carlo more and more.

However, Madlyn groaned. "Bad enough I have to put up with this line of bullshit in the courthouse. But at my family's Chanukah feast? Talk about cruel and unusual punishment."

"Madlyn!" Four voices united to turn her name into a rebuke.

"Carlo is an invited guest in our home," Papá chided. "Since you cannot seem to separate family life from work life, we have agreed you can air your concerns over the dreidel game, after we've eaten. Hopefully, we'll have a real dreidel miracle, and your behavior will turn acceptable."

Madlyn looked as if she wanted to stomp out of the room in a gesture of protest. But then she'd have had to forgo the latkes, a sacrifice even she wouldn't make. After another roll of the eyes and a muttered remark no one could understand, she filled her plate and ate silently, yet aggressively.

Putting up with Madlyn is like an acid test for any date I'm going to

introduce to my family. Since Carlo already knows her professionally, he has
an idea of what to expect. On the other hand, I can see why he wouldn't
want her to have any connection with his private life. She's my cousin and I
love her in the way you do relatives, but tonight I find her especially hard
to take.

They all ate and ate and ate. The phone didn't ring, and Mamá
tried to contain her nerves, not talking about Blanca and the
coming baby more often than every ten minutes or so. When
everyone swore they couldn't eat another bite, Mamá offered
dessert.

Tía Margarita jumped in. "Rosa, I'd walk ten miles for one of
your cakes. Actually, right now, I'd probably have to walk ten miles
to make room for your delicious dessert. Instead, why don't we
have the dreidel game now. Let the young people talk out whatever
they need to. We can work up some appetite for dessert."

Everyone agreed. Mamá and Tía Margarita cleared the table of
the still-abundant platters of food, and Papá got the big wooden
dreidel out. Tío Luís explained the game to Carlo and reminded us
all what the Hebrew letters stood for.

"Usually, you would play the game with pennies or chocolates,
something to gamble with. There are four letters for the four sides.
The whole message is, *Nes gadol haya sham.* That means: "a great
miracle happened here." Tío Luís pointed to each letter and then
named it. "The *nun* means nothing. The player does nothing. The
gimel means everything. That means a player who gets a gimel gets
the whole pot. If you get the *hey*, you get half the pot. And if you
get *shin*, you have to put something in the pot."

Then we modified those meanings to direct the talk between
Madlyn and Carlo. Papá said, "Whoever gets the most gimels wins.
The nun loses."

They both spun. Carlo got one gimel after another, and Madlyn
kept getting nuns.

"I suppose that means Carlo can talk, but you have to shut up,"
I said.

Carlo held up a hand. "No matter what the dreidel says, I say we should let Madlyn say her piece."

Wow. Just wow. I couldn't bring myself to disagree when he was being so diplomatic. A real class act.

Madlyn looked as if she'd won something. Just like when they'd been kids, Madlyn's needs and wants trumped all. "First of all," she said to Carlo, "I didn't know that you were single and dating."

Carlo smiled. "I didn't know you'd have any interest in this. Word around the courthouse was that you weren't single. That you and your boyfriend had been together for a long time. But I thought you wanted to speak about something professional."

Madlyn got pale at the mention of her now-gone boyfriend. "We broke up. I'm surprised your gossip hounds didn't tell you."

"Is this your professional concern?"

Madlyn scowled. "No. The divorce we were on opposite sides for recently. I'm not going to name names, but you know the one I mean."

Carlo made a face. "I do know. I'm not comfortable talking about details in front of other people, but I'll try to accommodate you if we can avoid identifying the principals. I'll also add right now that I take very few divorce cases. I don't like doing them. I'll only take one if I fear that my client is going to be treated unfairly by her spouse. That was the case this time."

"Unfairly? You thought my client was treating his spouse unfairly? I'd have expected someone like you to be fairer about the dad's rights to be with his child, but you've encouraged your client to impose so many blocks to her husband being with their son."

"How fair is it for the father to blame his son's mother for his diagnosis of ADHD? This same father who ignores the child whenever he's got a problem or is ill? This same father who abandoned his child to run off and shack up with a barely-legal young woman who subsequently threw him out?"

"My client tried to make amends, tried to go back to his wife and child." Madlyn looked as frustrated as a soaking wet hen. She actually waved her finger in Carlo's face.

Carlo remained calm. "After cutting her off financially and

threatening to continue to withhold support if she didn't take him back. No apology for having left. No assurance he wouldn't do the same thing again. How do we know he'd have made any effort to come back if his new little girlfriend hadn't thrown him out?"

"A sensitive guy like that? She never understood him, never gave him what he needed or wanted. They got married when they were both too young. I think she probably got pregnant intentionally just to trap him." Madlyn's thin lips clamped in a grimace.

"It takes two to make a pregnancy," Ana Maria muttered, though she knew she should keep out of the battle.

Carlo regarded her. "If I didn't know better..." He narrowed his eyes and peered at her. "You sound like one of those deluded women who dates married men and buys into the line that 'My wife doesn't understand me.' Madlyn, tell me you're not dating your client."

She swallowed hard. "I'm not dating him."

"Sorry I wasn't precise. You *were* dating him, weren't you?"

"Guilty as charged," Madlyn admitted in a really tiny voice.

"*Dios mío*," Tía Margarita shouted. "*Mija*, what were you thinking? Dating a bad husband and bad father, not to mention he's also a client."

Madlyn sighed. "Give me a break. I was so depressed after Gunnar and I broke up."

"You mean after he left you," Ana Maria pointed out.

Carlo caught her eye and, in a subtle gesture, shook his head. Then he said, "As far as I'm concerned, the game is over, and so is this conversation. Madlyn, if you want to discuss this further, let's meet in a more appropriate setting so we can figure out where you want to go with this topic."

"I'm done," Madlyn said. Ana Maria kind of felt sorry for her. How sad to be sad at the Chanukah table.

"I'd say it's time for dessert now," Mamá said, springing up. Ana Maria doubted there'd been enough time to build up more of an appetite, but she hated to disappoint Mamá.

Just then, the phone rang--the landline. Everyone froze. Then

Papá rushed to answer. From his responses, it was impossible to tell what the conversation was. But when he hung up, he smiled. "Jorge says things are moving along, and we can go to the hospital whenever we're ready."

Mamá crossed herself. "But we haven't had dessert. And I haven't prepared food to take to the hospital."

"Rosa, try to relax. Jorge said there's no big rush. I'll help you."

"I'll help too, Mamá," Ana Maria said.

"No, mija. Margarita will help. And so will Madlyn." Mamá turned and glared meaningfully at her niece.

"Whatever," Madlyn muttered as she headed to the kitchen with her mother.

"You stay here, keep Carlo company," Mamá finished before heading to the kitchen.

Ana Maria turned to Carlo. "Well, we're going to finish this Chanukah feast in the hospital. Nice night to welcome my niece or nephew. You're welcome to come, of course, but it's not expected of you."

He smiled. "I think I'll take a raincheck on holiday baby births, which I'd previously associated only with Christmas."

They both smiled.

"Thanks for being part of this tonight. I'd like to say that as wild and woolly as things got, it's atypical for my family, but tonight felt a lot like business as usual."

Carlo's smile got wider. "Please thank your family for me for a wonderful evening. I really enjoyed spending time with them and, most of all, getting to know you better."

Ana Maria hugged him. "Thanks for hanging in. Your being here made it special."

"Wouldn't have missed it for the world. And, with regards your family, all I can say is, I can't wait to introduce you to mine. They make yours look calm and simple."

"Feliz Chanukah!" Ana Maria said.

"Feliz Chanukah!" Carlo responded, right before he kissed her good night.

PART II
THE AUTHORS

Eva Moore

AUTHOR OF "DECKED OUT"

Eva Moore writes sexy contemporary romances in between soccer practices and glasses of rosé. She lives in Silicon Valley, after moving around the world and back, with her college sweetheart, her three gorgeous girls, and a Shih Tzu who thinks he is a cat. She can be found most nights hiding in her closet-office, scribbling away, and loves to hear from the outside world. Please visit her at www.4evamoore.com.

If you'd like to know about future releases and giveaways, you can join her newsletter here: http://eepurl.com/cosVKT

The characters in *Decked Out* are from the *Exposed Dreams Series*. *Opened Up* is Adrian and Sofia's love story, where you'll also learn more about his mother's condition and his sisters. Enzo and Natalie find their initial HEA in *Stripped Down*. *Decked Out* is essentially an extended epilogue. Frankie, Jo, and Dom's stories will be here soon.

facebook.com/4evamooreauthor

twitter.com/AuthorEvaMoore

instagram.com/authorevamoore

bookbub.com/authors/eva-moore

Adrienne Bell

AUTHOR OF "A PERFECT FIT"

ADRIENNE BELL LIVES ON THE FAR EDGE OF THE San Francisco Bay Area with her husband and kids. She spends her working days writing and reading and most of her downtime watching comic book-themed television and scrolling through Disneyland fan websites.

You can follow the minutia of her life on Twitter, or check out what she has coming out next on www.AdrienneBell.net. Oh, and she thanks you for reading.

facebook.com/AdrienneBellAuthor

twitter.com/writerbell

instagram.com/authoradriennebell

bookbub.com/authors/adrienne-bell

Kilby Blades

AUTHOR OF "CRAZY OLD MONEY"

KILBY BLADES IS A FRESH NEW VOICE in smart contemporary romance. Critics laud her "feminist fiction", noting empowered heroines and multi-dimensional heroes. Her debut novel, "Snapdragon", was a ten-time finalist and a five-time winner for honors including the HOLT Medallion, the Publisher's Weekly BookLife Prize, and the Foreword Indie Award. She has been nodded for a total of twenty honors for her complete library, including a win for Best Debut Author in the 2018 RSJ's Emma Awards.

When she's not writing, Kilby goes to movie matinees alone, where she eats Chocolate Pocky and buttered popcorn and usually smuggles in not-a-little-bit of red wine. She procrastinates from the difficult process of writing by oversharing on Facebook and giving away cool stuff to her newsletter subscribers. Kilby is a mother, a social-justice fighter, and above all else, a glutton for a good story.

facebook.com/kilbybladesauthor

twitter.com/kilbyblades

instagram.com/kilbyblades

bookbub.com/authors/kilby-blades

Kari Lemor

AUTHOR OF "STEALING CHRISTMAS"

KARI LEMOR WRITES CONTEMPORARY ROMANCE with a splash of danger. Her *Love on the Line* series—*Wild Card Undercover, Running Target*, and *Fatal Evidence*—debuted in 2017 to outstanding reviews.

Check out her other work and get notifications on her website: https://www.karilemor.com/

f facebook.com/Karilemorauthor

twitter.com/karilemor

instagram.com/karilemorauthor

BB bookbub.com/authors/kari-lemor

Preslaysa Williams

AUTHOR OF "TOUCHED BY FATE"

Preslaysa Williams is an award-winning author of women's fiction and romance with an Afro-Filipina twist. Her debut novel, a contemporary women's fiction, will release in 2019. Sign up for her free newsletter here: http://eepurl.com/NArOn

f facebook.com/preslaysa

twitter.com/preslaysawrites

instagram.com/preslaysa

BB bookbub.com/authors/preslaysa-williams

Marie Booth

AUTHOR OF "RINGING IN THE REEFER"

MARIE BOOTH IS AN AWARD-WINNING AUTHOR of spicy contemporary romance and hot paranormal romance. A musical theatre geek who loves to write about the arts, Marie also writes sweeter paranormal romance as Gayle Parness.

You can check her out and sign up for her newsletters at www.mariebooth.com and www.gayleparness.com

 facebook.com/marieboothauthor

 twitter.com/marieboothbooks

 instagram.com/marieboothauthor

BB bookbub.com/authors/marie-booth

R.L. Merrill

AUTHOR OF "THE THANKSGIVING PARADE
FROM HELL"

ONCE UPON A TIME a teacher, tattoo collector, mom, and rock 'n' roll kinda gal opened up a doc and starting purging her demons. Several self-published books and a debut gay romance with Dreamspinner Press later, R.L. Merrill is still striving to find that perfect balance between real-life and happily ever after. She writes stories set in the places she loves most and she loves connecting with other authors online at the RT Booklovers Convention and RWA chapter meetings, of which she's been a member since 2014.

A sucker for underdogs, Ro has adopted cats, dogs, rats, snakes, fish and a chameleon named Godzilla. Her love of horror is evident the moment you walk in her door and find yourself surrounded by decorative skulls and quirky artwork from around the world. You can find her lurking on social media where she loves connecting with readers, educating America's youth, being a mom taxi to two busy kids, in the tattoo chair trying desperately to get that back piece finished, or headbanging at a rock show near her home in the San Francisco Bay Area. www.rlmerrillauthor.com

f facebook.com/rlmerrillauthor

🐦 twitter.com/rlmerrillauthor

📷 instagram.com/rlmerrillauthor

BB bookbub.com/authors/r-l-merrill

Erin St. Charles

AUTHOR OF "THANKFUL IN PERDITION"

Erin grew up watching Star Trek and reading Barbara Cartland novels (don't hate), wishing she could create something that brings her love of science fiction together with her love of romance. Still a romantic nerd at heart, she writes sensual, diverse stories that blend fantasy, adventure, and love.

The *Thankful In Perdition* Playlist

- Almost Thanksgiving Day, *Graham Parker*
- Autumn in New York, *Billie Holiday*
- We Are Family, *Sister Sledge*
- Sweet Potato Pie, *Ray Charles and James Taylor*
- Thanksgiving Day, *Ray Davies*
- Family Business, *Kanye West*
- Home, *Phillip Phillips*

facebook.com/erin.st.charles.1

twitter.com/erinwritesbwwm

instagram.com/authorerinst.charles

bookbub.com/authors/erin-st-charles

www.ingramcontent.com/pod-product-compliance
Lightning Source LLC
Chambersburg PA
CBHW020941120726
47905CB00008B/2630